—Ken Kalfus, author of *Coup de Foudre* and *Equilateral*, finalist for the PEN/Faulkner Award, and author of three *New York Times* Notable Books of the Year

"Skwerer's careful psychological insights, expressed against the two young men's shared fascination with the seductive but problematic world of Wagner's great operas, reward attentive reading. Above all, his dense and atmospheric re-imagining of pre-First World War Austria, and especially of Vienna, the crucible of the very best and the very worst the new century would have to offer, will prove compelling for anyone interested in exploring the all-too-human roots of destructive totalitarianism."

—Frederick Taylor, author of *Exorcising Hitler: The Occupation and Denazification of Germany*

"It is hard to imagine a more delicate subject than the youth of the man who would later be identified with absolute evil. Skwerer explores this territory with great sensitivity and surprising wit. He is also a fine storyteller. Readers will be intrigued and appalled."

—Tim Parks, author of the Man Booker-shortlisted *Europa*

"The adolescent Hitler: school dropout, loner, megalomanic dreamer. Why would anyone want to be his friend? And yet he had one, August Kubizek. In his novel *The Tristan Chord*, Glenn Skwerer succeeds in bringing this friendship to life, and in doing so he confronts us with the human side of Hitler. All too often we see Nazis simply as monsters and tend to forget that they were able to commit their crimes precisely because they were humans. This is an uncomfortable read but it will make you think. I read it in a single afternoon."

—Meike Ziervogel, author of *Magda* and *Clara's Daughter*

"How does one write about Adolf Hitler without descending into cliché or caricature? Glenn Skwerer takes on this most difficult of

About the Author

Glenn Skwerer is a psychiatrist who lives and practises in the Boston area. He was inspired by reading August Kubizek's memoir, *The Young Hitler I Knew*, to look more closely at the psychology of the friendship between Kubizek and Hitler, and to recast it entirely as fiction. *The Tristan Chord* is his first book.

literary tasks in his debut novel . . . A fascinating picture of Hitler's youthful obsessions."

—John Boyne, *Guardian*

"An intelligent and engrossing account of Hitler's youth . . . In fictionalized form, [Skwerer's] antagonist has something of the dramatic charge of Milton's Satan or Iago, proposing the most heinous ideas with the appearance of reason. Yet what is so striking about Skwerer's conception of Hitler is how mundane he is . . . At a time when anti-semitism and intolerance seem once again to be on the rise, *The Tristan Chord* offers a sobering reminder that evil comes in many guises, and sometimes can be as banal as a humorless sixteen-year-old loner who venerates music more than humanity."

—Alexander Larman, *Observer*

"This is a remarkable first novel. With an extraordinary assurance and innate grasp of form and character . . . Skwerer has done much more than conjure up a Hitler of base emotion and unalloyed evil . . . Subtly but with growing power, the ability of Hitler to seduce and move an audience becomes obvious and frightening . . . *The Tristan Chord* deftly and persuasively shows this diabolical power is contagious, infecting even those who insist on innocence because their hands are not yet blood-stained."

—*Herald Scotland*

"Dazzling . . . Skillfully draws out our sympathy for someone we usually find simpler and more comforting to dismiss as a devil . . . As ever, fiction proves better for grappling with moral nuance and emotional complexity. A tremendous read."

—*Press and Journal*

The Tristan Chord

GLENN SKWERER

unbound

First published in 2018
This paperback edition first published in 2019

Unbound
6th Floor Mutual House, 70 Conduit Street, London W1S 2GF

www.unbound.com

Text Design by Ellipsis, Glasgow

A CIP record for this book is available from the British Library

IBSN 978-1-78352-846-2 (trade pbk)
ISBN 978-1-78352-574-4 (trade hbk)
ISBN 978-1-78352-575-1 (ebook)
ISBN 978-1-78352-573-7 (limited edition)

Printed and bound in Great Britain by Clays Ltd, Elcograf S.p.A.

For Peter J. Scotto

Glasenbach, outside Salzburg, September 1945

I HAVE BEEN INTERNED IN GLASENBACH now four months; one of the guards even calls us "interns." This has a bit of grim humor in it as the place was a provincial hospital before the Americans and British took it near the end of the war and fenced it in with chain link and razor wire. I am making life here sound worse than it is because, really, it is not a bad sort of existence.

We sleep in large open wards, in hospital beds separated by screens. The wards are guarded, but the guards, American soldiers, are not intrusive or overbearing. Actually, their manner is rather relaxed and even apologetic. We are allowed books and newspapers. (They encourage us to read newspapers as the news is sobering and I suppose they suspect this will leave us feeling reflective and freer to talk. And that is, after all, why we are "interned" here: to talk.) We are allowed packages from home, and mail. The food is certainly no worse than it was at home during the last year of the war. We are fed turnips—steamed, sliced and fried in skillets, boiled, raw, puréed, as filler in the occasional meat dish. It is practically all that will grow in the stubborn, arid soil of this part of Austria. Supplies from the outside are rare.

We are given writing materials. But we are told, quite frankly, that anything we write—correspondence or journals—will be read, and we may be questioned about it. I know this as I write now. This encouragement to write, I believe, is part of their plan to relax our understandable inhibitions and distrust, to make us more introspective, more confessional. But they are asking too much. How am I to know what I could have done, or should have done—or should have *known*—then or now? Colonel Lewis, one of my American interviewers, tells me that writing is one way of knowing. How much will I know after I have written this? I will let you decide.

I was brought here in June 1945 because I may be a valuable—even unique—source of information, and because it is believed I require "de-Nazification." *De*-Nazification! I have to laugh. Thirty years ago, when I was sixteen years old, he told me (and not without some affection, I think), "Reczek, in politics you are a dunce, a turkey!" In 1938, having met again after decades, five years after he became Reichchancellor, he invited me as his guest to attend the festival in Bayreuth with him, and as we stood in Wahnfried, Wagner's home and the final resting place of one of the most fertile and irrepressible minds the world has produced, he laughed and told Winifred Wagner that *No*, I was not a member of the party, that only music moved me, most especially the music of her father-in-law; in politics, he added, chuckling a bit, I was an "innocent," *unschuldig*, which can mean both "naive" or "innocent of a crime." The hefty, English-born dowager—whom I would later learn had for years been trying to persuade him to marry her—smiled, and, clasping her hands to her apocalyptic bosom, told me that it was her fondest wish that the music I would hear in my next four days there would move me to join. I simply smiled and nodded. Adolf laughed again to himself and glanced at me. I read recently that the Allies had bombed Bayreuth during the final days of the war. I do not know whether Wahnfried or the Festival Theater still exist.

I am a failure. I know that. And yet at the Conservatory in Vienna I received honors or high honors in almost every course, even composition—arguably the most difficult and stringently graded, open only to those who had distinguished themselves in the required subjects. I received more referrals for pupils than I could accept in order to supplement my scholarship; these were mostly sixteen- and seventeen-year-old girls from the wealthiest mercantile families in Vienna, families, many of them Jewish, with rooms or whole homes in neighborhoods like the villa suburb of Döbling. I would arrive in whatever decent clothes I owned at the time, my lessons in a scratched and faded leather briefcase, marveling at the swirling marble staircases and chandeliers of the palatial apartment buildings, some a full city block long, that had been built to fill in the neighborhoods around the Ringstrasse. Occasionally, if the lesson was in the late afternoon, I would be asked to stay for dinner. I was surprised that many of my pupils—my Emilie or Marta or Cecilie—knew as much as they did. And this was not today, when anyone with a cheap Victrola can get to know a little music. It took time and money then to cultivate an interest in music. Some of my pupils' parents, and not only the mothers, had taken up an instrument as adults. And they did not condescend to me—I am sure of this—because I was a boy with a provincial accent on scholarship. Rather they seemed to *admire* my ambition, they solicited my opinions of composers who lived in Vienna, wanted to know about my courses, who was being taught, who was revered. My mother—God rest her honest and devoted soul—would urge me in her letters, gently, laughingly, to marry one of these girls. I tremble to think what my fate would have been had I followed her advice. My American interviewers, as I tell them my story over and over, lose no opportunity to remind me.

And where was he while my star was rising at the Conservatory? He was, I know this now, living in the Männerheim, a men's hostel (ironically, funded by Jewish philanthropists, particularly Baron Nathaniel Rothschild) in the Brigittenau district in Vienna. He was painting watercolors, copying photographs of the city's "sights" and selling them as postcards on the streets or in cafés. He was making larger copies and selling them to furniture dealers to be framed and built into the backs of sofas, actually embedded in the furniture, which was the fashion amongst the lower middle classes. He was sleeping in an open dormitory, probably not unlike the one here at Glasenbach, and forced to have his few remaining articles of clothing fumigated and deloused each week.

I tried to find him after I returned to our room and Frau Zdenek said he was gone. I checked with the police in each of the surrounding districts—any move, any change of address, even to a rooming house, had to be registered—but they knew nothing. I had suspected he was running out of money; his inheritance from his mother was almost gone and his share of the state orphan's pension was being used to support his younger sister. I would have paid his half of the rent until he found some other source of income—my parents would have, they always liked him, even regarded him as a second son, despite his being disinclined towards working at a job. But he had probably gone straight to one of the city's many dosshouses, which was why the police had lost track of him; and from dosshouse to dosshouse or the street until he landed in the Männerheim, where one could have a bed and meals and use the library for only a few kronen a week. By then I had stopped looking.

I said I was a failure, didn't I? One measures that in part, I suppose, by examining one's ambitions and expectations, but also by comparing oneself with one's classmates and friends. We all do that. But how does one measure one's self against the most powerful man in the world, a man worshipped almost as a god? Or against dreams so vast it would take two world wars to turn them to rubble? Tell me.

Part One

Linz, 1905–08

I HAD SEEN HIM ANY NUMBER of times before. Always the same outfit: a neatly pressed salt-and-pepper tweed suit, a long black wool overcoat that made him seem taller, older, almost gaunt. Black kid gloves, an ivory-handled ebony cane that he would lean on with both hands, jutting his chin out just a bit. At times he wore a top hat. He parted his hair on the right, so that a dark forelock would fall across his eyes; he was always brushing this back with his hand, tossing his head, clearing his throat. There was a humorous touch: a wispy suggestion of a mustache on his upper lip. The face was long, the cheeks sunken, the skin pale, almost sallow. He never looked about him—he looked either straight ahead with a serious, almost stern gaze, or sometimes down at his hands as he leaned heavily on that sleek cane. I thought he was a university student; I did not know it at the time but he was eight months younger than I was. No matter how early I arrived to wait in line for my twelve-heller standing-room ticket, he was there, with the overcoat and floppy forelock, and that unwavering gaze. I was allowed to go to the opera two nights each week, Saturday night and one weeknight. He was always there. I would later learn he was there every night.

Once we had our tickets we would lean against the velvet rope at the bottom of the stairs, and when the usher released us we'd take those cushioned stairs two or three steps at a time, trying desperately to seem casual, and take our places beside the pillars on the mezzanine. There were only two and if you secured them, as we almost always did, you had a fine, unobstructed view and could rest against them during the performance and take the weight off your feet a little. As we reached the pillars we'd take a deep, relieved breath, glance at each other and smile slightly, and he'd turn away and brush that drooping lock back and raise his head. That was the extent of our unspoken brotherhood. I'd watch him at times during the performance, his gaunt face lit, the eyes shining pale blue and clear as glass, as though his brain were absorbing every image, note, gesture, glance. He never looked at me.

One night we met at the doors as the crowd was filing out. He held the door open and spoke. "What did you think?" More a command than a question. As we walked, the brass tip of his cane tapped against the cobblestones. He stared ahead, waiting. I was afraid anything I said would sound unschooled, obvious, stupid. I was painfully aware that my suit, my only suit, was too tight, my bowtie childishly small.

"I enjoyed the singing more than the acting," I said. My throat was itching and I had to suppress the urge to cough. "But the opera is enchanting." We had seen *Lohengrin*.

"Yes!" he hissed. "Why can't they see that what is coming out of their mouths is not pure sound but *dialogue*. This is drama. This is the story of the loss of a hero, a redeemer, through the foolish curiosity of a woman. And you'd think they were playing *The Merry Widow*. If they are not moved by tragedy and redemption, how can *we* be? Even his—Lohengrin's—arrival was botched, the lighting was all on Elsa, fretting and carrying on like a silly cow. Lohengrin seems to emerge from the river like a frog hopping onstage. Ahhh—" He let out a sigh of frustration and

4

scraped the tip of the cane back and forth across the cobblestones as though to punctuate his disgust.

"But the singing?" I said. "Good. Very good. Especially Friedrich. And he could act, too. I suppose it's easier to play the villain."

"Yes," he replied, cocking his head as though weighing my remarks. He nodded gravely. "Yes. Yes, you are right. But the whole heroic dimension of the story was diminished by how the thing was done. This was not necessary."

"You've seen better, I suppose."

He grunted.

We walked in silence, the only sound the regular tapping of his cane. The streets were empty at that hour, the cobblestones wet and slick in the sulfur-yellow glow of the gas lamps. He stopped suddenly and pivoted. "I will leave you here. I live on the Humboldtstrasse, number forty-one. Are you sure you will be safe getting home?" His concern seemed comically chivalrous, as the city was safe at all hours. I almost laughed. I assured him that I would be safe.

"Thank you for accompanying me." He paused, extended his hand. "Hitler, Adolf."

"Eugen Reczek. I don't live far."

He nodded and pivoted again, the oversized black coat swinging like a cape, and headed off, carrying the cane under his arm.

I felt light and important that night, walking home through the wet streets. At the time I was fifteen. I had begun my apprenticeship in my father's upholstery shop the year before, though I would still be compelled by law to attend school one day each week for two years. On Tuesday and Thursday evenings and

Saturday mornings I took music lessons—trumpet, piano, and now viola, which I'd been told by Bravratsky, my piano teacher, was a good "angle," as violinists were a dime a dozen. And, as I've said, I was now allowed by my parents to attend the opera one night during the week and on Saturday nights.

I had no friends; I had no time and, really, I think, no inclination. I was either in class, where I was a competent but uninterested student, or practicing, or stretching fabric over a musty, overstuffed sofa, or rapt and dreaming at my post in the mezzanine. The boys in my class had no interest in music and I had no interest in wearing the blue cornflower—the Kaiser's favorite flower and the symbol of their belief in a greater Germany—or in going on invigorating hikes into the countryside with the Union of German Students. Although my surname is Czech, my father was three-quarters German, my mother's maiden name was Hauptmann, we spoke German at home, and thought of ourselves as German. Yet, as far as I can recall, I had no political opinions. I still don't. This is a strange admission, I know, for someone whose life has been spent in the shadow of politics and war and has seen them turn his dreams and ambitions to dust; stranger still, when he can say honestly that his greatest friend and influence as a young man would become Chancellor of the German Reich. You don't believe me?

My father expected I would inherit his business—if it survived long enough—or eventually set up my own. I understand my father. He was a good man, reticent but kind. He had grown up on a farm in the Waldwiertal, Austria's poorhouse—a hilly, not unattractive province on the country's northern border, its rocky terrain carpeted with pines and blessed with the occasional ruined castle. No opera, no symphony, only unremitting, fruitless, backbreaking work. At thirteen, he walked to Salzburg and found an apprenticeship, living in a suffocating attic above the upholstery shop; he would eventually buy that shop. He married my mother and with her small dowry and his own savings opened a shop in the smaller, provincial capital of Linz, where there was less competition, I suppose, but still a healthy middle class with their predictable taste for dark, plump furniture and the thrifty inclination to repair and reupholster rather than replace.

He was nearly sixty by the time I was fifteen and had almost lost the business twice, once when the currency was devalued, and again when he was wheezing and bedridden with one of the many pulmonary ailments upholsterers are prone to. He wanted me to learn a *solid* trade—if you are competent, if you are reliable, he would say, then you can live, you don't need to be a wonder child, a prodigy fighting with hundreds of other prodigies for a single spot. I would nod, and sneeze, and continue stuffing fresh horsehair into a velour pillow, rearranging it, measuring it against its twin, pressing on both to make sure they had comparable resilience and loft before I delivered them. I was a thoughtful and obedient son, though there may be more honest words for this.

My mother had taken voice lessons as a girl and loved music; she placed me in choir at church when I was six. She'd taken me to daytime performances at the Linz opera, paid for individual lessons at Linz's only music school and with private teachers, and later she persuaded my father to allow me to attend the opera, which often ended well after midnight. She understood, or seemed to.

*

I did not have to wait long to see Adolf again.

Even though two evenings a week he was stationed less than twenty feet from me at his pillar, I had never even glimpsed him in town. Not even on the Landstrasse, the central promenade that ran from the town square to the river and where Linzers customarily took their evening stroll during the warm months. With his long, fashionably cut overcoat, top hat, and ebony cane with the ivory shoe-handle, and his correct, purposeful stride, he should have been an unmistakable sight. At the time, one of my jobs was to deliver smaller, finished pieces to customers and to pick up new work that didn't require laborers to bring it to the shop. So in the late afternoon I could be seen criss-crossing the town under a load of colorful sofa pillows or balancing a small mattress on my head like some coolie. On opera nights, I would hurry back, strip to my waist and sponge the lint, sawdust, and crumbled horsehair from my itching neck and shoulders and chest, eat a quick dinner my mother had waiting, change into my one suit, and head to the opera house, the *Landestheater*, to wait in line for my standing-room ticket.

The day after he first spoke to me I was running at a jog across the square after making a delivery and stopped suddenly. He was standing off to the side of the Post Office—a building slated by the city to be demolished and rebuilt—holding a sketch pad with one hand, drawing with the other, glancing from the building to the pad. He was oblivious to passersby. I took a step forward.

"Oh, Reczek, hello," he said without looking up. "Here." He turned and showed me the sketch. "I have added this projecting corner, and the columns and steps, and I was just starting this triangular pediment in the center. Across the pediment should be a frieze of some sort—you know, a Greek messenger approaching

8

the king, something appropriate for a post office. What do you think?"

I was no expert but I thought the sketch quite good, actually. It was detailed, the perspective was accurate. It showed a sure hand.

"I think," I said, squinting at the drawing like a prospective buyer, "it is—monumental."

He nodded. "Well, exactly! Every city center should have a few neoclassical buildings. Nothing wrong with that, nothing wrong with an impression of size and strength and purpose. You can't reserve this sort of thing for the capital of the empire. No one owns the rights to grandeur, Reczek."

"Yes, but it could seem . . . out of place here. Out of proportion, perhaps." I said this tentatively. I had already sensed that Adolf would not take criticism well.

"When the rest of the square is redesigned," he replied, and I could detect a visionary sternness in his face, "the proportion will come."

I was still winded and breathing hard. "I must go, or I'll be late. I have a lesson tonight."

He gave me a crisp nod, the forelock falling forward. "Until Saturday then?"

"Until Saturday."

When I got back to the house my father was in the shop on the ground floor. He was rebuilding a sofa frame that had warped from years of sagging under the weight of its owners. He methodically pulled out nails, grunting and wheezing, his broad forearms glistening in the early evening light. He pried the board loose, eyed it along its length with a disgusted squint, and tossed it aside.

"I'm going up to change, Papa."

"Of course. Yes, do." He used the claw to loosen and lift another board.

"You should stop," I said.

"I will, soon."

I climbed the dark, narrow staircase to my room, pulled off my boots, and for a moment lay back on the bed. As I've said, I had no friends; the few I'd had in *Realschule* were lost to me now that I worked in the shop. Oddly, I had none from the music school; my lessons had mostly been individual, and when I did practice with a small group, the others—even the students from the *Gymnasium*— seemed to be there from a sense of obligation. They could have been punching a time clock in a factory, diligent as they were.

And presumptuous as this may sound, I felt I was beginning to pull away: my technique on the trumpet (an instrument on which producing even the most basic, sustained sounds is frustratingly tricky) was sure enough for me to be admitted to the town's amateur symphony; learning the viola seemed straightforward enough, or so I thought at first; and on the piano I had undertaken pieces in three and four voices which were intricate and complex and produced in me a feeling of astonished delight and profound reverence. I carried this reverence in my head and in my breast as I stretched fabric and stuffed mattresses and staggered to and from our neighbors' homes, bending under today's work and picking up the next day's. And the nights! Two nights each week I lived in a world of vast and engulfing sound, of death and redemption, of unfulfillable and unsustainable yearning, where—finally—I was no longer alone.

The next day in the late afternoon I was repairing an old chairseat with rusted springs when there was a pair of sharp raps on the door of the shop. Customers rarely came by at that time of day and deliveries were usually in the morning. I glanced at my father, who had stopped what he was doing and was slowly straightening up. He nodded and I went to the door. There stood Adolf. He was wearing the same suit and overcoat he wore to the opera. He leaned on the cane and then spun it in his hand.

"Eugen," he said, "come with me to the Landstrasse and the river. The light is glorious. I'll wait for you to change."

I glanced at my father, and Adolf looked up. Transferring the cane to his other hand he strode past me into the shop with an almost military bearing; he halted a few feet from my father and nodded.

"Herr Reczek, I am Eugen's friend Adolf. Adolf Hitler. I live at Humboldtstrasse 41. I request the honor of your son's company along the Landstrasse to the river and perhaps beyond. It is a splendid, exceptional evening. Please pardon the intrusion."

My father, still holding the augur he was using, blinked. Then his pursed lips widened into a tolerant smile and he nodded at me. "Enough for today."

"All of this will have to be enlarged and rebuilt," he said, waving his cane in an arc that took in most of the square. "Space is crucial. The municipal buildings should flank the square. Each should be a real showpiece and not hemmed in; the residential buildings should be pushed back. The Landstrasse will"—this was characteristic, I would learn, this shift from the conditional *should* to the imperative *will*—"open up, be transformed into a real boulevard with a central island for strolling and a lofty canopy of trees, lined with the best homes in the city. This will run straight to the river and culminate in a bridge—a real one, not the puny thing we have now—that will sweep one up and over and provide a striking view of the river, the city, and the hills beyond."

We were walking past the fountain in the cobblestoned Hauptplatz, which served as a stage for Adolf, with the aid of his cane, to elaborate his vision of the rebuilt city. The sun was going down, spreading an amber dusk over Linz. Linzers were out in number—old men alone, entire families with nannies pushing perambulators and two or three older children in tow, younger couples, workingmen returning home. In daylight, Adolf seemed even paler than he had at night; the wispy mustache was more obvious. At the shop he had waited patiently for me to change, and when I came down he was talking politely with my father, who was showing him some of the more expensive and detailed pieces we were restoring. As we walked toward the center of town he inquired as to how my day had gone: was I tired, was it healthy for me to spend all day inhaling the fumes from the glue we used and the constantly swirling particles of old cotton batting and horsehair. He wondered how I managed to stay awake through the operas I attended on weeknights, and I told him—with a confidence and pithiness which surprised me—that inspiration was the best stimulant. He nodded deeply. "Yes, yes!" he said. "Would that more understood that!" And he grew quiet, perhaps to let the profundity of my observation sink in.

We walked in silence along the Landstrasse, Adolf scanning the avenue, his hands locked behind his back, the cane tucked under an arm, like a strict schoolteacher, inspecting. The windows on the north side were ablaze with the reflected orange light of the lowering sun.

Suddenly the cane swung up in a dismissive arc. "Sandstone next to granite next to brick, most of it nondescript, *every* cornice different. And the windows too small to really permit a view of the street, the passersby, the river. A public building, it is true, can dominate a landscape, but a home, a residence, should submit to the buildings around it—not try to distinguish itself with pathetic little details, a few gargoyles or angels, or ridiculous grillwork." He shook his head in genuine futility and disgust.

"Are you in school?" I was almost afraid to speak, and I think the question came out sounding timid, rather than a reasonable but indirect query after his credentials. It would not take long to find out what Adolf thought of most people's credentials. He could be unnervingly authoritative and emphatic in his opinions, even then.

He paused, actually stopped on the street for a moment, looked at me strangely and then into the distance, towards the river. My heartbeat picked up. "No, oh, no," he replied. "No. School has nothing to give me. I left six months ago. If you want to be an accountant, an actuary, a civil servant, to have a bread-and-butter job, fine. My father"—he said the word with a mixture of awe and mistrust—"was a civil servant, a customs inspector, of the highest grade. A servant of the empire! He even fashioned his side whiskers after the Emperor's. He used to take me to his office to give me a taste of what awaited me—*if* I was lucky, he said. Lucky! I could not breathe the stale and suffocating air in that cage."

"I am a simple upholsterer's son, an apprentice," I said, somewhat disingenuously. I offered my palms, which were cracked and scratched from prying loose thousands of tacks while taking down old pieces of furniture.

"Don't you see how much more honest that is?" he said, fixing me with his pale eyes. "You rebuild, repair, remake things that people use, and they pay you for it, as they should. You don't pose

13

in the uniform of the Emperor, with epaulettes, brass buttons, and—Good Lord, of all things!—a saber. And besides, it is not so simple—" He softened his voice. "You squirrel yourself away to practice not one but *three* instruments, and at night you stand at your post drinking in genius. You don't fool me. You are doing two apprenticeships, and one day you will have to choose. Besides, I think you are probably poisoning yourself in that shop."

I was stunned. I had not even told my mother—who loved music and, as I've said, had been taking me to concerts since I was a small boy—about my daydreams of being a musician, or even a conductor or composer. My father perhaps would have understood my ambitions, but considered it a foolish whim, and a betrayal. But Adolf knew. Better than I did, perhaps.

He pulled a pocket watch—he was the only person I had met my own age who carried one—from his waistcoat, glanced at it and took my arm. "Come."

We walked, almost trotted, down to the river and Adolf stationed us at the foot of one of the bridges crossing the Danube into the small Linz suburb of Urfahr. He leaned against the railing with a look of deliberate nonchalance. (Adolf was many things, but never nonchalant.) He brushed back that unruly forelock and scanned the crowd coming into town for their evening constitutional. I started to say something but he sternly shushed me, so I leaned back, slid my hands into my pockets, and tried to assume the same look of casual interest. After a few minutes of this posing, I began to feel an urge to burst into laughter and had to press my lips together to stifle it. He whispered, "Here. Here she comes."

A girl, maybe seventeen, approached over the bridge, arm in arm with an older woman. They wore similar floral hats and had the same ostentatiously erect, dignified carriage. The girl was indeed very pretty and wore her blond hair pulled back demurely in a bun. As they passed, Adolf closed his eyes slowly and nodded. The girl seemed to acknowledge this with a slight lowering of the eyes and a barely perceptible nod in our direction. Adolf maintained his pose and gazed after her as she and her mother (as I learned) disappeared into the crowd making its pilgrimage into town, to browse, to see and be seen. A signal, I thought. A secret lover.

Adolf turned and leaned over the railing. He stared down into the dark river. The effort of appearing relaxed seemed to have taken a good deal out of him.

"That was Stefanie," he said.

"Stefanie who?"

"Rabatsch. I am in love with her."

"Does she—"

"Know? Of course she knows. I have been in love with her for more than a year. I was at school with her brother."

"Do you—correspond?"

"I have never exchanged a word with her. But that is not necessary. She knows my thoughts. I know hers. She will wait until I have established myself."

I wanted to ask, until he had established himself as *what*, or how, but thought better of it.

"You've told her brother?"

"No, I have never exchanged a word with him either. He seems like a bit of a fool, frankly."

"Then how can she know? You must speak to her."

He was still staring into the distance over the river and turned to look at me. "Reczek, Reczek, you do not understand the nature of an extraordinary love."

I smiled to myself as he turned his gaze back to the river and the Freinberg and the hills beyond, burnished now in the light of the setting sun. I was coming to know the certainty with which Adolf held his opinions and I could sense how little he could tolerate question-ing. But somehow this did not bother me. I did not find it laughable or pathetic; it seemed to me endearing, in a half-amusing way, and rather impressive. What I did not know yet was how vehemently he felt about *everything*, from the way a provincial orchestra handled the overture to *Tristan*, to the design of the Post Office or the bridges spanning the Danube, to how excise taxes were levied or alms distributed to the poor. I suppose this was why he always seemed so tense, so tightly strung, and so earnestly serious: that overheated brain was constantly reacting, appraising, revising.

"She is a striking-looking girl," I said. "She has nobility and poise." I told him she could play Elsa, the wronged heroine of *Lohengrin*, that she had the look of the long-suffering and virtuous.

"Yes! Exactly! Here, listen. Listen." Adolf fumbled through the inside pockets of his coat and pulled out a long, rectangular note-book bound in textured black leather, the pages edged in gold. He leafed excitedly through it; the hand was sloping and precise, rather old-fashioned. "Here." He read:

She comes each day at the appointed time
On her mother's arm, for appearances' sake,
A disguise.
Her slender waist, sloping swan's neck, quaint quiet
    tread
Her steady, transcendent gaze,
Clear, strong eyes taking in everything before her.
She is the distant past in the present instant,

She is the future in the present instant.
You shall see.

I recall being amazed. Not by the poem, but that he would carry such a book with him as he navigated the city. That and a sketchpad in a large pocket sewn into the inner lining of his coat by his mother, so that he could catch ideas as they came to him. Or, appalled by a building or a whole block, could redesign it on the spot. I say it again: I have never met anyone who reacted to the world around him so strongly and instinctively and immediately. Though I would not have admitted it at the time, I imagined myself doing something similar, keeping a notebook of melodic ideas and passages in my head as I pulled nails and tacks from the frames of old sofas, ripped rusting coils and soiled cotton batting from chairseats, or gutted mattresses of the horsehair and even switchgrass and hay sometimes used as stuff-ing in those days. My second apprenticeship, as Adolf called it.

"You must speak to her mother," I said. "Gain an introduction. It might not be impossible or even difficult, for all you know."

He slid the leather notebook back inside his coat. "I am a poor devil," he said quietly.

And so this became our routine. In the morning I would change into a pair of muslin pants my mother had sewn and an old shirt and descend into the swirling motes of sawdust and horsehair of my father's shop for the day, knowing that at five thirty Adolf would be at the door in his tweed suit, leaning on his cane, and at times wearing a black slouch hat. My father would glance at me and nod, and after I'd scrubbed up we'd be off to explore the city, to discuss music and art, and, of course, to wait for Stefanie to make her appearance with her mother on the bridge from Urfahr.

I did not know what Adolf did with the rest of his day but by late afternoon he was fairly bursting with energy and ideas. The center of the city would have to be demolished to make way for a quadrangle of muni-cipal buildings and perhaps a university. The opera house would have to be rebuilt on a scale with the Court Opera in Vienna. There would be a symphony. Museums would sprout like mushrooms. Spacious avenues would run in spokes from the center of the town, lined with block-long apartment buildings with ornate facades and row upon row of enormous windows and ceilings higher than those previously found in residential buildings. From inside his overcoat would emerge a series of sketches—which columns did I prefer? Did I like the hundreds of terraced steps leading up to the new Town Hall or did I think it detracted from the impression made by the building itself? I knew nothing about architecture but I would frown over the drawings and make a few tentative suggestions I hoped sounded intelligent. I took out books on architecture from our lending library and studied photographs of the Ringstrasse in Vienna, which, although neither of us had seen it, Adolf took to be the supreme expression of neoclassical style and grandeur. Adolf was satisfied with nothing as it was in Linz: everything had to be changed, enhanced, enlarged, demolished, renovated, or—if he was in a tense or nervous mood that day—"blown to bits." Even the buildings he admired could use a new cornice or pediment or frieze. "We must reach into the past to find the future, Eugen," he would say, "because the present is unendurable."

On nights when we went to the opera, Adolf would often accept my mother's invitation to have dinner with us. ("We must fatten you up, Adolf," she would say, "or you will never sing tenor at the

Court Opera. Sit.") The stern, judgmental Adolf, the Adolf who would blow Linz to bits and start over, who regarded civil servants as "uniformed ants with pensions, ants in the anthill of this rotting empire," who would rail against the set design in a small-town production of *Tannhauser*, or recall with rapture the voice of a Berlin soprano touring with a local company—*that* Adolf vanished and in his place was a somewhat overdressed, shy, polite, slightly formal but obviously grateful, painfully thin boy who could still reveal his ambitions in endearing, and amusing, flashes: "I hope to become an artist, or an architectural painter, perhaps even a great one." My father would smile and say, "The waiting list for greatness is long, Adolf, and there is no job application."

"The artist, I think, Herr Reczek, must learn to eat air. That is why I consent to allow Frau Reczek to fatten me. When she is done I'll be able to live for years on the atmosphere alone."

My parents were tactful and sensible enough not to ask Adolf what work he did. They were simply glad I had a friend. I went to school one day each week, as required by the state; the other days I was in my father's shop. In the evenings I practiced. (I had a second-hand viola and trumpet, and we had an old upright.) On Saturday I practiced with the amateur symphony. Sundays were mass in the morning and more practice in the afternoon. In my free moments I'd drop into an armchair, fold my arms and legs like an Eastern potentate, and nap or slip into a daydream of playing in a professional orchestra. I don't even remember thinking about girls.

And now, at least one weeknight and Saturday nights, it was Adolf and opera; on weekdays at half past five, it was Adolf at the door of the shop, the raised eyebrows and amused nod from my father, and we were off—to redesign Linz, to enumerate the flaws in a production of *Meistersinger* we'd seen recently, to wait for Stefanie. With my growing knowledge of music, Adolf would put aside his monologues at times and listen and nod with a gravity that exhilarated me.

A few months after we met, Adolf asked me to have dinner with his family. Or rather he said, "My mother wishes me to extend to you our invitation to lunch on Sunday next. Can you come?" His building, at Humboldtstrasse 41, was solid but otherwise nondescript. Though I usually offered to accompany him home after our evening walks through the city, or after a longer production at the Landestheater had ended in the early morning, he insisted on taking his leave one or two blocks away. So I'd seen the building only once, out of curiosity, taking a detour one afternoon when I was delivering a set of pillows to a customer in his district. By that time, Adolf was already a daily visitor at the shop and stayed for dinner several times a week, so it seemed odd that I'd never been in his family's home.

I remember walking up through the dark, bare stairwell to the third floor. I had on my theater-going suit, which was starting to wear thin. I was carrying in both hands, like a ritual urn, a large jar of my mother's homemade jam, *Zwetschgenmus*, wrapped in colored tissue paper and tied with a bow. (Whenever he came to dinner Adolf would bring us sweets, a small plant, or some other gift for the house.) While I remember the Hitler family apartment and its details clearly, what struck me with an immediacy that remains vivid to this day was Adolf's mother's face. She, not Adolf, answered the door, and she stood inches from me. I was surprised by how young she looked. Her hair was pulled back in the traditional bun, her skin was smooth and un-wrinkled, her mouth small. Her eyes were large, pale, and transparently blue—clearer and more transfixing even than her son's. What added to the impression of youthfulness, even girlishness, I think, was her expression; it was open and guileless and sad. She was slender and wore a black silk dress corseted tightly at the waist.

"Herr Reczek," she said.

"Eugen," I said, lifting the jar in its colored wrapping, and bending from the waist. "For you and your family." I sounded to myself almost as formal as Adolf.

The apartment was spotless. The mahogany furniture shone and the rooms had the citrus-like, faintly acrid smell of wax polish. It was surprisingly small: the living room served as the dining room and also apparently as a bedroom where Frau Hitler slept with Adolf's younger sister, Paula; two small beds had been pushed into one corner. Off the living room was an equally spotless kitchen, and off this a tiny, windowless bedroom, which was Adolf's. He led me there after dinner: it was like walking into a vault. It was filled with books, in piles on the floor, on a small desk, under the narrow bed. Many seemed to be from secondhand shops, which gave the room its musty, pungent air. The rest had been borrowed—Adolf belonged to every lending library in the city. There were books on art and city design, an oversized "visual dictionary" of architecture, books on Germanic legend and myth, a whole set of translated American westerns. I remember seeing Carlyle's biography of Frederick the Great.

The sketchpad and leather-bound diary he carried with him were on the desk, and open alongside them the libretto of *Lohengrin*, which he must have borrowed from the library of the music school. There were unfinished drawings, a sheaf of them on the bed, and tacked to the wall at eye level, ringing the entire room. They were sketches for scenes in *Lohengrin*.

After we'd seen our first performance of *Lohengrin* (Adolf had

21

gone to all seven), he'd stayed up all night redesigning the sets for the opera. He'd devised an apparatus that, he said, would allow a three-dimensional swan to tow Lohengrin across the stage. The forest, rather than a mere painted backdrop, extended onto the stage and became a dark refuge from which Elsa would emerge or retreat to. The king's courtyard, where Lohengrin would kill Friedrich, was now a menacing Gothic arena sur-rounded by spiked turrets. Each rendering included detailed instructions for choreography and lighting. The energy and utter seriousness that had gone into all this work thrilled me.

In the main room, behind the dining table, was a dark, polished sideboard holding several framed photographs and, lined up like soldiers awaiting inspection, a rack of Adolf's father's smoking pipes. Next to the pipes was a remarkable photograph. It was of Adolf's *Völkschule* class, fourth form, in Leonding. He must have been aged ten or so. There are five or six rows of boys with their teacher in the center. The boys look—as boys do at that age— attentive, bored, wide-eyed with almost comic apprehension, a few sullen and distracted. In the middle of the top row, at the very apex of the group, is Adolf. He is flanked by three boys on each side, each boy slightly shorter than the next, so the row slopes downward on both sides, leaving Adolf a good inch or two higher than the others. His arms are folded, hair parted on the right, the forelock down to the eyebrows. His chin is up, head angled back a little. The mouth is turned down at the corners, the eyes narrowed, and the face is set in a look of utter and defiant certainty. I have never forgotten it.

The meal was more elaborate than I expected. Adolf's mother served me first, then Adolf and Paula. Her movements were slow, controlled, formal, but she had a kind, concerned way about her, and she would smile and glance at you when she doled out portions, as though asking whether you'd like a little more now or later. And those *eyes*. They lent her an air of having great but quiet powers of observation. No one lifted a fork until she had seated herself, glanced around the table, and nodded.

"Adolf tells me," she said, "that you have a considerable knowledge of music, play three instruments, and work in your father's upholstery shop, Eugen. That you have your own interests but are willing to learn a trade."

Adolf did not look up.

"We live above my father's shop," I said. "When I was a boy, I was with him always, pleading to be allowed to do something, anything. I must have thought it was an honor then." Adolf glanced at me. "It was not hard to pick up. It was not as though I had to go to school to learn it. Or, like my father, be shipped to some distant city to live in a garret with a strange family."

Adolf had taken out a pencil and was sketching on a paper napkin. I glanced over—it was a great, vaulted archway. He was always drawing arches, gates, doorways, ornate entrances, alleys.

"Can you sing better than Adi?" Paula looked at me, putting her hands on the table. She was eleven.

"Well, I—I don't know," I said. "The truth is I don't know if I can sing at all anymore. I used to sing in choir."

"Adolf was in choir once but he hated it," she said. "Now he sounds like he's imitating giants, croaking it out until he starts to squeak. *Seht! Seht! Welch ein seltsam Wunder! Wie? Ein Schwan? Ein Schwan!*" Actually, Adolf was always singing snatches of dialogue in the empty streets of Linz when we left the opera. He had a strong but unsettled voice, somewhat harsh, which could

23

unexpectedly skip into an upper register. "All night! Walking up and down his room. Have you ever *seen* his room? It's like a library! You can barely stand in there!"

"Quiet, goose," Adolf said, sketching.

"Paula," Frau Hitler said calmly.

By now, Adolf had risen from his chair and was pacing the room, stooped over the drawing in his hand with a look of grave concentration. He placed it against the wall, quickly erased and sketched, and continued to pace.

"Adi." His mother had clasped her hands in front of her and was staring down at the tablecloth. "Adi," she said.

"I will return in a moment," he muttered, striding from the room, napkin in hand.

"Eugen." His mother suddenly turned to me, placing her hand over mine—a gesture that made my heart race—and said, almost in a whisper, "Eugen, you are his only friend since he left school, even before that. He admires you—no, don't say anything. Your family is kind to him. I know he likes your parents. Watch him. He is difficult and strange and he lives in his head. No one can tell him anything, though perhaps you can. He was like this when his father was alive, though more so now. Perhaps I am to blame. He may have a talent, and I have tried to convince him to go back to school, but I get nowhere. He is stubborn, he is beyond stubborn. He has strong ideas, many of which I do not understand. But he is also lost. Be his friend, listen to him, perhaps he will listen to you. You seem to have a head on your shoulders. A musical head, but still a head."

I could not take my eyes from her face. I thought I could read there a deep suffering and forbearance, and I wonder now whether she knew, or sensed, even then that she was going to die. This was not the last time that she would confide in me. Later, when she was sick and Adolf was in Vienna, I would find out that before Adolf was born she had lost three children within five weeks of each other—one in childbirth and two to diphtheria. My own mother had lost three children before I was born, a fact that could only deepen my odd identification with Adolf, but the tragedy had not been concentrated in such a short time. And my mother was consoled by a husband who had always shown a reasonable and tender concern for her, while Adolf's father—the man in the Franz Joseph whiskers, whose image, in his imperial uniform, stared down at us during dinner—was a very different man.

Adolf came back into the room. He seemed a bit jaunty. He pulled his chair in and tossed back his hair. "Well, goose," he said to Paula, "did you miss me?"

Paula glanced at him and out into the room. "It's not polite to walk away from the table like that," she said quietly. I thought she'd been embarrassed by her mother's confession.

Adolf frowned and grunted softly. Not exactly an apology but, for him, an acknowledgement of some meaning.

Frau Hitler looked from Adolf to Paula, then smiled at me. "Eat," she said.

Adolf insisted on accompanying me home that evening.

"My mother seems to like you, Eugen," he said. "She thinks you will talk some sense into me. Will you?"

I merely shrugged and smiled. I wanted to ask who was influencing whom.

"Ahh," he said with disgust. "I told you that once my father took me to spend the day with him at work. He allowed me to miss school, so I knew this was quite an occasion. He and the two customs inspectors under him shared a small office on one side of the river. People would enter through one door, spread their goods on a table in the middle of the room, and leave through another door. The inspectors would scrutinize everything, making a show of leaning over each other's shoulders, holding the more interesting items up and asking my father to look, as though they were expecting to find diamonds in a piece of fruit. The man's name, address, and destination, and a description of every item, were dutifully recorded in a fair hand in an enormous ledger. These people were like monkeys in a cage. Monkeys in a cage." He looked up. It was past midnight. The night sky in the early spring was clear and strewn with stars. Adolf, scanning the heavens as though he were looking there for someone to address, said in a whisper, almost hissing, "God save me from such a fate!" He had just turned sixteen years old.

I have been accused of having an attitude of "uncritical devotion" towards my friend. The truth is I cared about one thing and one thing only: music. This was the secret I carried with me all day as I sweated alongside my father in his shop, and during every waking moment at home. If my mother suspected, she did not say. Adolf was the only one with whom I could share this. Adolf cared, as I've said, about—*everything*. He worshipped opera, art, architecture as the supreme expression of the human spirit, but he cared about everything. And he had started to read newspapers and political flyers, a habit that would become voracious once we reached Vienna. So, with what I have been told is my tolerant good nature, I was obliged to listen to his harangues on subjects ranging from the military policies of the Austrian monarchy to tariffs on imported meat. I would smile to myself as my friend abused mayors, generals, monarchs. Devotion? Yes, Adolf was a demanding and impatient friend. I would never be late for the opera or for our end-of-the-day walks through the city or along the river or at times into the hills beyond, if there was still light. I would wait for the whistled passage from the overture to *Tannhauser*, then the tap at the door, and Adolf would make polite conversation with my father while I hurried to sponge the sweat and horsehair from my chest and neck, changed, and still smelling slightly of upholsterer's glue, bounded down the stairs for our next adventure.

If my friend demanded devotion, he also gave it. How were the viola lessons progressing and did I think it truly easier to learn than the violin? Most people thought just the opposite. Was I nervous about the up-coming performance of the amateur symphony? Did I feel prepared? Were the other players well trained? How was my father's business, there seemed to be a half dozen sofas stacked to the ceiling that weren't there yesterday?

At times, I felt he was inhabiting my life as I lived it. When he asked after my musical studies, he never implied that I owed it only to myself to pursue these, but that I owed it to the future of musical life, to the continuation of the German genius for music. This was no selfish pursuit on my part (which I'd always felt, given how hard my dear father worked) but a sacred obligation, a sacrifice, the very opposite of purely personal ambition. He conceived a traveling orchestra that I would lead; it would visit smaller Austrian towns and perform excerpts from great German composers, and I would introduce each with a brief lecture explaining the musical content and "significance for the nation." He even presented me with a watercolor of the Villa Eugen, more fortress than villa really, built into the pine-covered hills outside the city and where I would live after I'd established myself as a composer and conductor.

My favorite, though, was the *Conservatoire*—as he called it—for which Adolf made elaborate plans and sketches. This was a kind of Italian renaissance villa in which we both would live as bachelor artists. Adolf would pursue his painting in a glass-enclosed studio in one wing, while I would follow my own muse in another wing, darker in tone, and acoustically sealed to screen out street noise and allow my friend the divine silence he needed to concentrate on his painting. There was a gallery in which Adolf and invited artists would display their work, and a recital chamber spacious enough to hold a small orchestra. And, of course, there was a library, which occupied an entire floor. This salon was run by a gray-haired, black-gowned matron; with selfless efficiency, she supervised the staff, arranged the showings and recitals, and served as a personal secretary and concierge to Adolf and myself, sheltering us, allowing us the privacy and freedom of mind needed for artistic ideas—those unpredictable blessings—to bubble to the surface. It was only later that I realized that this woman was a cultured and aristocratic version of Adolf's mother. At the end of the day, my back and shoulders aching from taking down old armchairs and sofas, the scent of rotting wood and soiled muslin and burlap still clinging to me, I would lie in my bed and inspect the floor plans and sketches my friend had drawn and lose myself in imagining the high ceilings and palatial rugs and book-lined walls of the *Conservatoire*.

Once, I had gone to the funeral of a classmate who had been killed in an accident on his family's farm. My former classmates—with whom I was still superficially friendly, even though

I was in school only one day each week—were asking me about my life as a workingman. And there, trailing maybe twenty meters behind the crowd, was Adolf. The figure he cut, with the long narrow coat, the cane, the broad-brimmed felt hat, was unmistakable. I dropped back until I was walking alongside him. Neither of us looked at the other. A few of the boys glanced over their shoulders.

"How did you know Mueller?" I asked.

"I didn't."

"Then how—"

"I don't like the idea of your having other friends. I don't like the idea of your talking with those boys."

"They're classmates, really, not friends. And the conversation is shallow and forgettable. You can imagine."

"Still."

We followed the mourners. Adolf stayed through the burial and we left the cemetery together. Somehow, this did not seem an odd thing for him to do.

Decades later, after I had failed myself, failed my friend, failed my calling and missed my *destiny*, Adolf would, on the very eve of the *Anschluss*, write and hand me a check covering the musical education, from secondary school through Conservatory, of my three sons.

Another time, I prepared a small concert for him. Bravratksy had been taking me through Bach's exercise books for the keyboard, written for his students, his wife, his children. These are short, simple pieces that still require precision and concentration, even as they train and discipline the fingers. As one masters them, they become complex and beautiful. At times they can be almost comically fast; at other times profound, reverent—a truly German music. I would never tire of practicing these on our old upright.

One evening, after Adolf had stayed to dinner, I suggested in an offhand way that I play a few tunes Bravratsky had been helping me with. "You might like them," I said.

Adolf, who always insisted on helping my mother clear the table, glanced at her. She waved him off. "Go ahead, Adi," she said. "I hear the same concert every night."

I had chosen the first, second, and ninth preludes and fugues from the first book of *The Well-Tempered Clavier*. The first was in the key of C-major, fairly straightforward and pleasant. The prelude of the second was devilishly fast, beyond my technique at the time really, but I'd practiced it so often I knew it almost by heart. The fugue of the ninth was towering and profound, something I thought would really appeal to him.

Adolf had drawn up a kitchen chair and sat awkwardly on its edge, his arms extended and palms resting on his knees. He placed his cane on the floor. This was the posture of the humble, somewhat anxious student, and it was completely new to me. I was used to the legs crossed, cane spinning, chin-in-the-air diffidence he sometimes affected, or the dead-seriousness with which he would explain one of his new ideas, or the righteous indignation of his harangues on the "botched" design of the city. But this awkward, attentive curiosity I had not seen. I introduced each prelude and fugue with a few pieces of information—the key, the different ways it might be played, the technical difficulties of counterpoint. I used the pedal a bit on the first, to give it a flowing, lyrical sound. I *raced*, eyes closed, through the prelude of the second, dropping a note here and there, not too noticeable in the virtuosic cascade. I gave the fugue of the ninth everything I had, playing louder, slowing it down just enough to heighten the sense of drama.

Adolf watched with a graveness that bordered on perplexity.

"How," he said, "do you manage to play all the parts with only ten fingers?"

I explained how the voices were divided up—the thumbs and forefingers taking one subject, the outside fingers taking others. "Here," I said, "I'll show you."

He looked at me.

"Give me your hands."

He extended his arms uncertainly and I motioned for him to sit on the bench alongside me. He half-rose from his chair and seemed to freeze, his knees bent like an old man's. I gave him an encouraging little wave and he ventured another step and lowered himself onto the bench. He lifted his bony white hands—he had long, delicate fingers which, next to his eyes, were his most striking physical trait—and I carefully spread them across the keyboard. His fingers were pale and cold and damp. Then, as Bravratsky would, I got up and stood behind him, leaned in, and placed my hands upon his, finger for finger. My arms were resting on his shoulders and my cheek was next to his. I could smell soap and scrubbed skin; his slender body seemed to have gone rigid. I guided him slowly through the opening subject of the first fugue and the introduction of the second subject.

"The fugue in C-major is almost all white keys," I said, "which makes this easier—no stretching for the black keys. Good." I stepped back. "The second voice takes over but the first keeps repeating in the background—not every note repeated but enough, and the rest are implied. You don't have to play all the notes all the time, even though it can sound as if you are. Often,

Bach *does* have you play all the notes."

He squinted at the dense hieroglyphics of the music, and slid his hands quickly into the pockets of his suit jacket. He cleared his throat. He was sweating. "There are many notes," he said.

I laughed. "Yes, there are a lot of notes in Bach. Many more than in Wagner. For a long time, it is nothing but drudgery to practice. Then one day you realize—I am *playing* this! It is quite a feeling."

"You play well," he said and again cleared his throat.

"Well, I'm so-so, I think, at this point. But I have been well taught."

"Do you think Bravratsky would take me as a student? I know my mother would buy me a piano, if I asked her."

"Oh, you needn't do that. My father's customers are always offering him good used uprights at a bargain. Learn on one of those. But it is very time-consuming, ask my mother. What about your studies? You have more than you can handle now. I've seen your room. I don't know when you sleep."

He sighed. "Yes, yes, I know."

At that moment, he seemed to me, for some reason, sad and defeated. I could feel my stomach drop with fear. I had seen him inspired, jaunty, excited, aloof, righteously angry, silent, contemptuous. But defeated? He had left school, he said, to avoid defeat, to avoid being herded into the civil service, an accountancy, a solicitorship—a "bread-and-butter job," as he called it. He would teach himself. He belonged to every lending library in Linz. He went to every opera, knew every stone of every public building, had drawn them all, over and over. But that would only get him so far. Sooner or later he would have to allow himself to be taught, *submit* to being taught, even well taught, or he would remain a perpetual amateur. He would stay in that cell of a bedroom in his mother's apartment, remaking the world in his head. This fearless, arrogant boy who had given *me* hope.

I do not know if I could have put this into words at the time, but I felt it. And I felt sharply disappointed for another reason. I had played well, I thought. I'd succeeded in slowing the fugue of the ninth to emphasize its depth, its profound sentiment, without becoming ponderous. Adolf paid close attention, he was impressed, but he was not moved. The architecture of the music, the technique, interested him, not the sound. The scale was too small, too intimate. Adolf liked his art big. Huge. Monumental, heroic, tragic. Oceans of sound washing over him, engulfing him, carrying him away from his tense, pacing self.

Two weeks later, we were to get an unexpected dose of the heroic. One of the traveling companies was putting on a production of Wagner's *Rienzi*. This was his first operatic success, but rarely performed, then or now. It had been overshadowed by the lush, mesmerizing chords of the later works, and had not even been produced in Bayreuth. So it was a real curiosity. We met as usual in the Hauptplatz an hour early and ran the two blocks to the opera house in time to get our standing-room tickets and a place close enough to the front of the line. The moment the ushers released the ropes, we vaulted up the burgundy-carpeted stairs to our leaning-posts in the mezzanine.

Quite a surprise! More in the tradition of Grand Opera than the myth-laden music drama that so hypnotized us. But well done—a splashy, exciting overture, lots of battles, processions, marches, predictable villains, and a fairly conventional hero. Rome is in a state of chaos and decay; Rienzi—refusing a kinship and preferring to accept the title of "Tribune of the People"—rallies the citizens of Rome, and for a while it looks as though he will succeed in restoring the city's virtue and grandeur. But the Church, choosing to believe the slander of Rienzi's enemies that he is a heretic, excommunicates him. The people turn on him. Rienzi appears on a balcony with his loyal sister and makes one last attempt to persuade the crowd, but they riot, the city burns, and Rienzi perishes.

There is one splendid scene—Rienzi's Gethsemane—in which, the night before the final confrontation, he kneels alone before an altar and prays for strength. He declares that his mission is to transform his people's shame into greatness. He will never marry; Rome is his bride. I glanced toward Adolf then, but he was no longer at his pillar. He was standing at the railing, chin raised, hand on his cane as though he were grasping the hilt of a sword, those transparent eyes liquid and glistening.

At the very end of a performance I was used to receiving some signal from Adolf—a tilt or waver of the head, a nod, an uneven gesture of the hand—indicating what he had thought of the production. Tonight was different. With a stern, impatient expression, he clutched his overcoat and headed down the stairs. I followed him out into the street. We walked for several minutes in silence. He had still not looked at me.

"When Rienzi—" I began.

"Shut your mouth."

My face burned. He had never spoken so sharply to me. We walked on, the only sound the steady tapping of the brass tip of his cane. He had still not glanced at me.

"Come with me to the Freinberg."

The opera had run for four hours and it was past midnight. One of my jobs in the shop was to start the fire each morning at seven o'clock. Still, I walked with him over the bridge and up the slick, grassy slope of the Freinberg. The sleeping city below us was enveloped in the pale-yellow haze of the gas lamps. Adolf stopped, finally looked at me, and began to pace. (How I was to get to know that pacing, that determined, relentless nocturnal back-and-forth!)

"We live today in a state of deep humiliation," he said, waving his arm in a slow arc to include the city, the hills, and the country beyond. "We ourselves don't even know how deep, how profound, how shameful. Yes, yes, I know, you have a comfortable"—he said "comfortable" as though he could chew the word and spit it out—"life. We all have comfortable lives. You have enough to eat, your mother is kind, even your esteemed father is kind. You will have a reliable trade. And then off to the side, with what energy you have left to devote to it, you have your music. But that music—you yourself have told me this, Eugen—plays in your head all day long, while you wipe the sawdust, the bits of horsehair and coconut fiber from your neck and eyes and hair and the insides of your mouth. If you could wipe it from the surface of your lungs you would. If you don't watch it, you yourself will become stuffed. An upholstered man! Don't laugh! At least you are aware of this. You see, first you laugh, then you *cough*, because you are eating the air in that shop. But you are aware, you are aware of something greater. I can see that. Look at the students in the cafés along the Landstrasse every evening, with their fat faces, scheming, praying to remain—*comfortable*! Please, God, let me become a comfortable accountant, solicitor, civil servant, with a comfortable pension and easy chair! Maybe even a comfortable small manufacturer or merchant with a house in town and a carriage and nannies. Please, Lord, I do so want to be a *slave* to comfort. And while we are at it, why not a little filthy fun on the side with so-and-so's sister, the one with the big, voluptuous bosom? Or a whore in another town?"

He paused and dug his cane into the moist earth.

"Why do we—we, I mean you and me, Eugen, and a few others—go to see Wagner performed? For the costumes? For the *entertainment*? Entertainment is for the comfortable. No, we go for a glimpse of another world, an extraordinary world. Not a comfortable one. But a world that did exist and may again exist. He, Wagner, reminds us. He reminds us that we have less to fear from death than from never having lived. The Church, too, gives us a glimpse of another world. But you can have the Church and its heaven. I will have Wagner, he is my religion. Do you understand me? Of course you understand me. But know this: to be with me, to want a new world, to destroy the world as it is—you must first declare *war* on everything comfortable."

He crouched, ran his hand over the wet grass, and looked out over the city on the other side of the dark wide river.

"This bastardized, humiliated empire can't last. It will come apart at the seams. If not this year then next, or the year after that. *That* will not be comfortable but it may lead to something . . . greater."

I looked at him—bent close to the ground, gazing at the city, the city whose streets I had walked with him dozens of times, listening to his plans to redesign and rebuild. He was using the cane now as a pointer: Linz would have the tallest steeple, the longest frieze, the greatest art museum. The new cultural capital of Europe. He stroked the grass, a gesture of ownership, like some adolescent visionary or general planning his assault. I said nothing. With Adolf, there was never anything left to say.

Later that week, over dinner at our house, Adolf recounted for my parents the story of *Rienzi*—his accepting the title of Tribune, his betrayal by the Church, by the populace, the fire that consumes the city. I chimed in with a description of the orchestral highlights and a moving, though partial, rendition, from memory, of "Rienzi's Prayer" on our piano.

For the next few weeks, my parents took to referring to Adolf as "the Tribune" or "our Tribune." My father, with good-humored affection, would call "Eugen, the Tribune!" when Adolf arrived at the shop in the late afternoon, and Adolf would smile a bit shyly and cock an eyebrow. In private, my father would say, "Well, at least our Adolf now has a job!" Adolf managed to find the libretto and score at one of his lending libraries, and I would accompany him on our upright while he struggled in his cracked, unreliable tenor:

> *You strengthened me, gave me supreme power*
> *To raise up what had fallen into dust*
> *You transformed the people's shame.*

On "shame," or *Schmach,* I recall, his voice wavered, broke, and jumped an octave. I could see my mother, on the other side of the room, turn away and cover her mouth.

At the conclusion of the prayer, Adolf, like Rienzi, abased himself, touching his forehead to the floor. "I am praying for a new voice," he announced, prostrate. I remember this because it was unusual—rare—for this grave young man, who lived with dreams of unlimited success, to laugh at one of his own failings. He had, I felt, become a second son in our home, a brother, a comrade, a co-conspirator in my own plans to escape the world through music—to escape my *life* through music—as I conspired with him to change the world through art or simply to make it over entirely.

I know now, from an article in the *Berliner Zeitung* (which we have in our "library" here at Glasesnbach and the accuracy of which I have no reason to doubt), that decades later Adolf had the original manuscript of *Rienzi* taken from the library in Bayreuth and placed in a vault, where it was found, undamaged, amid the smoking ruins of the Chancellery in 1945.

Late one afternoon, a few weeks after seeing *Rienzi*, Adolf came to the shop, excited. I was wearing my apron and canvas trousers. I think he may have grabbed me by the shoulders. This was unusual—as extravagant as he became during his monologues on Linz, architecture, the empire, the tariffs on livestock, and virtually everything else, the physical display of emotion was foreign to him. He said he was going to Vienna for three or four weeks and planned to stay with his god-parents. His mother had agreed to fund this trip. "I have told her I must study the paintings in the Art History Museum—the technique, the use of color, of different materials. Without such examples, one can make no progress." I knew, though, that he would quickly exhaust the art museum and spend his time sketching the renowned buildings of that imperial city and, if he could find affordable standing-room tickets, going to the opera every night.

My father nodded at us. I removed my apron and we went into the kitchen. I insisted on taking his overcoat. He was still talking as he gently slid out of it. He always treated his clothing with great care.

"I will be eyes and ears for both of us, Eugen. There is much that will be of use to us, perhaps more than we can know or imagine. But while I am gone, you must be my eyes and ears for Leydenhauser"—Leydenhauser was our code name for Stefanie; I think it was the name of one of his old classmates. "If you are at the bridge later than five thirty, you may miss her. Does she betray any trace of worry or surprise at my absence? What is she wearing? Is anyone accompanying them—her brother, a female friend, or even some officer?" Occasionally Stefanie and her mother would be joined by one of the uniformed officers who liked to flirt with the attractive young women in Linz, sending Adolf, wild with jealousy, into a rant over "These useless good-for-nothings with their starched uniforms and clanking sabers and heads filled with cement. They are duller than mannequins!" At that time, even during peace, Austria seemed overrun with regimental officers, decked out in gold braid and epaulettes, riding boots, plumes, capes, sabers. The Emperor's Gentlemen-at-Arms, the Austrian Lifeguard Cavalrymen, the Special Lifeguards, the Light Dragoons, the dismounted Lifeguard Cavalrymen! Often, they were the sons of the aristocracy. Adolf detested them. "Here," he said now, "is my address in Vienna if you need it. Or simply record your observations and date them. Do not speak with Stefanie, unless seeing that I am not there and perhaps curious or concerned, she addresses you directly." I considered this unlikely.

I was, of course, used to my friend's obsession. After all, idealized love—love at a distance—was a staple, really, of German Romanticism in Austria and Germany at this time; we were saturated with it. It was celebrated in lyrical poetry, including Adolf's own, for that matter. In stories, it often had tragic consequences, but not always. Once, when I was in Adolf's room at the Hitler household and he had stepped out to help his mother with something, I noticed on his desk a dialogue he was engaged in writing—in fact, as I realized after a moment, a dialogue between him and the young woman he waited for every day at the bridge from Urfahr and with whom he had never exchanged a word. He was instructing her, explaining that she was a true soprano *coloratura*, telling her what roles were open to her as a result, how she must train her voice, and that he would consider writing a libretto for her which his trusted colleague, Eugen Reczek, could both score and conduct. Well, this was a fantasy I could appreciate.

I told him I would keep watch.

Four days after Adolf left, I received a card, an elaborate, beautifully produced postcard that opened out into three panels, forming a panorama of the Karlsplatz with the Karlskirche in the center. It was titled "Vienna, Karlsplatz, as seen from the Technical High School." In the margins, Adolf had scrawled "Greetings to your esteemed parents!" On the card, he had written:

> *In sending you this card I must apologize for not*
> *having let you hear from me sooner. I arrived safely as*
> *you see and am now having a good look at everything.*
> *Tomorrow to the opera, to "Tristan," the day after to*
> *"The Flying Dutchman," etc. To the Stadttheatre today.*
>   *Greetings from your friend,*
>   *Adolf Hitler*

In one of the photographic panels he had drawn an arrow pointing to the building which housed the Vienna Conservatory of Music and along the arrow had written "CONSERVATORY!"

The following day I received another card, a photograph of "The Stage of the Imperial Opera House." He had written:

The interior of the edifice is not very inspiring. If the exterior is mighty majesty which lends the building the solemnity of an artistic monument, the interior strikes one as rather unimpressive. Only when the mighty waves of sound roll through space and the whistling of the wind yields to the frightful rushing billows of sound does one feel nobility and forget the gold and velvet with which the interior is overloaded.

Adolf H.

The handwriting was flowing, slanted, oddly mature. The misspellings and often missing punctuation, though, took me aback. It was at almost comic odds with his formal diction, the winding yet forceful sentences of his tirades, the ferocious eloquence when he got going on one of his more emotional monologues. It contradicted what I regarded as his obvious intelligence and his constant reading, which surely exposed him daily to correct German spelling and grammar. Was it the lack of formal schooling? I doubted it, though it suggested that even in the earlier grades he took his schooling as casually—or as contemptuously—as he did later, before he left it behind altogether. Perhaps, consciously or not, he was still trying to get the goat of his pompous, detested teachers.

He sent several cards with views of the Academy of Fine Arts. It was one of the neoclassical jewels of the Ringstrasse, its massive doors interspersed with Doric columns each supporting a different, casually draped Greek god, the ceiling frescoes by Feuerbach, the upper stories lined with huge arched windows overlooking the magnificent Schillerplatz. It had been designed by Theophilus Hansen, whose buildings included the Parliament, the Vienna Stock Exchange, the Ringstrasse *palais* of the Archduke Wilhelm, and the Musikverein, one of the finest concert halls in the world.

I checked the box several times each day and rifled through the mail as soon as I had it in my hands. I received four or five more cards over the next month. Each contained questionable spelling or syntax. Every card was, of course, of a building, a square, a monument, a boulevard. There were mentions of "Leydenhauser" ("How is Leydenhauser?" ". . . thinking of Leydenhauser," "Despite the splendor, I cannot wait to return to Linz and Leydenhauser and to that daily exchange of understanding, that vision.") They contained not just descriptions of admiration and ecstasy but also the usual criticisms. The buildings surrounding a plaza were "wonderful in themselves but not positioned for maximal effect," the Hofburg Palace was "splendid, but situated too close to a shopping district, which shows evidence of haphazard planning," a university building on the Ringstrasse was "magnificent, perfect, but simply not big enough!"

My friend had rebuilt Linz; he was starting to rebuild Vienna. I stood the three-paneled card on the small table next to my bed. At times, before falling asleep, I would reread it and study the Karlskirche and other buildings on the Karlsplatz, and the hand-drawn arrow pointing to the Conservatory.

I did keep an eye on Stefanie, as I'd promised. I'd be at the bridge from Urfahr at five o'clock each day, in the same spot, and assume my pose of practiced nonchalance. I'd survey the crowd coming from the far side until I caught sight of them. When they were abreast of me, I'd incline my head, glance and nod, then quickly look away, raising my chin and narrowing my eyes as though scanning the crowd for other familiars. The first day she smiled and dipped her head. I thought I could detect, though, in the mild tilt of her head, a trace of perplexity. The second day, she did not smile. The third or fourth day she looked straight at me in a questioning way—worriedly, I thought—and held my gaze for several beats, even though she was forced to swivel her head rather awkwardly as she continued walking. She was holding a parasol.

I was excited, though not too surprised. After all, practically every day for better than a year she had seen at this same spot a gaunt boy in a long, dark overcoat, immaculate white shirt, collar, and tie, holding an ebony cane, who would nod formally, almost ceremoniously, at her. He couldn't have been more conspicuous if he'd dressed as one of the Emperor's Gentlemen-at-Arms and bowed with a sweep of his plumed hat. That night, lying in bed, I thought—I really *did* think—I would put an end to this charade, this dumbshow. Like some courtier, I would approach the girl and her mother. I would apologize for the intrusion and explain that I represented an admirer. At that moment, he was in the capital arranging admission to the State Art Academy, the first step in establishing himself and proving his worth. He would return for her, she could be sure of that. Stefanie and her mother would be impressed with his devotion and determination, moved by his shyness and old-fashioned reticence. I knew that Adolf's marrying Stefanie would, of course, interfere with our plans to live together in chaste companionship in the *Conservatoire* while pursuing our respective disciplines. Perhaps the architectural plans could be altered, redrawn. Perhaps it would not matter.

Even as I write this now, I find myself shaking my head. Could I really, even at that age, have been taken into this fantasy in such a way? That together, in an unshakeable, immortal friendship, we would conquer the disciplines of art and architecture and music; we would destroy the world as it was and create it again. It was a dream verging on reality for us. In 1938, when Adolf took me to Bayreuth and we walked in the garden behind Wahnfried, Wagner's home, he said to me quite seriously, "I have work to do now, but I will finish it, I will see it through to the end, and when I am done, Reczek, you will be with me forever." He still believed it! Everyone around him seemed to believe it.

Later that week, Stefanie and her mother were accompanied by an officer, a cavalry officer, I could tell by the uniform—the striking green coat which came to the waist in front, the field of gold braid over the chest, the epaulettes, immaculate white breeches, and riding boots. He even wore the cap with the regimental plume. A real peacock. I don't need to tell you that one year later Stefanie actually *did* marry an officer and moved to Vienna. I imagine they led an utterly conventional life, if her husband did not perish in the Great War. My friend, the pathetic dreamer, would return to Austria, and to Linz, in 1938 and destroy that very footbridge. He would replace it with a structure that was more like a boulevard over water; it rose gracefully over the river and continued through Urfahr, exactly as he'd described it to me then, more than thirty years earlier. Close to the Linz bank, where he would wait for Stefanie, he would place a different couple: a statue of Krimhilde on one side and Siegfried on the other. It was the only one of his many plans for Linz he had time to realize before he put a bullet in his head last April in Berlin. I have read that he may have taken cyanide first, leaving an adjutant to shoot him and place the gun in his hand, making it appear that he'd taken his life in a manlier way. I don't believe this. He was perfectly capable of putting a bullet in his head. Anyone who knew him, who knew his unyielding nature, would realize this. With Adolf it was everything or it was nothing. Always.

Adolf returned after slightly more than a month. He was strangely quiet when I met him at the station. I expected him to launch into an immediate, exhaustive account of the architectural and cultural splendors of the capital. Instead, he was silent. "I must see Leydenhauser," he said. "Come." As it was already late afternoon, we walked to the Urfahr bridge and waited for Stefanie and her mother to appear. We exchanged with them the usual glances and cursory nods, and mother and daughter moved with the flowing crowd into Linz. Suddenly, Adolf swung around towards the river and leaning over the railing he ran his hands, shaking, through his thick, lank hair. "I cannot continue to see Stefanie under these conditions," he said, "or I will lose my mind. I must leave. I must move to Vienna. I will go to the Academy of Art. When you are ready, you will join me."

It is difficult for me to say what I felt at that moment. I knew Adolf was not joking, and I knew his mother would sponsor him. My first reaction was one, I think, of alarm. For a time, I would be left behind, choking on the dust and fumes of my father's shop while he studied in the city—really, the European capital of artists and musicians. Even with the prospect of entering the Vienna Conservatory—if they would have me, an upholsterer's son who dabbled in the viola, piano, and trumpet in his spare time and knew almost no music theory—this sense that I could be left behind was terribly distressing. I was heartened, in a way, that Adolf realized, or seemed to, that he couldn't spend his life reading and drawing at night in his room, wandering the city with his sketchpad during the day, and exchanging glances with a girl to whom he had never spoken and who didn't know his name. "What am I to say?" he would ask me when I urged him to introduce himself. "I am an unemployed amateur who lives with his mother, didn't finish *Realschule*, and has no prospects? That would be the end of it, Reczek." I hoped that he had come to his senses: If he wanted to go further, especially if he chose architecture, then he had to submit to being a student, an apprentice. Very, very few artists and musicians are truly self-taught, and even then it is probably only vanity for them to think so. Adolf must stop rebelling against his dead father or he would end up a possibly brilliant but unfinished, thwarted personality. An eccentric, passionate failure.

I did have another reaction to Adolf's vow to go to Vienna to study. I hesitate to mention it because it involves speculating about an intimate aspect of my friend's life, and it is not an easy thing to discuss. It is a subject that would emerge again and again once we were sharing a room in Vienna. In the end, it would nearly drive us apart.

Adolf was a personality in tension. I don't have to tell you this. One could see it in his ecstatic reaction to music, the pacing in his room, the brooding, the compulsive reading and sketching for hours, the talking, the need to idolize and to denounce, the inability to sleep until he had exhausted himself. This was the reason, I think, he reacted so strongly to everything around him. There was something impossibly stubborn and radical in his nature. I do not follow politics and later I did not bother to familiarize myself with the specifics of Adolf's program, but I remember a Munich journalist's observation that Adolf radicalized everything he touched. I can understand this.

Adolf also had something—how can I put this?—Puritan-like—or is it Puritanical?—in him. Sexual jokes, bawdy humor of any kind, made him uncomfortable and even angry. I think this is one of the things he most disliked about the boys in the *Realschule*, aside from their ambitions to become actuaries and civil servants. Boys of that age are often avid masturbators, despite the horrid stories we were fed about blindness, idiocy, and the other supposed medical consequences. Boys would even joke about masturbation and talk roughly about girls and women. Adolf hated this. Even then he was preoccupied with syphilis—and this in *Linz*, which had no red-light district and where the closest thing to pornography was the "adult" section of the local wax museum. Once we got to Vienna, syphilis was to become more of an obsession with him, as well as a social and (strange as it seems) racial problem. I recall he thought it could be inherited, although this was not an unusual belief at the time.

Once, in Linz, I got a taste of this myself. In those days, upholsterers also designed and hung draperies and wallpaper; they were interior decorators of a sort and in Germany and Austria were even licensed as such. And it *was* something of an art. My father had a client who lived in a castle outside Linz, beyond the Freinberg, and he would take me there to help him line the walls with felt and hang wallpaper, a difficult and dangerous job given the size and height of the rooms. He'd told me the owner, Frau von Branitsch, was rich and eccentric and not to mind anything I saw or heard. In fact, I rarely even saw her when we went. When

I did, she seemed to be gliding through the rooms, lost in her thoughts, and clutching at the neck a robe that trailed after her along the cold stone floors. Once, though, we had finished lining a chamber with felt and I was high on the ladder struggling to hold up lengths of wallpaper samples.

"Yes, yes, that is a wonderful design," I could hear him saying in the tolerant, mildly pleading voice he used with important customers. "But, you know, this is a large room with high ceilings, and rather dark. The pattern is small and could easily be lost. In fact, you might hardly see it unless you were standing with your nose to the wall, no? Something bolder, larger, but still elegant, still to your taste, with a brighter background. Look at this."

"In candlelight, Herr Reczek, the rooms look quite different. You are always here during the day. That is the problem."

"True, yes. But look at this."

My neck and arms ached, and I was lightheaded. I glanced over my shoulder. My father was going through his book of samples. Frau von Branitsch was standing there, arms folded, calmly discussing his recommendations, nodding and skeptically wagging her head—and not wearing a stitch of clothing! Still talking, my father gave a little wave of his hand indicating that I should not look and just hold up the paper while they continued to discuss color and design and what could be bought from suppliers in Vienna.

I told Adolf this story once, in a way, I think, that conveyed my unfathomable surprise, as I tried to keep my balance on the ladder, rather than any real dirty-mindedness. I expected *some* response—a disbelieving (or even disapproving) shake of the head, a smiling glance, an amused grunt. But there was nothing, silence. When I looked at him he was staring sternly, even angrily, ahead. I suffered in this scalding silence until we could change the subject.

Now, Stefanie was no girl or young lady to Adolf. She was not Stefanie Rabatsch but a Wagner heroine, a perfect mezzo-soprano without having sung a note, and the object of dozens of adoring poems. In truth, she was pretty, I thought, in a plain sort of way, narrow-waisted, with long blond hair that she at times wore in tresses down to her waist, like a schoolgirl. I do not know if even my friend was beginning to find exchanging glances at the bridge a little silly, but I do know he had begun to suffer an intolerable tension. Going to Vienna would not only help him establish himself as an artist, it would also remove him from an impossible situation.

The months after he returned from his reconnaissance trip to Vienna were worrisome. I expected endless stories about the Court Opera, the Burgtheater, the imperial buildings of the Ring-strasse, the museums, the Art Academy. But no. He stopped coming to the shop every day, and when he did he would quietly address my father and wait for me to change.

He no longer had dinner at our house. On our walks he was either withdrawn or brooding and irritable. Even his monologues—which I'd learned to attend to with the right mixture of interest and brotherly indulgence—stopped, or were at least less frequent. He did not carry his sketchpad with him. We went to the opera, but afterwards, instead of engaging in our customary and spirited critique, he would excuse himself and either head home or towards Urfahr and the hills outside the city. Once, when he failed to meet me at the opera house, I walked to the apartment on the Humboldtstrasse. His mother said she thought he had gone out to look for me. She was beside herself.

He had begun to stay out all night at times and once had been gone two days. When she asked where he'd been, he muttered, "Walking." All she wanted, she said, was to hear the reassuring sound of Adolf pacing his room at night, singing snatches from Wagner, drawing, reading out loud, memorizing passages. I sat her down. I said that Adolf had likely told the truth—he was out walking. He felt he had a decision to make and needed more space than his tiny bedroom allowed. I assured her he was not involved in anything sordid or unseemly, and that he was not losing his mind (although this is what he himself had told me). I lied and told her we were still taking our early evening walks together and attending the opera.

Frau Hitler looked drawn, unwell, and she seemed thinner.

How convincing I was I can't say. I wondered whether a glimpse of the capital had ruined Linz for Adolf, whether it had shaken his astounding certainty, his sense that he was destined to go there, to study at the Academy of Fine Arts, to establish himself, even to become great. After all, as much as I admired his work, he had to know I was no judge of the extent of his talent. The only other person who saw his drawings and plans was his mother, and mothers, of course, make awfully unreliable critics—although I know Frau Hitler had every reason to believe Adolf had talent. I did not envy her, though. Adolf was an unusual and worrisome boy to have for a son.

I wondered, too, whether this had something to do with Stefanie, whether under the strain of this unremitting obsession he had given in, and soiled the purity of his "extraordinary love," or felt continually tempted to. This would have been terribly humiliating for him, to allow himself to turn his Beloved, his future partner in the pursuit of all things high and noble, into the fantasy of a lewd, dirty-minded boy. It would have made him no better, in his own mind, than the snickering schoolboys in the *Realschule* he felt he had left behind. I could have told him that only recently I, too, had become a fellow sinner and that we would become blind, drooling idiots together. I don't think he would have found this reassuring. Besides, Adolf didn't believe in sin, he believed in humiliation, defeat, and dishonor.

One evening as I was helping my mother clear the table, he appeared at the door. He looked tired and grim. I knew that he had decided to go to Vienna, to apply to the Art Academy, to take part of his patrimony now (an ironic triumph, spending the legacy of his father, a life-long civil servant, on art school). He had come, I was sure, to say goodbye. Holding his black slouch hat in his hands, he greeted my parents and nodded to me. My father folded his newspaper and rose from his easy chair. My mother, seeing how pale and drawn he looked, took his overcoat and guided him to a seat at the kitchen table and lit the stove for tea.

"My mother," he said, "is seriously ill. She must have an operation. She is in excruciating pain."

My own mother placed her hands on his shoulders, but he stiffened and she stepped back.

"What is the problem, Adolf?" my father asked, sitting down across from him and resting his thick forearms on the table.

"It is cancer of the breast."

"When is the surgery?"

"The day after tomorrow. At the Hospital of the Sisters of Mercy."

"Does she have medical insurance, through your father's civil service pension, perhaps?"

Adolf shook his head. His eyelids were fluttering. He looked as though he had not slept in days.

"This can be a tremendous financial burden," my father said. "I know from my own problems."

"It doesn't matter. She must have the operation. She will have her own room as well. I have seen to it."

"Does your family have a doctor?" My parents exchanged glances.

Adolf stared down at the table.

"No. I took her to the hospital when the pain became too much to bear. This is what they told me."

"Would she allow our doctor—Dr. Bloch, you must know him—to examine her? Just to confirm that this is indeed the problem?"

Dr. Bloch had seen my father through his long pulmonary illness. He was known in Linz as "the people's doctor," but in fact he lived in a large Gothic house on the Landstrasse, where he had his consulting rooms. He had his own hansom, which he would drive himself at all hours to visit patients who were too sick or weak to come to his office. He often adjusted his bill to what the family could afford and in certain cases would even forego payment. He was a Jew, but people seemed not to care. There were very few Jews in Linz anyway.

My father went on. "Your mother will need someone to look after her once she returns home, and she may require additional treatment."

"I can help nurse her after the surgery, Adolf," my mother said. "I have done this before. More than once."

"You are kind, Frau Reczek, but my mother's sister will come from Spital for several weeks." As he said this his eyes fluttered and closed, and for several moments we sat there watching his chest rise and fall slowly until we realized he was asleep. My father helped him get his suit jacket off and despite his groggy protests we got him up the stairs and laid him down on my bed. He had become thinner and was surprisingly light. My mother followed with tea, and I was dispatched to check on Frau Hitler and tell her Adolf would be spending the night at our house.

When I knocked, Paula answered and without a word opened the door for me. Frau Hitler was propped up in bed in the living room. A teapot, several cups and dampened washcloths were on a small table beside her. Her face had already lost some of the youthfulness that had stunned me when I first met her. She indicated with her head that I should sit in the small chair that was drawn up to the bed. I told her that my father was arranging for Dr. Bloch to examine her the following morning.

"That is probably wise," she said. "Thank you. I will be glad to pay his bill."

"My father—"

She raised her hand and looked at me. Even in that drawn, exhausted face, the clear grey-blue eyes were alive and penetrating.

"How is Adolf?" she said.

"Tired. He fell asleep while he was telling us. Sitting up. We had to keep looking"—I stretched my neck forward and goggled my eyes to mimic a kind of staring disbelief—"to make sure he was really asleep. We took him upstairs and put him to bed."

"This has been difficult for him."

"My mother says she is going to stuff him like a goose."

Frau Hitler gave me a slight smile and closed her eyes. "I wish her luck. He has never eaten much."

"Yes. He lives on his . . . enthusiasm."

She nodded, her eyes still closed.

Lying there, perfectly still and with hands folded on the coverlet, she reminded me of the figures carved into the lids of sarcophagi, their hands resting on the hilt of a sword. I knew she had lost three small children before Adolf was born. Later, I would discover she had lost a fourth, a boy, Edmund, who was born several years after Adolf. He had died of measles at five. Death must have felt like a constant undertow in her life. Once or twice, Adolf had addressed me as Edmund, without correcting himself.

Dr. Bloch sat in our kitchen at noon the following day. He was a big man with a walrus mustache and a down-to-earth manner; one sensed in him a natural optimism tempered by a long and instructive acquaintanceship with death. He had grown up in a small village in Bohemia, which at that time was still under the Austrian flag, and studied medicine in Prague. His suits were always well made but a little too large, and this gave him the slightly rumpled look of a man who was simply too busy or preoccupied to wonder or care how well his clothes actually did fit. My father said this was one of the reasons he trusted him, as a doctor should avoid all appearance of vanity.

My mother had let Adolf sleep while my father and I worked in the shop. She'd woken him only for a large bowl of potato-and-cabbage soup, which in her mind was not only filling but the substrate of all human life.

We were all there, though, at the table. Dr. Bloch glanced at us but spoke directly to Adolf.

"The tumor is large. One can't say how long it has been there, but your mother says she has been in pain or discomfort for some months. I don't expect you to have noticed this. She seems the type of lady, you know, not the type to let on, or worry others. Uncomplaining. Despite all this, there seems not to be a speck of dust or fleck of mud in the entire home. Your mother is a superb homemaker. I suppose I'm not telling you anything you don't know, Adolf."

Dr. Bloch paused, placing the palm of his hand softly on the table.

"The tumor appears to have spread to the chest wall and perhaps to the bone. I believe this is why it has become so painful and come to our attention now. This will complicate surgery somewhat and there is no telling about the future. You needn't worry that she will be operated on by some know-nothing. I will speak with Dr. Urban, the chief of surgery at Sisters of Mercy and one of the best-known surgeons in Upper Austria. Despite the advanced stage of the tumor, I am quite sure he will take her."

Adolf bowed his head slightly. "You have my eter—"

Dr. Bloch lifted his bear's paw of a hand from the table and nodded.

"Here's where you and your aunt must help us, Adolf. After the surgery, she will be in bed for some weeks. You must treat the wound the way your devoted mother keeps the home—it must be perfectly clean and dry until it heals. In the beginning, after she comes home, I will see her each day on my rounds. I will leave exact instructions."

"May she have her own room while she is in the hospital?" Adolf's eyes were wide and pleading.

"Yes, of course, but the cost will be somewhat higher. This is another matter. Your father's pension leaves no provision for medical insurance. You must go over each bill from the hospital and the doctors carefully. If you have any questions, ask me. This is no problem. Eugen's father has dealt with this before, too. If the household budget is strained, and especially if this compromises your mother's care, we will see whether the hospital can reduce its charges. This is never an easy matter— the sisters are not always merciful, if you understand me—but it can be tried. And I will keep my own charges as reasonable as possible."

Here Adolf did something that surprised all of us. He was still very tired but had listened to Dr. Bloch's explanation without fidgeting, his hands in his lap, chin up. Suddenly he sprang out of his chair to rigid attention, his arms at his sides, and closing his eyes he bowed his head. The kitchen chair almost tipped over. It was a gesture half-military, half-operatic. Bloch was taken aback for a moment. Then he smiled and stood and placed his big hand on Adolf's shoulder. "I know," he said, "you will be a great help to your good mother."

Adolf gave him a brisk, decisive nod, the forelock flopping obediently.

In Linz in 1907 most cabs were horse-drawn and the street lamps were still lit with gas; the electrification that had been spreading across Europe had not quite reached us yet. Adolf borrowed a narrow mattress from the shop and laid it across the seat of the rented carriage. His mother's incision, he said, ran from her upper chest to her abdomen. An attendant wheeled Frau Hitler out the hospital entrance and, with Adolf nervously directing him, laid her carefully on the mattress. Adolf sat at her feet, holding a carton filled with gauze, dressing materials, sterilizing solution, and other supplies. After an agonizingly slow drive over the cobblestones, we arrived at the apartment on the Humboldt-strasse. The two of us, with my father, carried Frau Hitler up the three flights; I could see her trying not to wince with each step. Her bed had been moved into the kitchen, which was the only heated room in the apartment—it was early May but the weather had remained quite cool. Since Adolf's small bedroom was off the kitchen, he could remain available to his mother day and night.

Johanna, Frau Hitler's hunchbacked older sister from the family village of Spital, was already there. She seemed eager to wait on her sister, and her nodding, smiling manner, with the bent back and stooped walk, gave her the look of an agreeable crone. Adolf told her to put up a kettle for tea and immediately began building a nursing station in one corner of the kitchen, clearing out the dishes and replacing them with the boxes of gauze and sterilizing solution, and tacking the instructions for the care of the wound on the wall next to the bed.

My father looked at me. I knew what he was thinking: This will make a man of our boy Adolf, he will take control of the finances, he will get a job, he will give up his fantasies of being a great artist, or Tribune of the People, or Designer of Cities, or any of the other hundred notions that filled his teeming adolescent brain. He will grow up. His mother's illness will shock him into adulthood. He will bend to reality. I recall at that moment feeling a keen anger and despair. I suppose I could see my viola and trumpet, and my own crumpled first attempts at composition, tossed as well on the junk-heap of Adolf's dreams.

Well, it did not turn out that way. Adolf kept his promise. He scrubbed the floors, he cooked, he kept the kitchen infirmary spotless, he emptied the bedpan, he helped his aunt Johanna clean and dress his mother's surgical wound. His eyes were bloodshot from lack of sleep; if anything he seemed even thinner and taller than before. I returned his books to the lending libraries and brought back new ones he'd asked for, always the same subjects: history, art, architecture, war, biography, German mythology. Perhaps from exhaustion he was quieter. He sketched, but without the feverishness I was used to. He talked less, but the scope of his thinking had not changed. When I brought him a new stack of books, he'd simply rub his eyes and nod. As far as I could tell, no one he had known at the *Realschule*, or elsewhere, came to see him. His mother was right: I was his only friend.

In the beginning, Dr. Bloch came every day. He inspected the incision, asked about diet, left instructions, sometimes injected morphine. Adolf's mother never complained, but it was clear she was, at least right after the surgery, in a good deal of pain. You could tell simply by the way she narrowed her eyes. At each visit, Adolf would stand at attention and ask gravely, "And so, Herr Doktor?" And Dr. Bloch would say, "And so? And so we wait. Think in weeks, not days. But the wound is clean and healing nicely. I must say, you and your aunt are doing a splendid job. The patient is starting to regain her strength and eats well, even with the nausea from the morphine. Your presence, in particular, Adolf, seems to be of great help to her. It would not surprise me if that is one reason that despite the extent of the surgery, she is making such a quick recovery."

A few weeks after the operation, Adolf presented Dr. Bloch—who at Frau Hitler's request had been present during the surgery—with the gift of a watercolor depicting a part of the Landstrasse which featured Dr. Bloch's home and office. This might seem excessive, but at the time in Austria it was not at all unusual for grateful patients to present their physicians with gifts, often food or something decorative. It was the largest painting I'd seen him do, actually a pen-and-ink drawing he'd colored in. "Ah, you've gotten my old barn of a home just right!" Bloch said, inspecting it. "The detail is right and the perspective is right, and you've chosen some flattering colors. Get some wrapping paper or something to protect it and we'll take it down to my hansom. This is good. Perhaps with some formal training, Adolf, you could go somewhere. What do you think?"

"Yes, yes, I think so, I hope." Adolf mumbled this and went to get a sheet of brown packing paper which he carefully folded around the watercolor. I think this must have been the only encouragement he'd ever received, other than from me and his own mother. The rest of his family never lost an opportunity to remind him of the security of the civil service, and Mayrhofer, his father's friend and Adolf's legal guardian, had arranged for him to become a baker's apprentice. Adolf once showed me a letter from Mayrhofer exhorting him, in his father's "sacred memory," to take up "an honest and decent trade," as though an artistic vocation were simply a sly trick for avoiding work. ("These Philistines are trying to ruin my life!" I can still hear him shouting to the sky on one of our expeditions through Linz.) To this day, I have to laugh when I imagine Adolf in a white apron and hat, dusted with flour and shoveling loaves into a brick oven in the back of a sweltering bake shop on the Landstrasse.

At Dr. Bloch's suggestion, Adolf found a ground-floor apartment in Blütengasse 9, a respectable old building. It was in Urfahr, on the other side of the river. The building was owned by the widow of the former postmaster of Linz, a helpful woman who liked everyone, it seemed—but then everyone liked Klara Hitler, with her kind, reserved manner and the air of something tragic about her. The new place was almost identical to the old, with a kitchen flanked by a small bedroom on one side (which would again become Adolf's nest of drawings and books) and a living and dining room on the other. From the kitchen and bedroom it overlooked the countryside in Urfahr, which was lovely and dotted with farms. Dr. Bloch felt it would be beneficial to Frau Hitler to convalesce in the open air and take walks as she regained her strength. Also, I suspected, the medical costs were straining their budget and Urfahr was cheaper—it was technically another town, with none of Linz's excise and sales taxes, goods were cheaper, and one could easily get vegetables and milk and meat from the surrounding farms. My father and I organized the family move; as Adolf helped his mother—dressed again in her customary black silk, her dark brown hair now streaked with grey—from the hired coach and walked her into her new home, I thought of the aging aristocratic hostess who would run the *Conservatoire* (drawings of which still decorated the walls of my bedroom) while Adolf and I labored at our separate artistic disciplines.

I began again to hear the overture to *Tannhäuser* whistled outside the door of the workshop at the end of the day. We went back to the opera. At times, we even waited at our stations for Stefanie and her mother to appear on the bridge, although Adolf made no attempt to talk to her or to gain an introduction. I began to think he was not just a "poor devil" who feared rejection, but actually preferred it this way, despite his brooding complaint that it was causing him to "lose" his mind. Stefanie was a muse, inspiring but unattainable. To touch her would be to soil her. Perhaps he was simply inviting me to join him in contemplating an imagined and unapproachable beauty—despite the jealousy, the rants against the officers with their sabers and gold braid, the grand talk of establishing himself and sending for her. As for Adolf's attitude towards women of the more approachable sort, I couldn't begin to imagine what he thought until we reached Vienna together, and the whole issue of women—real women of flesh and blood—confronted us on all sides and in all shapes.

In early summer, the amateur symphony gave a concert on a Saturday afternoon, a series of folk songs orchestrated by Bruckner, a native of Linz and a kind of local hero to us. My mother came; Adolf came; Frau Hitler wished me luck but was still too weak to make the outing; my father had to stay in the shop.

The concert was held in the *Landestheater*, where we attended the opera and which was as close as we had to a true concert hall in Linz. I still remember looking out into the audience and seeing my mother in a floral-print dress and hat, and Adolf, gloved, with cane and top hat for the occasion, taking their seats in one of the first few rows. After the performance, I waded into the audience with the other players—all adults—to greet our families. My mother kissed me, and Adolf peeled off one of the calfskin gloves, pumped my hand—then, ballooning his cheeks, his eyes popping from his head, brought his hands to his mouth to play a few imaginary notes. "Like one of Rubens' angels," he laughed, "trumpeting the entrance of the Lord!" He *laughed*! It was one of the few times I remember his laughing. He usually ridiculed people who laughed in public; it was a sign of bourgeois complacency and idiocy.

To celebrate, my mother took us to Landtmann's on the Hauptplatz in the center of town. She allowed us to order coffee with whipped cream and any pastry we liked. I ordered a slice of *Apfelkuchen*, and Adolf *Nussstrudel*, filled with sweet cherry sauce and nuts. He looked up from the menu, wide-eyed, and thanked her. She had been feeding this strange gaunt boy for more than a year. More than thirty years later, in 1944, still living in Linz, she would call to tell me she had received a basket of sweets and fruit from Adolf on her eightieth birthday. She was in tears. We were near starving then; the state had calculated our daily allotment of food, based on sex and age, down to the fraction of a kilogram, a fraction that seemed to decrease each month as the situation in the East became more desperate and more food was required for the troops, who were said to be eating their horses. My mother offered to send the basket to my family. I said no.

"You were excellent, Eugen," Adolf said, after we had taken our seats in Landtmann's. "Bruckner is so surprising. He can take something so small and primitive, a country song, and make it large and impressive." He sipped his coffee and closed his eyes for a moment as he let the whipped cream melt on his lips.

"Your hat, Adi," my mother said. He was still wearing his top hat.

"Mmmm," he said, opening his eyes and smiling. "I have your permission? I wore it only so Eugen could spot us in the audience when we arrived."

"It worked, all right," I said. He nodded and placed the silk hat with his cane on the chair next to him.

"How is your mother?" my own mother asked. She regarded Klara Hitler as a near-saint, not the least for putting up with her unusual and unemployed son. (She, of course, was fond of Adolf and a co-conspirator in encouraging my own subversive musical interests.) Her recollection of Adolf's father, whom she'd known distantly, was of a pompous, overbearing ass who would hold forth on politics every evening in the taverns with his cronies. He drank too much, she said. Adolf, of course, would not say much about him, except to describe him as "the servant of a dying and diseased empire."

Adolf paused. His manner became grave and deliberate, as it often did when discussing his mother.

"She is getting stronger. Little by little, yes. The wound is healing, the fevers are gone. Dr. Bloch, though, says she must not attempt housework for at least another month."

"Is she in much pain?" my mother asked.

Adolf was silent and looked down at the table. He spoke with difficulty. "Some, yes. But less. Dr. Bloch does not want to give her morphine too often, though, for obvious reasons."

My mother nodded towards his empty plate. "Go on, Adi, have another. You like the *Nussstrudel*?"

He looked at her with those petitioning eyes.

My mother motioned to one of the waitresses. Adolf's appetite for sweets was almost a joke in our family. He ate punctiliously, as though he were suppressing any temptation to relish his food and could not quite trust what was on his plate. He remained thin. But his craving for sweets was unstoppable, almost canine. When he was on one of his favorite subjects, it was the only way to get him to stop talking. He became entirely unselfconscious. Once, at our house, I watched him consume a whole *Dobos Torte*—a five-layer sponge cake, each layer drenched in chocolate buttercream, covered with caramel, and topped with hazelnuts—by himself.

My mother and I glanced at each other and watched Adolf wolf down another *Nussstrudel*. She was both appalled and gratified, I think, by his helplessness around the tortes and cakes and strudel our country was famous for. She motioned again to the waitress.

Adolf sat back, daubed at his mouth with his handkerchief, folded it, and slid it back into the pocket of his suit jacket. "Thank you," he said, almost out of breath. "I haven't told you. I am leaving. I am going to Vienna in the beginning of September."

I tried to look merely concerned, but I felt my heart drop into my gut.

My mother turned from the waitress. "When? Adolf, your mother—"

He placed both hands on the table and stared at them. "A young man of almost eighteen," he said rather too loudly, "must not be kept by his mother!"

A few customers glanced in our direction. My mother looked at my friend. I could see she was somewhat shaken. "Adi," she said quietly, "your mother . . . does she approve of this plan?"

"My—mother," he began, as if hammering his words, "wants—what is—good for me. If I stay in Linz, I will—I will *rot*." He smoothed his unruly hair with his hand. "Forgive me, Frau Reczek. I did not mean to raise my voice."

"That is all right, Adi. But you know your mother takes a great—a real comfort in your presence. And you have been so good to her. Herr Reczek and I, and Eugen, and especially Dr. Bloch, have been impressed by your devotion. It is genuine. We know this, Adolf."

"My first loyalties are here. One day Linz will be the cultural capital of the Reich. Besides, the Art Academy does not begin its year until September. My mother will be much stronger by then, at this rate."

My mother smiled. "Spoken like a true Tribune of the People"—Adolf allowed himself a small smile, a little ruefully, I thought—"But you've heard Dr. Bloch. Your mother remains a gravely ill woman."

"I know," he said. He stared at the table.

We were silent for a moment, in the gay din of the shop. It was Saturday and there were several families with small children.

Finally, Adolf spoke. "May I have another *Nussstrudel*, Frau Reczek?"

"Of course! I was just ordering when you startled us with your news."

My friend and I looked at each other, and I gave him a quick, firm nod, as if to say, I know and I'm with you. But what I thought was, I am being left behind to swelter and choke in my good father's shop and to play my small role in the amateur symphony of Linz. I will lose my nerve. *I* will rot.

It was clear that Frau Hitler had not yet agreed to Adolf's going to Vienna to study at the Art Academy, and that without her support he would not have a bite to eat, much less *Nussstrudel*. (He would eat the air, as he had already declared to my parents.) Nor would he be able to pay the academy's fees. He would have to convince his mother and his guardian, the sturdy, practical Mayrhofer, to release part of his father's legacy, which in Vienna might last him a year at most.

Adolf's tone, whenever he asked something of his mother, always surprised me. He was no longer the uncompromising artist, the scourge of bourgeois Linz. The belligerence was gone. The need to be right was gone. It was as though he simply could not bring himself to expose her to the harshness of his own thinking, to that side of his personality. He was soft-spoken and rational. He pretended to be practical. Artists could hold many jobs, he told her: They could design operas, they could hire themselves out as portraitists to the middle and upper classes, even the most ordinary products—a tin of tobacco, a bottle of cough syrup—could not be packaged and advertised without the help of an artist. And attending the Art Academy would allow him to return to school, to pick up where he left off, but in a way consistent with his own interests and talents (never mind the question of why he hadn't sought out instruction in art or mechanical drawing in the years since he had left school).

Now his mother, I think, did not doubt the intensity of Adolf's interests or his devotion to them, or that he had some measure of talent. In her own worried way she was proud of him, though she did not always understand his feverish enthusiasm for his "projects." But she regarded herself (and I knew this better than Adolf) as a dying woman about to send her only son, a strange, grandiose boy without a skill or trade to fall back on, who had never earned a penny in his life and seemed to live in a dream world, into the capital of a country of 45 million people—a city of imperial splendor, of the finest academies, of royalty. It was also a city of loose morals, prostitutes, syphilis, filth, and misery and poverty of a sort the average citizen of Linz could scarcely imagine.

That summer we resumed our routine as though nothing had happened. We took long walks to the Freinberg and the surrounding countryside, we went to the opera, we took up our posts for the eternal exchange of glances and nods with Stefanie as she crossed over the Danube with her mother in the early evening. Adolf sketched an impressive series of castles which, he said, would one day dot the hills outside Linz; these would be owned by the city and lived in by townspeople who would be paid to dress and live as Germans did centuries ago, and to cultivate the surrounding land. Linzers could stay for days or weeks at a time to get a taste of the soil.

Frau Hitler was now stronger and managed to cook dinner for us in the apartment on the Blütengasse. The intense brooding and irritability of recent months was mostly gone. I assumed this was because things were settled and Adolf had convinced his mother and guardian to give him access to part of his father's small legacy. Though one could never tell with my friend, for whom grand dreams became personal reality with surprising ease. He still believed that without speaking a word he had somehow "won" Stefanie, and that once he secured his place in the ranks of the world of art all he had to do was send for her. I winked at this, because I was a tolerant and indulgent friend and perhaps because I half-believed it. After all, once Stefanie assumed her place at Adolf's side and was developing into a fine soprano, I would be installed in the Villa Eugen (the sketch was still on my wall), composing furiously and accepting invitations as a guest conductor. Perhaps there would be a role for Stefanie in one of my productions. Stranger things had happened. Stranger things *would* happen.

Then, one evening in late August, Adolf was again at our door. He was leaving for Vienna the following night, he said, could I help him carry his luggage to the station? He did not seem excited, which surprised me, but rather grim and determined. My mother gave him tea and *Apfelstrudel*. My father asked him if he knew where he was staying and warned him against being swindled; he would go to Vienna on business, usually to buy fabric for special commissions, and said that if you ignored the advertisements and didn't buy impulsively, you could find the necessities at a reasonable price, especially in the outlying districts of the city. We are counting on you for reports, Adolf, he said, clapping his thick upholsterer's hand on Adolf's bony shoulder. *Good*, I thought: I had shown my father the postcard of the Karlsplatz with the arrow pointing to the "CONSERVATORY!" Maybe he thought Adolf was testing the waters for his own son. Perhaps.

Was I jealous? I don't think so. I realized that one had to take a seat in the back, so to speak, in any friendship with Adolf. Possibly this was the result of an unfortunate lack of assertiveness in my own personality. But I was also willing to do this because I admired what I saw as boldness and undeveloped talent, and because I knew that he needed a—how do you put this?—a wide *berth* to express his hundreds of opinions and often violent emotions. And because I valued his encouragement. I also sensed, I think, how solitary and tormented he was (I was lonely too, I don't deny this) and that beneath his grandiosity and fantastic ambitions was a cauldron of insecurity and self-doubt. Was he selfish? Of course. But he was taking me along. He could be selfish for us both. Vienna would be his first real test.

When I went to Blütengasse 9 the next evening, Adolf was standing in the living room with not one but *four* suitcases. One was filled with clothing, sketch pads, his watercolor supplies, and, carefully wrapped, his portfolio for presentation to the academy. It was fairly heavy. The others felt as if they were filled with lead. He was taking his entire library with him! Little Paula was crying and his mother was crying. I gathered they had said their good-byes, and so we carried the lighter suitcase to the front steps and slid the others along the tiled floors and down the steps to the street, where we hailed a cab.

"Don't make jokes," he said as we helped the coach-man with the suitcases. "You will find a trumpet and piano weigh as much when you join me. Perhaps you will consider renting a piano. No?"

We were silent at first during the ride. The cab jostled as it bounced over the cobblestones, and Adolf's hair flopped over his nodding forehead. He did not look at me.

"I did not want my mother coming to the station," he said at last. "I cannot stand such scenes. She would cry. She would think she was seeing me for the last time. A train pulling out of a station at night in a cloud of steam, the hissing and screeching—it makes me shudder."

"When you visit me at the Villa Eugen, you must come by motorcar then."

He glanced at me but did not smile. It was a warm September evening, but he was wearing his overcoat of stiff, heavy wool.

"My parents asked me to wish you luck."

"Yes." He nodded and closed his eyes.

"Send us your address once you know it. My mother says she will send you a food package. She says to remember not to spend too much on the opera and on confections. To remember you are a starving student. I said I didn't know which would tempt you more in Vienna, the Hofopera or the cafés."

"I know how to starve," he said.

When the porters, looking very put out, finished stowing the suitcases, Adolf and I stood on the platform for an awkward moment.

"It's too warm for that coat," I said. "But I suppose your mother insisted."

"In fact, she did." He squinted at the ground as though looking for something he'd dropped. "But you shouldn't have mentioned her."

We shook hands quickly and I watched him get on the train and find his seat. He sat by the window but did not look out or wave, and as the train was pulling out the light from the gas lamps caught him for a moment: the sallow, sunken cheeks and the frightened, pale, electric eyes staring ahead. Perhaps I was seeing him for the last time.

Adolf had been a demanding friend and with his leaving I had more time to fill than I expected. It was not hard to keep busy. My father was receiving more commissions from those who could afford to redecorate entire houses, and there was a steady flow of sofas and chairs to be reupholstered. I went to the opera. I had become more proficient at the viola—a beautiful, melancholy instrument and somehow trickier to play the better one got—and I joined an amateur chamber group at the Music Society in Linz, which practiced two evenings a week. As Adolf had asked me, I kept tabs on the construction of the new mortgage bank on the Hauptplatz, and once a week I took up my post on the bridge from Urfahr to make sure "Leydenhauser" was still taking her evening constitutional with her mother, and the occasional officer.

After a few weeks, I noticed something. Life had become flat, stale, routine, without depth, without purpose. Music could relieve this sensation of drab everydayness, but only for short periods of time. At first, I thought this had to do with my being busier, going from one thing to the next to the next. But it did not. It had to do with Adolf's absence. And it was not just that I missed being whisked from the shop at the end of the day, followed by an impassioned account of whatever he had dreamed up since our last meeting, the new sketches, new resentments, attacks on the empire.

It had to do with the way my friend saw the world. He saw the world as fallen, disgraced, filled with oppressors and fools, cracking under the strain and spinning towards some cataclysm out of which it would emerge redeemed and renewed, or perhaps utterly destroyed. This view had cast its dramatic shadow over my inner life for three years, perhaps longer. It had created suspense—literally a world suspended over an abyss—and it had rescued me from the tyranny of the mundane.

This is one reason, despite the absence of a father and with the indulgence of his mother, that Adolf did not work. Work, any job, would have buried him in the details of the everyday and would have become a prison, like the "iron cage" of the civil service of which his father had been so overbearingly proud and against which Adolf never tired of railing. It would have depressed him terribly.

For the same reason, I think, he never married or had children; the details of domestic life would have been overwhelming to him, fatal. This was also the reason he was so attracted to German myth and legend, to war, to the lives of Frederick the Great and others, and to his god Wagner, whose stories often involved the cataclysmic struggle for control of a kingdom, or the world, or simply one's life and deepest love. There is a chord Wagner uses in the opening phrase of the prelude to Act I of *Tristan* (I know what you're thinking: More German bombast; everything bloated with significance! Wait.), also as part of the Tristan motif, and again in the prelude to the third act, after the wounded and dying Tristan flees to France. It consists of an augmented 4th, an augmented 6th, and an augmented 9th, above a base note. There were critics at the time who considered it "the beginning of the end of tonal harmony" and a "descent into chaos"! One of my professors in the

Conservatory in Vienna would later tell me he considered it the most significant chord in all of music. It is the so-called "Tristan Chord," a chord in no particular key and which contains two internal dissonances, creating a powerful feeling of brooding anticipation, of suspense, of gathering doom.

I can see Adolf listening to it alongside me, pressed against the railing of the Landestheater mezzanine; his eyes are pale and glistening; he is stunned, as if by a miracle some inner tension of his own nature had been turned into engulfing, spectacular sound. Hearing it in my mind still makes me shiver, a distantly remembered thrill—even here, in this bleak, empty room they have given me to use as my "writing study," with its long bare table, concrete floors, and whitewashed brick walls.

After four weeks I still had not heard from Adolf, and I went to see his mother in the apartment in Urfahr. Her hunchbacked sister Johanna had returned to Spital and she was alone with Paula. Each time I saw her I was alarmed by her appearance. She used a cane, she had gone from youthful and slender to bony and angular, and her hair, once dark, was dull and streaked with gray. Her roundish face, which had reminded me more of an older sister than a mother, was wrinkled and her cheekbones visible, as though through some trick of cinematography her skull was slowly emerging from beneath her skin. The whole effect made me sad and anxious. But the eyes—Adolf's eyes—the transparent ice-blue eyes were alive and vital. She seemed isolated and alone out in Urfahr, especially with Paula now in school. She apologized for having to rest on the bed in the kitchen while we spoke.

It turned out she had just received a pictureless postcard from Adolf on which he had written that he was well, very busy, and that he would write at length as soon as he had permanent living quarters.

"He has been away from school so long," she said, "able to do things in his own way, that it will take time for him to change. I know I am to blame for this, but he is stubborn and willful. But you know this, too. Do you want some tea? No? There is some if you change your mind. Your mother told me you passed your journeyman's examination. I am so glad. So, you see, if you go to study music, you can earn some money on the side, and in any case you have a trade to fall back on. You don't always have to be walking on such thin ice."

She rearranged the pillows behind her head and sat up. Although Urfahr was just on the other side of the river, there was no noise from the street. We could have been deep in the countryside.

I stood. "I will have some tea," I said, "but I think you should, too."

"All right, yes, but not too strong."

I poured myself a cup and stood by the bed while she sipped; she nodded, and I took the saucer and cup from her and placed them on the counter. "You will tell me when you'd like more?"

"Yes."

She lay back and closed her eyes. I had the feeling she wanted to tell me something she considered important while we were alone. While she still could. After all, aside from her, my parents and I were the only ones truly committed to her son.

"Yes," she said, "Adolf gets this from his father. The terrible willfulness, the inability to admit when he is wrong. In all other ways, he is the opposite of his father. Time, obligations to family, being punctual mean nothing to him. My husband saw to that. Rather than study, he went out every afternoon and Sundays to play with boys two and three years younger, so he could always be the leader. Constantly playing at war, Cowboys and Indians, the Boer War, the Franco–Prussian War—the Silesian War! You, Eugen, are the only friend he has ever had his own age.

"So the reports from school came and with each he got a thrashing. Alois would slap him about the shoulders and head. So what did Adolf do? He stayed out later and got *more* thrashings. My husband made study curfews, and Adolf broke them and got thrashed. Alois was never intoxicated during these; he drank at the tavern and talked politics but was never drunk. It was his way of doing things. I never tried to stop it, I waited outside the door until it was over. To this day, this moment, I reproach myself with this. In some part of him, I'm sure Adolf holds this against me. Though he would never say.

"He was always reading American westerns—the books by Karl May, you know them?—and he loved Old Shatterhand, the hero, who would refuse to talk or react when he was tortured by his enemies. 'The next time Father hits me,' he said, 'I will refuse to cry. And he did! He did not utter a sound, he was silent. He even made his face blank, like a dummy. He was like a rag doll. He would not even shield himself. It was very strange. My husband didn't know what to make of it. Adolf would count the blows, then run to the door—since he knew I was there listening— and report, 'Mother! Father has delivered me twenty-three or forty-two blows,' and then run back and accept more! The thrashings became less frequent and eventually stopped. I think they stopped entirely after Alois slapped Adolf hard on the side of the head and Adolf fell and was limp and did not move or respond for a minute—though he might have been pretending.

Alois was afraid he had killed him. After that there were loud threats and warnings, but no thrashings.

"My husband was a formidable man. He was illegitimate and grew up poor as dirt in the Waldwiertal, like your father. He was thirteen when he went to Vienna to become an apprentice to a cobbler. To apply to the Imperial Civil Service he had to take a special examination because he had never gone to the *Gymnasium*. Only a lack of formal education kept him from going beyond his rank as a chief customs inspector, first class.

"Rules, regulations, routine were everything to him. Things had to be on the mark, not a fraction of an inch one way or the other. He even grew long side whiskers like the Emperor! And like any other civil servant of first rank, he thought education sacred. Self-education had got him where he was and lack of education kept him from going further. So when Adi disobeyed his teachers, and he started wearing the blue cornflower like the other boys and mocking the Emperor, it was as though he was mocking everything my husband lived for. To make things worse, Alois had no ear for music or eye for art, though he encouraged Adi in his drawing when he saw that the boy had a good hand, thinking this might lead to his being a draftsman or engineer. In a way, this is something I respect about my son—that you must do what you love, what will contribute to life and culture. But he takes it too far, as he takes all things too far.

"Of course, I could not oppose Alois. Not even when he beat Adolf. You see, Eugen, I came to work for my husband when I was sixteen. He was twenty-three years older than I was, and married to a woman who was almost twenty years older than him. She was ill and bed-ridden by that time and really did not seem to have ever been much of a wife to him. I believe he married her because she was the daughter of an official and well off. Well, I can't say I blame him.

"I do not have to tell you what you already suspect. And I thought, Why not? His wife was old and sick and seemed to hate him, and Alois—well, he expected obedience but he was confident, even charming at times. And I was terrified of having to go back to the home of my family. What I did not know was that he was seeing still another woman—woman? Girl! The seventeen-year-old maid at a local inn, the daughter of the innkeeper. And when Alois's wife died, leaving her money to her son by a previous marriage, this girl was already pregnant and of course he married her. She could not abide my presence in the home—I don't know what she suspected—and so I was sent back. I don't blame her.

"Her name was Franziska Maltzberger. She had two children by Alois, became sick with tuberculosis, and I was called back to run the house, and to care for her and the children. By the time she died I was pregnant. I am not proud of this. When I gave birth, Alois and I were already married. It was . . . convenient, if nothing else. I was already his cook, his mistress, his maid, the governess of his two motherless children, and the mother of his new child. An hour after the ceremony, my husband was on duty again. What? You look surprised? You think I am, how do you say, cynical? I am not cynical, Eugen, only disappointed.

"A few months after the wedding, I gave birth to my son Gustav, and then to my daughter Ida. Beautiful, healthy children. Even Franziska's children loved them. And then another son, Otto, whose name was chosen by Alois. But Otto died after only five days and a few months later Ida and Gustav, who were not yet three years old, contracted diphtheria. They died within four weeks of each other. This you know. I am sure Adolf has told you. I was too stunned even to cry. My knees would give way when I tried to walk, I had to be held up.

"Adolf was the next child, and sickly at birth. I was constantly afraid he would die too. I am guilty, I know, of indulging him, and perhaps in encouraging his feeling that he is in some way special. He is not untalented, as you know. But I am afraid this sense of specialness will not be of help to him in a world where we all struggle in very ordinary ways to survive. He feels too special even to work at an ordinary job. This is why I allowed him to have a small part of his father's legacy to go to the art school in Vienna. At least it is a school. He will have to allow others, older and more knowledgable, to tell him what to do, how to practice. He will have to obey. He will have to listen. He won't be able to jump from one thing to another. It won't all be just in his head. He will have to come to terms. Maybe he will find a girl he likes, an educated girl. So far he has not shown the slightest interest in girls. Why are you smiling?"

"I'm afraid I'm no help in that. Girls, I mean."

I was certain Adolf had said nothing to his mother about Stefanie.

"Of course! You are either in your father's shop, practicing your music, or with my son! You will meet someone and then you will see. It will be clear. Perhaps that is why I bought Adi new clothes when he started to attend the opera. I hoped he would join an opera society or club. But he did find you, Eugen, and your mother and father. I am grateful for this. You understand his enthusiasms, but you also have one foot in the real world. At least one! You are his only influence."

She closed her eyes and massaged her brow with the tips of her fingers.

"I have always felt that the deaths of my children—and there was another boy after Adolf, Edmund, who died of measles when he was five and Adolf was ten—were my punishment. I even believe that my cancer, the surgery that took away part of my body, and my approaching death, are in a way the second and final stage of this punishment. But a punishment is also a penance, and I thank God for this opportunity. I rejoice in it. I know I should not tell you this because your good mother lost three children before having you, and I do not want you to think that this was somehow deserved. There is a mysterious line between fate and punishment, and one can only begin to tell the difference by looking closely at a person's life."

Throughout this, Frau Hitler had remained propped up in bed, her voice controlled and deliberate, at times wincing in pain. My mother had told me she was taking as little morphine as she could in order to avoid becoming overtired. The house, as usual, was spotless.

"I think," I said, "you are being very hard on yourself. You have always been kind to me."

"Perhaps. But that has nothing to do with this."

I was a little shocked, I admit, by Frau Hitler's confession of her relations with Adolf's father. But how ironic. There I was, steeped to the eyeballs in the Wagnerian repertoire of incest, parricide, murder, greed, overpowering desire and sexual ambition, idolizing a man who, I would later learn, seduced the wives of his patrons, who had even raped the fifteen-year-old daughter of Lizst, then had three children in succession by her while she was still with her husband who had refused her a divorce. And I was *shocked* that a poor housemaid and serving girl from Spital would find herself involved with her domineering employer more than twenty years older than she, whose wife was an invalid twenty years older than *he*. Frau Hitler was right: I was young. Vienna, I thought, would cure that. Vienna, where at that moment I imagined my friend, in the art student's traditional smock and beret, standing in a room with enormous windows, matter-of-factly studying a naked female model, the only sound the scraping of charcoal on sketch paper.

"You are a good listener, Eugen," Frau Hitler said. "Of course you are, or you could never be friends with my son."

"Everyone knows your good nature," I said, aware of a note of both pomposity and uncertainty in my voice, "and your devotion to your children. And of the exemplary way you have dealt with this—this terrible illness. Dr. Bloch has often commented on this. He considers you one of his bravest patients. My father told me this."

"All of us, I think, are a mixture of good nature and bad," she said. "Probably more bad than we care to admit. A life cannot be undone, or done again. Only paid for."

"Adolf," I said, stumbling a bit, "Adolf—if he were to take a routine job, would have no time or energy for his studies, painting, opera, architecture, history, biography—"

"—yet you, Eugen, have found time to learn three instruments and a trade. And you earn money for your family."

"My situation is different. I grew up in the shop. And my father has always supported my interest in music. In his way."

"Yes, a different father." She half-smiled, winced, and shifted position. "You speak up for your friend. You are loyal. That is a good trait."

Frau Hitler's eyes closed. The river, which I could see through the window behind the bed, had grown darker, and against the

79

pillow, in the late September light, her face seemed round and girlish and smooth, the face with those unnerving pale eyes that surprised me when I'd arrived just two years before for that first dinner.

I have thought many times since of this conversation with Frau Hitler. During the 1920s and 30s I would see images in the newspaper and in newsreels of Adolf reviewing his troops, at attention, arm extended, his face a mask of defiance, harsh, resolute, unflinching. I would think of Frau Hitler's description of his standing at attention to receive his father's blows, counting, giving a report to his mother, and returning for more. I thought of this story again in 1938 during the *Anschluss*. Adolf's father had been born in the poor village of Strones in upper Austria and baptized in the neighboring town of Dollersheim, since it was the home of the parish church. A few weeks following the *Anschluss*, Adolf ordered all 350 families moved out of both villages, and a division of the German army moved into the area, where it took artillery practice and blew both towns off the face of the earth.

> *My dear Rezcek!*
> *You must forgive my long silence. I am living only*
> *three blocks from the railway station, at Stumpergasse*
> *31 in the Mariahilf district. My landlady is a Frau*
> *Zdenek, who is Polish or Czech, I think. Her German*
> *is laughable!*
>
> *If the room were any smaller I would have to sleep*
> *standing up.*
>
> *We spend endless hours studying and copying the*
> *paintings in the Art Museum. Frankly I think some of*

*these masters are less than masterful but the collection
is vast and has whatever you would want (we must be
more discriminating when we build our museum in
Linz!).*

*They have a small architecture library where I have
been able to study to my heart's content the original
blueprints of Hansen, Kemper, etc. for the buildings on
the Ring. This as you can imagine is a great
temptation.*

*Let me know how the Post Office renovation and
the new bank is coming. And Leydenhauser.*

*My mother will have my full address. My greetings
to your esteemed parents!*

Your friend,
Adolf Hitler

*P.S. I have found a place the Dorotheum where one
can rent a grand piano by the month at a very
reasonable cost. I can hear you pounding away
already!*

I received this postcard—another large fold-out, this one
displaying the Parliament, the Art Museum, and the Court Opera,
all venerable Ringstrasse buildings—in mid-October 1907. There
was no mention of his mother's health. I didn't think this odd, as
Adolf regarded cards and letters as ways of conveying opinions,
reactions, mere information. I showed the card to my parents,
who often asked after Adolf; my father nodded, read the post-
script, and handed it back with a skeptical but benign grunt.

I made plans to visit in early January, when I understood that classes were not held. I would approach the admissions office at the Conservatory about their requirements, perhaps speak with a few students. I had not yet told my father about this, but business was quiet during the first week of the new year and he had no reason to refuse me. I worked hard, I lived frugally, my trips to the opera cost me only a few heller and sleep. Bravratsky, my piano teacher, was encouraging; he had spoken with me about Conservatory training even before I met Adolf. I was playing Brahms with the Music Society's chamber group. I studied the score of every opera I saw, if there was time (and with Adolf gone, there usually was). Still, I thought of myself as a dreamer, an imposter, a provincial amateur. I had never gone to the *Gymnasium*, I had not finished *Realschule*, I had one suit that was becoming embarrassingly tight and was fraying at the elbows. I would show up on the doorstep of the Conservatory, and they would tell me politely to go back to Linz and wheeze myself into an early grave. But I *would* show up, I would not lose my nerve, and for a simple reason: if I did, I could not face my friend. My friend who had endured, and defied, the derision and beatings of his father, the puffed-up man in pince-nez, a double-breasted tunic, boots, and a saber on his belt.

I never made the trip, but for reasons I did not foresee. Frau Hitler's condition had worsened. The cancer was back; it had created a terrible inflammatory reaction across her chest, according to my mother, and had burst through her surgical incision like some suppurating monster. She was confined to bed and her hunchbacked sister was recalled from Spital.

Dr. Bloch had begun treatments with iodoform. I gather this was a last resort. Gauze strips soaked in iodine were laid across the open wound in order to prevent overwhelming infection and to "burn through" the cancer. Surgery was of no use; the cancer had burrowed into the chest wall and exploded through the skin, draining pus and blood. I tell you, it was a bloody, stinking mess. The iodine causes searing, excruciating pain, and intense thirst— and yet the patient, during the treatment, is unable to swallow even water. Dr. Bloch was coming every day. He would apply the iodine strips and inject Frau Hitler with morphine to dull the pain.

Frau Hitler refused to call Adolf back from Vienna. He was finally in school, she said, and she would not interfere with that. My mother insisted, and at last Frau Hitler allowed her to send a telegram to the tiny room at Stumpergasse 31.

Two days later, I went to visit. The door was ajar and I gently pushed it open. There was Adolf, in his good trousers and a starched white shirt, wearing an apron, on his hands and knees scrubbing the living-room floor. He had rolled up his sleeves and placed a folded hand towel fastidiously under each knee. He was scrubbing furiously and his hair hung in his face. He looked up and put a finger to his lips, then pointed to the kitchen and waved his hand, indicating that I should go in. I took off my shoes.

The sharp, vinegary smell of the iodine—a smell I was to get to know too well ten years later during the war—permeated the kitchen. The sofa had been moved back into the room so Adolf could again sleep in the sickroom while he looked after his mother. Aunt Johanna silently padded in, bearing a metal basin of water that she placed on the counter, and left. Frau Hitler lay there, eyes closed, quite still except for the barely perceptible rise and fall of the sheets over her chest. Her eyes opened to a slit, and she looked at me. "Eugen," she whispered, "the good friend of my son."

"Don't try to speak, Mother." Adolf was in the doorway, untying his apron. "Opening your mouth just makes the dryness worse."

Frau Hitler nodded. She placed her finger to her mouth and ran it over her lips. Adolf reached into the icebox and withdrew a cup. He bent over her and said "*Mach' den Mund auf.*" She closed her eyes and opened her mouth as though she were taking communion. Adolf took a sliver of pulverized ice from the cup and placed it on her tongue. The muscles of her face and throat worked gently as she sucked on the ice. She took a deep breath, and grimaced.

This was something I had never seen. I had never seen the angry, righteous critic, the would-be Tribune, the aesthete, the loner, the stern devotee of Wagner and his murderous gods, display this kind of tender, selfless devotion, and I suspected I would never see it again.

We sat on the sofa alongside the bed. Adolf massaged his closed eyes with his fingertips. "For several hours after the bandages are applied," he said, "she cannot drink or swallow. It is a torment, but she does not complain. Come, let me show you something."

He had set up an easel in his bedroom off the kitchen. He had begun to sketch what looked like the Landstrasse as seen from the river. He crossed his arms and studied it. "Dr. Bloch has commissioned another watercolor. His house is here, on the right." He paused. "I do not know what time of day this should be. That is crucial. Light is crucial. I think it should be late afternoon. The sun is low and the buildings stand out, they are illumined as if from within. The details stand out." He sat on the bed and sighed. "They have us using only oils. It is very difficult, very slow. I do not yet have the confidence."

"How is the academy?"

He looked up at me. The bony face was somber and drawn, but the eyes shone. "Vienna is . . . majestic," he whispered. "You will see. You must see."

"Your mother is quite ill."

"Yes, I did not think it was this bad. But she would not tell me! Always, 'Things are getting better, slowly,' 'I can get about more easily,' and so on. She never complains, I have never seen her complain. Not when my father was alive, not now." He ran his hands through that lank, unruly hair. "I took a late train. It was a terrifically uncomfortable ride. No one slept."

Three weeks later, as I came into the kitchen from the shop for lunch, my mother, who was setting the table, said without looking at me, "Dr. Bloch wants to see you. Today. This afternoon. He said to come when you can get away from your work. I would go later in the afternoon—he is very busy with office patients in the middle of the day. I do not know what this is about." Her expression was blank, rather grim, and I knew not to ask. She had been visiting Frau Hitler almost every day.

Dr. Bloch, as I've said, had his office in his home, a drafty old Gothic house on the Hauptplatz near the center of town. Two scowling, thick-lipped gargoyles flanked the front entrance; as a boy I used to stick my tongue out at them and run inside whenever my mother took me for a visit. The rooms were imposing and the largest of them, with a massive fireplace and tall windows opening onto a balcony, had been converted into his office using hospital screens to partition it into a consulting area and an area for examination.

"I am worried about your friend," he said. He was wearing his white physician's coat over a rumpled tweed suit. With the walrus mustache, the impression was of a careworn but avuncular, and quite serious man. He slouched in his desk chair. I was sitting in a leather armchair, and I thought as I sat that it needed to be stuffed and resprung, and perhaps my father could offer our services as a courtesy. "I don't mean concern over his future," Dr. Bloch went on, "although I suppose there is reason for this, too, as his mother has told me. You know this as well. He has chosen a hard road, going to school to become an artist. But that is not the immediate concern. Rather—well, you see, Eugen, I am there almost every day now. Frau Hitler is an exceptional patient. Despite the horribly painful treatments, she will only breathe more deeply and close her eyes. A kind, disciplined woman. But the son, when I apply the iodoform—he goes *rigid*, he grimaces, his face twitches, his hands clench and unclench. Once, he almost did faint and I had to help him to a chair. He was shaking. Rigid and shaking. Now he stays in his room during the treatments. But I can hear him pacing, and at times exclaiming, awful, guttural exclamations. He is tortured. Once, I was concerned enough to open the door— he was on the bed, doubled over, rocking, his hands clasped behind his head." He sighed and ran his fingers along the edge of his desk, which was covered with flasks and vials containing different-colored powders, and on which sat a pharmacist's balance. "Smaller things as well. I inject the mother and the son winces. I push the morphine and he swoons. Once, he grabbed my arm and asked, in a truly desperate tone, 'Does my mother suffer, Doctor?' What am I to say? I say, 'Yes, she suffers, but less than some and less than I would expect.'"

I felt odd listening to Dr. Bloch, as though I were hearing something I had no right to hear, something intimate and obscene. I suppose at that time anything that contradicted my view of Adolf as isolated and fearless left me feeling strange, uncertain about my own life. Dr. Bloch sank a bit into his chair and rubbed his forehead with the heel of his hand.

"In my business, I have been witness to many such scenes. More than I care to say. But I have never seen this kind of . . . connection . . . between a son and a mother. I do not mean to say I consider Adolf a mother's boy. If that were so he could never have taken off for art school in Vienna. But it is as though mother and son share the same nervous or circulatory system. In my experience, this is unusual.

"Here is the point, I am afraid. Frau Hitler is going to die. In a few days, perhaps; perhaps in a few weeks. But not longer. I doubt she will live past Christmas. I believe Adolf knows this and I am concerned that when it comes he may do himself some harm. I find myself keeping my medical bag at my side to make sure he will not be tempted to slip out a bottle of morphine, and I make sure never to leave a hypodermic there. He is a good caregiver and support to his mother, but still I am afraid.

"You are his friend, Eugen. I would ask you to watch him closely. Ask him about plans for the future, see if he can imagine life after his mother's death. If he talks as if he himself has only a short time left, tell me. Or if he gives you artifacts that belong to him, mementos, objects to remember him by. Urge him to get more sleep. He looks more haggard each time I see him. I have told him to sleep in his room, but often he insists on sleeping on the sofa by his mother. Tell him to let his aunt do most of the work, after all that is why she is there. Of course, say nothing to him of our talk."

Dr. Bloch folded his hands over his ample stomach and sighed. He seemed weary and I suspect he found himself, once more, presiding over a series of events whose course he was helpless to alter. After all, hope is for the patient, not the doctor. I thought of hearing his hansom in the street at night, when he was making urgent calls, cracking his whip and calling out in a gruff voice to his nag.

"I think," I said carefully, "that his dedication to being— becoming—an artist will see him through this."

"Well, I hope you're right," he said. "Certainly being in school again is a help. It provides structure and direction. For a time." He stroked that enormous mustache. "I saw you. The town symphony, at the *Landestheater*. The Bruckner. I thought it quite good. Do you think you can make a go of it? The music, I mean? I suspect your lungs might be better off for it in the long run. You already have traces of your father's bronchitis. Your parents tell me that every minute you're not in the shop or with Adolf, you are practicing or at lessons."

"It takes training."

"Well! Everything takes training, as you know better than most your age. My daughter's fiancé, who is a medical student in Prague, is also a clarinetist. They have a little symphony of their own that he plays in, just the medical people—the students, those in hospital training, the professors, some in practice."

"More Dvorak than Brahms?"

Bloch smiled. "Oh, no! Everything! He writes that right now they are practicing a symphony by Brahms. But then you also have a profession, or trade. Maybe one can have both, no?"

It seems odd that only now, decades later, I remember distinctly what I must have noticed when I walked into that cavernous office. Dr. Bloch had hung Adolf's first gift, the watercolor of the Landstrasse seen from the town center, in one corner of the room. There were other paintings, some of them no doubt gifts from patients, not all of them terribly good. In 1938, the Gestapo seized both watercolors Adolf gave Dr. Bloch, as well as several hand-painted postcards he would later send from Vienna "in eternal gratitude" to the good doctor, and which Dr. Bloch had kept.

That month I visited almost every day after work, taking the bridge I thought of as Stefanie's Bridge, in the early dark, over the broad stretch of the Danube. My mother visited, bringing meals for Adolf and his sister and aunt, and soup for Frau Hitler, who could no longer swallow solid food. Frau Hitler was unfailingly polite and grateful, even as she continued to waste away. She would only whisper, either from fatigue or because the treatments had affected her voice. She developed headaches from the iodo-form, and even during the day the curtains were drawn and the room kept dim. Once I brought my viola and played a sarabande by Haydn, which I had transcribed from a piece for violin. She smiled—a thin smile on that tired, serene face—her eyes, the Hitler eyes, alive, lit from within.

Adolf himself hardly ate and I suspect he hardly slept. He always looked exhausted and when my mother brought him pastries and sweets, he would nibble at them, distracted. When she insisted, he allowed her to bake him an entire ham, which he barely touched. He hovered over his aunt when she tended his mother and sometimes ordered the silent woman from the room. He reminded me at times of a squirrel, reacting with quick, frantic movements of his head and eyes to every sound his mother made. He said little, which made me awkward and uncomfortable; I was so used to his being an indefatigable talker.

Two weeks before Christmas, Dr. Bloch stopped the treatments. They were not working and were extraordinarily painful. The wound continued to ooze pus and blood. The rolls of gauze were saturated almost as soon as Adolf's aunt applied them. The smell in the kitchen was awful and the hunchbacked woman would wash the floors with vinegar in an attempt to disguise it. Yet Frau Hitler continued to appear calm, her eyes closed, a tired smile on her face, sipping water or a little soup when she could. She would communicate with the merest nod or shake of the head, or whisper a few words. As I sat on the sofa with Adolf, watching her, I recalled her confession and I wondered whether the fire of her illness and its terrible treatment had burned through her guilt over her relation with Adolf's father during his first marriage and again during the fatal illness of his young second wife—as if losing her first three children, and later a fourth, wasn't penance enough. Perhaps her serenity was simply a result of the morphine, which Dr. Bloch had continued giving her even after withdrawing the iodoform.

Adolf was inconsolable. The sedative Dr. Bloch had given him made him appear more sleepless and ex-hausted. He wore the same trousers and white shirt, with the sleeves neatly rolled, exposing his thin upper arms. He had stopped washing. He sat on the sofa with me, rubbed his face, and ran his fingers through his increasingly slick, dirty hair. He would let his head fall back and doze; I remember the odd sensation of watching his eyes move back and forth under his eyelids as he slept. Then he'd wake with a little gasp, spring up, and pace the room. I thought about my conversation with Dr. Bloch. Although my mother came as often as I did, we stopped talking about Frau Hitler or Adolf.

Two days before Christmas, I left the shop early, while there was still light, and crossed Stefanie's Bridge into Urfahr. The door to the Hitler apartment was ajar. I eased it open and saw Dr. Bloch. He was sitting on the sofa in the living room, the black leather bag at his feet. Paula and Johanna were sitting in chairs in the living room. Dr. Bloch looked up at me and motioned towards the sickroom, the kitchen. I paused and he motioned again; I went in.

Adolf had set up an easel alongside the bed, so that it caught the light from the window behind his mother's head. He was sketching in charcoal and pencil, glancing down at her every few seconds. I stood back. He had drawn his mother's shoulders and face. I was stunned. Given the circumstances, of course, I should not have been, but of the hundreds of sketches and watercolors Adolf had shown me, none had contained a single human face. He drew buildings, stage designs, occasionally scenes of nature. When he drew people, they were simply mannequins, anonymous, almost stick figures, climbing the steps of the "new" post office, standing in front of the "new" bank building, or strolling through the huge plaza in front of the art museum he planned for Linz when it became the "cultural capital of Europe." Also, the scale was often wrong—the scale and perspective of the buildings was accurate, but the human figures were either too large or too small, and the position of the limbs seemed unnatural, either too stiff or slouching, not the way people ordinarily walk or climb stairs, even in the abstract. In the stage designs, he omitted the characters or when he drew them he focused on costume design and the faces were seen from an odd angle and shaded.

He had drawn his mother from the shoulders up, staring straight out of the canvas. Her eyes were open wide and she was wearing her usual black dress, which billowed a little at the shoulders and buttoned up at the throat, ending in a small frill under her chin. He had softened the edges and lines that illness had etched into her appearance. The face was rounder and smoother, it was the face that had greeted me at the door two years before. Instead of filling in the details—something he did endlessly when drawing buildings—he had left the image rather rough. But he had caught, in his mother's open, strong, younger face, the girlish reserve, the kindness and discipline that were so much a part of her nature.

Dr. Bloch was standing behind me, looking at the drawing. He grunted softly. "*Lebensnah*," he said, "as in life." Adolf stepped back. He was out of breath, his arms hung at his side, staring at the image. "My God," he whispered. Dr. Bloch placed his bearish hand on Adolf's shoulder. It was only then that I realized, in the silence of the apartment, that Frau Hitler was dead.

The funeral was two days later. Adolf spared no expense, which my mother said was foolish as he needed the money to continue his schooling in Vienna. There were three coaches, all dark polished wood, black silk, and leather inside. Adolf rode alone in the first, my mother and I in the second, and in the last coach

Angela (Adolf's half-sister by his father's second wife) with her husband Leo, little Paula, and Mayrhofer the guardian. Leo was an overweight civil servant whom Adolf detested and in turn regarded his young brother-in-law as a deluded, spoiled boy. The casket, polished mahogany with brass rivets, was drawn ahead of us in an open carriage. My mother fingered the silk curtains and shook her head. "He put Paula in the back," she said, "with Angela and the men."

The carriages bumped and jostled their way along the packed dirt roads for an hour or two before we reached the small cemetery in Leonding, the town outside Linz where the family lived before moving to the city, and where Adolf's father was buried. The day was dreary and gray and there was snow on the ground. Adolf spoke to no one, not even the priest who had been retained on his mother's instructions to pray for her soul. (Given Adolf's opinion of priests, the poor man would have been lucky to receive his small honorarium.) He pointedly avoided even looking at Angela's husband and Mayrhofer.

My friend stood at the foot of his mother's grave, hollow-eyed, in his top hat and long overcoat, looking even thinner than when he'd returned from Vienna, and watched as the gravediggers slid the rough planks from under the casket and lowered it with ropes. There was a steady wind in the graveyard which, like most rural cemeteries, had been placed in the shadow of the town church. Adolf shut his eyes and seemed to sway, and for a moment I thought he was going to faint and fall forward, straight into the grave. Paula, who was standing next to him, stepped back and looked at her brother, not so much in alarm, I recall, as in real terror. Still, no one spoke. No one stepped forward to steady him or console him. I know I was afraid to. The only sound, apart from the low rush of the wind, was of shovelsful of dirt slapping against the mahogany casket.

My mother had offered to cook a meal for all of us at Adolf's apartment in Urfahr after the burial, but he declined—mostly, I think, because he could not bear being in the same room, much less at the same table, as Leo Raubal and Mayrhofer. But he agreed to come to our home that evening to share dinner with us, which surprised me. Since he returned at the beginning of December I had not seen him leave the apartment or even the sickroom.

My mother had asked him to bring Paula, but he came alone. He was still wearing the suit and topcoat he'd worn earlier that day. His manner, which at our home was usually one of polite reserve alternating with a jaunty, amusing haughtiness, was slack, drained. His stiff white collar hung loosely around his neck. Normally a bit sallow, he was ashen. I tell you, he looked fit to be buried with his mother.

As always, he offered to help my own mother, who removed his coat, turned him around and steered him toward the dining table, which had been set with the linens and china usually reserved for Christmas and Easter, and sat him down. "Have you eaten today, Adi?" she asked. He shook his head slightly, without looking up. In a moment, he had in front of him a steaming bowl of oxtail stew, a winter staple of shredded meat and root vegetables, thick as lava. I watched him hunch over the bowl, taking small, fastidious spoonfuls. He did not look at me. He did not speak. That disobedient hair, which he had managed to slick back and keep in place during the funeral, hung over his eyes.

We ate nearly in silence. My father, who had washed and put on the suit he wore when he travelled occasionally on business to buy printed fabrics, asked a few practical questions about the apartment in Urfahr, where Paula would live, how Adolf would make up the instruction he had missed in Vienna. Adolf mumbled polite answers. No one mentioned his mother. I suppose we were afraid that if we did he'd simply collapse under the weight of his grief and exhaustion. My parents looked at each other when he declined dessert. My mother had prepared *Apfelstrudel*, which he normally devoured. "*Komm, iss' schon,*" she said softly.

He shook his head. "I have something to say," he announced. He pushed back his chair and rose as though this required his last ounce of strength.

I don't know what I expected. Would he eulogize his mother, or thank us, or bow to convention and offer a prayer? He seemed so frail that one had the impression the stiff wool of his suit was holding him up. I did not expect what he said would change my life.

He leaned forward and with outstretched fingers braced himself against the dining table, his head drooping and the hair again in his face. "Eugen," he began, "is my brother, both in an artistic and a proper spiritual sense. You know that." He pushed himself up, drawing to his full height and tossing back his hair. "What he does now is crucial. Fateful. If he does not enter the Conservatory, or at least make an application, he may not receive a second chance. I know this because many of my fellow students come from artistic families and have brothers and cousins in the Conservatory. The training is long and arduous and if one does not begin at university age, or even sooner, one is finished. Hopes are shattered. Dreams turn to dust. One is doomed to remain an amateur for life."

Adolf closed his eyes and drew a long breath. I glanced at my father. I expected him to betray skepticism and impatience, or to be making a clear effort—under the circumstances—to suppress these.

I was certain he was thinking (once again) "The Tribune speaks!" Instead, he seemed to be listening with a curious gravity and earnestness. I do not imagine he was simply being polite because Adolf's mother had just died.

"It is but a short step from artisan to artist, from artisanry to art. Both require training and technique. Both require one to work with one's hands and with great care. Both require, in varying degrees, inspiration and aesthetic judgment. But art crosses the boundary from the economic to the spiritual, from the individual to the collective life of man. To my shame, my own father was a creature of the economic world entirely. He made nothing. He contributed nothing." Adolf closed his eyes, with an expression of pain and fatigue, and shook his head. "He was a sterile functionary, a bureaucrat. His work could have been performed by a machine or monkey. Forgive me my disrespect, but I must speak the truth. This is no time for lies. Not for me, not for Eugen."

Adolf, who a moment before had looked stern but earnest, rolled his head in a circle, and his eyelids fluttered—we thought he was going to swoon and fall! My father started from his chair, but Adolf held up his hand.

"My mother understood. Despite her instinct for obedience, even obedience to the dead, and her concern for my physical welfare, she allowed me to enter into artistic training. Give Eugen one year. If he is temperamentally unsuited to the demands of Conservatory life, it will show itself. The cost will not be great. What you have taught him of your trade during his life will not evaporate in one year, and he has already passed his journeyman's examination. His musical talent is undeniable. Vienna is a vast and morally dangerous city, but for music it is the only city. In this time and this place. I will make sure he finds a safe place to stay."

My father looked at Adolf and smiled a little to himself. My mother had folded her hands on the tablecloth and was staring at them.

Adolf seemed about to go on, but paused. "Please inform me of your decision before I leave for Vienna," he said quietly. "I will need to make arrangements."

He lowered himself into his chair. His shoulders slumped, his eyes closed, and then his head fell a little to one side, like a puppet with its strings cut. For a moment, I thought he'd fallen asleep.

I had never discussed applying to the Conservatory with either of my parents, and I had not discussed it specifically with Adolf, despite his repeated hints and the arrow on the postcard that sat on my night table. I suppose I was too good a son. I wanted to avoid facing what I knew it meant: abandoning my father's trade and family business, my legacy. And as her only surviving child, I would be abandoning my good mother. There was no need to have this discussion now.

Two days later, my father said simply, without preamble, "You may go."

My mother said nothing.

Within a month, I was on a train to the troubled capital of my country, with a trunk and a suitcase stuffed with my mother's smoked meats, cheese, preserves, and pastries. The nearby passengers shifted uneasily and glanced in my direction, annoyed and hungry. My father had packed my viola and trumpet with his usual thoughtfulness and care and sent them separately to a fabric dealer in the Mariahilf district, where in a few days I would pick them up, and my new life would begin.

Glasenbach, outside Salzburg, October 1945

GLASENBACH IS A RATHER QUIET PLACE. We don't talk much, with each other, I mean. There are no restrictions on this, but . . . still. I suppose we're afraid we'll be overheard, or spotted talking with someone who will turn out to be an important Nazi, a higher-up. Or if we say anything faintly incriminating, or something unflattering about our hosts, it will be passed on. This is a shame, really.

We have more contact of a social nature with the guards— although supposedly this *is* forbidden, or at least discouraged. I myself have struck up a friendship of sorts with a young guard, a Mr. Robert Hardie (his great-grandfather was "Hardeinger"; two generations of exposure to the American talent for simplification and it has been whittled down to "Hardie." Americans seem to prefer short, muscular names.) He is a teacher of mathematics in a high school in Lexington, Kentucky, and has a wife and two small children. He arrived in Europe late last year, when German resistance was already petering out, was assigned to a camp for displaced persons, mostly Germans, outside Frankfurt, and then assigned to Glasenbach. I have tried to teach him something of the theory of harmonics. Once, at one of our Friday afternoon "parties," he gave me a taste of American bourbon from a small metal flask. It almost burned a hole in my throat and set my brain on fire. He laughed and clapped me on the back until I stopped sputtering.

The silence, though, can be oppressive. Hours go by with the only sound that of the doors swinging open and one of us being called to another "interview." The wards we occupy have two rows of ten beds facing each other, with high windows on either side. Each of us has a locker against the wall behind our beds where we keep our one change of clothing, an extra pair of shoes, toiletry articles, and in my case a small stack of books from our little lending library. None of us has anything of value. No one wears a watch (there is a clock on the wall of every room in this place) or keeps a wallet. There is nothing to buy in any case.

My bed faces west-northwest and I make a point, unless I am being interviewed, of spending the late afternoon here each day. I unbutton my shirt and luxuriate in the warmth and light. It seems to dry out my viscera and I feel lighter, less waterlogged; the building is dank and cold at this time of year, and a fine film of mildew grows on the walls of some of the corridors. We are allowed one walk each day along the perimeter fence, which bristles with barbed wire. On bright days, I am glad to get additional sunlight; on overcast days, the black, twisted wire against the gray sky is a little discouraging. There is a rumor that in the spring they will allow us to cultivate individual garden plots. This would be nice, if not for what it might say about how long the Americans plan on keeping us here.

My fellow internees are a mixed lot. On my ward, there are several lawyers who were involved in a Nazi legal association; a judge who had become a specialist in interpreting the Nuremberg Laws, determining the degree of tainted ancestry that could void a marriage between a German and a half-Jew or quarter-Jew or eighth-Jew; a minor actor in anti-Semitic films made by Goebbels' propaganda ministry; an engineer who I'm told designed one of the first Porsche sport automobiles; the personal chef of Erich Koch, the Gauleiter, or regional party leader, of East Prussia and supposedly one of the most brutal of the party bosses; a university administrator who was thought to have been somehow involved in the assassination of Chancellor Dollfuss by Austrian Nazis; a number of petty bureaucrats; a chemical engineer employed by the firm responsible for Zyklon-B; and the president of the National Socialist cycling association. And, of course, me—The Friend of the Führer's Youth and leader of a local chapter of Strength Through Joy. Under de-Nazification "critieria," we have been classified as *Hauptschuldige* ("chief culprits"), *Belastete* ("incriminated"), *Minderbelastete* ("less incriminated"), or *Mitlaufer* ("fellow travelers"). I doubt Glasenbach holds any "chief culprits." Most of us have been given the designations "incriminated" or "less incriminated." Anyone who is a "chief culprit" or "incriminated" is an "automatic arrest." I am "incriminated"; this is due to my direct acquaintance with Adolf Hitler. The chef and the Nazi cycling enthusiast are "less incriminated." During my first weeks here I met a university professor, Wilck, from Graz, who was a member of the Party and "incriminated." He had gruesome stitches the length of his forearms. He and his wife had tried to commit suicide before the Americans came to arrest him. They administered morphine to their young daughter and took morphine themselves; the dose was enough to kill the wife and daughter, but he did not die. He then opened his veins the long way, up the arm, and nearly died himself later in hospital of blood loss. He is gone now; he was taken from the camp a few weeks ago, to be tried for the murder of his wife and daughter.

*

I can understand why the Americans want to talk with us. If they are going to put money into rebuilding, they will need to make sure—after the newsreels, the torchlight parades, the *Sieg Heil*-ing, the German Doctors League, "Strength Through Joy," the League of German Maidens, the National Socialist Motoring Association—that we are not all lunatics, brainwashed. I am *Hitlers Jugendfreund*, "The Friend of the Führer's Youth," and so I am a possible lunatic. Jobst the lawyer, who like me is "incriminated," says that one of the plans being considered for Germany is "pastoralization." German cities, those that aren't already rubble, will be leveled and the country turned into farmland. Everyone will be a farmer growing his own food, and the country will be "pastoral," like a painting or a Bach pastorale. No cities, no trains, no factories, no army, no universities, no Conservatories. I can't say I blame them. Perhaps Austria will be "pastoralized" as well, or turned into a permanent zone for vacationing skiers. They will allow us to manufacture confections, of course: our tortes, tarts, *Knödel*, marzipan roses, *palatschinken*, *Mozartkugeln*, *Kaiserschmarrn*, strudel. That we are good at.

One internee, Dincklage, who sleeps on the other side of my ward—he was an archivist, essentially a librarian and clerk, for Kaltenbrunner (who is to be tried at Nuremberg, I recently learned) and SS intelligence—has been able to measure the length of the ward in meters. He has a whole itinerary: a walking tour of Austria based on the exact number of kilometers from town to town. Eyes half-closed, he spends two to three hours each day pacing off the distance from one end of the ward to the other. Now and then, he'll call out "I can see Moosbrun!" or "Two kilometers from Wiener Neustadt! A glorious, warm day!"; we roll our eyes and turn over on our bunks. He is continually shining his boots, and they creak. It drives us crazy. When he gets to "Vienna," I will tell him to keep going east, into the Russian zone, where they are sure to steer him due north towards one of the labor camps. (I'll even supply the exact number of kilometers to Omsk, if he needs it.) Colonel Lewis, with whom I have spent more time than with most of the other interviewers, tells me that these camps are filled with German prisoners of war; the Americans and British have been unable to negotiate their release or transfer to prisoner-of-war camps in the West. In 1941 and 1942, he says, the German army took vast numbers of Russians prisoner—to call them "soldiers" wouldn't be accurate, they were mostly poorly trained conscripts, villagers and farmers. They weren't housed in prisoner-of-war camps but rather herded into open enclosures, tens of thousands in a single fenced-in enclosure. The Germans packed them in so tightly they could not sit. They weren't fed, and most, if not all, died of starvation, exposure, and disease. Nearly three million men died in this way. There were outbreaks of cannibalism.

Practically the only conversation I have here, aside from the interviews and with Mr. Hardie, is with a younger internee named Ernst Schlosser. Schlosser is my bathing partner. Since the water in the showers is invariably cold, we are allowed one hot bath each week. One week, my partner sinks into the hot, clean water first; the next week, the order is reversed. The guards are hardly ever around. And I suppose soaking in the water with our eyes closed and the steam rising, our heads resting against the old ceramic tub, loosens the tongue. Schlosser says he was an administrative assistant to Friedrich Rainer, the Gauleiter of Salzburg and Carinthia. He says he had no real power or responsibility (of course) and was not responsible for deportations (of course). I suppose this might be true. There were few or no Jews to deport in Salzburg anyway.

"What I enjoyed, really," he said this morning, while he was soaking and I was waiting, naked, rubbing my arms in the steam, "was running the Klessheim Palace, outside the city. Hitler loved the place. It was close to Munich, quite beautiful. He met there with King Boris of Bulgaria several times, with Horthy, the head of state of Hungary, with Prime Minister Antonescu, and a few times with Mussolini. We maintained the grounds, hired the staff, made all the arrangements, cleaned up their mess afterwards. The SS would hold conferences there. Rainer, who was SS himself, went to some of these but would never talk about what was discussed. What's your case?"

I told him I was a clerk in the registrar's office in Eferding.

"Yes," he said, "but how were you—connected?"

"I was a leader of the local 'Strength Through Joy' organization."

He smiled. "Well, then, they can charge you with 'Strength' or 'Joy,' or both. Don't look so shocked! When they are done with the big fishes at Nuremberg, they will get to the small fry. By the hundreds. I've heard the trials will last two or three years, or longer. In the meantime," he sighed, "I wish they'd stop asking me how many times I've read *Mein Kampf*—as many times as everyone else! None! Zero!—or 'Are you glad Hitler is dead?' or 'How do you feel now about the Nazi program?' What am I to say? It was a good idea poorly carried out?"

"You mean," I said, "we lost."

"I mean that if we'd not lost, we'd be asking *them* the questions. Or perhaps we wouldn't even bother. The Americans are so patient and well meaning. Are you getting in? You'd better, before it gets cold."

I have to admit I *am* shocked. It had never occurred to me I could be charged with a crime or find myself facing a tribunal. Endlessly interviewed and "de-Nazified." "The Trial of the Führer's Boyhood Co-conspirator"! This is hardly credible. I should be careful. In saying this, of course, I am being reckless. But I no longer care. I started writing this after I had been here two months. Next week it will be six. The food is poor, and my teeth are starting to loosen.

I hear footsteps ricocheting down the long brick corridor. Through the small, square window in the metal door, I can see the guard coming. I must relinquish my writing room.

Part Two

Vienna, 1908

WHEN THE TRAIN PULLED INTO THE Westbahnhof, I saw him standing on the platform, a solitary figure, his hands thrust into the pockets of his overcoat. It was a cold night in early February. His head was bare, and the ebony cane hung from one coat pocket. I rose from my seat and moved through the car as it glided past, trying to keep him in view. His head turned abruptly: he had seen me. Hauling my trunk and suitcase, I got off.

He did something then that startled me. He walked up to me and halted. His usually stern face softened into a gentle, almost sly, grin, and letting the cane slide down his arm, he grabbed me by the shoulders. Then he kissed me on both cheeks and clapped me on the shoulders. "Your future awaits," he said.

We looked at each other and nodded and each took a handle of the trunk. In my other hand I carried the suitcase full of food, which he kept glancing at. The streets were lit with tall electric arc lamps, and Adolf, of course, launched into an account of the electrification of Vienna—the costs, the plans, the political controversy, which districts had electrification of streets and residential buildings, which had only the streets lit, and so on. I listened.

The Stumpergasse was only a few blocks from the station. His room was as small and grimy as he'd promised. Books stacked neatly against one wall, a narrow cot, a chair and small wooden desk, no closet. This was a typical "basin flat"—the lavatory down the hall and a single cast-iron spout on each floor from which all the residents filled their basins and jugs. The place stank of kerosene. The address—Adolf Hitler, Vienna VIII, Stumpergasse 31, Second Staircase, Second Floor, Door 17—said everything one needed to know. And there was an added, uncomfortable irony. I never mentioned it and tried not to think about it. In colloquial German, a *Stümper* is a pathetic, almost comical fellow who tries and tries but—usually due to a lack of talent and luck—is doomed to fail. It often refers to people with grandiose artistic ambitions. *Stumpergasse*, then, is "*Stümper* Street" or "The Street of the *Stümpers*." Not a good omen.

We undid the straps of the suitcase and fell on my mother's food like a pair of wolves. When we were done, I sat slumping on the cot, exhausted from the trip, barely able to keep my eyes open. It was past midnight. I looked up. Adolf was standing before me, his coat over his arm and cane in hand. "A taste, Eugen, just a taste," he said. "You've come all this way." As usual, my protests did no good and soon we were out under the tall lamps for our first foray together into the new terrain.

Well, it was more than a taste! As always with my friend, it was a twelve-course meal. I could hardly see anything, not even the enormous spire of St. Stephen's. The boulevards were slick from a recent rain and shrouded in a thick yellow fog that seemed to cling to the pavement and buildings like some living, creeping substance. Adolf was undeterred. He took me to the Palace of Justice, the Burgtheater, the University, the Art Museum, the Town Hall or *Rathaus*, the Court Opera. Gothic, neo-Gothic, mock-Gothic, Italian Renaissance, German Renaissance. Semper, Wagner, Hansen, Hasenauer, all the architects. How many tons of granite and from where, secret entrances and exits, the number of years under construction. ("I'm just giving you the basics, Reczek. When we come back tomorrow in the daylight you will see what I mean.")

All this detail swirling through my sleepy brain! But aside from the looming Imperial presence of those buildings in the fog, I can recall only two things from that first night.

As the sky started to lighten toward dawn and the fog lifted, we stood under a huge chestnut on the green before the Parliament with its hundreds of steps rising in tiers, the big semi-circular drive, and Pallas Athene in front holding Winged Victory in her hand. All of which, of course, I had seen in photographs.

But there, on the roof, flanked by the stamping, rearing steeds and the bare-breasted female charioteers which stood on opposite corners of the building, were dozens of half-naked male and female Greek gods! As though they'd just dropped from the sky! They seemed unposed (one hand on a thrust-out hip, the other holding a staff), placed almost at random, as though waiting backstage for their cues. "My welcoming committee!" I said.

Adolf was staring at these human forms materializing in the pale sky the way one might contemplate another universe. "Some are marble, some bronze," he murmured. "Tomorrow I will tell you who they are and who did them."

"Well," I said, "I hope one of them is Aphrodite. I would like to meet *her*. It's about time."

Adolf did not reply.

The second thing I recall happened after we'd been out only ten minutes or so. We were walking towards the Ring. Adolf was talking and I was trying very hard to stay awake and not trip on the cobblestones or the curving trolley tracks that crisscrossed the vast boulevard. Out of nowhere, a woman was standing before us. She was wearing a turban-like hat and long elegant coat, and when I looked at her powdered face, white and ghostly under the lamps, I realized she couldn't have been more than fifteen years old. She'd blocked our way and without a trace of shyness said to me in that soft Viennese accent "Well, boys, are you—" Adolf stepped between us, his arm raised, and for a moment I thought he was going to strike her across the face with the back of his hand. But he spun, grabbed my shoulder, and pushed me ahead of him, barking "Come, Eugen!" I glanced back at the girl, who stood there with a hand on one hip, looking like a child in her mother's clothes and heels. She said something obscene which I could not quite make out.

This was my first hint that Vienna at that time—even aside from the Spittelberggasse or red-light district, which I had heard about—was a city teeming with prostitutes. Young, very young, middle-aged, even old. Some registered with the police, some not. On the street, in doorways, leaning against store windows, beckoning from alleys, in coffeehouses smoking cigarettes as they waited for their regular clients. When I had lived there a while, it made sense to me. Social sense, economic sense. It would furnish plenty of material for discussion between us. But I remember most Adolf on that first night, with the righteous anger of an avenger, stepping between that young girl and me. "Come, Eugen!" Imagine: Adolf driving the prostitutes from Vienna, like Christ chasing the moneychangers from the temple. A good joke, I thought, but not one I would have said aloud.

When we got back to Stumpergasse 31, Adolf's room was so cold I could see my breath. He lit the kerosene heater, which in minutes filled the room with its rancid warmth. Adolf had borrowed another mattress from Frau Zdenek and laid it on the floor, but he insisted I take his bed. The room was so small we had to stand my trunk on its end and stack the suitcase on top. We hung our clothes from a pipe which ran across the ceiling. Adolf lifted his mattress and laid his trousers over the wood slats and pressed the mattress back down, "to keep the crease." He grabbed a whiskbroom, brushed out the mattress, and covered it with a sheet. Then he sprinkled the bed with a white powder he said contained boric acid. "Vienna," he said, "is a splendid city, but unfortunately we must share. *Bettwanzen*." Of course, in Linz we had bedbugs, but usually in rooming houses and in the poorest sections of town. Well, where did I think I was now? I climbed into the bed and pulled the scratchy wool blanket over me. Adolf seemed filled with energy and was moving back and forth in the little available space. I remember Adolf pacing and describing the lobby of the Court Opera, which he thought "impressive but overdone." I fell asleep in seconds.

When I woke late in the morning I could feel something moving over my lip. I spat and ran a finger around the inside of my mouth. There were tiny brown bugs on my neck and chest, and as I yanked off my nightshirt I could see them scatter from my hips and thighs, leaving behind their mates who were still attached and bloated and enjoying their blood meal. I swiped frantically at them until my thighs were streaked with red. Then I rubbed myself down with the vinegar-soaked rag Adolf had shown me the night before. I took the soap-and-brush kit my mother had bought for me, wrapped myself in a towel, and headed down the hall to my first cold-water bath in Vienna. *Willkommen*. There were far more effective ways of dealing with the *Bettwanzen*, I would learn, than boric acid and vinegar. But for the years I remained in Vienna as a student they were my frequent bedfellows.

I dressed. Adolf was still asleep, his dark hair dusted with the boric acid powder. I recall thinking he was too slender and pale to make much of a meal for our little friends—they must have already drained from him whatever they could! I had a good cheap breakfast at the Café Aida (good omen, I thought) on the Mariahilf Strasse, drank my first cup of the dark, aromatic coffee I would never have had at home, and scanned the listings of rooms to rent. I knew I could not afford more than ten kronen a month. If I were to stay, I would need to rent a piano (a grand, not a decrepit upright), and that would cost as much or more than the room. Adolf was paying ten kronen for his closet and its inhabitants.

The Mariahilf district was heavily commercial. Wholesale butchers, tailors, fabric dealers of the sort my father dealt with on his visits to Vienna, shops selling and even renting furniture, produce warehouses, typesetters, cobblers. Plenty of cheap restaurants and cafés, where the coffee was as good as it was anywhere in the city. And noise: boys pushing racks of clothing over the pavement, the squeal and rattle of the tram on the Mariahilfer Strasse, men calling to each other as they unloaded their lorries, Eastern Jews hawking cheap leather goods, pots and pans, old boots, twine. Anything one wanted could be gotten quickly and inexpensively in the Mariahilf. The residential buildings, like Adolf's, were depressingly similar: five or six stories, with shops on the street level and a sooty little courtyard in back.

I found the fabric dealer without difficulty and picked up my viola and trumpet in their cases, shipped in a sturdy wood box my father had built and padded with horsehair and straw. I bought a postcard of St. Stephen's to send to my parents. When I got back to the room, Adolf was still asleep, and I decided to walk some twenty blocks to the Conservatory on the Karlsplatz.

*

Motion and chaos: this was my first impression of Vienna by day. Trolleys with large black automobiles riding right alongside and horse-drawn carriages alongside the autos. People streaming in either direction and wading into traffic like sleepwalkers. In the cafés, German—much less guttural than the German one heard in Linz—and some Czech; on the streets, German, Czech, Hungarian, Polish, Italian, Eastern tongues I did not recognize, and the yiddling of the Jewish street vendors. And in the alleys, even on some of the main boulevards—at ten o'clock in the morning!—the girls and women in the long coats and hats and heavy make-up slouching against doorways. Every other building seemed to display a sign advertising the name of a physician, and under the name, *Specialist in Dermatologic and Venereal Diseases.* I had landed on another planet.

The people in the Admissions Office of the Conservatory had my application and letters of recommendation. If I were kind enough to come back the following afternoon at one o'clock, I could sit for the examination, which would consist of a short written section, a performance section, followed by an oral examination. Or I could choose a day later in the week. If I required a piano, not to worry, they had plenty. Imagine! I had expected to be coldly informed of a date some weeks in the future. Then I could hire a tutor to help me prepare or go to one of the special "examination schools" for a crash course. (Adolf said there were several that sold their services to students preparing for the entrance examination to the Art Academy and that he had actually gone to one.) On the day of the exam, clutching my viola in its case, I would stand in line with hundreds of other examinees, too nervous to talk or share a joke.

I must have run the twenty blocks back to Room 17, Stumper-gasse 31. Adolf was *still* sleeping. I shook him awake and told him I would be examined the next day. Excellent! he exclaimed groggily. We must find you a room, there is no time to lose, and then to the Dorotheum to rent the piano!

I treated him to lunch, or breakfast, at Café Aida. He seemed desperately hungry—I had never seen him eat anything other than cakes and strudel with such abandon. We pored over the "Rooms to Let" listings in the newspapers. It seemed as if anyone who owned a home or had rented an apartment in Vienna was letting one or more of its rooms. We spent the rest of the day and evening looking at them—not only in the Mariahilf but in other districts—and they were dreadful. Those in private homes were often in the cellar. Many were tiny rooms in apartments with dirty, squalling children, and the women who answered the doors often had an exhausted, beaten-down look. In some, the arrangement required me to share the room at night with a *Bettgeher* or *Schlafgeher* (literally, bed- or sleep-goer). These were "tenants" who rented the room to sleep at night but were not allowed there at any other time. In short, they were homeless but had some marginal income, or at least enough to keep them out of the dosshouses. None were less than the ten kronen Adolf was already paying on the Stumper-gasse. None would allow me to bring in a piano, even if one fit. Most were filthy. In some, the *Bettwanzen*, who usually made themselves scarce during the day, retreating into every crack and crevice, were lounging in the open, unconcerned, probably busy digesting last night's blood meal.

In a single, exhausting day, I learned something I could prob-ably have learned in no other way. Vienna, despite its palaces, its imperial grandeur, its reputation as a center of culture, was a city sitting above a vast lake of poverty and despair and filth. Every day, people without money or prospects streamed into it. They came from other parts of the decaying empire, from rural upper Austria, from Bohemia, Moravia, from the desperately poor lands of Galicia and the Bukovina. They didn't even know if there was space for them.

In reality, there was an acute housing shortage. The *Bettgeher* at least had the means to rent a bed of his own at night. But there were others, entire families, who for a few heller crowded into dirty attics and slept on blankets on the floor, surrounded by strangers. Some of these people, I heard, would allow other "tenants" to engage in sex with their children for a small fee, and adults would engage in sexual relations in full view of others, including children. It would have been better, no doubt, to spend the warmer nights on the street or in one of the city parks, had this not been illegal and strictly enforced by the police. To those living on the margins—students, small artisans, manual laborers—the existence of these conditions was a constant source of anxiety. A little bad luck, the loss of a job, the loss of income sent by one's family in another part of the empire, and one could sink quickly into the wretched underclass of night-goers and bed-renters, or worse. When it was cold and wet, thousands descended into the vast network of sewers and tunnels beneath the city. Some practically lived down there, Adolf told me, fighting off the rats and clawing each other as they scrambled after the coins that philanthropic pedestrians would drop through the grates.

Well, we returned to the room on the Stumpergasse and Adolf went to work. He persuaded Frau Zdenek to switch rooms; she would take Adolf's room and we the larger room, large enough to accommodate a piano, for ten kronen each, double the rent she was now receiving. He assured her that I was a serious student, from a family well known to him, and that I would not bring women or girls back to the room. (I had my reservations about this last guarantee.)

Frau Zdenek, a good-natured older woman, seemed rather pleased that she would have an artist *and* a musician as tenants, and not at all disturbed by the prospect on my "pounding away" on the piano or "screeching," as Adolf put it, on the viola. (We did not tell her about the trumpet.) We helped Frau Zdenek move her belongings and few small pieces of furniture, and then carried in Adolf's books, our beds, and my trunk. Adolf "tried out" the room, walking off its dimensions, pacing and pivoting, head down, his hands behind his back, his expression so serious you'd think he was considering purchasing the place.

Adolf paced whenever he spoke at length or was lost in thought. In fact, the only time he did not pace was when he was reading, drawing, or asleep. He really was extraordinarily restless; I don't think I've properly conveyed this aspect of him. I attributed it to the tensions in his nature and his ceaselessly active brain.

"It will do," he said. "Though once the piano arrives, who knows?" He dusted the corners of the room with boric acid powder, then hung our clothing in the narrow wardrobe Frau Zdenek had left for us—our claim to respectable lodging.

Adolf took a whisk to our clothes and to the mattresses, to chase any stray *Bettwanzen*. Then he got down on his knees and inspected every crevice in the room, poking with the whisk, plugging the larger seams in the floor and baseboard with a claylike caulking material. "They are there, Reczek, I know it. Waiting for us to close our eyes and sleep, the little devils. I know their tricks. I will teach you. Ah! It is the fate of struggling artists to deal with such creatures. Luckily, we have no room—especially after the piano arrives—for a sofa, or they would take that over too." We took the bedsheets, and kneeling next to the bathtub down the hall, washed them in a solution containing ammonia (an ablution, I would learn, that Adolf performed every other day). He pointed out the small brownish streaks where the *Bettwanzen* had smeared their feces, something I actually had seen before on the fabric of the shabbier furniture which came into my father's shop to be reupholstered. We twisted the water out of the sheets and carefully hung them to dry.

It wasn't the *Conservatoire*, as Adolf had sketched it back in Linz, and Frau Zdenek was no slender, aristocratic matron, but our aspirations, I thought, lent it a kind of grubby dignity. It was a start.

Thirty years later, as Adolf's guest in Bayreuth, I would stroll with him over the deep green lawns of Wagner's estate and joke about my being appointed Reichminister for the Control of *Bettwanzen*. Adolf sighed and said, "Yes, we were poor students and that was just one more insult. But I tell you, there are *Bettwanzen* the size of Mime or Alberich. They are crafty, they infest, they hide, they make themselves invisible. And they are secretly draining the blood of the nation. This is a matter of survival. But, as always, Reczek, only music fills your head—and don't think I do not envy you. You were always an innocent in these matters."

Perhaps he should be here to tell that to my American friends.

The next morning, I breakfasted again at the Café Aida, read the Vienna papers, and strolled through the Mariahilf. The rich smell of horse dung hung over the streets with their small shops, and rivulets of black liquid flowed around the cobblestones into the city drains. I did not care. In my head I rehearsed everything Bravratsky had taught me about harmony, counterpoint, orchestration. When I got back to the room at noon, Adolf—who had been up all night reading by candlelight, at times mumbling or reciting to himself—was, of course, asleep. I changed into my one suit and overcoat, picked up my viola in its case, and went out.

Now, there is not much written for solo viola, even today, and there was less then. I had decided to play the third of Bach's cello suites, transcribed for viola (the viola is tuned just like a cello, only an octave higher, and Bravratsky had helped me with the transcription). These pieces are, of course, famous today, and with the Victrola the average fellow in the street would recognize them even if he had no idea who wrote the music. But then things were different. They had been lost and only discovered ten or fifteen years before by Casals in someone's attic or cheese shop or some such place. They had no markings suggesting articulation, dynamics, tempo—in fact, no markings of any kind, no indication of *how* to play them.

I got there early. I was the only one. I had expected a mob. I sat on a bench outside the administrative offices, my viola case over my lap like a schoolboy. I stared at the marble walls, marble floors; a gilded mural of Orpheus stared down at me from the domed ceiling. A woman from the inner office walked out and, placing her hands on her knees, bent and whispered, "They'll be coming for you in fifteen minutes."

I opened my viola case and tightened the bow; my hands were shaking and the bow knocked against the case as if it were tapping out a distress signal in code. I ran my resin block along the taut ribbon of horsehair and tested its tension against my index finger. I turned the pegs on the viola, and tried to draw the bow in long, steady strokes; the tremor produced a somewhat wavering tone, making it harder to satisfy myself that I was in tune.

"Herr Reczek? Are you ready? I am Professor Schauffel. Come. We don't have far to go."

I looked up at a rotund man in an ordinary dark suit, with a neatly cropped beard and polite smile. He led me into a surprisingly small room on the same floor contain-ing only a long table with three chairs and before it a single music stand. There was a Bech-stein grand in one corner.

"Professor Epstein, Professor Zweig—both string faculty. Herr Eugen Reczek, our young Linzer." Epstein, Zweig, Schauffel. To this day I can remember their names like an incantation.

We shook hands, I bowed to each and thanked them.

Professor Epstein gestured to the lonely stand in the center of the room, and they sat. "What have you got for us, Herr Reczek?" he said.

"I will start with the first three movements of Bach's third cello suite. If you wish me to go on, I will."

Eyebrows raised. Schauffel and Zweig glanced at each other and nodded, bemused, perhaps a little doubtful. Epstein closed his eyes and simply smiled.

"Herr Reczek is better mannered than our Viennese appli-cants," Zweig whispered.

Schauffel said, "Does that surprise you?"

Their low laughter echoed in the room. I moved the music stand to one side.

"You will play without music?" Professor Epstein said.

I nodded. He returned my nod and gave a little wave of his hand. I let my bow touch each of the strings to make sure I was still in tune, and launched into the first movement of the third suite.

When I finished and had paused before the second movement, Epstein held up a finger.

"You have played like a true purist, a man of the modern age," he said. "No frills, no embellishments, easy on the vibrato. The opening measures were com-manding and a bit agitated and severe, as they should be, and the agitation persists through the quick, repetitive runs later in the movement. But now imagine that after the return to the opening gesture, as the pace slows a bit with those halting and somewhat dissonant tones, something happens. You have worked through the agitation and fury, and emerged into the light—with a sudden smoothness, even tenderness, and in the closing measures a sense of serene, soaring confidence. You can be a little freer with the vibrato, if you'd like. Please play it from the return to the tonic. We'll take a few liberties with Herr Bach, no?"

I played the section again and, as I did, I could see Epstein nod slowly and steal a glance at the other two.

"Good," Epstein said when I'd finished. "You see? Still baroque, still Bach, but the emotional tone has shifted, the character of the music is emerging. Now take it from the beginning with this perspective, of—transformation."

I tell you, it was so interesting I forgot I was being examined. When I had finished the suite, they asked a few more questions about the music, and chatted with me. *Chatted.* I had expected, I don't know, an inquisition! Something typically formal and German, with the threat of disapproval and rejection hanging like a cloud over my poor provincial head. Not so. They had read the application and letters, wanted to know how far I had gone with Bravratsky, what I had played with the chamber group, whether I had switched from the violin or had gone straightaway for the viola, whether I was interested in composition, conducting, teaching. Zweig even asked quite seriously about my training as an upholsterer!

The room got quiet and Professor Schauffel said, "You know, you might enjoy studying composition with Professor Tausk. This is his period. You should ask today whether he has any space for first-year students, and tell him we told you to ask. We have two violinists on the string faculty who teach viola, and we will have to put our heads together to figure out who will be best for you. And, of course, who has time. Both may want to speak with you."

They also required me to take a course in music history and one in music theory at the University (the Conservatory had an arrangement with them) since I had had no truly academic training in music.

I walked out into the cold bright February sun. I did not feel excitement, only an extraordinary, buoyant calm. And a tremendous clarity, as though some constant, nagging, hectoring voice in my head had become still and I could hear only the beating of my own steady heart. I remembered Adolf, his eyes hollow and his face drained after his mother's funeral, barely able to support his own slight weight, in the kitchen of our home in Linz—which now seemed to me a *village* next to Vienna—persuading my father to allow me to apply, and my father two days later, frowning and saying simply, "You may go." I walked the twenty blocks back to the Stumper-gasse, the pedestrians and traffic flowing past me like a silent film. I went to the Post Office on the Mariahilfer Strasse first and sent a telegram to my parents: *I am in. Starting Monday. Eugen.*

When I got back to the room, Adolf was up and hanging the wrung-out sheets to dry. There was a semi-circle of opened books on the floor, surrounding dozens of sketches of courtyards at night. When I told him I was in, he paused and sat down slowly on his bed. For a moment, he seemed upset and looked up at me with a grave, almost mournful expression.

"In? Just like that?"

"Yes. I am to start Monday. Although there are things to be done, arranged, before then."

He studied the array of books and sketches on the floor as though searching for something he had lost or misplaced.

"I have a talented roommate," he said.

After a moment I said, "I'm not so sure of that. But they have a place for me."

He slapped his thighs. "Well. The piano," he said. "Come."

We went not to the Dorotheum but to a small piano shop in the Mariahilf, Fegelein & Son, where we found, of all things, an old Boesendorfer grand, in good con-dition, perfectly tuned, for two kronen a month. In no city other than Vienna could one have found such a deal. And this included several enormous Poles who delivered it straight to our room, removed the legs to angle it through the door, screwed them back on, and oriented the thing properly. I raised the top, and Adolf inspected every chink and corner for signs of our friends the *Bettwanzen*. I refused to allow him to sprinkle that awful powder on the strings or inside the body of my beautiful Boesendorfer. I could just see the plumes of white powder rising from the grand as I pounded my way through a transcription of Siegfried's Rhine Journey.

We went to a nearby café to celebrate. I treated us to *Nussstrudel* and *Kaiserschmarrn*, and I offered to buy Adolf unlimited *Bierkuchen* but he turned me down because, of course, it contained ale. I wasn't sure if he objected to the alcohol (I had never seen him drink alcohol, even on those occasions when my parents offered him a dessert wine or beer at our home) or if he felt the ale diminished the intense sweetness. He craved only pastries and strudel and cakes, and a little tea.

That evening we went to our first opera in Vienna—my first, not Adolf's, for he had been standing through dozens of performances since he arrived the previous September. Of course, it was a production of *Lohengrin*. We spent more than two hours in line outside to make sure we got, for two kronen each, tickets for standing room on the ground floor, under the Emperor's box. There, the acoustics and view were excellent and women were excluded, a condition Adolf insisted on. (Women, he said, treated opera as a social occasion and were by nature incapable of assuming the proper, reverent attitude.) We didn't wear our topcoats, even though it was February, so we could avoid paying the required ten-heller coat-check fee once we got inside.

The lobby of the Court Opera, if one could call it a "lobby," was a vision of marble, granite, frescoes, sculpture, chandeliers, sweeping staircases, and dozens of softly lit vaulted alcoves on each floor. It felt more like walking into a cathedral than a theater and was almost as hushed. Theater-goers whispered, ushers whispered or simply gestured and nodded. Unlike the *Landestheater* in Linz, which seemed to me a place where livestock had taken a liking to opera! Of course, my friend provided his own whispered commentary: what was well done, overdone, omitted, the fresco artists, how many thousands of tons of marble and from where, the secret entries and hidden stairwells, which he knew from studying—memorizing—the plans kept in the architecture library of the Art Museum. I am almost ashamed to admit that what really captivated me—while Adolf went on about the five types of Carrara marble from quarries in Italy and the twenty years of construction—was cleavage. Evening gowns displaying bare shoulders, long sloping necks, upswept and piled hair, *décolleté*, pearls, diamonds, rubies. So much exposed, blushing female skin! To this day, I have never seen so many beautiful, bejeweled women in one place. A wonderful complement to the neoclassical architecture.

When those with reserved tickets were seated, we were allowed to make our way to the standing area. As we were waiting for the orchestra to assemble, an usher shouldered his way through the crowd and held, before Adolf, a silver tray on which lay a small envelope. Adolf gave the expressionless usher an annoyed look, took the envelope and removed and unfolded its contents. He smiled and handed me the note, which was written on expensive paper, you could tell. The handwriting was cultivated and unmistakably feminine: "Meet me under the chandelier by the balustrade on the right at the end of the second act. I am wearing a floral hat and veil. You won't disappoint me, will you?"

I looked at him. "Do you know—is this someone—?"

He smirked and shook his head. He took the note back, crumpled it, and tossed it at his feet. I would discover that this was the not the first time Adolf had received this sort of unsolicited proposition at the opera. He seemed to regard them with a kind of outraged, sneering contempt, one more reminder that there were moneychangers in the Temple of German Art, purveyors of sex and syphilis, that even in our capital of culture one was swimming in filth. I could not know it then, but that note, delivered by a liveried usher who arrived like some messenger from the gods, was a harbinger of the rift that would open up between us before six months had passed.

The music that night was close to perfect. The orchestra, rather than compete with the singers, precisely underscored and expressed every thought, sentiment, and action of each character, pausing in suspension at exactly the right moments, moving through a tremendous dynamic range, embodying the constant tension of character and story, its living substance. For me, the difference from my previous experiences is hard to describe. It was like going from a horse-drawn carriage to a well-tuned sports automobile. Mahler had become director of the Court Opera only two years before and conducted all the Wagner and many of the other productions. From where we stood we could see his head above the rim of the orchestra pit, the hair swept back, pince-nez glinting, the hands, baton, shoulders, eyes turning a collection of over one hundred individual players into a disciplined machine of sound and musical vision.

We did not have time to applaud him. We left in the middle of the third act and ran back to the Stumpergasse so we could be there by eleven o'clock, when the doors were locked and one had to pay a 20-Heller *Sperrsechserl*, or entrance money, to the old caretaker to let us in. In those days tenants were not given keys to their own buildings. But Adolf, who knew the drill, had gotten hold of Lizst's transcription of *Lohengrin* for piano from one of the several lending libraries he belonged to, and whose fees came to twice his monthly rent. I played the rest of the opera on the Boesendorfer and we took turns singing the roles. When Lohengrin had finally ridden off on the swan, it was well past midnight.

Adolf, though, was just getting started. By the time I had washed, made one last check for *Bettwanzen*, spread clean sheets, and laid myself in my narrow bed, he had folded his suit neatly, spread several open volumes of illustrated German legends across his bed, and was on his knees on the floor sketching new stage designs by candlelight. He kept humming to himself, asking me without looking round what *I* thought, jumping to his feet to frown at something he'd just sketched, pacing back and forth in the little space in our room not taken up by the piano and our beds, and then as though struck by divine inspiration he would throw himself down on the floor to continue sketching in the flickering light. When I woke at seven or eight in the morning, the books and sketches were stacked next to his bed, and the top of the Boesendorfer was covered with unfinished sketches. Adolf looked as though he'd just fallen asleep. The bed was surrounded by a halo of white powder. He slept as he always slept—on his back, neck extended over the pillow, mouth open, arms rigid at his side. He looked as though he'd sketched himself to death.

It didn't take long to notice that Adolf's breath had become somewhat foul. Standards regarding this sort of thing were different then. What we would now call "bad" breath was common and hardly noticed. We had yet to become addicted to American Pepsodent. But Adolf's breath was rancid, and I attribute this to diet. During my first weeks in Vienna, we often ate at the nearest soup kitchen, where one could get a substantial midday meal— roast pork, potatoes, cabbage soup—for 30 heller. Usually, though, I had to persuade Adolf to come with me, and I soon realized that he was subsisting on sour milk, stale biscuits, at times *Mehls-peisen,* a pudding made from oatmeal flour, and an occasional piece of poppy- or nut-cake. Certain days he would declare as "fast" days, and then he drank only milk, usually not fresh. His breath often smelled to me like sour poultry. Of course, I never mentioned it.

There was something else, and I attribute this, too, to diet. Adolf had become flatulent. Terribly so. This had not been the case in Linz. Of course, in Linz we were usually out of doors, where it would have been less noticeable, or in my father's shop, which smelled strongly of old fabric and horsehair, or more recently in his mother's sickroom, with its penetrating smell of iodine and alcohol. But he had eaten dinner at our home many times and it was not noticeable there, even though the heaviness of the Austrian diet and the richness of the pastry leant themselves to such effects.

In our room on the Stumpergasse, Adolf's desk was directly in front of the piano and his back was towards me while he studied and sketched. At times, I would be lost in my playing, or furiously making notes in my composition books, and suddenly realize I was being engulfed in a silent, sulfurous wave. At other times, there was warning—a sudden rip, like the sound of heavy cloth or fabric being torn with a jerk, followed by Adolf's coughing loudly or clearing his throat, which I took to be a kind of unspoken "Pardon me." This sound was more frequent when he was engaged in strenuous reading, say, a volume of Wagner or Schopenhauer or Chamberlain's *Foundations of the Nineteenth Century*. Still, I felt it had to do with his drinking large quantities of milk, the tensions inherent in his character, and his isolated existence. When he became excited and paced and went off on one of his longer monologues, the effect—between the halitosis, flatulence, and the ever-present stench of the kerosene—could be overpowering. I was not happy about this. I considered suggesting he consult a physician, but of course said nothing. Years later, I read that he, like Wagner, had become a vegetarian and still drank liter upon liter of milk.

The classes at the Conservatory were a combination of tutorials (viola and piano in my case) and small classes, sometimes no more than seven or eight students, in harmony, composition, counterpoint, and at times so-called "master classes" in performance. There were no female students. Almost all of us were from families of modest means, although over time I would learn there were boys whose fathers owned distilleries and paper mills, and who for many reasons were not anxious for us to know this. Most lived in cheap accommodations dominated, like ours, by rented pianos in the poorer, outlying districts, often two or three to a room, trying to ignore the sound of the trolleys, motorcars, dray horses, street vendors, not to mention the domestic racket of the neighbors. Very few of us had grown up in Vienna, and most, like me, came from smaller cities like Linz and Graz. A few even came from country towns, particularly in Moravia, for some reason. There were also a number of Jewish students, who tended to be among the best trained, most talented, and at times the most arrogant and opinionated, though I must say I often found the arrogance justified and the opinions intelligently and passionately defended. They had a rebellious streak in them, the Jewish students, and enviable ambition. The Conservatory had its own cafeteria where most of us ate and the food was cheap and reasonably good.

The Conservatory also maintained an office where students could obtain tickets without charge to concerts around the city. We could also attend, for no charge, rehearsals of the Philharmonic, the People's Opera, and even plays at the *Burgtheater*—though not the rehearsals of the Court Opera, as Mahler had forbidden this.

There were offers for us to play, for a fee, in small chamber groups at soirées in the homes of aristocratic and upper-middle-class patrons, who tended to live in the districts closer to the center of the city. Often, we would be joined by a member of the family, as it seemed every physician in Vienna was an amateur violinist or oboist. These jobs were especially coveted, as they gave us a chance to mix with—*and* be treated respectfully by, consulted by, and *fed* by—a better sort of people, a musical sort, rather than the landlords who were perpetually hounding us for rent money (although I must say Frau Zdenek was good about this) and complaining about our practicing at night. Most importantly, these evenings were a source of referrals for piano pupils, often the sons and, more often, the daughters of the families who hired us to play.

Adolf's schedule remained a mystery to me. He was asleep when I woke and went off to class, and he was sketching feverishly, pacing, or reading when I went to sleep. The drawings seemed to be of buildings on the Ringstrasse, or the Hofburg, Belvedere, and other "palaces," or stage designs for scenes in opera—the sorts of things he was doing in Linz. When occasionally I returned to our room in the afternoon, he had just woken up or was still asleep, looking a bit ghostly, his dark hair and shoulders dusted inadvertently with the boric acid powder he used to disinfect the bed. The sketches had been collected and stacked neatly, the books put back, the charcoal and pencils and pens in their trays. Often there was a collection of pins on the small desk, a single bug impaled at the end of each—trophies from the night's hunting.

I did not question him about his classes at the Academy, or his progress there, as he seemed disinclined to talk about it. In fact, he never mentioned the classes or the other students, and I thought this odd as he invariably had strong opinions about everything and everyone with whom he came in contact. I expected this to be especially true regarding his teachers. I knew from my years of friendship with Adolf that he talked—endlessly—about what he wanted to talk about and not much else. Whatever was preoccupying him gathered force like steam under pressure and found its release. Any questioning had to be gentle and good-humored and carefully timed, or he would suspect it implied criticism and become aloof and distant, or even enraged. It was no accident that he did not have many friends. It was not even a matter of "many."

Once, as I was returning to the room in the middle of a sunny afternoon, I saw him from a distance. He had spread his papers over a park bench and was sketching the *Burgtheater*, a building he thought "perfectly classical" and whose architectural plan he had studied. This was the time of day when the sun was high, Vienna's chronic gray morning haze had dissipated, and when, I imagined, many of the studio art classes at the Academy were held. What Adolf was doing on a park bench at that time of day was beyond me. I worried that he was cutting class. I worried that he had been on his own so long that he could no longer function as part of a group, that his inability to take direction, his natural abhorrence of teachers and authority, had got the better of him. Now that he had his chance, he would destroy it. I stood in the middle of the boulevard, the trolleys clanging past me, staring. I never disturbed him when he was sketching or reading. He was bound to be irritable and abrupt, and would answer, if he did, without even looking at me. My own situation could not have

been more different. My good father was patient but still a perfec-
tionist, and after years of apprenticeship in his shop—where one
must use the correct needle, the correct stitch, the proper stuffing,
or else the fabric would bunch up, the pattern would not align, the
seat would not have the desired bounce and resiliency—I could
breathe. True, this was a German-speaking Conservatory, there
were plenty of rules and right and wrong ways of doing things,
every teacher was *Herr Professor Doktor*, and so on. But even in
the most technical subjects, for instance, the teaching of counterpoint, there was choice, interpretation. I was expected to have an
opinion. The part of me that before this had been free to express
itself only with Adolf, at least with regard to *music*, was unbound.

And it was easy to make friends. The Brahms–Wagner controversy was still raging, the conservatives siding with Brahms and the
"rebels" with the Master of Bayreuth. Although I loved Brahms, I
don't have to say which camp I was in. One would think Mahler's
near-perfect productions of Wagner would have settled the issue.
But, no, walk into the Conservatory canteen and the war was still
on. Brahms was the natural inheritor of Beethoven; Wagner was the
beginning of the end of classical music, an over-rated blowhard.
Sometimes I would try to moderate, but really I was a partisan, a
true Wagnerite. Then I wished I had Adolf with me, to quote at
length from Wagner's prophetic "Work of Art of the Future," which
he had almost memorized, and to launch into his powerful defense
of Wagner's music not merely as music but as a way of seeing and
transforming the world and one's self: in other words, music as
redemption. Wagner, alone among composers, had produced sixteen
volumes of sprawling, difficult prose—sixteen *volumes*—and Adolf
was hunched over them night after night, by candlelight, copying
passages, reading out loud, pacing, running his fingers through his

hair as though he could massage the very ideas into his brain, coming back to the open volume on our small wooden desk.

I once asked him to come with me to one of our lunchtime brawls, but he grunted without looking up from the newspaper he was reading (he was now reading newspapers every day—spending his own money on them rather than reading them free in any coffeehouse—several of them, front to back, which he had not done in Linz) and he said no, it wasn't his "sort" of thing. A debate, a fight, over the revolutionary meaning of Wagner's music, what could have been *more* his sort of thing? Once, in the months after he had become Reichchancellor, I read an interview with him in the newspaper in which he said that to understand National Socialism one must first understand Wagner. Only I knew what he meant; only I had *seen* it at its conception. My American and British hosts here at Glasenbach know this, they question me endlessly about it. But will they ever understand that his ambitions were born out of the spirit of music? Colonel Lewis smiles when I talk about this. He asks whether, after all that has happened, I still believe it. I don't know what to tell him. At times I no longer know what I believe, about the present or the past. I wish only that we were in our Italianate *Conservatoire*, Adolf in his studio, me at the piano, improvising, notating. The matron knocks and quietly reminds me that luncheon will be in a half hour and there is a guest recital in the afternoon, not to forget. As I lie on my cot in our ward, thinking about this, I can see through the tall windows across the grounds to the fence. The day is bright and cold. Two men are out there, with a spool of barbed wire. They seem to be repairing something.

At the Conservatory, I learned something about myself, and I learned it quickly. I could speak. I had been playing second fiddle (or viola) to Adolf for several years, in part because I had no real interest in some of the subjects that set him off on his monologues, and in part due to his overbearing personality when we were alone. The give-and-take that is the currency of normal human exchange was foreign to me. I was used to being an audience, not having one. Part of this was knowing how to "handle" Adolf, how to give him the platform he needed, and allowing for his eccentricity. Part of it was an enjoyment of his enthusiasm, his emphatic nature, his gift for imbuing any subject with an apocalyptic importance. But part of it—a larger part than I care to admit—was something else.

There is a word in German—*hörig*—which has no real equivalent in English. It is a word that comes more naturally to a culture that (for better or for worse) values obedience and hero-worship. *Hörig* can have a range of meanings: servility, submission, an obsequious bowing to authority, even a helpless passivity. But it can also suggest something different and less craven: a response or thrall-dom to charisma, to charismatic authority, an inspired loyalty and devotion. With me, I'm afraid, it was all of these. Often, it was a failure of nerve. A weakness in the knees, as you say. How many decades has it taken for me to see this? Did it really take the self-abasement of a whole people to make this obvious to me?

Now, without Adolf but surrounded by people, by *musicians*, whose ideas and opinions were detailed and intelligent and passionate, my brain lit up, my tongue loosened, and I spoke. And the more I spoke, the better spoken I became. My fears, quite strong at first, of remaining the bumpkin from Linz, evaporated.

My piano students were excellent, well-bred girls, and often serious about music, too. The Conservatory would allow us to use their practice rooms to give lessons, usually in the late afternoon or evening. If the girls were from outside Vienna—from the Tyrol, Graz, often Bohemia and Moravia—they would usually live in one of the many "women's hotels." These were well-appointed dormitories with their own dining facilities, maids, and practice rooms, and, as you can imagine, a source of endless stories among my Conservatory classmates. Most of these stories were either obviously false or the product of elaborate wishful thinking. Lessons were given in the late afternoon and one might be asked to stay for dinner, which was an experience both flattering and intimidating. My pupils would tell me, in a good-humored way, that a single appearance of a Conservatory student at dinner could produce weeks of coy speculation and questions.

If the girl lived in the city, then one was obliged usually to go to her family's apartment or home. Often, this was in one of the palatial buildings off the Ringstrasse or, if the girl was Jewish, in the affluent Eighth or Josefstadt district, or in the lovely villa suburbs of Döbling and Hietzing. I knew that Jews were thought to be obsessed with money. In my experience, nothing could be further from the truth. The commitment of these families to music, theater, and the arts in general was astonishing to me. My own parents often talked nothing *but* business—new customers, old customers, a commission that could be profitable, deliveries of bales of coconut fiber and horsehair, a sofa that stank of dog's urine. The parents of my Viennese piano students, when they happened to be at home, would interrogate me. What was I studying? Was Bruckner still at the Conservatory? What did I like? What did I recommend? Had I heard any of the Rose Quartet's performances of Beethoven? I'm sure they talked about money or they couldn't have lived the way they did, but it was never discussed in my presence. One of my favorite pupils, and my only viola student, was a Jewish surgeon in his fifties, maybe older. He was already an accomplished pianist.

There is a story I heard about the famous *Wiener Werkstätt*. In 1903, the young architect Josef Hoffmann and the designer Koloman Moser were sitting in the Café Hermannshof, across from the Court Opera. They were discussing their fantasy of creating a workshop that would combine all the applied arts—architecture, interior design, furniture, textiles, metalwork, ceramics, carpentry, typography, graphic arts—in pursuit of the *Gesamtkunstwerk* or "Total Work of Art," an environment in which everything down to the last detail was consciously designed and coordinated. Fritz Warndorfer, a Jewish businessman and passionate admirer of William Morris and his Arts and Crafts Movement, came in, spotted them, and sat down. He listened, and when he had heard enough he pulled 500 kronen from his pocket—in those days, a staggering sum to be walking about with—slapped the money on the table, and said *Anfangen!*—"Begin!" Supposedly, this was how the *Werkstätt* was born. I don't doubt it.

All of this only strengthened my sense of leading a double life. During the day, it was the neoclassical architecture of the Conservatory, with its marble floors and columns, its painted murals of Pallas Athene and Orpheus with their gilt highlights, my professors in their waistcoats and high collars. In the afternoon, the vast apartments and homes off the Ringstrasse, with the heavy, dark furniture and lace, some even with vaulted ceilings. And in the evening, back to our cramped room on the Stumpergasse with the lavatory down the hall, toilets encrusted with feces, the sooty airshaft outside our one window, and Adolf stalking the *Bettwanzen*. And the stench, always, of rancid cabbage boiling in the rooms above us. It surprises me now to say I didn't resent it. I didn't question it. This was how a student lived, this was how great art was made. Forget Adolf's plans for our *Conservatoire*, with its greenhouse and library and recital room. That was for later.

One of my favorite students, and certainly my most conscientious, was a seventeen-year-old named Emilie Sachs. We had our lessons in her family's grand apartments on the Josefstadt Strasse. Once, Emilie came by the room on the Stumpergasse. She must have got the address from the Conservatory as it was not something I normally handed out. (Adolf, in fact, had specifically forbidden this.) She wanted to drop off composition homework that was late, with a note explaining that she hadn't fully understood the assignment, and a list of questions for me to address at our next lesson. She came during the early afternoon. I imagine Adolf was asleep or had just woken up. In any case, he was furious.

"This is our room, our sanctuary," he lectured me when I returned later that day. "It is where I read and think and write and draw! It is where you practice and compose. It is a world of higher things"—a higher world populated by *Bettwanzen?*—"and I would expect you to be sensitive to this. This is not a place for women or girls, for some little rendezvous—"

He was starting to pace (the four steps from the piano to the door and back), hands in the air, head down, eyes blazing. I knew I was in for a real harangue. This was common enough, as you know, in Linz. But in Vienna the speeches were becoming more frequent and even more forceful and strident as my friend became more irritable. I was starting to think he really might be losing his mind.

I must stop here and tell you something. I digress, yes, but you will forgive me. We were living in a world that is lost to us now almost entirely in some respects. Now one can see young men and women walking together openly, with a bearing relaxed and healthy and self-confident. Men no longer wear the stiff, high collars that made every turn of the head seem unnatural and mechanical. Women are no longer laced into whalebone corsets that create an hourglass shape, making it difficult to move and breathe normally, and even on the warmest day in summer covered from toe to neck by layer upon layer, buttoned right up to the chin. Things were different then. Young men and women lived in separate worlds. A girl from a respectable family would never be seen with a young man without an escort, as though the absence of her mother or a trusted family servant put her very life in danger. Her education was limited to whatever would make her seem more companionable and pleasing. I benefitted from this as music lessons were considered desirable, even a necessity. She was expected to be abstinent and even sexually ignorant until marriage. A giggling girlishness in manner was encouraged, or excused, so that her comportment seemed anything but serious and adult.

Expectations were different for young men, *or* older men. Ignorance in sexual matters was considered neither desirable nor manly. With respectable girls and young women cordoned off by their families, the result was, as I've said, a city teeming with prostitutes as young as twelve or thirteen. Some could be had for as little as a few heller. If you had money, you could go to a "hotel"—a brothel—and dance with nicely dressed women to piano accompaniment in a furnished parlor, and in this way enjoy the farcical appearance of polite society before adjourning to one of the upstairs bedrooms. If you could not afford to be seen— that is, *recognized*—in such a place, there was always a back stairway that would take you to a private sitting room adjoining a bedroom. The bedroom closets held whips, riding crops, harnesses and other equipment to accommodate the tastes of more eccentric clients.

But there were other, more legitimate ways of meeting young women. The city was filled with waitresses and shopgirls, and any middle-class home could afford to keep domestic servants. The girls were from the poorer classes and often their parents had never even been legally married. They usually had no immediate expectation of marriage and were flattered by the attention. But you paid. You paid for the room, you paid for dinner and a play, and you paid with a little bit of your soul for the uneasy pretense of being interested in their lives, their tastes, their jobs, their cheap dreams. They expected gifts—perfume, scarves, dresses, handbags, sometimes straight cash. If you did not want to be seen dining with the girl, some restaurants would offer you a *chambre séparée*, a private dining room opening onto a bedroom. It was all a charade—a form of prostitution, really—without the simple, honest transaction. If the girl worked as a domestic, she could be expected as an unwritten provision of her employment to furnish the young man of the house with experience, and perhaps service the appetites of the old man as well.

And the risk of infection was constant. Syphilis was rampant. Prophylactics were expensive and unreliable. They were made from sheep's guts, like sausage casing; they would often tear as you tried to put them on. One could see older men in the streets, with their topcoats and canes, heads held unnaturally erect, their knees rising almost to their chests with each step, barely making progress, their eyes fixed ahead of them, frowning with an expression both severe and perplexed. These were the "high-steppers" in whom the disease had advanced to its third and final stage. They were grotesque reminders of what could be in store for you. In those days, many—even doctors—thought the disease could be inherited, so that in allowing one's self to risk infection, one could be dooming one's children and one's children's children, male and female.

Even satisfying one's self in private had its supposed medical risks. Gastrointestinal disorders, blindness, hair loss, atrophy of one's genitals, impotency after marriage, loss of ambition, and a permanent mental dullness only slightly above idiocy were some of the reputed consequences. In my case, I was simply never alone. When I was supposed to be asleep, Adolf was up, reading, writing, drawing, pacing, reciting passages and dialogue from Wagner. When I woke, he went to sleep, on his back, his arms rigid at his sides, his hands sometimes actually balled into fists, his face a frowning mask of exhaustion. Now and then I got back to the room in the late afternoon, while he was still in class, but you could never tell when he would walk in. His schedule—apart from his agitated night-time studies followed by sleeping until midday—was still a mystery.

"These girls you teach," he said the day Emilie Sachs had come to the room, "do you think they are truly serious, dedicated? I see how carefully you prepare the lessons, with the same care you take with your work at the Conservatory. But this is *wasted*, don't you see? Woman as a being is incapable of dedicating herself to a higher goal, artistic or moral. This is as much as to say that she is intrinsically soulless. What you teach them will be worn as a bit of social adornment, like clothing, first to impress, yes, then to seduce and entrap. In the end to satisfy Woman's lust for conformity! Because she lacks the intrinsic value of the human personality, she must supply that value from the outside, in the form of money, possessions, successful children, the best box at the theater, the envy of other women, the social position of her husband. Her vanity, which is bottomless, can only be satisfied by the attention of a sexually aroused male.

"This is the crude truth. I have watched you struggle, I have witnessed your tireless devotion. Do not allow yourself to be distracted, to be dragged into the filth of failure and disappointment, to wallow in the sty of so-called domestic bliss. A man *can* remain pure, Eugen. His desires can remain pure. But he must devote himself single-mindedly and with the utmost seriousness to a higher goal, which I know you to be capable of. Otherwise, the consequences can be disastrous, even fatal. Don't tell me you don't know that. Of course you know that."

I was sitting on the piano bench. I thought of what I usually thought of when Adolf got going on the subject of women: Stefanie. The woman-hating of a young man disappointed in an "extraordinary," and extraordinarily one-sided, love.

A few weeks after I arrived in Vienna, Adolf had taken me to an exhibit of paintings and sketches by von Stuck, a favorite of his. I was a bit stunned at first. Most of the pen-and-ink drawings, which were technically quite good, depicted a naked woman enjoying the attentions of a slick, glistening python. In one sketch, titled *Sin*, the woman is arching backward as the enormous snake slides between her legs and over her genitals, encircling her neck. The woman is beautifully drawn; her eyes are closed and lips parted in frank ecstasy. The effect of *Sin* is not one of simple condemnation, but of feverish eroticism and disgust. At one point, I found Adolf in front of von Stuck's drawing of the head of Medusa: the woman stares directly at the viewer, her face round and expressionless, her pale transparent eyes wide open, the hair a mass of writhing snakes. He was riveted. Still staring at the face, he grabbed my arm. "My mother's eyes, Reczek!" he said in an agitated whisper, and we left the gallery.

Adolf was now standing at our "window," looking out into the perpetual gray light of the airshaft. I ran my finger along the edge of the piano bench.

"Are you done?" I said.

He did not answer.

"It's three o'clock," I said.

"And so?"

"You're missing class."

Again silence. He did not turn to look at me.

I stared at my hands. "Where is your—devotion?"

"There is nothing to devote myself to," he said. "I was rejected."

"You were—"

He sat down on his bed and rubbed his face. "My portfolio was well received and I was admitted to the examination, which was two days—two mornings and afternoons—of freehand sketching. They gave us the subjects: 'Expulsion from Paradise,' 'Hunting,' 'Spring,' 'Construction Workers,' 'Death,' 'Rain,' and so on. Beyond that we were on our own. At the end of the second day, they informed us."

I did not speak. I must have expected another outburst—the unfairness of the judging, a bias against applicants from the provinces who lacked the right academic pedigree. But he sat with his hands between his legs, staring at the floor in the dimness of the room. The smell of the kerosene was almost overwhelming. Of course, it made sense—his continuing to draw and read all night and sleep until the middle of the day, my seeing him in the Prater during the afternoon, his never mentioning his classmates or professors. I had been afraid the same contempt for instruction and the classroom that had led him to drop out of *Realschule* in Linz was resurfacing at the Academy. It honestly had not occurred to me for a moment that he had been rejected.

"Was there some explanation? Did they say anything?"

"'Drawings unsatisfactory. Too few heads.' That is all that was written on my sheet. I went to the dean the next day and that is what he said. 'Too few heads.'"

I knew instantly what that meant. Adolf, as usual, had stuck to scenes of nature and buildings, even if the given themes called for people. Or if he had included them, they were indistinct or odd, or grotesque.

"Did he . . . say anything else?"

"He asked what school of architecture I had attended. When I said I had not, he said I should become an architect or an architectural painter."

"Well, of course! He's doing you a favor. He's pointing you in the direction of your true talent. That happens all the time in musical training. Performance or composition or conducting or teaching—"

"—a school of architecture will only accept applications from a graduate of an *Oberschule* or *Gymnasium*. I would have to go back and finish my secondary education. That is impossible. I don't have to tell *you* that." His voice, which had become quieter, had again begun to assume its familiar hardness, its defiance and contempt.

"What will you do?"

"I have myself," he said. "I will always have myself."

The next day when I returned in the late afternoon, he was gone. There was a medical text on the desk, which he had no doubt borrowed from one of the lending libraries he belonged to, a constant drain on his dwindling funds. The large volume, bound in thick textured leather, was open to two pages of detailed illustrations. There were several of male genitals erupting with the ulcerating chancres of primary syphilis. Another—a splendid pen-and-ink drawing by a French medical illustrator—depicted the awesomely beautiful and naked body of a woman covered from head to toe in the roseola pustules of the second stage. Others depicted the "monster infants" of syphilitic parents, the terrible reminder of past transgressions: infants with the wizened faces of old men ("syphilitic runts"), infants without limbs, infants with internal organs growing outside their bodies. He had bookmarked a page with this quote from a medical pamphlet, lightly underlined in pencil:

And all it takes is a single contact. Beware, young man. Provocation will reach you in all its forms, and in particular in its worst form, which is that of clandestine prostitutes. How dangerous they are, these little factory girls, who pass up and down the boulevard pretending to put off going back to work!

I looked at the bookmarks. They were a pair of tickets to *Spring Awakening*, the Wedekind play which was being performed in Vienna for the first time after years of being banned. I did not think the pair was for my student Emilie and myself. The performance was that Friday evening. It was part of Adolf's campaign to keep me from ruin.

The production of *Spring Awakening* was at the Burgtheater, a magnificent building and one of Adolf's favorites. We attended in our opera-going outfits. It surprised me that the play was so funny. Wendla promising to hide her head under an apron while her prudish, flustered mother tells her the truth behind the story of the stork. Hans bidding a reluctant and lascivious farewell to Vecchio's *Venus*, one of a series of classical reproductions he has been using as an aid to a habit he thinks is beginning to dissolve his brain. The bumbling headmaster and his faculty—Kuppeldich, Affenschmalz, and the others—discussing how to deal with Melchior after his illustrated opus *Copulatio* is discovered. The audience was in stitches. But Adolf sat through it with an unwavering look of stern and sober curiosity. I spent most of the play biting my lip. Each time I started to laugh, Adolf's eyes would dart disapprovingly in my direction, and I would massage my mouth.

We did not discuss *Spring Awakening* in the manner of our critiques after the opera.

Outside the theater, Adolf simply grabbed my arm and said, "One more stop, Eugen." And we took off in the direction of the Spittelberggasse, Vienna's single block-long red-light district. My Conservatory classmates at times would casually mention having stopped off there, but I doubt they did more than play the tourist.

The Spittelberggasse was more a side-street than a true street. It was a narrow, poorly lit way, almost an alley, flanked by one- and two-story houses. The windows on the ground floor were either opened or the shades were raised. Inside, you might see a half-dressed woman sitting at a cheap vanity combing her hair, powdering herself, applying make-up, all the time glancing towards the street to keep an eye on the evening's business. The "girls" ranged from fat, scowling middle-aged women with creased, painted faces and huge pendulous breasts shifting under their lingerie, to flat-chested girls barely in their teens who sat expressionlessly in stiff-backed chairs, some of them likely the children of prostitutes. I don't have to tell you what a sad and grotesque sight this made.

As we sauntered past the houses, I felt repelled and queasy, and yet my heart was beating fast. A chemise would lift and there would be a flash of bare breasts. A leg would lift and a stocking would be unrolled and clipped to a garter. Men, many in long coats and top hats, streamed in both directions. The women would pretend to ignore the "shoppers" until one tapped softly on a window, the light would turn off, the shade would come down, and then the front door would open for negotiation. The gentleman would stand at the threshold until terms were agreed on. It was accepted that men would not stand in front of the windows and stare. The whole procession was oddly quiet and solemn.

I was tense and very conscious of how I walked, letting my arms swing or clasping my hands behind my back, my head forward a little as I glanced from side to side. I became uncomfortably aroused, and I'd think of the medical illustrations, of the genitals with the erupting sores. That was enough. Adolf's tactics were working. Adolf himself walked beside me, his chin up, a smirking, derisive smile playing across his face. He kept his eyes fixed ahead of him. At the end of the block, he pivoted, placed his hand on my arm and said "Again," and we walked the little street in the other direction, Adolf thinking God knows what, and me conjuring the terribly disfigured genitals like Professor van Helsing fending off Dracula with his crucifix.

When we reached the boulevard, we walked in silence for a few minutes. Adolf still wore that somewhat proud smirk. Finally, he lowered his head and said, "Well?"

"It's quite a scene."

"Yes."

"Have you been there before?"

"Of course not. Once is enough, don't you think? I have heard."

"Where are the police?"

"There is no need for the police. It is perfectly legal. The whores have cards issued by the city which allows them to practice their trade as long as they submit to examinations by a police physician and are at least eleven years of age. I'm sure some customers find their billfolds and pocket watches gone afterwards, but they do not complain. In a society that values and protects the flame of life, there will be no need, and no desire, for places like this."

The "Flame of Life." Again! The pure, sacred, incorruptible, and eternal flame. He had talked in Linz of the flame, but in Vienna this had become a regular theme. I think he had picked it up from the *völkisch* newspapers and leaflets that seemed to be everywhere, in the news kiosks, hawked on the streets, in smoke shops, littering the gutter, even in the cafés, which were a stronghold of the more legitimate press. There were flyers for seemingly dozens of groups devoted to cultivating the flame in young people—the Wandervogel, the League of German Youth, the Knights Templar of Aryan Youth, various sports leagues. They sponsored prayer groups, football teams, choral societies, camping trips, but mostly daily hikes into the hills west of Vienna in full Bavarian costume. I could never really tell what the "flame" represented—racial purity, sexual purity, or simply the desire to distinguish themselves from the Czechs, Magyars, Ruthenes, Jews, and everyone else. Adolf, who never joined any group beyond a lending library, had begun to collect these, and they were stacked in a growing pile alongside the borrowed volumes of Wagner and Schopenhauer and Chamberlain.

Some of these leagues required their members to abstain from sex and marriage until the age of twenty-five. This would not have been a hit with my classmates at the Conservatory. When we weren't battling over Brahms and Wagner, or mimicking our professors, we were exchanging information on where and for how much one could obtain reliable prophylactics, which coffee houses had the prettiest and most accommodating waitresses, the aphrodisiacal properties of powder made from the horn of the rhinoceros, the best brothels (as if any of us could afford to frequent these places), and which matrons of the Society for the Friends of Music—the philanthropy that founded the Conservatory and still ran it in name—were known to bestow their favors on the most talented students (as far as I could tell, this was *pure* fantasy). Naturally, I didn't discuss any of this with Adolf.

When we got back to our room, Adolf changed into the old trousers and collarless shirt he wore to study and draw and pace at night. He set up his candle, selected the volume he would read, got out his sketch pad and charcoal and pens, and dusted both our beds with boric acid powder. He placed fresh cloves of garlic in the corners of the room, a new weapon against the *Bettwanzen*.

I lay on my bed and closed my eyes. My blood was racing, pulsing in my ears. I could not stop the images: a chemise being lifted over a head, a corset undone, hair combed and shaken out, eyelashes rolled, bosoms powdered and plumped. I hugged my arms to my chest. In a moment, I heard the frantic scratching of charcoal on paper. Stop, start; stop, start. The scuff of chair legs against the wooden floor, the sound of pacing, four or five paces to the door, and back. Ten or fifteen minutes of this, then the scuff of the desk chair once more, a page being turned. At last, quiet. But I could not sleep. Even imagining the ghastly medical illustrations was of no use. An hour later, I got up and went down the hall to the lavatory. I do not think Adolf watched me leave the room. I could hear him humming to himself, lost in his night-world.

He wasn't entirely wrong about Emilie Sachs. She was a pretty girl with a broad, open face and frank eyes. She attended one of the many girls' academies in Vienna, a watered-down *Gymnasium* really, with some mathematics and science, only modern languages and literature, and plenty of art and music, which was often supplemented with private lessons in the home. She was by far my most serious student. That she spent hours each day in disciplined practice was evident, always. When I criticized her playing, she grasped the point quickly, corrected herself right away. Her seriousness somehow made me more relaxed with her because we could concentrate on mechanics and technique in a very matter-of-fact way, without my having to soft-peddle my criticisms. If I complimented her playing she would nod politely without smiling, or at times reply, "Good. I'm glad," in a soft, even voice. I remember she wanted to apply to the small women's college of the University of Vienna and was thinking of studying medicine. Already at that time there were many Jews on the faculty of the medical school, and a few female students, mostly in pediatrics, as one might expect.

But what was most striking about Emilie was her complete lack of girlishness. My other students—and they were all girls of good families of about the same age—were in the habit of covering their mouths and looking away as if to stifle an outburst of giggling, over what I could never say. Perhaps over their playing. It seemed prudish and flirtatious at once. I learned to smile indulgently and gesture to the sheet music, as if to say, May we continue, Fraulein?

Emilie Sachs presented no such distractions. During lessons she was calm and focused. Her walk was unaffected, more of an adult stride, at times almost masculine. My classmates at the Conservatory—those experts—said you could tell whether a woman had known a man by the way she walked. And so married women walked with an unselfconscious and purposeful stride: they had left the ghetto of girlhood, with its hysterical, pent-up energies, behind. I could not imagine—I felt *ashamed* imagining—Emilie with a man.

When I swung the heavy brass knocker (the head of Pallas Athene) against the massive door of the Sachs's apartment on Thursday in the late afternoon, I would hear her brisk steps across the living room and the door would swing open, and she would nod and bend from the waist—"Herr Reczek." She would never allow one of the servants to answer. She was already developing the quiet authority and discretion I have always associated with physicians, especially the admirable ones like Dr. Bloch. I was not surprised that she had come to our room to deliver a late assignment, infuriating Adolf. A woman—a *girl*—attempting to violate our sanctum of Art and Music and *Bettwanzen*!

Emilie's mother was often there—taking in packages, talking quietly with the servants, stretching to reach a book from the shelf-lined walls of the living room or the library. There were more books in that vast apartment than I had seen in any home. It was the first thing I noticed when I walked into the Sachs's apartment for our initial lesson, and I thought immediately of Adolf's borrowed books and newspapers stacked against the walls of our dark little room, stinking of kerosene, on the Stumpergasse. Occasionally, I would be startled by the grinding ring of a black telephone, which sat on a pedestal by the window. Frau Sachs would glide in, speak a few words into the mouthpiece, and hang up; then she would nod apologetically at Emilie and me, and leave. I had seen telephones in offices and public buildings, of course. I had never seen one in a private home.

Sometimes at the end of a lesson Frau Sachs would bring us *Palatshincken*—beautiful light crepes filled with fruit and served with a vanilla and raspberry sauce—and dark, bitter coffee in tiny porcelain cups. She would smile, excuse herself, and disappear into one of the other high-ceilinged rooms without a word.

"Don't your servants *do* anything?" I once asked Emilie. "You answer the door and your mother brings the food."

"We have servants but don't like to make them work," she said. "It is a form of hypocrisy, really, or guilt. Don't ask me to explain. It is too complicated."

Frau Sachs did not dress in a way I associated with adult Viennese women, corseted gowns narrowing the waist, pushing up and exaggerating the bosom, gathering in folds under the chin. Women often seemed unnaturally stiff and erect when they walked, encased in linen and silk, with hundreds of buttons up and down the back. Instead, Frau Sachs wore the "reform" fashions I had seen in magazines and associated with Secessionist artists, like Klimt. These often fell loosely from the shoulders, gathered a bit under the bosom, then draped down to the floor, with no waist at all, doing away with who knows how many layers of undergarments. Devoid of lace or frills, Frau Sachs's dresses had rather bold geometric patterns in black and gold and other striking colors. She wore her hair up and had an interesting longish face with large deep brown eyes and a warm tolerant smile. She was tall, maybe seven or eight inches above five feet, and the long waistless dress that flattened the chest made her seem even taller. She was also more slender than most women, and the whole impression was attenuated, languid, graceful, unhurried. Ever since, I have associated affluence with a pleasant, unhurried—and un*worried*—manner, as though nothing on earth could go wrong that couldn't be fixed and made right.

My own mother was short and stout—*stämmig*, as we say, "like a tree trunk"—as solid as my father, and while she was quite a competent woman, she was always worried about *something*, rushing about in a brisk, muscular way. And, of course, there was Frau Hitler, younger but also a busy, fretful housekeeper, suffering over the past and constantly worried about the future. How Frau Sachs dealt with her worries, if she had any under that languid surface, was not apparent to me. I should add that she was an important member of the Society for the Friends of Music, or *Gesellschaft der Musikfreunde*, which is how I came to teach her daughter. She would also hire student chamber groups from the Conservatory to give recitals at her home, Emilie said, or simply to play following a dinner party.

Once, when our lesson had run late, Frau Sachs asked me to stay to dinner with her and her daughter. I made a show of having assignments for my Conservatory classes and lessons to plan, but really I didn't want to seem ill-bred and too eager to take advantage. In fact, the thought of having dinner with Emilie and her slender, cultured mother in this home filled with books and artwork and splendid furniture and vast Oriental rugs was nothing short of a dream come true. Frau Sachs simply bowed her head, clasped her hands together, and said with polite urgency,

"Oh, please *do*!" and I threw up my hands as if to say that I, for one, could not refuse such a charming plea.

"My mother is going to interview you," Emilie said. "Beware."

"There's no reason why I shouldn't politely ask Herr Reczek—I'm sorry, *Eugen*—about himself. Common curiosity. Consideration."

We were at one end of the long table in the dining room, having soup. There was no mention of Herr Sachs joining us.

Emilie raised her eyebrows at her mother. "Herr Reczek has not proposed to me, Mother. He is a proper piano teacher."

Frau Sachs sipped her wine. "I thought Herr Reczek was a student at the *Conservatoire*." And she looked at me for confirmation.

I laughed. "Well, I'm not Viennese. That alone is a topic for conversation."

"No one in Vienna is Viennese," Emilie said. "They become Viennese, or pretend to."

"No, but I'm especially boring and provincial, from Linz, where the whole town goes to bed at ten o'clock, except for the handful who run off to the small opera house."

"Did you study opera in Linz?" Frau Sachs asked.

"Music was a hobby then. I'm an upholsterer. I even have my journeyman's certificate. My father is a real master, and I was his apprentice. Until he concluded it would be more humane to allow me to starve as a Conservatory student than to die an early death breath-ing horsehair and sawdust." I had decided, as a policy, to be unembarrassed about my apprenticeship since everyone at the Conservatory seemed to find it the most charming and novel part of my resumé. "You have splendid furniture," I said. "I've noticed."

"Ah," Frau Sachs smiled at her daughter. "I'm going to have to borrow Eugen."

"We are redecorating," Emilie explained. "Again, my mother is interested in what is fashionable."

"I am interested in what is *new*, yes." Frau Sachs seemed to treat her bright and opinionated daughter with an amused tolerance and forbearance—which I liked, frankly. I imagine this was a measure of how truly provincial I was, siding with the mother against her rebellious offspring. "Do you know Schroedinger's?" Frau Sachs went on. "The fabric store on the Mariahilfer Strasse? No? It is a remarkable place."

"My father would travel to Vienna now and then to meet with fabric distributors and designers for special clients, but I never went with him." I thought of mentioning our eccentric and naked client in the castle. I should have, Frau Sachs would have found it amusing. But I couldn't have known that then. "I was in the shop or I was waiting in line for standing-room tickets to the opera. I rarely left the city. I told you, I'm a bumpkin."

"Oh, that's not true, of course, Mama."

"You know, the *Conservatoire* provides discounted tickets to students. That is an old policy, and we make sure they keep it, even as prices have risen terribly."

"But not to the Court Opera. I'm still standing in line for standing room. I must be destined to stand."

"But the productions—" Frau Sachs placed her hands on the table. "Mahler is an indisputable genius. Did you see the production of *Tannhauser*? With Leo Slezak?"

Emilie closed her eyes. "Are we going to hear about this now?"

Frau Sachs turned to me confidentially. "I'm afraid my daughter is opposed to *true* sensuality in music."

"I'm opposed to, to—kitsch! To bombast! To everything that is overdone, food that is overcooked, books that are too long. Fat women in helmets with horns bellowing about dragons and sacred treasures. The stories are like Viking comic strips. All that Teutonic—*flatulence*! Hours of it! And those horrible dwarfs digging for gold, they're just horrid little anti-Semitic caricatures."

I almost burst out laughing. I knew Emilie the good student, not the *enfant terrible* of the Sachs household.

I held up my hands and frowned, like a fond older brother. "I know the scale of the work seems oversized. But, you know, well, my roommate—"

"Your roommate—!" Emilie gasped.

This time I did laugh.

"Last week, Mama," she said, "I went to Herr Reczek's room to deliver an assignment which was overdue and about which I had a number of questions. I knocked on the door and I waited and waited. Then it creaked open a few inches and a face—hollow eye sockets, sunken cheeks, and eyes, pale eyes like a Weimaraner's, glaring at me as though they would bore into my brain. His hair was hanging over his face and he was breathing as though he had been doing calisthenics. And he says *nothing*, just stares. So I explain myself and he takes the papers from my hand and says, 'I will see he gets this.' The door creaks closed again. Then suddenly it opens and he says, 'Please do *not* come back.' The door closes again. What a ghoul! I am sorry, Herr Reczek, I don't mean to be so harsh."

I smiled. I liked playing the older brother indulging his precocious sister. After all, I was an only child and had never enjoyed this kind of seniority.

"Don't be offended," I said. "He must have been reading or drawing. He is very serious about these things. An artist. Painting, architecture, music, set design for opera, city planning. Everything. He must have committed to memory the plan for every building on the Ring by now. But don't interrupt him when he is working. He can be a beast. I know this from Linz. We have known each other for years."

Frau Sachs was listening intently. "Where is this young man enrolled?" she asked.

"Nowhere, I'm afraid. He—he teaches himself. In fact, he shuns teachers. He has never been a joiner of groups or schools or anything else. But without him I would not be here. I would be stuffing sofas in Linz."

Frau Sachs nodded and narrowed her eyes. "What is his instrument?"

"None. For him, music, I mean Wagner"—here I raised my arms and wiggled my fingers, as though appealing to the gods, and Emilie laughed—"is a way of seeing the world, of regenerating the world. Don't ask me to explain that, I don't understand it fully. Yet. I have not read Wagner's writings. Perhaps they are too—abstract—for me. I am an upholsterer and an upholsterer's son, I need to have the instrument in my hands. I need to feel the bow biting into the strings, the vibration of the instrument against my cheek. So my appreciation is purely sensory, or perhaps, sens*ual*. It has not gone to a higher plane. That is my limitation. Or so I'm told."

"That is no limitation," Emilie said. "It just means you are not a pretentious aesthete."

"I'm not so sure of that."

"Well, I am your student and I am sure of that."

"No false humility, please, Herr Reczek." Frau Sachs smiled when she said this. The smile was not without a little irony and wisdom (wisdom, yes, although you may come to doubt me). It filled me with confidence. "Perhaps," she said, "that was your friend's message. Or one of them. Your friend with the sunken cheeks and eyes of a Weimaraner."

"Perhaps," I said.

I opened the door to our room quietly. It was late and I had had to pay that near-blind *Hausbesorger* his twenty hellers to let me into the building.

The room was shadowy in the candlelight and the kerosene heater was on, its fumes rippling in the air. After the mahogany and high ceilings of the Sachs's apartment in the Josefstadt, it was like crawling into a hole in the ground. Adolf was sketching. He seemed to be copying something from a book next to him at the desk. There were sketches strewn over both our beds and covering the piano. On the floor, arranged in a semi-circle around the desk, were other volumes open to pages displaying photographs of buildings.

He continued to draw. He did not even glance in my direction.

"Where have you been?"

I hesitated.

"I was at the Sachs's. You know, the one who came by here last week. It was the last lesson of the day and I was asked to stay for dinner. This happens at times. They are only being polite. The mother and daughter."

Silence. The scratching of pencil on paper.

"It has happened before?"

"Before, I have said 'No'."

I slipped off my collar and necktie and sat on the bed. He sketched, glancing often at the photograph in the volume on the desk. Alongside it, a half-eaten biscuit and an empty glass of milk, his dinner.

"Did you enjoy the attention, Eugen?" He had still not turned to look at me. He was silhouetted from behind by the flickering light from the candle, bent over the small desk, the image of a copyist in a monastery.

"I liked the food, actually." I said this with, I believe, an indifferent, even hostile, edge.

"They want you to think they are bestowing their attention when in reality it is just the opposite." He sighed, and continued drawing. "*They* are flattered, though they would hardly betray this. They need your thoughts, opinions, reactions, your whole response to the world, to fill their inner emptiness and create something resembling a true personality. It is like a transfusion of blood."

I almost laughed. I thought of Stefanie not bestowing a word on Adolf in the nearly two years he spent waiting on the footbridge from Urfahr. But I suppose that was the point, wasn't it? The moment she opened her mouth she would no longer have been the glowing incarnation of German girlhood, an inspiration to Art and Poetry. She would have become an ordinary girl with ordinary, even trivial, dreams and ambitions, on her evening stroll, her arm encircled through her mama's.

"Well, the girl already has enough opinions to fill a book. I think you might hear some of them, too. Frau Sachs has invited you there."

Ah! That got his attention. He shifted in his chair and glanced over his shoulder with a mixture of perplexity and contempt. I think he was flattered.

"I'm serious. The husband is an amateur violinist. He hires students from the Conservatory to play chamber pieces with him at their apartment. There are guests, too. And a good dinner. And dessert! I told her about your studies. She thinks what you are doing is difficult and admirable, and she would like you to come. Even though you scared her daughter half to death! She knows your Professor Roller, too. Not well, I think, but she has met him." I dangled this plum carefully, trying to sound casual. Roller was Mahler's set designer and Adolf revered him. The possibility of an introduction would be too much to resist. Almost thirty years later—even as I write this, I can hardly believe it—Adolf would bring Roller, then an old man and quite ill, to the Chancellery and ask him to stage Wagner's *Parsifal*. He kept the ambassador from Great Britain waiting *two* hours while they discussed Adolf's ideas and sketches for certain scenes.

"They have a library, Adolf," I said. "A separate room. A large room with high ceilings and no windows. Like a vault, really. It is lined with books from floor to ceiling. The smell of the paper and ink and leather binding is overpowering." I thought of his sketch of the Villa Eugen, which was still on my night table at home. "Not just the usual literature and history. Big books. Books containing photographic reproductions of works of architecture and art. Books that are difficult to even lift. There is a ladder on wheels. It is attached to a rail built into the shelves and runs along all four walls. You wheel it to the right spot and climb up and choose the book you want." I sighed and let my hands dangle between my legs. "We must get one, eh?"

Adolf stared at me—not really at me, but in my direction—his head tilted back, eyes narrowed, blinking furiously, massaging his chin with the palm of his hand. It was his Big Idea look. He rose from the chair and began to pace, hands clasped behind his back, bent at the waist, frowning at the floor. Now I knew things were really cooking: The future of Art, Music, and the German people was at stake.

"I am going to write an opera," he said.

I looked at him.

"An opera?" I said flatly. Adolf had taken a handful of piano lessons from my teacher Bravratsky in Linz and then quit. Practicing scales, he said, was boring, a waste of time. He had committed to memory nearly every word of every opera Wagner had written, he could whistle every line of dialogue and all the orchestral passages. But he had no formal knowledge of music, of harmony, orchestration, counterpoint. He couldn't *read* music.

"I know what you are thinking," he said. He was still pacing, talking at the floor.

"Professors and classes may be useful for some but not others. Intuition and inspiration—the inspired idea—count, too. Besides, you have taught me much. Listen to me! In 'The Work of Art of the Future,' Wagner describes the legend of Wieland the Smith, which he says is an essential legend for the *Volk*, especially now, a story of talent, yearning, captivity, humiliation, and revenge. And freedom. Ultimately, freedom. It speaks directly to our present-day loathing of the shallow, cowardly, and inhuman culture in which we exist. Now, Wagner wrote an incomplete libretto for *Wieland*. He gave this to Lizst, asking him to finish the libretto and compose the opera. Lizst, perhaps from a lack of talent and *inspiration*"—he almost shouted "inspiration," *Eingebung* in German, with a kind of guttural contempt—"never took this up. But the unfinished libretto exists. It exists in *this* book." He stood to attention before the desk and ran the tips of his long, white fingers over one of the leather-bound volumes.

He pivoted. "I will complete the libretto, design the sets, indicate the melodic content of the music, the motifs for each character. You will elaborate on my musical ideas, orchestrate them, and provide the climactic orchestral themes." He looked away for a long moment, as though listening for some distant sound—the opening strains of the Prelude, perhaps. He was still at attention, hands clasped behind his back. "Are you with me?"

I knew the price of *not* being with him. If I refused Adolf, or if I agreed but told him I thought the plan was impulsive, unrealistic, bound to fail, verging on the ridiculous, I would destroy our friendship. I was not prepared for that. He could not tolerate criticism, I knew this. I had become expert in working around these aspects of his character without, I thought, compromising myself. I would help out. I would do a bit of teaching. I would not discourage him. But I would watch the whole scheme collapse under the weight of its own grandiosity.

And this saddened me. I knew he had been crushed by his rejection from the Academy. It must not have been easy to watch me go off every morning—well, he *was* asleep—to the Conservatory to study, play, conspire, and joke with my classmates, to teach the spoiled daughters of the bourgeoisie, to be deferred to by their mothers and fathers, to be asked *my* opinion on musical matters. While he, a talented amateur, paced the night away in our room at Stumpergasse 31, Second Staircase, Second Floor, Door 17, isolated, ignored, sinking into poverty and oblivion. This business with *Wieland* was the desperate and pathetic resort of someone who saw himself in exactly this way. I tried not to think about it.

The following four weeks seemed endless. I knew the basic story of the legend: Wieland is a metalsmith who forges miraculous tools and weapons. Out of the blue, three swan maidens arrive. Wieland instantly falls in love with one of them, Schwanhilde. They marry and live happily until the men of the envious King Nieding capture

Wieland, torching his home. Schwanhilde manages to fly off. Nieding enslaves Wieland—cutting the tendons in his legs to prevent his escape—and forces him to forge weapons for his soldiers. Eventually, Wieland forges a pair of wings which enable him to fly; he swoops down on Nieding, kills him, is reunited with Schwanhilde.

Wagner clearly saw Wieland as an inspiration to the German *Volk*, and "The Work of Art of the Future" ends with the exhortation: "O sole and glorious *Volk!* Thou art thyself this Wieland! Weld thus thy glorious wings and soar on high!" I knew this not because I'd read a word of Wagner's writings—which at the Conservatory were considered rather eccentric—but because I'd been listening for months to Adolf ecstatically recite passages from Wagner's long and barely comprehensible essay in which he announced his credo as a composer and which Adolf knew almost by heart. He would quote it at length night after night while I fought to stay awake, tried to practice, complete my composition homework, or simply fall asleep at a reasonable hour.

Adolf barely slept. He wrote furiously, using as much of Wagner's unfinished libretto as possible and writing in the same stilted, formal diction. He paced, humming and muttering to himself, pausing to read me passages from the more violent and climactic scenes. He forgot about the *Bettwanzen* and neglected to sprinkle the boric acid powder (which had never done much, anyway). He sketched literally hundreds of set designs, in charcoal and pencil-and-ink. They covered the piano, the beds, the desk, the floor, and sat in piles alongside his books. He was pacing and humming when I fell asleep and hum-ming and sketching or writing frantically at the desk when I woke up. Empty glasses of milk and crumbs of dried biscuit were everywhere in the room. I was afraid we would soon have not only *Bettwanzen* but rats. After all, there were more rats than people in Vienna. At the Conservatory, I could hear them moving inside the walls of the practice rooms. You could catch them scampering between storm drains in the gutter in broad daylight.

The third day, I came back to the room to find Adolf at the keyboard "composing." He was humming and plunking the keys with one finger. His eyes were half-closed and his head tilted back in a posture of inspiration. As far as I could tell, the thing was in no particular key and seemed to lurch from one hackneyed, melodramatic passage to another.

"I was working on the Prelude," he said without turning around.

I listened a little more, put down the briefcase in which I kept my own compositions and homework, and took off my overcoat. I sat on the bench next to him. I could feel him going tense and rigid, and I remembered the time at home when I placed my hands on his to show him the fingering of one of Bach's fugues. In Vienna, Adolf used to bathe every day—which was rather unusual back then, when heating the water was not so easy—and he used a harsh, abrasive soap that often left him looking red in the face and neck. He hadn't bathed in days and there was a sharp, feral smell coming off him.

I played a few chords and tried to hum the melody I'd heard him working on when I came in. I added the notes to the chords and tried shifting keys and improvised a bit.

"Okay, no?" I said. "Why don't you start from the beginning and show me what you're thinking of, and we'll try it in a few keys, vary the melody a little, and get this to hold together. Are there different motifs you've worked out?"

He jumped up from the bench and started to pace. He brought both trembling fists together under his stubbled chin; his whole slender frame seemed to shake.

"Who is the composer?" he shouted. "Whose composition is this? I will play and *you* will write down what I play!"

I waited and looked at him. He lowered his fists and rubbed his face with quick, jerking motions of his hands.

"All music," I said slowly, "has structure. At times, Wagner's music abolishes keys altogether, but it still has order, organization, progression, harmony, repetition. I will incorporate all your ideas, but it must be done in an orderly way."

He was massaging his eyes and seemed to be trying to steady himself. There was a crop of bristles on his chin, which he kept touching with the tips of his fingers as if in disbelief. He had always been careful about shaving.

"Yes, yes. Of course. You are a musician. You know these things."

And so it went. He developed motifs for each character and the melody, if one could call it that, for each line of dialogue. I notated, orchestrated, changed many things. The orchestral passages were lifted almost without alteration from *Rienzi*, *Tannhäuser*, *Tristan*, and the other operas. All of it lacked the wonderful, cumulative tension of Wagner's music. Sometimes we worked all night and I simply washed my face in the morning and went to class, while Adolf continued to plunk away at the keyboard.

As far as I could tell, he spent most of the day working on the libretto and sketching designs for the sets. He incorporated scenes from the original Nordic myth of Wieland that Wagner had omitted from his sketch for the libretto, violent, bloody scenes of

Wieland's revenge. The thing began to take on a scale that was enormous, beyond all possibility. I would argue against this, but it was useless. There were plans for a hundred swans to be released in the theater following Wieland's climactic reunion with Schwanhilde. The orchestra included over five hundred musicians and the chorus over a thousand singers. I thought I would fail my courses and my friend would lose his mind and be taken to wherever one is taken when ambition exceeds talent and training by a fantastic margin, and one goes weeks without sleep and lives on stale biscuits and sour milk.

One night, still in my clothes, I lay down on my bed to rest for a moment and fell asleep.

Suddenly Adolf was holding me by the shoulders. My heart was pounding and I was looking into his moist, excited face, sallow, almost orange in the light from the kerosene heater, which hissed quietly. His eyes glistened. The room was filled with the sulfur smell.

"Listen, Eugen!" he whispered. "Before Wieland fashions the wings and flies to Nieding's palace and runs him through with the magic spear, Nieding's two sons, without informing their father, will visit Wieland on his island to learn the secrets of his miraculous craft. Wieland welcomes them and allows them to examine the tools he uses to fashion gold, which he keeps in a heavy chest. Secretly, the edges of the lid have been fitted with the sharpest of blades, blades as sharp as any of the swords he has forged for their father. As they peer into the chest, Wieland slams the lid down, neatly severing their heads. The kettle drums boom as the heads bounce inside the chest! Wieland plants his boot on each kneeling, decapitated body and shoves them aside. He tosses away his crutch, symbol of his servitude, throws open the lid of the chest, and taking a head by the hair with each hand, he limps to the front of the stage. He holds the dripping heads aloft and sings:

> *"Blood-payment for my crippling,*
> *Blood-payment for the weapons I have so toil-*
>   *somely wrought*
> *for thee, thou cursed King!*

"Here, Eugen, the vapors of Wieland's smithy thicken and darken, until only Wieland is visible, holding aloft the severed heads in a column of light:

> *"These skulls shall I boil the flesh from, until they*
>   *glisten!*
> *And from these fashion two goblets inlaid with*
>   *rubies and emeralds, with rims of gold.*
> *The bodies shall I sever at the joints, cleave flesh*
>   *from bone*
> *And from these limb-bones fashion flutes of the*
>   *sweetest melody.*
> *These shall I present to Nieding as worshipful gifts*
> *And, as most melodious flutes of bone play, shall*
>   *we drink to his present victory over King Rothar.*
> *O, vengeance! Even to imagine such a scene warms*
>   *the very sickness in my heart."*

Adolf looked up from the sheet of paper. His hands were trembling. He said softly, "Eugen, I will finish this tomorrow, sketch the scene and the presentation in the court, and when you return from school we can work on the music. I have an idea, yes, a very preliminary one, for a blood-payment motif which we may want to insert into several scenes, slight traces of it perhaps into the Prelude. It could serve as the theme for the Murder of Nieding. What do you think?"

I nodded, and he released my arm and I fell back, filled with images of severed heads, skulls, vapors, Adolf's face in the glow of the kerosene heater, his lips whispering ecstatically. The rotten-egg smell filled the room. I was asleep in minutes. When I woke, for a moment I did not know whether this actually had happened.

I had begun to doze in class, even in the raucous canteen with my classmates. I told them what was going on. They were amused, mostly. I had mentioned Adolf and his studies before, and they had asked me to bring him to lunch at the Conservatory, but as I've said, he always refused. They had taken to referring to him as "The Invisible Wagnerian" and "Eugen's imaginary friend." But a few were concerned about me and offered to let me stay with them while I looked for new lodgings. Even von Stueben-Harzburg, a talented violinist from an aristocratic home in Vienna and one of the few who had finished the *Gymnasium* before starting his Conservatory training, offered me a room with his family. Emilie Sachs, the future physician, was worried about my fatigue and obvious difficulty concentrating and told me her mother would certainly pay for me to see their family doctor, one of the best in the city. I had never thought I would leave Adolf, who needed my half of the rent in order to continue to live at Stumpergasse 31, but I began to consider this seriously.

Two weeks after this marathon of "composition" had begun, I left the Conservatory early one afternoon. I simply had to sleep. I planned to tell Adolf that if we did not work at a more reasonable pace, one that allowed me to keep up with my Conservatory assignments, I was out. It was hard enough to finish my own work and exercises and still listen to his monologues on everything, from the need for new housing for the working classes (rather funny, when you think of our own housing as students) to Franz Josef's foreign policies to the need for chastity in the young German male. When I got to our room, though, Adolf was gone. The volumes that contained various accounts of the Wieland legend were gone—returned, I suppose. There were no sketches covering the floor, the piano, the beds. Both beds were neatly made and once again surrounded by the circles of white powder.

I took my coat off and sat on my bed. He had given up. He had given up and returned to his routine of camping out on park benches in the afternoon and sketching architectural masterpieces. He knew that composition of a full-scale opera was a hopeless fantasy, that he had neither the training nor ability for this kind of undertaking, that the music was warmed-over Wagner, that the libretto was grotesque and silly, when it wasn't appallingly violent. He would come back to the room that evening and resume his "studies."

The sketches for set designs had been collected and stacked alongside his own collection of books. I had never looked at these closely; I was too busy at the piano, trying to organize Adolf's musical notions into something coherent and remotely original. I walked over and knelt before the pile of sketches and began to go through them one by one.

They were done mostly in charcoal and pencil or pencil and ink. Again, few faces ("too few heads") or faces seen obliquely and in shadow. There was Wieland, seen from behind, kneeling and hammering before the glowing forge, his tools at his side, splinters of light outlining his crippled, hulking form and penetrating the dark fumes gathering at the ceiling of the smithy. There was Wieland, in agony, his tendons cut, being rowed by Nieding's soldiers to the small island where he is exiled, the moonlight rippling on the water and the island looming in the mist. There was Wieland again, having crawled to the front of the stage, holding aloft like an offering to the gods the bloody heads of the two sons, illuminated in a column of light and surrounded by the dark, swirling fumes of the smithy.

In others, Nieding's court was depicted as cylinders of light flanking a ziggurat-like throne on which sat the draped and menacing figure of Nieding himself. Nathor's army could be seen snaking through the hills by torchlight on its way to destroy Nieding's empire. Wieland and Schwanhilde, reunited, kneeling in a moment of intimacy before the hearth in Wieland's cottage; the fire highlighted their forms and threw light on walls hung with Wieland's tools, spears, swords, and other creations of the genius smith. Wieland, having swooped down on Nieding's throne, his forged wings enveloping the panicked king as he ran him through with a spear. This appeared especially frightening as Wieland's face was partly hidden, and one saw only the outstretched arm of the king as he sank to his knees, pinioned between the realistically drawn metal wings, and Wieland's fist gripping the end of the spear as he drove it in.

There were other, unfinished sketches—of a triple wed-ding between Wieland and Schwanhilde and Wieland's brothers, Helferich and Eigel, and the other swan maidens; another of Wieland's winged form rising through the island's mist, the smithy glowing beneath him. It was often hard to know from the drawings what would transfer directly to the stage and what would be used as painted backdrop. Of course, I had seen hundreds of Adolf's architectural sketches, which were often surprisingly detailed and precise for someone without a background in mechanical drawing. These were different. They were rougher and intensely emotional. He had captured the dark, foreboding, violent atmosphere and the terrible, soaring ambition of the Norse legend. I thought they were brilliant.

I put aside several. Adolf usually made two or three copies of each, often with minor changes. I chose one of Wieland spearing Nieding, then another of Wieland triumphantly holding aloft the boys' heads. In a third he is confronting Nieding as Nieding sits on his throne, and lastly I took a drawing of the crippled Wieland being rowed by moonlight to the island rising out of the mist. I opened the piano bench and slid these under the loose sheet music and notebooks I kept there. I had been doing this since I got to Vienna: When I saw a sketch of Adolf's I liked, of which I knew there were copies, I would make a note. When he was out or asleep with his fists clenched at his sides, I would quietly choose the copy I wanted and add it to my collection inside the bench. I took very few of buildings—his architectural sketches were impressive, but they struck me as overly detailed and rather lifeless. But the rougher sketches from opera or from legend and myth—most in charcoal or pencil and ink—were often striking; they had the drama and dark energy I associated with our favorite works. I don't think he ever noticed, or if he did he said nothing.

The American psychiatrist was back yesterday. He doesn't wear a white coat but a regular officer's uniform. He speaks fluent German, which surprises me since he is not a refugee and none of the other Americans seem to speak a word of it and rely entirely on translators. His manner is different—quieter, rather bland. He is the only American who does not shake hands with me in a strenuously friendly way, smiling, before we sit down. He simply motions for me to sit, and then he sits. He does not lean forward like the others. I suppose I expect him to smoke a pipe, but that is a cartoon, a stereotype, am I right? At times, he taps the fingertips of both hands together and nods, or he runs the tips of his fingers across his lips thoughtfully. He still calls Adolf "der Führer," as though this were a polite and considerate form of address. I find it amusing. Usually, he asks about our friendship in Linz and about Adolf's relationship with his mother, which I suppose is par for the course, as you say.

Yesterday, he asked if I had any "homosexual stirrings" towards "der Führer" when we were roommates in Vienna. I laughed. He asked, "Is that really a humorous question?" and held his palms in the air in a kind of helpless, perplexed appeal. I told him that except for a single occasion, which occurred as a kind of accident, I never even saw "der Führer" naked. He slept in a full-length nightshirt which he would pull over himself first, before removing his trousers; he found the most private times to use the lavatory and to bathe; he took fastidious care of his body and clothing, especially as it began to fray and unravel; and he engaged in the never-ending war with the *Bettwanzen*. No, I told him in a manner both ironic and serious, the Führer and I shared a mutual attraction to a higher reality. The white-helmeted MP was at the door at this point and the meeting ended. I am going to let him chew on that one.

Only once during the weeks we'd spent working on the opera did Adolf and I leave the room on the Stumpergasse together. I had come back during midday, expecting to spend the rest of the afternoon at the piano, drawing from Adolf the music for the dialogue and notating it. "Don't take your coat off," he said as I walked in. "We have an appointment."

We left and in the freezing Vienna drizzle walked toward the center of the city. The sky was gray, people walked with their heads down, the blare of the automobile traffic and the rumble of the trolleys seemed muted. A miserable day. Adolf would not say where we were going, then finally, after a long, impatient silence, he told me we had a four o'clock appointment at the Hofburg, the royal palace of the Hapsburgs, where Franz Josef himself lived. For a moment, I thought my friend had finally lost his mind and believed we had an audience with the Emperor. But it turned out to be much less momentous. He had made an appointment for us to view the relics in the Hofburg Treasure House, a little museum, really, where people could come to see all sorts of royal paraphernalia. The center of attraction was the *Reichkleinodien*, mostly a bunch of jewel-encrusted sceptres and crowns and swords that at one time had been kept in Nuremberg and used in the coronation of the Holy Roman Emperor going back to the fifteenth or fourteenth century. They were removed to Vienna in 1807 to keep them from falling into the hands of Napoleon when his armies entered the city.

What Adolf really wanted to see, though, was the so-called *Heilige Lanze* or "Spear of Destiny." All sorts of mystical nonsense swirled about this decrepit thing. Some claimed it was the Spear of Longinus, the Roman soldier who pierced the side of the body of our Lord on the cross, which then miraculously spilled bright red blood and water. Some said it had been forged by the ancient Jewish prophet Phineas and that it was the spear he used when, on finding a Jew copulating with a gentile woman, he raised it and—as the couple was lying together engaged in the sex act—ran it through both of them, pleasing the Lord greatly and preserving the racial purity of the tribe. (I don't need to tell you that the notion of a Jew copulating with a non-Jewish woman would become quite a potent thing.) Some said the spear had been passed from one Germanic ruler to another, including Frederick Barbarossa and Friedrich II, two of Adolf's favorites. According to one legend, St. Francis of Assisi borrowed the spear to go on a mission of mercy. In 1906, only the year before Adolf and I came to our room on the Stumpergasse, the Germans in the Austrian Parliament sponsored a motion to return the spear and the other *Reichkleinodien* to their "sacred keeping place" in Nuremberg. The motion did not pass.

What one heard most often, though, was that the spear conferred on its owner the power to conquer the world. Adolf insisted that this was the very spear that King Amfortas had dropped when he became weak and sick, and which had to be retrieved by Parsifal in Wagner's opera. Wagner and his friend Nietzsche, the philosopher of the Superman, had visited the spear in the Hofburg Treasure House not long before their falling out.

What struck me, though, was how primitive the spear seemed, compared to the glistening gold knick-knacks that filled the Treasure House. It looked as though Wieland himself could have forged it! The head of the spear was slender, made of blackened iron, and tapered to a sharp point. A groove had been carved in the iron and in it rested a nail, supposedly one of the nails that had been driven through Christ's hands. The nail was held in place by loops of gold, silver, and copper wire, and a hammered dull silver sheath had been fashioned which slid over the head, including the nail and wires. The shaft was also dark iron and must have been six or seven feet long. The spear lay under glass on a bed of burgundy velvet and against this rich, soft background it looked ancient.

We stood staring at the *Heilige Lanze* for a long time. Adolf folded his hands in front of him and bowed his head, and for a while I thought he had fallen into a trance. There were tourists in the Treasure House, milling around the exhibits and murmuring. Finally, Adolf spoke. The spear, he said, had been identified by Wagner with the Grail in *Parsifal*. A man named Guido von List, who ran a "blood lodge" of some sort, had written a book titled *The Invincible* in which he claimed that the Icelandic Edda—the epic poem on which Wagner had based the Ring cycle—predicted the coming of "The Strong One From Above" (presumably, from the North, where all the Strong Ones seemed to live) who would redeem the spear from its current degraded state. List also claimed that the swastika was the sign of "The Invincible."

"The lance doesn't belong here," Adolf said. "None of this does. They are like lithe, powerful animals imprisoned in a zoo." He took my arm and led me out.

I learned from an article in the *Wiener Zeitung* that thirty years later my roommate went back to see the spear. (I have no doubt that while he lived in Vienna, and as long as his good clothing lasted, he must have visited the thing dozens of times.) On entering Austria in 1938, during the *Anschluss*, he went first to Linz. From Linz he drove to visit his mother's grave in Leonding, in the small country cemetery where I had stood watching him sway in the wind, afraid he would pitch straight into the grave. From there he went on to Vienna. Apparently, despite the deliriously happy and adoring crowds that greeted him everywhere, there was concern he would be assassinated and so he was constantly surrounded by officers and bodyguards. He had been told to remain in his Vienna hotel until his climactic speech on the steps of Parliament the following day, but sometime after midnight—still the night owl I knew—he insisted on being taken to the Hofmuseum, where the lance and the other *Reichkleinodien* had been moved to a special room years before. There, while Himmler and the bodyguards waited nervously outside, he spent an hour alone with the spear, still on its velvet cushion under glass. I cannot imagine what must have gone through his mind in that hour, alone in the night with that prehistoric-looking thing in the darkened museum, at the moment of his triumph, in the city where as a half-starved nineteen-year-old in our room at Stumpergasse 31, door 17, he had been—as he saw it—ignored, tossed aside, humiliated, and rejected.

Apparently, on leaving the room he ordered Himmler to have the lance and the coronation crown and sceptre returned to St. Catherine's in Nuremberg, where they had been kept in previous centuries. Several years later, during the Allied bombing of the city, they were moved to a vault well below ground. Expecting, no doubt, to find some great military secret, the American Seventh Army under General Patton blew the two-foot-thick steel doors off the vault and found the lance on its velvet cushion, along with the other *Reichkleinodien*. They were a little perplexed, I imagine, and only a few months after the war ended in May, politely returned the items to the city of Vienna, where they are now being kept in a safety deposit box in the Austrian Postal Savings Bank. I like the Americans. They have been kind to me and I understand entirely why they have interned me. But when confronted with the unusual and the profound, they often seem puzzled.

A few days after the *Wieland* episode ended, I was called out of class. This was unusual. I remember my fellow students watching me with envy and apprehension as, trying to seem casual, I followed one of the administrative secretaries out of the room. I was sure I was going to be scolded for my recent inattentiveness—well, falling asleep!—in class. All my teachers had remarked on it and one had started referring to me as "Sleeping Beauty," and made a point of calling on me the moment my head began to droop. When we reached the Conservatory offices, a messenger in livery bowed and handed me a small envelope from which I retrieved a note in a feminine hand written on vellum:

Dear Herr Reczek,
My daughter has need of your ear and I have need of your eye.
　I am reupholstering the second floor and replacing the draperies. I liked your ideas. Can you meet me at the cloth merchant's shop on the Albertinaplatz just round the corner from Sacher's Hotel today at four o'clock? I will reimburse you for your time, of course.
　Most sincerely,
　Adele Sachs

I had no students that afternoon. I scratched my reply at the bottom and handed the note to the messenger, who thanked me, turned on his heel and was out the door. The secretaries seemed impressed. I smiled at them like a man with a secret.

I was becoming a regular retainer of the Sachs's. I would teach their very serious daughter, consult with Frau Sachs on upholstery and drapery, and soon play chamber music with Herr Sachs, when he returned from his sugar refineries in Bohemia. I was moving among the *haute bourgeoisie*—a sight far better than boring, stale aristocrats. *They* were the cultural aristocracy of the city, heavily but not entirely Jewish. They put their enthusiasm and their money, of which they seemed to have an endless supply, into everything new, exciting, and even radical in art, music, literature, architecture, and design. They read the criticism in the *Neue Freie Presse*, as I did whenever I could; they wrote the criticism in the *Presse*; one of them *owned* the *Neue Freie Presse*. Adolf would have thought them phonies, but they supported everything he revered, especially art and architecture and opera, although they were a bit wider-ranging in their tastes. Often quite devoted to Wagner, they were Mahlerites like us. And they collected art, which Adolf dreamed of doing.

Walking into the fabric store on the Albertinaplatz was like walking into one of the private libraries on the Ringstrasse—hushed, reverent, with an air of quiet efficiency. One heard the rustle of silk, the murmuring of the salesmen and clients as they inspected lengths of fabric on long dark tables. The place was lit by a glass chandelier and the fabrics were stored in bales on shelves built into the walls from floor to ceiling. Hanging from each bale was a white tag specifying design, quality, price, and country of origin.

I must have been standing inside the door gaping like a real country boy because before I realized it Frau Sachs had swooped down and taken me gently by the elbow.

"Eugen, let me show you what I've been looking at. Here."

She led me to a table where three bales had been unrolled to display a length of several feet. I remember one was a common floral pattern, like chintz, but the others were stunning: a delicate pattern of leaves and filigree in blue and gold, like a design by the Englishman William Morris, and a more striking, colorful, geometric pattern of the sort one associated with artists like Klimt, Moser and Roller.

Frau Sachs touched my shoulder. "Well?"

She was wearing a long, narrow dress, obviously made to be worn without a corset, with a striking mantle of gold and black triangles that came right up to her chin. Modern, Secessionist in spirit, the kind of thing I had seen in the pages of the *Presse*, never on the street. Not the sort of dress one saw even in the more expensive department stores in the city center. I was sure it had been made for her in a salon. I noticed again the sad, mahogany eyes which drooped a bit at the corners, giving her expression a quality of world-weariness; they seemed kinder and sadder when she smiled. That she would pretend to defer to my judgment—well, I was quite flattered. I recall feeling that my collar was too high and my overcoat a bit shabby and tight in the shoulders.

"It's to cover the furniture in the room where Emilie takes her lessons," she said.

The salesman stood on the other side of the table, watching us with a patient, impassive, but still polite, expression.

"In that case," I said, "you should have the sofa re-sprung as well. The other pieces are fine." Pretty confident for a journeyman apprentice, no?

I reached for the delicate leaf design and massaged the fabric between my thumb and forefinger, as I had seen my father do. Cotton, but thick, densely woven, soft as silk. Like nothing that came into our shop. "This, Frau Sachs. *This*"—I touched the fabric with the so-called Art Nouveau design—"is nice, too. But this sort of bold pattern is hard to align when it is being stretched and fitted. If the alignment is off in the slightest, it will be very obvious." The salesman looked at me curiously.

Frau Sachs nodded and told the salesman to cut off a few feet of each. "We can look at them in the room and decide," she said.

"That will be easier, don't you think? Now do you want to go to Demel's? It's only on the next block." She looked at me and laughed. She had a marvelously spontaneous and sudden laugh that almost lifted the corners of those melancholy eyes. "It's just a coffee and pastry shop. It will fortify us for the strenuous decision. And the climate in *here* is terribly formal and funereal, don't you think?" At Glasenbach, lying on my cot in the afternoons, I find myself thinking of Frau Sachs. I hear her making a pronouncement and asking, charmingly, "Don't you think?" as though she knew she was right, but out of consideration and good breeding was inviting your confidence, without really expecting an answer. I miss this.

A "pastry shop"! You walked into this place through a pair of swinging doors with engraved glass panels and *Demel's Söhne, K.u.K Hofzuckerbäcker* in gilt lettering. Marble floors, a huge brass fan turning lazily and circulating the heady aroma—it hit you instantly—of coffee and baking pastry dough. They must have used a crock of butter in each pastry. And confronting you as you came in the door, heaped on silver platters on an enormous buffet, was a mountain, a Matterhorn, of pastries, tarts, truffles, strudel, flans, millefeuilles, cakes, canapes.

Behind this display, like porcelain dolls, two pretty girls in black-and-white uniforms stood with terribly bored expressions. People would come up and point, and one of the girls would place the desired delight on a small plate, never losing that same placid face. Other customers were at marble-topped tables or in booths eating or squinting at the impossibly long menus. Frau Sachs nodded at a passing waitress who seemed to know her, and we were led to a booth away from the commotion. Without a word, the waitress left and quickly returned with two delicate, gold-rimmed cups of coffee topped with a dollop of whipped cream dusted with cinnamon. I can't recall what I ordered that day—I imagine something embarrassingly ordinary, something I would have ordered at home—but the first thing I thought when I saw that mountainous buffet was that I must somehow wrap one of the pastries in a linen napkin and slide it into my pocket for Adolf, who was getting leaner by the day, to wolf down behind door 17 of Stumpergasse 31.

Frau Sachs lifted her cup, sipped carefully, and put it down.

"This isn't a part of the city you get to very often, is it?" she said.

"No." I sighed. My hair was dirty blond then, with streaks of lighter blond, and my skin pale. I'm sure I was blushing.

"Why should you? You have better things to do."

She said this in such a frank, definite way that I put down my cup and looked at her. I thought of Frau Hitler and her honest, transparent eyes, a peasant's eyes; Frau Sachs's were, as I've said, a deep brown, almost black, a complex, liquid color. Where Frau Hitler's eyes made one think of simplicity and devotion, Frau Sachs's were gently ironic, but also serious. I think she was saying she knew I came from a family of craftsmen, working people with no real money, and that it didn't matter. She wasn't about to pretend she was introducing me to "the better things in life." I will tell you something I know about Jews, even rich ones. The notion that all they care about is money, their own and others, couldn't be further from the truth. There isn't a fat, prosperous Jewish merchant who wouldn't rather marry his daughter to a poor intellectual, an artist, or a university lecturer than to another prosperous, or soon-to-be-prosperous, businessman.

"Well, it's true, isn't it?"

"Yes?"

"That you have better things to do?"

"I—I suppose so. But I don't mean to say, Frau Sachs, that those who do spend their time here are wasting it."

She seemed to smile to herself, sipped and winced slightly. "Emilie says you have the right attitude—there are many rights and wrongs in Emilie's view of things—towards music," she said. "That it is a noble and true calling, but that its nobility is available to everyone. She says that you are serious but unaffected, and that your seriousness does not get in the way of your enthusiasm for the music. She does say that unlike her last teacher you have not tried to seduce her."

I must have smiled involuntarily. "I am afraid I do not have the charm or energy, or money, to seduce anyone."

"Of course, that's nothing to be ashamed of, if it's true. Money you can't help, at least not right now. Charm? Charm is the great Viennese curse." She said this with an edge of bitterness, and this unnerved me. I have always been afraid of adult revelations. I don't know quite what to say when I hear them.

I said, "Emilie is a serious student, a good student, and talented."

"Well, that's no reason not to try to seduce her, is it? Oh, I'm embarrassing you, Eugen, I'm sorry. But she *could* be a little less serious, a little less convinced of her own opinions. At seventeen. Although I suppose this will stand her in good stead if she plans to go to university and then for medical training. You can already see her in that white physician's coat, can't you?"

"Well, I think she would be good at it. She does seem to enjoy telling others what to do. That's what doctors do, isn't it? She is kind enough to take direction from me."

Frau Sachs laughed. I remember my heart jumped. I could make a sophisticated woman laugh! I must have been learning *something* at the Conservatory. "Of course, the only reason she lets me tell her what to do is she knows I know more about music than she does. But she would be a perfect Conservatory teacher. All my instructors enjoy their authority. We spend our lunchtime doing impressions of them, when we're not fighting over Brahms and Wagner, or Wagner and Brahms." I pretended to think carefully for a moment. "I think it might be very difficult to be married to Emilie."

"Well, she would never marry someone like *you*, Eugen. Don't look that way! You're simply too mild and obliging. Too tolerant. Too *polite*. If Emilie marries at all, and she swears she won't, she would marry some firebrand. One of those men you see addressing the Social Democrats' rallies. A reformer. Someone who would like to change the world. Someone with even stronger opinions and even more convinced of their correctness than she is of hers. Emilie would have to meet her match."

"Then she should marry my roommate."

Again, that bright, airy laugh. I was learning that for Frau Sachs to laugh, there had to be a strong element of irony—very different from her daughter. "You mean the one who terrified Emilie when she came by with her assignment, the one who made her promise never to come back?"

"Yes. That one. He would match her opinion for opinion. She could never out-talk him. But—You see, he doesn't like women. He told me so himself. He feels that they are a corrupting influence on men, that by nature they are incapable of—how did he put it?—'serious cultural sacrifice.' When we are at the opera, in the men-only standing area on the first level, he sometimes receives notes from women requesting a meeting, women who have only seen him waiting for the standing-room tickets. *I* never receive such invitations. No doubt I must appear too mild and obliging. Not a challenge." Another soft, musical laugh! "He never responds. He shows me the note, shakes his head, crumples it, and tosses it on the floor."

"Oh, my," Frau Sachs said, framing her face by placing her hands over her cheeks in a comical way. "The fellow sounds even more—unusual—than you described him. Well, I'll tell you what, since you are a couple of 'standers.' My husband has a customer who buys a row of seats by the orchestra for the whole season. And a good deal of the time he is away from Vienna and offers us tickets. The next production of Wagner, I will take you both. However, I can't promise your friend he won't receive any unsolicited invitations. Though not from me."

"And Emilie must come with us."

"Yes! Of course. She not only dislikes Wagner, she reviles opera. She thinks it is far too long and a horrendous waste of her time, but perhaps she will make a 'cultural sacrifice' if we insist. What do you say?"

I was right, of course, about the fabric. We went back to the apartment and spread the samples against the sofa and armchairs. The chintz was ordinary, the "Nouveau" pattern too large and bold, the leaf-and-filigree just right.

With a look of regret, Frau Sachs ran her hand over the Nouveau design. "I love this, but it's just too big! It's not for furniture. And you're right. If the pattern on the seat doesn't align exactly with the back and the arms, it will look shoddy. Ah! It always looks so striking in the store. It is like the dresses at the Flöge salon. The designs are always so original and new, you forget the thing was meant to be inhabited by a human form, not hung on the wall."

I nodded. I had no idea who "Flöge" was.

I placed my hand on the seat of the sofa, pushed down, made a face.

"Yes, it's shot, isn't it?" She tilted her head to one side and pouted.

Fritz, the servant, appeared just then to say someone was downstairs with yet another package and wanted to speak directly with her.

"Oh, all right," she said, as if the act of receiving a package was the worst sort of drudgery. "Will you wait, Eugen? I appreciate so much your coming. You've been a great help."

She gave my hand a little squeeze and left the room quickly. Her fingers felt slender and cool and very soft, like a child's. My mother's hands—she was in the habit of placing my hand in hers and covering it with the other whenever she wanted to wish me well or simply tell me to remember to do such-and-such—were calloused and reddened and thick. And yet somehow I think Frau Sachs would have been able to talk with my mother without difficulty, as one mother to another. She had that way about her— understanding, a *guter Mensch*.

I went to the piano, the feel of those small fingers in my hand still lingering, and standing over that gleaming grand, a Bechstein, kept impeccably in tune, I began to play with one hand— Debussy, something I usually did not play around Adolf, who called it "French tinkling." The abstract *langueur* of that melody suited the room perfectly in the late afternoon light, and I hoped Frau Sachs would reappear while I was playing the few passages I knew from memory. Emilie had told me, with some contempt, that her mother "loved everything French, as one would expect her to," and had taken her to Paris for two weeks when she was fourteen "to see what life without true seriousness was like."

Even as I played I could not lose the sensation of those slender fingers gripping my palm. I stumbled over a passage I couldn't quite recall, and stopped playing.

I noticed that the sliding doors to the library were open and, a bit hesitant, I went in. The room had a completely different atmosphere, even a different scent, from the sitting room, and I imagined that this must be the domain of Herr Sachs (when he was home, whenever that was). Emilie told me that she spent a good deal of time in there. A palatial Persian rug covered nearly the entire floor, and the chairs and large sofa were covered in rugged, riveted leather the color of oxblood. My father had a customer, the banker Heissmeyer, who had furniture like this, covered in old cracked leather so thick we had to use needles the size of small spears to repair it. The room had a massive fireplace, and you could tell from the charred stone that it had seen use.

I had been in the library once before, briefly. There were shelves of history and literature and philosophy, complete sets of the usual heroes—Schiller, Novalis, Goethe, Schopenhauer, Rilke. Books on botany with marvelous illustrations. Complete sets of Shakespeare in English, Voltaire in French. And a wonderful framed engraving of Frederick the Great and Voltaire on a bench in the garden at Sans Souci, deep in discussion, surrounded by the Italian greyhounds Frederick kept by the dozens and even insisted on having buried with him. How could I *not* have absorbed all this, living with Adolf? He worshipped the man, had read a translation of Carlyle's heroic biography when we were in Linz, and insisted on giving me stirring accounts of Frederick's impossible last-minute victories as he paced the tiny bedroom in his mother's apartment. Frederick, who had Bach's son as his court musician and challenged Bach himself to compose a six-part fugue on the spot! Adolf had shrugged off Frau Sachs's invitation to the chamber concert, but I would carry him here on my back if I had to.

And the smell—like a drug. A musk, a mixture of leather, ink, and old paper.

There was a long bureau against one wall, with dozens of shallow drawers, the sort of thing draftsmen and architects kept their work in. I carefully slid out a drawer: Japanese prints, woodcuts. Colorful, cartoon-like scenes of nature and peasant life. An orchard of cherry blossoms; snow falling into a stream while a straw-hatted peasant trundles his wagon over a small, arched bridge. Beautiful prints, each labeled with a title, the name of the artist, an approximate date.

I pulled open a drawer towards the bottom: a Japanese woman, her robe undone, lies naked on a beach, at the water's edge. Rising from the sea foam, an octopus with huge goggle eyes. His massive lips are clamped over the woman's private parts, and his tentacles caress her buttocks and breasts and encircle her nipples. She has taken one of his tentacles in her mouth and her head is thrown back, eyes closed in a sort of genteel swoon. The print was labelled "Hokusai, 'Awabi Fisherwoman and Octopus' from *Pangs of Love*, 1814." My heart was beating like a hare's.

I lifted the print and under it was another of a Japanese man and woman, their robes opened, copulating on a bed of pillows spread over a bamboo mat. Their faces wear an expression of polite engagement, their eyes do not quite meet. The print, on the whole, was rather bland, except for one detail: the man's organ is monstrously large and outsized, marbled with veins, purplish, and simply—bursting. It is being received by lips equally engorged and detailed. Beneath this print, a whole set of prints depicting the same couple (as far as I could tell) in a variety of positions, the genitalia always gargantuan, the man and woman wearing the same sweet, placid expressions.

I heard steps. I slid the drawer closed, grabbed a biography of Otto the Great from the shelves, and pretended to be engrossed, poring over an account of the First Italian Expedition. Frau Sachs stood in the doorway of the library.

"Why is it," she sighed, "that men are always drawn to the library and always seem to know in which drawer they are kept? Like hunting dogs on the scent." She smiled slightly. "That's how I know you are not Viennese, Eugen, you are red-faced and speechless and won't look at me. I must go out again. Feel free to browse. Fritz will let you out. If you would like to borrow a volume, go ahead. I trust you to take care of it. There is an interesting story behind the lithographs, but—some other time."

The following week, when I came for Emilie's lesson, the furniture on that floor had been entirely recovered in the leaf-and-filigree fabric. It looked splendid. The work was marvelously done—tight, careful, meticulous work, perfectly aligned and finished. I sat on the sofa—re-sprung, with good support, quite comfortable. The next day, I received a check drawn on the account of Victor Sachs for 60 kronen, fully one-half of one year's rent. I took Adolf to Demel's, where he stuffed himself with *Nussstrudel* and *Kaiserschmarrn*, talked about his plans for the electrification of Linz, and glanced suspiciously and uncomfortably at the mothers and their teenaged daughters who filled the place that weekday afternoon. I did not tell him where the money had come from.

*

By June, Adolf's own money seemed to be running out. He continued to eat nothing but stale biscuits and *Mehlspeisen* and drink sour milk, which did nothing to help his breath. I started to find bits of colored wax on the desk—the merchant at the nearby cheese shop was selling (or giving) him rinds from large wheels of cheese, which he nibbled while he studied and drew, often consuming some of the flavored yellow wax as well. At times, when I woke at night, I would find him with needle and thread, the stub of a candle burning on the desk, carefully darning his salt-and-pepper suit jacket or trousers, or his overcoat, which was starting to pull apart along the shoulder seams. Despite oiling them, the gloves he always wore to the opera were cracked and splitting, and he had begun to keep his hands in his pockets as we waited in line for standing room. Of the whole outfit his mother had bought him—and which she hoped would get her aloof and eccentric son out of his room and into the world—only the ivory-handled cane and silk top hat were in good shape.

He didn't talk about it, of course, but I knew he was running low. The orphan's pension he shared with his younger sister came to 25 kronen per month, and this took care of rent and basic food costs and kerosene. But membership in the lending libraries, in the Vienna Museum Association, which allowed him discounted entrance to any of the city's state-run museums, and the frequent trips to the Court Opera, even at standing-room prices, were a constant drain. I knew he would rather eat the rinds from wheels of cheese than give them up. The remainder of the modest inheritance from his father was being held by the guardian, Mayrhofer, until he was twenty-four. His mother's savings, and the money from the sale of the house and farm in Leonding, had been all but consumed by her medical expenses—on which Adolf spared nothing, despite Dr. Bloch's suggestions—and by the relatively lavish funeral, the mahogany casket with brass fittings, the coaches and drivers, all of which Frau Hitler, a simple woman, would have frowned upon.

His reading shifted that late spring and summer. He began to read newspapers regularly, several a day, front to back. This had started in Linz, but Vienna was awash in newpapers, flyers, magazines, weeklies, journals, booklets of every sort. Every group—Czechs, Poles, Ruthenes, Slovenes, Jews, even Italians—had newspapers in its own language. At the University, the Italians, Germans, Jews, and Hungarians all had their own cafeterias. The Germans started this, of course, by refusing to eat with the rest of the rabble of nationalities, and soon all the others had their own canteens, fraternities, and even their own informal sections in lecture halls. Since almost all of us at the Conservatory, Jews included, were German-speaking and Germanic in outlook, this sort of thing never arose.

Every political party, and there were dozens, had its own organ. The Austrian Parliament was a mess. It was like a sporting event. Shouting matches would erupt daily, the insults would start to fly, fights would break out and ink-splattered and blood-splattered Parliamentarians would be carried out on stretchers. Nothing got done. Every motion was a useless gesture and probably intended as such. When one of the new, motorized ambulances would roar past in the street, horn blaring, attendants in white uniforms riding "shotgun-style," bystanders would throw their hands in the air and exclaim, "Ah! Parliament must be in session!"

Of all the sheets one could buy from hawkers, or at the tobacco kiosks and newsagents, the *völkisch* newspapers were the most numerous and the most aggressive. The organizations and parties that put them out also sponsored activities and events—lectures, rallies, summer solstice festivals, meetings in beerhalls—meant to promote the solidarity of the *Volk* and eventual union of Austria and Germany, or of Germany and all the ethnic Germans throughout the empire. (One of my classmates, a violinist from a politically prominent and aristocratic family, used to refer to them as "lederhosen loonies.") The most popular of these papers, the *All-Deutsches Tagblatt* or *Pan-German Daily*, had its editorial offices two blocks from our room on the Stumpergasse. Adolf had started to read this every day, along with the *Wiener Deustches Tagblatt*, *Der Hammer*, and one called *Unverfälschte Deutsche Worte* or *Unadulterated German Words*. These would accumulate for a few weeks, then he would throw them out. Adolf, being a reader and thinker and not a joiner, never went, as far as I know, to any of the hikes or spring festivals or even lectures.

One he kept, though, was *Ostara*, an irregularly published half-magazine, half-newspaper, named for the Germanic goddess of spring. It was often open on the desk alongside the volumes of Wagner, Schopenhauer, and Nordic mythology. I first noticed it because of a striking illustration on the cover of one of the numbers: a handsome Crusader knight bringing his sword down on the head of a very unappetizing-looking fellow with bulging lecherous eyes, a big nose, big low-set ears, a fat double chin, and in need of a good shave. This was, of course, the all-purpose stereotype of Jews, Slavs, and southern peoples or "Mediterraneanoids." Under the banner "Ostara" ran the subheading "The Only Periodical Dedicated to the Research and Cultivation of Heroic Racedom and Men's Rights." Inside *Ostara*, which was printed in a very stylized Gothic font, one could find illustrations of hairy, broad-backed men menacing or actually raping fair-haired women, who wore expressions of exaggerated surprise or, in some cases, a kind of narrow-eyed swooning submission. There were illustrations of various noses and heads drawn from different angles. Some issues even included collectible coupons for a "race beauty prize." If one accumulated enough of these one could obtain a "racial certificate," no questions asked.

Ostara's articles ran along similar lines: "Race and Woman and her Predilection for the Man of a Lower Nature," "The Dangers of Women's Suffrage and the Necessity of a Master Ethics Based on Men's Rights," "Judging Character by the Shape of the Skull," "The Love and Sex Life of Blond and Dark People," "Introduction to Sexual Physics," and even an article titled "Callepedics, or the Art of Deliberate Conception," which claimed that Aryan couples, by adopting certain sexual positions and copulating at particular times of the day and year could increase their chances of producing blond-haired blue-eyed offspring.

"I was looking at several issues of *Ostara*," I said one evening, casually. "This is not Schopenhauer." I was sitting at the Boesendorfer. Adolf was drawing by candlelight at the desk. The kerosene heater was hissing away near the piano and the smell stung the inside of my nostrils.

Adolf grunted without looking up from his drawing. "Well, what did you think, Herr Reczek?"

"Is it really scientific?" I tried to say this in a tone of voice that was one of genuine curiosity, not so critical-sounding. He continued to draw.

"Dr. von Liebenfels is a learned man. He was a Cistercian monk, but he has left the Church. He knows Sanskrit, Sumerian, Hebrew, Latin, ancient Greek. The articles are well documented, as you can see if you read them carefully. He has bought a castle on the Upper Danube at Struden near Grein, Castle Werfenstein, where he plans to revive the Order of the Knights Templar, or Teutonic Knights devoted to the Grail. He is not a member of an *august* university faculty, but that is no matter. All sciences begin with the individual, with individual ideas, not with 'approved' doctrines. I would rather produce one brilliant idea than a life-time of steady office work. Dr. von Liebenfels' knowledge is immense and his intuition is keen."

"You . . . know him?"

"I have met him. He gave me some earlier issues of his journal which are no longer available, as well as some of his other writings."

I had been playing a passage of Ravel's—more tinkling—while we spoke, and I stopped. As far as I knew, this was the first contact Adolf had had with another human being in Vienna besides me since he arrived the previous September.

"I am going to see him again this week. He said he would give me a copy of his new book. This was published last year but there have been no additional copies until now. There has been genuine interest in it. Come with me. It would do you good to spend a few minutes away from your professors at the Conservatory."

Von Liebenfels, it turned out, lived in the Leopoldstadt district, which was crowded, largely poor, heavily commercial and Jewish, and as one might expect, overrun with "line-girls"—prostitutes who could solicit on the street at all hours but had to stand back against the buildings, never crossing an invisible "line" deter-mined by the police. They were still calling out to us—"Boys! Twenty heller for a fine experience! You look like you could stand to relax a little, eh? Look at me!"—in the nasal accents of the Eastern Jews (yes, there were Jewish whores) as we turned into Dr. von Liebenfels' building. It was an older building, shabby, but judging from the decorative filigree on the spiral stairwell and ceilings, and the elaborately tiled floors, it must once have been rather genteel.

"Yes, yes, come in, boys!" Von Liebenfels clapped his hands together as he led us into his apartment on the top floor. "This must be your roommate—"

"Eugen Reczek, sir."

"Ah, the compositional student at the Vienna Conservatory. Here, sit. Would you like some *Topfenstrudel*? Of course you would. And strong coffee. Ah! I forgot, Adolf, you drink only tea. I don't know what I would do without coffee. I could barely stay awake, much less continue to write and publish. My doctor tells me that if I keep this up I will soon have a hole in my stomach."

Von Liebenfels was a tall man, strapping but slightly stooped. He wore a smoking jacket over trousers, several layers of sweaters, and corduroy slippers. He had a big bald head, wore tiny glinting spectacles, and was perpetually clapping and rubbing his hands together. He shuffled about the kitchen, talking while putting together our desserts. I could have been watching a character out of a burlesque skit. The apartment was a mess—crammed with books, papers, back issues of *Ostara*, figurines, and reproductions of primitive drawings. His smoking jacket billowed behind him as he emerged into the small living room carrying a tray with a pot of tea, small cups of coffee, and strudel.

"Here is what you wanted," he said, placing a slender volume carefully on the table before Adolf. I craned my neck and he smiled and slid the book in my direction. The title, in Gothic script, read *Theozoology, or the Science of the Sodomite Apelings and the Divine Electron: An Introduction to the Most Ancient and Modern Philosophy with a Justification of the Monarchy and Nobility, by Dr. Jorg Lanz von Liebenfels.*

Dr. von Liebenfels gathered the smoking jacket about him and lowered himself onto one of the chairs. He closed his eyes and sipped.

"A long and obscure title, I know, but the argument is simple, Eugen. Your roommate is familiar with some of it already from his reading of earlier numbers of *Ostara*."

Dr. von Liebenfels guided a sliver of *Topfenstrudel* into his mouth and dabbed at his lips. "In short, there is good evidence, anthropologic and literary, that the Germanic race existed originally—either at the North Pole or on a now-submerged continent in the North Atlantic—as a race of electric god-men. By 'electric' I mean exactly that—suffused with an electric substance which may have allowed them to communicate without the use of language and even to perpetuate the race without the intermediate of sexual congress. Even today there is growing scientific evidence that the female ovum can be fertilized through direct electric stimulation. There may well have been organs specialized for the reception and transmission of electricity but which today exist only as shrunken and degenerate remnants, in the comparatively tiny hypothalamus and pineal gland of the human brain. Ah! But why *degenerate*?"

He placed his warm, moist hand on mine. "Listen to me, Eugen. These Germanic god-men were ambitious. They pushed south and east, through southern Europe into ancient Egypt and Mesopotamia, where they were responsible for virtually every achievement of culture and civilization, from mathematics and language to the great architectural accomplishments of the ancients which your roommate so admires. Look at the sculptures of the ancient Greeks. Habitus, musculature, eyes, forehead, cranium—beautifully proportioned and classically Aryan-German. They bear no resemblance to modern-day Greeks because they are the product and reflection of an entirely different race.

"The question then," he said, "is: What happened? What happened, indeed."

He slid his hand from mine. The smooth face became grave, almost despondent. He took a felt cloth from the pocket of his smoking jacket and massaged his spectacles. Then he smiled, suddenly.

"Would you like more? I thought so."

He padded into the kitchen and returned with another slab of *Topfenstrudel* and a small dish. "Here," he said. "Try some raspberry sauce. It goes quite well with the cheese. Try it, no? Of course you'll try it."

He sat down again, assuming the same grave expression. He gathered the folds of the silk jacket about him and fixed his clear blue eyes on me.

"Mixing, Eugen. Interbreeding. Promiscuous relations with the indigenous races. And even, perhaps, with an intermediate race of ape-men." He opened *Theozoology* and leafed through the pages. "Here, figure sixteen. This is an Assyrian drawing from the year 1500 before Christ." It showed an ape-man—it looked more like a panther balanced on its hind limbs—half-standing, with a long tail and a large penis, prominent and upward-curving. "The Assyrians even appear to have bred a race of love-pygmies purely for the purpose of deviant sexual pleasure. They had Sodomite relations with Aryan males and copulated with Aryan females. The result: All cultural progress ceased and a reverse migration began. The Germanic peoples withdrew into what are now the countries of central and northern Europe and Scandinavia. The race of Sodomite apelings disappeared. But the ape-nature persists, in Slavs and Mediterraneans, principally. Those races that have flooded Vienna and much of Europe.

"Now. In the development of the Aryan male, eroticism plays a subordinate role, as it does in all creators of culture. Even the Aryan penis is smaller and better-proportioned, as you can see in Greek statuary of the Classical Period. This is the tragedy of the erotic life of the heroic man: that Germanic women, the bearers of his own race, do not find him primitive and sensual enough. As in Ezekiel, chapter twenty-three, verse twenty, where we find that 'the women were crazy for the voluptuousness of fornication with men whose members were like the members of asses and whose flood of semen was like the flood of semen from a stallion.' The primitive-sensual dark men of inferior races—the so-called 'interesting' men—have thoroughly spoiled our women's erotic tastes both psychologically and physically."

Adolf was spooning the raspberry sauce over his strudel, looking up at von Liebenfels between bites and nodding as though he had heard this before or simply knew it to be true. It occurred to me that this audience with Lanz, as Adolf called him, had been arranged for my benefit, and that von Liebenfels regarded me as another potential recruit.

Von Liebenfels lowered his eyes and looked especially somber.

"There is something else quite disturbing," he said, "which genetic science is only now beginning to appreciate. Even if a woman eventually joins herself to a German husband and bears children, the traits of all her previous lovers—of all the sensual men of inferior races who have copulated with her and deposited their semen within her—will be seen in the offspring. Think of that. The genetic constitution of offspring thought to be purely Aryan could contain, secretly, as it were, the traits of descendants of the pleasure-apes, whose lasciviousness and lewdness, whose raging Sodomite lust, exceed all imagination. The most valued features of our race—blue eyes, blond hair, a ruddy complexion, a small mouth, healthy teeth, small slim hands and feet, and a tall, well-proportioned form—will vanish. Our culture will vanish. Our ability to create immortal, spiritual works, which you as a student of German music know intimately, will vanish. We are on the verge of catastrophe."

Dr. von Liebenfels brought the tips of his fingers together in an attitude of prayer and stared at the table.

"There is only one conclusion to be drawn. The solution lies in direct intervention in the erotic life of man and woman. The war against the apes of Sodom begins with *you*, especially in your choice of wife and in your abstaining from relations with non-Germanic women. The peculiar preference of many German women for lusty, satyr-like men should be diminished. These women, who seek out copulation purely for the purpose of enjoyment, these she-creatures, these nymphomaniacal baboons, the so-called 'modern women' of free love, depressed by melancholy and vague longings, who burn for the love of Sodomite monsters, of Slavs and Mediterraneans, these women who have drunk the wine of lust, who would become mothers to broods of lascivious, bloodthirsty beasts, must be prevented from ever bearing children. Their only goal is to breed humanity downward."

Von Liebenfels was sweating and out of breath. He slid a monogrammed handkerchief from the pocket of his smoking jacket, folded it, and patted his glistening forehead and around his neck. Throughout his lecture, with its nymphomaniacal baboons and Sodomite love monsters, I'd been trying to listen with an expression of polite, earnest concentration.

"We must just as intensely fight the intrusion of women into public life, Eugen. The ultimate outcome of their efforts will be, and to some extent already is, to turn the world into a big brothel in which everything revolves around penises and vaginas in a silly and absurd satyr's orgy. These women, with their lascivious apelike nature, destroyed the cultures of antiquity and will bring down our culture as well if men do not stop to think. Just as different races of men have unequal rights, so too do men and women have unequal rights. The old and true custom which allowed the Lord of the Manor to sleep with every virgin proves that the ancients knew it is the man who is responsible for breeding the race upward.

"Ultimately, on a larger scale, the inferior races must be annihilated—either gently, through restriction and sterilization, or through harsher means. Along these lines, the invention of a functional sterilization device or agent would be the greatest boon for mankind."

He looked at Adolf's empty plate and clapped his hands.

"Ah! Your friend's hunger for *Donauwellen* and strudel is surpassed only by his thirst for sacred knowledge. I have some Benedictine liqueur, if you would like? It clears the passages of the head, I can tell you. Ooof, I forgot: no cigarettes, no coffee, no alcohol. Only a thirst for learning. Perhaps *that* should be the prescription for our German youth. When Adolf first came and asked for back issues of *Ostara*, I was, of course, impressed by his obvious sincerity, but I was surprised by his comprehension and retention of detail.

"Oh, yes, one thing, Eugen. Through my Vienna friends I have purchased the Castle Werfenstein, perched on a sheer rock cliff above the Danube at the village of Struden. True, it needs a little cleaning up, but the location is perfect. I plan to hold there a Germanic Mass for which I am composing a liturgy. It will begin with soft harmonic music after which the brothers will sing the 'Pilgrim's Chorus' from *Tannhäuser.*"

I nodded as though I recognized his musical intentions; I tried to imagine this crazy blend of Wagner and the Latin Mass wafting from some decrepit castle on the outskirts of Vienna, and a chorus of chanting "brothers" in monks' cowls, all as smooth and clean as von Liebenfels. I felt an oppressive tightness in my chest. What, I thought, if my professors knew I was here?

"But there is much more," he went on. "And all of it will be accompanied by music. You are a Conservatory student and perhaps you can help me with this. I have a number of questions. Also, the fencing associations at the University, among whom *Ostara* is widely read, have invited me to speak. Perhaps you and Adolf will come? These are closed associations, but if I vouch for you there will be no trouble. Lastly, my friends, you have come all the way here on foot, like pilgrims—here is two kronen for your transportation home."

He stood and made a small waving motion with his hand.

"Now go, my good friends, my future god-men, or I will lecture forever! I can only tell you what I already know, so now I must return to my work."

"Dr. von Liebenfels is a strange man," I said.

We were sitting in a tram that ran along the Mariahilfer Strasse. The street was crowded with men in top hats, messengers on bicycles, the Jewish street vendors in long dark coats, wide-brimmed hats, and sidelocks, hawking their wares—rags, pots and pans, cheap gloves—with a certain jumpy nervousness. It seemed very odd to me that only moments before we had been in von Liebenfels' little apartment, stacked with papers and books, talking about Sodomite pleasure-apes and regenerating the German race. Adolf was staring out the window at the crowds with his usual severity.

"Lanz," he said, "is a learned man, completely devoted to his researches. Perhaps it seems strange, such devotion to a cause without an obvious economic motive."

"He charges for *Ostara*."

"Only what he needs to live modestly."

"Do you believe it?"

"Believe?"

"His theories, Adi. Do you believe all this is true?"

Adolf held open *Theozoology* in his lap and leafed through the pages of footnotes and references in tiny Gothic print and the appendix, which included drawings of ape-men with large, curving penises.

"Anyone can find documentation," I said.

"It is not a matter of scientific truth. After all, science changes from day to day, year to year. It is a matter of essential truth, even spiritual truth, of what one sees and knows and feels to be true. Of what intuition suggests and experience confirms. Should we reject the work of an individual scholar because it happens not to be in agreement with academic science? With the science of the professors? Only mediocre and uninventive minds can bear to breathe the stale air of the academy for long. You know that."

As soon as he got going about "the professors," I knew not to argue. He hated institutionalized education in all its forms. He had his reasons, and I understood. I was compromised, too. I went off every morning to an approved—revered—institution, where our professors often lectured us wearing full academic gown, just as Adolf was collapsing into sleep after a night at his studies and impaling *Bettwanzen* on pins.

From our seats on the tram, we watched the crowds hurrying along the Mariahilfer Strasse. The black motorcars alongside choked the street, trying to nose past us, honking and creating quite a racket. It was a typical gray Viennese day, and the smoke from burning coal and kerosene and the factories that had sprung up just outside the city hung thickly in the air, like something you could scoop with your hand. On some days, you could almost feel it coat your tongue and the inside of your mouth.

"Look at them," Adolf said, staring out the window. "No doubt they are on their way to their bread-and-butter jobs, in the cold pursuit of profits, more profits, *always* profits. As though the soul of man, or of a race, could subsist on profit. Do you think that *Ostara* is published for profit? You yourself saw the way Dr. von Liebenfels lives, in his tiny apartment in the Leopoldstadt, filled with books and journals. The streets teeming with whores and other syphilitic rubbish."

He leaned back and closed his eyes.

"There is a man, an engineer, Hans Goldzier," he said. "He believes, and has produced evidence to support it, that the core of the earth is filled with an electrical substance, a liquid under great compressive forces. This core substance sends out projections to the earth's surface where, released, it is converted to electric currents which can actually be detected by living organisms. Who is to say that the sensory organs that Lanz postulates were present in ancient man, whom he termed 'god-men,' were not adapted to receiving these currents? Those structures that have since degenerated into structures the size of a pea, the pituitary and the—the—"

"Pineal."

"Yes. The pineal gland. And who can know whether the subjective life of men might not have been different under the influence of these currents—more divine, energetic, profound, even heroic."

What was I to say? That von Liebenfels (if that really *was* his name) seemed to me an outrageous quack? That I wouldn't have minded a little share of the profits the horde in the street was after? That in middle age I hoped not to be living in an apartment in some whore-infested part of the city? That I'd prefer *not* to stand through four hours of *Parsifal*? That I'd like to sit through all four acts without worrying about paying some hoary old *Hausbesorger* a few heller to let me back into my own building? More to the point—despite dearly loving my good parents—that I'd rather have grown up in a family like the Sachs's and come home after a day of studies at the *Gymnasium* to a lesson on my viola from a truly first-rate teacher? Rather than spend my days stuffing sofas that smelled of urine from a poodle!

That night, he read *Theozoology, or the Science of the Sodomite Apelings and the Divine Electron* from cover to cover—it was a slim book, not like the tomes and oversized art books he got from his lending libraries. He was at the desk with the book and a candle, while I, a secret, lascivious pleasure-ape, fell asleep imagining my piano students and Emilie Sachs and Frau Sachs, and the sweetly smiling couple in those Japanese prints, trying to keep my paw from stroking my tragically under-sized Aryan penis. At one point during the night I was startled to hear Adolf shout "Is Wagner 'true'?! Scientific? *Science!*"

*

201

Occasionally, in the evening in our room, I would give in to the desire to be a little subversive and I would play a passage from Debussy or Chopin, that pair of tinklers. "What is wrong," I would pretend to muse to no one in particular, "with sound for the pure, simple pleasure of sound, of listening?" Adolf would cough and glance at me from the desk. "Debussy says '*Le plaisir, c'est la droit*'—'Pleasure is the law'." Now he would really turn around and I could hear the chair scrape against the floor. Yes, yes, I know! The purpose of music is to serve the Total Art-Work of the Future and the purpose of the Art-Work of the Future is to serve the regeneration of man and the purpose of the regeneration of man is—

I would allow the last notes of some languorous passage to linger, and Adolf would be staring at me, expressionless.

"You worry me sometimes, Reczek." Then back to his book.

It saddened me, too, to see him poring over street-flyers, the *völkisch* tabloids, the privately published pamphlets, or a journal printed on cheap, pale-yellow paper depicting a medieval knight bringing his sword down on the noggin of some ape with leering, heavy-lidded eyes, a hooked nose, and a three-day growth of beard. I preferred to think of my friend, my fellow artist and future collaborator in our *Conservatoire*, beating his poor brains in against the sprawling, impenetrable prose of Wagner or Schopenhauer in heavy leather-bound volumes. And taking a little holiday from these labors to sketch great buildings or scenes from *Götterdämmerung*.

Not that I doubted Dr. von Liebenfels' sincerity or dedication or learning. He understood dead languages. He tunneled through ancient texts like a starving rodent. There were more footnotes in his books than notes in a sonata. But I could not *really* believe that we Germans were descended from a race of god-men inhabiting a city beneath the North Pole, that we were involved in a war for survival with a swarthy array of inferior races sporting fleshy noses and big penises, and that a messiah-like "Strong One From Above" would arrive to annihilate (or sterilize or enslave) these races and not only restore our former Teutonic glory but also lead us to world domination.

I was perfectly happy, despite my affection for the French tinklers, for German *music* to dominate the world. In fact, I felt it already did. Richard Wagner provided the most blissful non-economic experience available to human beings in a squalid world obsessed with money and overstuffed furniture. I would have preferred, and would still prefer, to live in a world that understood this. But, for me, the Villa Eugen or our *Conservatoire* would have been enough. To do our own great and difficult work, to share it with a small group of like-minded artists or an adoring public, to open the eyes and ears of artisans, bankers, and laborers to the glories of German art and music—this would have been just fine. I am afraid I would have to add to this a few selected and talented students, mostly beautiful young women who considered sharing the bed of a talented composer to be an essential and necessary part of their musical education and with whom I could share my private collection of Japanese lithographs. That would have been plenty. I had no need to go to war against the descendants of the sodomite apelings or to "breed the race upward."

But Adolf could not leave the world alone; not its art or buildings or cities or peoples. Of course, at the time, he saw it the other way around—that the world would not leave *him* alone, would not stop subjecting him to endless humiliations, whether it was through nightly visits from the *Bettwanzen,* or by rubbing his nose in his poverty and ignoring his talent, surrounded as he was by the "unheroic" vulgarity of modern art, here, in the ancient German capital of Vienna, now swollen with the descendants of strange, dark races, more of them streaming in every day.

And this is why I am sitting in this drafty brick warehouse of an internment camp, with my hair starting to fall out, trying to explain myself to a parade of military investigators, who are insistent but polite, and to a psychiatrist who does not understand me, who wants to "de-Nazify" me, whatever that means. They tell me, You were with the Führer in the beginning, in Vienna, where his ideas "germinated" (that is the word of the psychiatrist, he loves to speak of ideas "germinating" and "fertilizing" and "flowering"), you consulted with him when he reentered Austria in 1938, you were with him in Bayreuth in 1938 and 1939.

And I ask them, Do you know that Alberich, who can only seek to dominate the world because he has renounced love, is both doomed and tragic? Do you know why? They seem stymied. They look at me as if I have three heads.

Adolf agreed to come to the recital at the Sachs's apartment. I had taken him to a performance of Brahms's *German Requiem* at the Conservatory, which he thought stirring and beautiful, and I told him he needed to hear Brahms's chamber music, too. We were going to play the first piano quartet, a fine early piece, and first performed with Clara Schumann—with whom Brahms was said to be hopelessly in love—at the piano. This was not the Total Art-Work of the Future, but I told Adolf that it would do him some good to see that one can be transported by beauty on a smaller and more intimate scale, and that certain aspects of music only become apparent on this scale. "You are the musician," he said, a little more ironically than he needed to.

I loaned him one of my white shirts, as his were becoming soiled and threadbare, acceptable among our crowd of standers at the Court Opera, but not at a dinner recital. He reinforced the stretched shoulder seams of his suit jacket and overcoat, and took a long bath. He was very fussy about his body and his clothing, a trait I think he got from his mother. This, of course, was one reason the *Wanzen* drove him into a frenzy.

I received a kind note from Herr Sachs, thanking me for teaching his daughter and for "agreeing to participate"—even though I *was* being paid—in the recital, and although he said he knew the Brahms piece well, would I be kind enough to humor his presumptuousness in performing with students from the Conservatory.

When we arrived at the Sachs's apartment, I carried my viola case under my arm and Adolf stood stiffly alongside me, his face reddened from the abrasive soap he always used, and his hair thickened with a little chicken fat and combed back so it would not flop down over his eyes the way it habitually did. Fritzl the servant actually answered the door and bowed, and I saw Frau Sachs coming towards us with Emilie behind her.

"Herr Reczek!" She smiled and lifted my hand lightly. She tapped the viola case with a finger. "Yet another of your instruments. Herr Adolf *Hitler*!"

She now lifted Adolf's hand—he almost drew back instinctively and I winced inside—and she placed her other hand on top of his. He flushed and a thickened strand of hair sprung loose and hung drooping over his forehead.

"I have heard of the impressive range of your studies, of your devotion to music, and of your love of our Court Opera. I think you will enjoy yourself tonight."

Emilie was standing a few paces off, watching Adolf with apprehension. I glanced at her and made a little private gesture with my hand as if to say, Not to worry. She didn't seem reassured.

Then Adolf did something I did not expect. Tossing his head, he brushed the errant strand of hair back with his free hand. He announced, *Küss die Hand, gnädige Frau!*, then, bending from the waist, he smartly kissed the back of the hand Frau Sachs had placed on top of his, closing his eyes as his lips touched her skin—and snapped back to attention. Now, in Vienna, it was common for a man to kiss a lady's hand. But it was usually the man who lifted her hand first, met the woman's eye with a charming half-smile, and barely brushed his lips over the back of her hand. He might then simply resume his original position, or perhaps after the "kiss," pause and meet the woman's eyes briefly and smile again or nod before pulling himself up. There was a lightness about it. Instead, Adolf bent slowly and with a grave expression, planted his lips fully as he closed his eyes, then snapped back up. It was a gesture both solemn and military, as though he were reporting for duty. I was surprised he didn't click his heels.

Frau Sachs laughed.

"I don't flatter," she said. "I've only said what I've heard as truth, Herr Hitler. Come with me to the library. The other students are there now."

As it turned out, the guests were already eating. This would be followed by the recital, then the students, having played for their supper, would be fed. After this, we would rejoin the group in the library for a reception and dessert and coffee.

Frau Sachs led us to the library. The center of the room had been cleared for the Bechstein and three simple wooden chairs and music stands. Our cellist, Julian Schaub, and pianist, Otto Wagener—both third-year students—were there. Wagener was playing random passages to get a feel for the piano and Schaub was tuning his cello. I placed my case on one of the chairs, opened it, and lifted out my instrument in a way, I'm ashamed to say, I had actually rehearsed, gently but not overly respectful, the way I imagined a practiced journeyman musician might. Wagener pointed across the room and looked at me. "The Invisible Wagnerian, finally? A little Brahms won't bother him?"

Frau Sachs had paused as we came into the library and turned to Adolf, I imagine to chat and put him at his ease, and to give him a sense of how the library was organized and had grown over time. Adolf had slowed but simply *kept* walking—sleep-walking, really, in mesmerized steps. His palm was placed over his nose and mouth as he scanned the shelves. I could actually see his skinny chest—in our room, in an undershirt, one could discern the outline of every rib—expanding, contracting, expanding, as if he were breathing in some divine afflatus. He was like a pilgrim who'd wandered into St. Peter's. Wonderstruck. I looked from Adolf to Frau Sachs just as she turned to look at me, as if to say, My God, you were absolutely right.

Adolf had approached a wall, taken his hand from his face, and placed it gently—like a caress—against the spines of the books.

Schaub, busy adjusting the pegs on his cello, whispered, "Is he going to fall to his knees and weep?"

"I must get back to the guests," Frau Sachs said politely. "My husband will be in."

A few moments later, Victor Sachs did appear. I knew he was trained as a chemical engineer and had made his money from several successful patents as well as the sugar refineries in Bohemia. I suppose I'd expected a short bespectacled man whose mother had not known which to praise more, his school grades or his violin-playing. Well, he was tall—over six feet—and slender but broad-shouldered, which gave him an almost strapping, athletic appearance. The line of his hair was receding but he made no attempt to disguise this and combed it straight back. He had a lean face with a hawkish but aristocratic nose. And he was charming and self-effacing.

"You'll accept my apologies for even allowing you to accompany me," he said. "But you are students and undoubtedly need the money and to be stuffed with good food, and I am an aging man who needs to be humored. My technique is still acceptable but I'm afraid my timing is off, so you will have to cover for me. Especially Herr Reczek. I do know the piece well, though."

He sighed and lifted his hands.

"There was a time when I could have been in your place, but did not have the courage, and perhaps I was only humoring myself in believing I had the talent." He laughed. "Well, there is not much time to rehearse, is there? Back to my guests. In fifteen or twenty minutes I will return, then the guests will follow and pretend to humor me as well."

He was right. His timing *was* off, but not too badly. He was a little fast during the slow movement and a bit slow during the fast movements. I had to drop a few notes and extend others. Wagener, the pianist, played more vigorously than usual to disguise the problems with tempo. But it was a passable job, and it's a pretty piece of music anyway.

The guests turned out to be mostly family, including Herr Sachs's two brothers—one a surgeon at the medical school who had developed a procedure for treating pancreatic cancer and was also an amateur violinist, and the second an engineer like Herr Sachs. They gave us a better hand than we deserved, and Dr. Sachs laughed and whispered to me that my playing made his brother look good. Dr. Sachs's daughter, a few years older than Emilie, was a student at the Vienna School of Arts and Crafts under Professor Roller, Adolf's hero and Mahler's collaborator at the Court Opera. She later married the violinist Karl Rankl, whom she had met in the same room at one of the family concerts. They were fortunate enough to be able to emigrate to England, where Rankl became the director of the Covent Garden opera.

Many of the children who were there that evening, and who went on to become physicians, professors, and even musicians, were, like their parents, less fortunate. I know that now. During the recital, they sat in the chairs and sofas which had been arranged around the perimeter of the library. The boys wore knickerbockers with matching Tyrolean jackets and drooping bow-ties; the girls wore identical dark frocks. They were remarkably attentive, almost solemn, as though they were aping the expressions of the adults. I was amused, as nothing could be more tiresome to the ears of an eight-year-old than exquisite chamber music.

There was a fire in the fireplace and the chandelier had been lit. Adolf, I recall, stood throughout the entire piece, his back against the bookshelves, wearing a slight frown of very deliberate and earnest concentration, yet entirely unmoved by the music. He seemed terribly self-conscious. Perhaps he was aware that his suit, with all the stitching and sewing, had begun to look a bit shabby. I remember feeling bad for a moment that I'd kept after him to come.

Herr Sachs had his student accompanists take a separate bow

to more applause and announced "Enough! They must eat!" Everyone laughed and applauded again. Frau Sachs led us, and Adolf, into the dining room, where the table had been entirely reset. The food! Small succulent capons nestled in beds of rice, glazed asparagus, creamed onions, tall glasses of champagne, then flaming bowls of rum pudding.

"Where are you studying, Adolf?" Schaub said.

Adolf looked up, blinking, and went back to his capon.

"Herr Hitler, do you speak?" Schaub smiled.

I intervened. "Too much! All the time, in fact. But not when the food is so good and there is so much of it."

"Well, then, Adolf, you will not mind if I drink your champagne for you, since you haven't touched it?"

"Of course not. Of course not." Adolf then rose, uncertainly, and handed his glass to our cello player. The pale liquid glittered in the light from the chandelier.

Schaub took the glass and raised it.

"The arch-Wagnerian," he said, "bows graciously to the disciples of Brahms of Vienna."

Adolf seemed to panic for a moment. He looked from Schaub to Wagener to me, his eyes darting like a startled bird's. Then he said, "Why, yes, of course!" and he lifted his water glass and met the fluted crystal in Schaub's hand. The glasses clinked, Adolf nodded, and another few strands of hair sprung loose and fell over his eyes. I must confess I ate Adolf's rum pudding, which he did not touch either, because it contained alcohol.

When Fritzl the servant led us back to the library, *there* they were: the two girls from Demel's in their fetching black-and-white uniforms and caps. Frau Sachs had hired them for the evening. And in the center of the room, a smaller version of the Everest of tortes, tarts, truffles, strudel, and cakes that had greeted me when Frau Sachs had first taken me there. This time, the pastries were surrounded by liqueurs of every conceivable color—apricot, pear, cherry, apple, plum. The girls were pouring these into tiny glasses and dishing out the desserts with the same attitude of bored efficiency and politeness.

I glanced at Adolf, half-expecting to have to catch him as he collapsed in a delirium of expectation and craving. He simply stared.

"From Demel's," I whispered, "The waitresses are the very ones who served us."

He did not look at me, but nodded, and began moving, again like a somnambulist, towards the display.

Emilie Sachs was suddenly beside me.

"He is on his good behavior this evening," she said.

"Yes. You are not indulging yourself?"

"I have no intention of becoming a stout Viennese matron."

Again, I could hear the steeliness in her voice, that adolescent rejection of bourgeois comfort and sensuality. Emilie knew what she was about.

"Your mother is not stout," I said.

She glanced at me and I wondered for a moment whether I had somehow put my foot wrong, so to speak. The drawer containing the Japanese prints was directly behind us.

"She is still a matron," she said.

"Well, yes, of course."

"You did well by Papa."

"For someone who evidently has little time for practice, he is rather good."

"Yes," she said. There was a trace of considerable bitterness in her voice, and I chose not to pursue it. Emilie could be remorselessly frank, and I did not want to hear the truth, whatever it happened to be. Not then.

"Look," I said.

Adolf was standing in the corner with Herr Sachs, his plate supporting a towering slice of double chocolate cake with whipped cream and fruit. Herr Sachs was making sweeping gestures along the wall of books, talking in an animated, explanatory way, pulling out one volume then another. Adolf was managing to both stuff himself and barrage his host with questions. At one point, Herr Sachs shook his head and laughed aloud and clapped Adolf on the shoulder. It was the only time that evening I saw my friend engaged in something resembling conversation, an exchange.

Emilie looked at me and said, "I can't begin to imagine."

"Your roommate is an interesting young man," Herr Sachs said to me later. Some of the guests had left, and Wagener and Schaub and I were packing up.

Herr Sachs tucked my viola under his chin. "My God," he said, "this is two or three inches longer than a standard violin! How do you manage it? You need the reach of an ape. Perhaps you should simply hold it between your knees."

He lifted the bow and, closing his eyes, ran up a scale.

"Yes. Tricky, as I recall. Hard to hold a note, they tend to decay, slide into one another. Ahh."

He laid the instrument in its case and folded the felt covering over it with a delicacy that suggested a long familiarity with fine objects.

"The only bad thing about youth, Eugen," he said, "is you have to keep remembering it."

Adolf was across the room, working on a plate of *Guglhupf* and continuing to inspect the shelves.

"Your friend, he is like a *Yeshivajunge*."

"Yes?"

"You know, a Yeshiva boy. A young scholar of the Talmud. Not a *Bücherwurm*, really, better than that. A real mania for books and learning and what he thinks he will find there. Where does he study?"

"Nowhere," I said, quietly. "In our room. In libraries. He will not allow himself to be taught. It must all be on his own terms."

"Then he will come to nothing." Herr Sachs watched Adolf carefully slide a volume from the wall and inspect the frontispiece. "No degree. No systematic training. That is a sure, long descent into poverty and eccentricity."

"Not so long from where we are now," I said, "in our room on the Stumpergasse."

Herr Sachs smiled.

"My wife says you are also an upholsterer, by way of your father. Yes? The new fabrics in the music room, as we call it, are intricate, tasteful designs. They're English, aren't they? You know, before she goes to University I think it would be good for Emilie to learn how to extract and refine sugar, don't you? Can you see her doing that? My daughter?" He laughed and nodded. "I am lending your roommate a few things. No, no, he was too polite to ask. A biography of Frederick Barbarossa and Fichte's *Addresses to the German Nation*. Apparently, he belongs to several of our lending libraries but hasn't found them. I'm sure he'll take good care of them. Oh, I am a bit *under*, Eugen. Alcohol brings out different things in different men. In me, it seems, sadness, generosity, and inextinguishable regret. Not always in that order."

He placed his large hand on my shoulder and squeezed.

"My good wife beckons."

On the tram back, I sat with my viola case across my knees and Adolf sat alongside, the two volumes in his lap. It was drizzling and he had taken off his overcoat and wrapped it around the books.

We said nothing. I remember being very tired. I'd been worried about performing before Emilie and Frau Sachs (I thought this had gone rather well), and about meeting the man whose daughter and only child I was teaching and whose wife I was accompanying to fabric stores and cafés, and on whose bank account my exceedingly generous payments were drawn. But I was worried mostly about my friend. As his money dwindled, he had become even more isolated and irritable, if that was possible, his rants longer and more strident. His interests had expanded to encompass the emotionally violent politics of our beset empire, and he referred more often to the faithlessness and "diseased soullessness" of women, or "Woman," as he called them collectively.

Our agreement was that I could practice in the evenings until midnight while he studied and sketched at the desk. For the most part he had been good about this. And frankly I had been good about interrupting my composition exercises to listen to Adolf's feverish accounts of Frederick's strategy in the Seven Years' War or his endless opinions of the Vienna sewer system or a planned building renovation on the Ring.

One night, though, I heard him tossing the pages back and forth. I looked up. He was running his hands over and over through his lank hair, something he did when he was really stymied and had ground to a halt in his reading. I imagined he had just run up against some especially obtuse passage in Wagner or Novalis or Schopenhauer. (*Ostara* must had been a welcome relief after such fare!) He kept glaring at me over his shoulder as I played. I was working on and notating one of my own compositions, which wasn't *that* hard on the ear.

He seemed to know exactly when I was about to play. I would take a deep breath, and the moment my fingers were poised over the keys, he would turn and glare. I would glance at him, resume playing, improvise a bit, then go back to scribbling. At one point, as my fingers were hovering over the Boesendorfer's immaculate keyboard, I closed the lid, sat back, and said, "*What?*"

He turned away.

"What?" he repeated. Then a pause, and he held both fists above his head. They were shaking. "What, nothing. *Nothing, nothing, nothing! Neusicht!*"

He stood and walked out of the room without taking his coat. It would have been interesting to get up and take a look at what exactly he *was* reading, but I was so stunned it didn't occur to me. An hour later, he was back.

A week before the Sachs recital there had been another outburst. We were in line outside the Court Opera when a group of fraternity students—in full gear, with riding boots, cavalry-style jackets with the tricolor sash across the chest, sabers dragging at their sides—came along. This was not too unusual on a Friday or Saturday evening. They were loud, backslapping University boys, and after a few beers they would sweep along the sidewalks or even through the streets singing their fraternity or drinking songs, often predictably bawdy. They were obnoxious but really they bothered no one. Many already had *schmiss,* or deep facial and cranial scars, which they wore with great pride as a sign of their willingness to defend their own and their brothers' honor. They dominated social life at the University and even the police weren't allowed to discipline them.

Adolf, of course, despised them. They were younger versions of the "frankly stupid" officers who would turn up in uniform at the Opera half-drunk, bypass the rest of us waiting in line, claim their ten-heller tickets and head to their private standing section in the mezzanine, and from there keep a look-out for unescorted ladies. Whenever a group of fraternity brothers passed us, Adolf would simply turn his back. This time he did the same—but then he stepped toward them and in a surprisingly guttural voice, as if some robust demon were speaking through him, shouted "*Schmiss*-face! Where did you buy your toy swords?"

The brothers stopped singing and slowed.

"What was that?"

Adolf stepped out of line. I was too astonished to speak. I put a hand on his shoulder and he shrugged it off.

"I said, 'Where did you get your toy swords, little boys?'"

The brothers looked at each other. A few smiled as though they were trying to keep from laughing. One of them stepped forward.

"Is that a challenge, friend?"

"Never mind, Matthias," another said. "Look at him. Breathe on him and he'll fall over."

The one named Matthias nodded thoughtfully, drew his saber, then turned and cried "Onward!" We heard them singing something about everlasting comradeship as they marched off into the night.

The other "standers" had moved back. Adolf resumed his place in line and looked away from me. His hands were trembling and he jammed them into the pockets of his coat. He cleared his throat and said nothing. I, too, said nothing, and I didn't bring up the incident even after we had returned to our room later that night.

So I had reason to be worried about the evening at the Sachs's. I had known Adolf for more than three years, and for long periods I had seen him every day. During that time, I had not seen him—with the exception of our afternoon with that character von Liebenfels—in the close company of anyone other than his mother and sister, Dr. Bloch, and my own parents. That was it. That was the extent of his contact with the world, I suspect. So, at the Sachs's—would he get into a shouting match with Schaub or Wagener? Launch into one of his monologues, surrounded by the Sachs's surprised guests? Would he be icy and defiant and aloof, or perhaps only mildly aloof and somewhat snobbish? How would he treat poor Emilie? I suppose I didn't expect what I got. Polite, deferential, shy, awkward— "touchingly, painfully awkward," as Frau Sachs later put it. To Emilie, it was a polite nod and a whispered "Fraulein," after his dramatic and unexpected smooching of Frau Sachs's hand.

"Well, what did you think?" I asked. We were still sitting on the tram on our way back to our room, rocking from side to side as the car bumped and lurched its way towards the Mariahilf. I suppose I expected some comment on the Brahms or the inexhaustible desserts. He hugged the books wrapped in the coat on his lap, stared down, and said, after a moment, "Tonight, we have seen a family of highly refined tastes."

We continued to sway as the tram moved forward, and I watched our reflections in the dark window of the car. He sat up, without expression, clutching the books. I leaned back. The evening had gone well. The Brahms was luminous, and playing it inside that private library for barely more than a dozen people was a treat. The guests were pleasant and appreciative and discerning in a way concert-goers rarely are. The food was marvelous. The money was good. I had to struggle at times to keep from being distracted by the two serving girls in their black-and-white-lace uniforms. But none of this came to mind as the tram bumped along, taking us back to our kerosene-stinking room. Instead, I found myself thinking of Frau Hitler—her round, simple peasant's face, her guilelessness, her disciplined acceptance of an excruciating death, her love, and her unrelieved concern for the uncertain future of her only surviving son.

Not long after the concert at their home, Frau Sachs went on a decorating binge. She reupholstered, replaced drapes, repainted, had the wallpaper in many of the rooms of the vast two-floor apartment steamed off, bought rugs, and even bought a new set of cutlery designed by her niece at the Vienna School of the Arts and Crafts. At the end of my day at the Conservatory, I would take the tram to the Josefstadt and we would pore over reams of fabric samples and wallpaper designs. Later, we would repair to Demel's or to a café inside the Hotel Sacher.

Sacher's café had an older clientele; it was filled with smoke, a place where elderly men pursed their lips and wagged their heads as they concentrated on a game of chess, or frowned at the late edition of the *Neue Freie Presse*, where older women maintained their correspondence and somewhat younger men talked busi-ness, where even younger women would come by themselves to read and have a dessert and sip dark coffee from elegant cylin-drical cups. In short, no one seemed to take anything seriously and yet everything serious in life seemed to go on there. The only group not represented was the military, which I found rather strange since one saw the gaudy uniforms of officers, especially of the cavalry, wherever one went in the *Innerstadt*.

I learned that Frau Sachs was forty-two years old and the daughter of a dry goods merchant who had con-verted to Protestantism, which she regarded as "reasonable at the time but in the end utterly useless." (Could she have known how useless, utterly, in the end?) She'd had a good education, mostly in the private academies for young women. This was inevitably the case, since public education beyond *Volksschule*, or primary school, was available only to boys. Girls, if they were inclined and their parents had the money, could then attend the private *Mädchenlyceum*.

She spoke French and, oddly for the time, excellent English, and read Dickens, Shakespeare, and Thackeray, and was very fond of John Galsworthy, whom I'd never heard of. Of course, I'd *heard* of the others, but had never read a word by them, even in translation. She had intended to raise Emilie "like a man since anything else was pointless" and felt she'd more or less succeeded. She devoted much of her time, and some of her money, to the predictable charities, including a progressive men's hostel built by Baron Rothschild (where Adolf would live during his last years in Vienna) and a girls' orphanage. And, of course, she sat on the board of the Society of the Friends of Music, which had run the Conservatory since its founding in 1807, when Salieri was appointed its first director. She was violently opposed to the state's plan to nationalize it. She revered Wagner's music and was a devoted Mahlerite. She had even met Mahler briefly when he granted a five-minute audience to the board of the *Gesellschaft* and allowed them to sit in on a rehearsal of Gounod's *Faust*.

"He seems like a hard man," she told me. "All edges and angles. Thin, soft-spoken but very precise, entirely devoted to his work. I doubt he ever relaxes. I think he will die of nervous exhaustion, no organism can exist at that pitch for very long." She had published a letter in the *Neue Freie Presse*, defending Mahler from the attacks of anti-Semites, who were constantly trying to dislodge him from his post as director of the Court Opera even though he had converted to Roman Catholicism to get the job in the first place.

Her attitude towards her daughter was strange to me. She approved of Emilie's strong-headedness and her disciplined approach to her studies, but was also amused by it and encouraged her to "cultivate a sensual appreciation of life" and not to be so "anti-Viennese." What I found especially odd, in an affluent and recently successful Jewish Austrian family with only one child, is that she seemed to apply no pressure to her at all. If anything, it ran the other way. Emilie had devised a "curriculum" for her mother to compensate for the flaws in her education. This included general reading in science and the social sciences, in history and politics, and the demand that she take up an instrument. I approved of this last and offered my services.

Not surprisingly, I found myself falling into daydreams in which Frau Sachs provided *me* with instruction. After all, this was the stuff of literature, or French literature at any rate. An older, married woman of liberal sensibility and a younger, inexperienced man, a student usually. I was well brought-up, polite, considerate, provincial, and endearingly (or so I hoped) awkward in such matters. I tried to flirt in a mild way. I told her some of the stories that circulated among my classmates, which she found amusing and typical. I even told her about Frau von Branistch, my father's naked client in her castle, and my struggle to hold up the wallpaper. She laughed and patted my hand. "Your father sounds like a wonderful man," she said.

Once she came to a recital at the Conservatory of a student quartet I played in; we were performing an early Beethoven piece, not terribly interesting but still difficult. She was there with the other ladies of the Board. Afterwards, the Board, Conservatory donors, guests, and families surrounded us and peppered us with questions about our studies and plans. Frau Sachs, her hair swept up, bejeweled and striking in one of her "Flöge" gowns, rather than give me a quick, proper handshake like the other Conservatory board members, shook my hand and still clasping it rested her other hand gently on my forearm; then, in a gesture that would only come easily to one on intimate terms with another, she brushed my hair from my damp, glistening forehead.

Well, this produced a minor sensation among my classmates. I had all but proven the legend that ladies of the Board bestowed their favors on talented students. I received admiring glances and sly nods and smiles from my fellows as I passed them in the hallways; I was clapped on the back by third-year Conservatory students I'd never spoken to before. I was the "lapdog of the ladies of the Board." "Well, Reczek," Michael Oberhupel, one the violinists in our quartet, said to me, "it is always the quiet ones, the modest ones, who have something good to hide. This should be a lesson to all of us." My classmates speculated about the anatomy of violists, and a rumor circulated that the liveried messenger who had pulled me from class that day was carrying a demand from Frau Sachs that I service her immediately. I didn't have the heart to tell them that I appeared to be the son, the second child, that Frau Sachs had never had.

In the meanwhile, Frau Sachs kept track of every minute I spent going over fabrics and designs and accompanying her to the fabric emporium near the Hofburg. She sent me checks covering all of it at the "professional rate." I protested, half-heartedly. In truth, I had more money than I knew how to spend. I treated Adolf to *Nussstrudel* and *Sarah Bernhardt Torte*. (He thought my parents were sending me an allowance or the money came from my piano lessons.) I bought a new bow. I bought no new clothes as that would only have made it more obvious that Adolf's were falling apart. I bought Adolf no new clothes because he would never have allowed it. We were still "standers" at the Court Opera.

I had enough in my account to rent a dozen *chambres separées*, but frankly I had no idea how one went about attracting the attention of a suitable shopgirl or waitress, and I was terrified of disease. Still, I bought a package of expensive French prophylactics (they were sold behind the counter at certain cafés) and carefully opened it one rare sunny afternoon when Adolf was sketching outdoors. They indeed looked just like the casing my mother used in making sausage, but thinner and translucent, with a smoother surface. They actually *smelled* like cows. The instructions were in French. I broke one of them simply handling it. At last I got one on but it kept slipping off, and it occurred to me that I didn't know their size (or mine, which was variable). I couldn't tell inside from out. Finally, I went to a medical dispensary, where one of the older salesmen gave me a few tips and suggested I practice, of all things, by unrolling one over a peeled banana. I wondered aloud whether it was better to put it on beforehand or at the critical moment. At the moment, he assured me, and smiled. In short, I needed instruction badly.

On a Thursday afternoon, I arrived at the usual time for Emilie's lesson. Frau Sachs answered and told me Emilie was visiting her father in Warnsdorf, in the Czech-speaking part of Bohemia where he had his factories. This surprised me. Emilie was meticulously organized and would certainly have told me if she needed to reschedule. But come in, Frau Sachs said matter-of-factly, there is always work. And indeed there was. She wanted to reupholster the dining-room chairs, which were covered in a conventional damask fabric and had started to wear after many dinner parties and under the strain, she said, of "too many bourgeois posteriors." She was having second thoughts about the drapes we had chosen for the Music Room, which were a simple bold stripe, blue and gold, no pattern or filigree. She had wanted something more striking, a more involved pattern with more color, something "Secessionist." I told her that drapes were backdrops, that there was a thin line between the striking and the vulgar, and if she wanted to "secede" from common sense and good taste that was her business, but I wouldn't encourage it (exactly the sort of high-handedness my father, always anxious to please clients, had cautioned me against).

We inspected the sitting room off the dining room, and then she showed me Emilie's bedroom. It was just what I would have expected—dark, masculine, un-adorned. A red-and-black Oriental rug, four-poster bed with dark bedspread, and burgundy drapes. There was a small writing desk and a good-sized bookcase filled with volumes and bound notebooks, which was unusual as in those days books, even a personal collection, were usually kept in common areas. Emilie should have had a shelf of her own in the library. The heavy velvet drapes, even on this bright afternoon, gave the room an enclosed, cloistered feeling. There was a sheaf of neatly stacked papers on the desk, several fountain pens arranged alongside it, and an inkwell.

What happened next I recall with frightening clarity, nearly forty years later. You know Rousseau's advice that in writing a memoir one should write as though everyone one had known in one's life were dead? Well, most of those I did know *are* now dead, swallowed by the events of the past five years. My mother died only a few months after receiving Adolf's basket of sweets during the middle of the war; she had lost a good deal of weight as a result of the war-time rationing and succumbed to a heart attack. My father died of his worsening lung ailments more than twenty years ago. Frau Sachs and Emilie, I know now, are gone.

Many of the men I knew in my small town of Eferding either volunteered or were conscripted, were sent to fight in the East, and few have returned. Of the older ones at home, some died of starvation in the last year of the war. Adolf has taken his own life. Perhaps my story will die; I do not know whether these pages will ever see the light of day. They still take them, and the writing utensils, from me after each session in this cold, drafty room and give them back when I return. You would think I was divulging military secrets of extraordinary importance and they were holding their breaths waiting for each installment. And yet there is no evidence that they have even bothered to look at this. Perhaps the American psychiatrist, that bland creature, will read it.

Where was I? (As if I didn't know.) I was standing with Frau Sachs in the late afternoon light of Emilie's room. We were examining the drapes and the nondescript wallpaper, which had begun to peel and tear. Suddenly—I had not planned this, perhaps I had simply grown tired of waiting for my Conservatory classmates' fantasies to fulfill themselves—I turned to Frau Sachs and took her by the shoulders.

"Frau Sachs—"

She looked at me with a benign but unsmiling expression.

"Yes."

"Frau Sachs—"

Her eyebrows lifted, her head inclined forward a bit.

"Yes?"

I knew at once I had made a disastrous mistake. I was a provincial. A Conservatory student in the most musically sophisticated city in Europe, but a provincial to the bone. I was inexperienced. I could not even manage my own impulses in the quasi-intimate and subtly flirtatious relationship I had developed with Frau Sachs. I saw cues where they didn't exist. The only thing that had saved me with her daughter was Emilie's stern devotion to her studies and the rigid nature of our relation as teacher and student. I would lose her. I would lose Frau Sachs as a friend and sponsor, I would lose Emilie as my favorite student, and I would lose Herr Sachs, whom I was told had taken a paternal liking to me. I would lose this opening into a world I had never known. *And* I would lose the money.

"Yes?" She paused. "You have a sudden and passionate idea about this dreadful wallpaper? Or the drapes?"

I must have simply stared at her as though I were about to say something, my eyes pleading with her to rescue me—us—from the mortifying awkwardness of my advance. I realized I was still holding on to her shoulders. I let my hands drop.

She looked at me a moment, and then turned. She reached behind her and undid the top button of her dress, a smock really, that buttoned down the back to her waist.

"Go ahead," she said. "You can do the rest."

I was glad she was facing away because I am sure my expression

225

must have been one of mortified glee and embarrassment at what I had done and absolute terror at what I would be called on to do next. You'd think I would have been relieved, and relaxed, and gratified at my astonishing good luck. I was a provincial, as I've said.

When I was finished with the buttons, she lifted her dress at the shoulders and it simply fell away from her. She stepped out of it, folded it and placed it over the back of the chair at the desk. She was wearing some sort of lightweight shift beneath, and a camisole, and an undergarment beneath the camisole. Despite the layers, I could see her breasts shift slightly when she moved.

She turned again and raised her arms and waited and said, "Well?"

"Yes, of course."

"Yes, of course, Frau Sachs?" She laughed gently.

I lifted off the camisole and she laid it over the dress. Then she removed the shift and undershirt, and in what seemed like a fraction of a second she was standing naked in the dimness of Emilie's bedroom. Against the dark drapes and rug and bedspread her skin looked white as chalk. Her breasts were slightly pendulous, but full and pleasantly round, very pretty and well preserved, really—women of that class, of course, did not suckle their own children. The nipples were large and pink, and I remember this surprised me, as her eyes and hair were dark brown and I had assumed that all Jewesses had small, dark nipples. (Such were the things that occupied my mind at the time.) Without clothing, she appeared even more slender than in those untailored Flöge dresses. Partly, this was her height, eight inches over five feet. Her limbs were long and soft and pliable (but that is a rough word for what I mean), and her feet seemed to me comically— endearingly—small.

She cocked her head a bit and smiled. "Well?"

I suppose I'd been gaping like a true idiot.

"Hmm? Oh, yes, of course. Frau Sachs."

I removed my jacket and quickly laid it over the seat of the chair.

"Please relax, Herr Reczek. You have time."

"Yes."

Staring at her, I laid my trousers and shirt and underclothes on the seat of the same chair, and then placed my high collar, the one I wore to the Conservatory each day, on the desk alongside the fountain pens, where it sat like some stuffy Victorian guardian of culture and civilization. I must have indeed relaxed a bit because my Aryan and uncircumcised penis, in all its dusky glory, was practically saluting Frau Sachs. She looked down and made a soft clicking sound with her tongue.

"Do you have anything?" she asked.

"Have anything? Yes, well—"

She placed her hand on my cheek and kissed the other, said, "Wait a moment"—and left the room. She walked very naturally, as if she and Emilie, as part of their normal routine, strolled about the apartment without wearing a stitch of clothing. She reappeared a minute later with a prophylactic in a square of cellophane. I thanked her and started to open it.

"You needn't put it on right now. Here, come sit on the bed."

As you can no doubt tell, she knew what she was dealing with. Or perhaps she merely sensed what was needed. In any case, her approach was patient and slow and filled with preliminaries. There is no need to go into great detail. When she indicated, with tact, that the moment had arrived, I slid the prophylactic from its clear wrapper, unrolled it, and tried to put it on inside-out.

"Here," she said, and she knelt, inverted the thing, and pulled it on expertly and snugly, tugging a bit from side to side. It reminded me of watching a mother kneeling before a six-year-old boy, arranging and buttoning up his coat before leaving the house. She was kind enough not to betray exasperation, and what should have been embarrassing for a young fellow like me was rather amusing. What was upsetting was what happened next.

Each time Little Wotan (as she called it) approached the Cave of the Giants, he shrank until he resembled the shriveled, mean-spirited Mime or one of the Nibelungen dwarves, and the rubber, which had been snug and shiny, wrinkled up and slid off.

I apologized profusely. I must have seemed perplexed and desperate. She placed her hand on my thigh.

"You can talk to me, you know, Eugen. You can tell me."

She pinched my ear lobe and tugged on it—again, a maternal gesture.

"What is it? Hmm?"

I rubbed my face and debated in my head whether or not to tell her.

"A 'who,' not a 'what,'" I said.

She looked at me.

"Adolf," I said.

"Your roommate?"

She continued to look at me with an expression of quizzical concern. Not a trace of condescension or surprise. She would have made a fine psychoanalyst.

"Yes," I said. "You see, it is—it is like a betrayal. No, a series of betrayals. Over and over. I was admitted to the Conservatory, but the Academy of Fine Arts rejected him. So he must watch me go off to my Temple of Music every day, and listen to me talk about my classmates and teachers, and practice on that mammoth Boesendorfer—a real beauty, though it takes up two-thirds of our room—*and* run off to teach my students, almost all young ladies in women's hotels or lovely homes, while he ruins his eyes sketching away and reading all night in our bedbug-infested room. Yet if it weren't for him I would not be here. I would not have come. I would not have applied to the Conservatory. I'd be stuffing sofas. Also, you see, his parents are dead and his money is running low, and mine are alive and helping me to some extent, whenever they can. And *you* are helping me. His mother, whom he adored, died in December, at Christmas, of a terrible, terrible illness—I don't know which was more terrible, the illness or the treatment—just before I joined him here. He also loved a girl once, too, from a distance, for years. They never exchanged a word. A few weeks ago, we heard that she'd moved to Vienna and married, of all people, a cavalry officer. 'Peacocks of the empire,' Adolf calls them. The sort who are allowed into the Court Opera practically for nothing and are simply on the prowl for rich women. The kind of women who send him the notes he tears to bits."

"And here you are in bed with a—comparatively—rich woman, yes? You are a good and loyal friend, and so you feel guilty."

"Yes. In part, yes. And there are other things."

She again looked at me in an encouraging way, a look that promised understanding without judgment, concern without criticism or scorn. I told her about the display of medical texts Adolf had arranged, the photographs and explicit drawings of chancres, sores, pustules, of ulcerated and necrotic flesh.

"I realize he was only warning me off the prostitutes and 'working girls,' of course. But it has gone beyond that now. He says that sex is 'the realm of pigs.' He has become a kind of—

woman-hater, really. I attribute it to his disappointment with Stefanie, the girl he loved. But it is odd. It worries me. He has said such things as 'women lack souls,' that they lack all capacity for heroism and honor—as he calls it—that they try to steal the characteristics and substance of men to mask their soullessness, and in particular that they have a bottomless need—a terrifying need—for sexual satisfaction which can damage a man in some way. He says that they 'contaminate men in the paroxysm of orgasm.' I don't fully understand it, really. It is recent, since he has begun to read the *völkisch* newspapers, *Der Hammer*, that sort of thing, and especially a journal called *Ostara*, which says it promotes 'men's rights.' He even took me to meet the man who publishes and writes most of it. I think Ostara is the Germanic goddess of spring, actually." I didn't mention Dr. von Liebenfels' explanation of the tragedy of the Aryan penis. I simply couldn't.

"Is he an anti-Semite?"

Frau Sachs asked this in a curiously neutral way, as if she were asking whether he was left-handed.

"Adolf? No—I mean, I don't think so. At least I have never heard him say anything specifically against Jews. He revered Dr. Bloch, his mother's doctor, who is a Jew, a very dedicated man. Even now, he sends him small watercolors of Vienna, you know, on his birthday and so on, and signs them 'With eternal gratitude.' The surgeon who operated on his mother, Dr. Urban, I think, was a Jew. Otherwise, there are no Jews in Linz. Everyone is worried about the Czechs! Czechs moving in, taking our jobs. Mass being said in Czech! Foolish stuff, really. No, Adolf is a 'pan-German.' He seems to believe in a greater Germany celebrating all things German—music, art, culture, history, myth. He believes Wagner is quintessentially German, and he reveres Mahler—even though

Mahler is a Jew, although a convert for the sake of his career—because Mahler understands Wagner's intention perfectly and realizes it perfectly. God, I feel like I'm sounding off in the Conservatory canteen. But you know what I mean. I'm sure other Austrian Germans feel the same way."

"Are you anti-Semitic—I mean, are your parents anti-Semites?" Again, the same oddly neutral tone.

"I have never heard either of them even mention it. My father doesn't like the German nationalists, the 'blue-cornflower-in-the-lapel crowd,' he calls them. He says they are blowhards, looking to blow their horns about something, anything. My father is a modest, rational man."

I felt a heaviness cover me like a blanket, and I looked away from Frau Sachs and her stunning white nakedness in the fading light of the room.

She placed her finger under my chin and turned me back to her and lifted her eyebrows.

"What?"

"There is your husband," I said.

"Yes?"

"He has been—generous to me. I like him. This is how I repay him."

She spoke very deliberately.

"My husband and I have not had sexual relations for years. This is by arrangement. It is understood. You look shocked."

She sighed and lay back, folding her hands over her white belly, which seemed even whiter with the dark patch of hair below it.

She looked up through the top of the four-post bed at the ceiling. "Victor," she said, "is syphilitic."

"But he—"

"He is mostly without symptoms now. He is beyond the first phase of the illness. Whether he is infectious is unclear. But I will not take the risk. He has a woman, a mistress, in Reichenberg near Warnsdorf. An intelligent woman, though, not a peasant or an assembly-line worker. What she understands, what she is willing to risk, I don't know. There is no evidence that I have been infected, Eugen. But I have been ill before. When we were first married, I contracted gonorrhea from Victor, even taking precautions. I don't blame him. He was a man before he married me, he had his needs, even if the risks were obvious. But the illness was devastating. I suffered from abdominal pain, almost constant, and a persistent catarrh. We consulted doctors, specialists—none of them knew what they were doing.

"I was sent to Franzensbad for a 'cure'—it is not as well known as Karlsbad or Marienbad, but perhaps even more beautiful. Their specialty is 'women's disorders.' Every guest has her own physician who prescribes a regimen 'customized' to her disorder, although all the regimens are suspiciously similar. At five or six in the morning several glasses of mineral water from the spring, then a soak in one of the cold springs. This is followed by an excellent breakfast, then more baths—mud and gas baths, with giant bubbles rising and bursting at the surface. It was like being inside a volcano. Carbonic acid baths, electric water baths, steam baths. All of it, supposedly, a powerful treatment for everything from spinal atrophy to neurasthenia. Then there is the house specialty— dark, sulfurous baths made from the earth of the peat marshes in the nearby hills. And the buildings! All Greek Revival and massive Beaux Arts style. There were recitals every evening featuring supposed virtuosi, renowned pianists, violinists, divas. Why are you smiling?"

"I'm sorry. At the Conservatory, whenever one performs badly or gives a dreadfully wrong answer in class, the professor might say, 'Now, don't worry, you can always find a place in a sanatorium orchestra.'"

"Well, the whole thing is a sham! There were rich Jews and non-Jews from all over central Europe and even Russia. There was the wife of a famous Russian rabbi with a whole entourage. The food at the hotels, of course, is splendid and plentiful. They eat like pigs and brag about their successful husbands and children. It makes me sick to think about it. It is a front for empty, frustrating marriages and venereal disease."

She sat up and unpinned her hair. Extending her neck, she pulled it back with both hands, lifting up her white-and-pink breasts. One could see what she must have looked like as a girl— large alert brown eyes, reserved but questioning.

"Gradually, the illness seemed to recede of its own volition," she said. "Although the doctors said it likely left scarring, internally, which is why Emilie has no brothers or sisters."

She took my head in her hands. I was staring at her breasts, which seemed to be looking at me like a second pair of eyes.

"I like you, Eugen, not because you are young and 'clean'"— she used the German *sauber*, which means both physically and morally clean—"but because you are talented, *and* good company for shopping, and, I think, without pretense. Not full of yourself."

She leaned forward and kissed me, and she knew just what to do because Little Wotan awakened from his Teutonic slumber, donned his armor, and spent the rest of the afternoon in glorious and uninhibited combat.

Afterwards, I helped her dress. I must say, of all the things we did that day, this made me feel most like a "lover." She raised her arms and I lowered the camisole over her, then buttoned her blouse, and after she put her arms through the shoulders she turned and with the aplomb and objectivity of a tailor I did the row of pearl buttons that started at the neck of her "reform" dress and ended at her waist. I dressed quickly and she straightened my collar.

"The collar is too large," she said, tugging at the shoulders of my jacket. "You need one that is smaller and not so high. You are an artist and student, not an assistant bank manager. Would you like a glass of wine before you leave? I'll have one. I think you should, too. You should celebrate"—neither of us referred to the demise of my virginity directly—"after all, I don't think your roommate is going to approve and he certainly won't share a bottle of wine with you. After the concert, you hardly touched your wine and he had none at all, although he practically ate us out of the whole display from Demel's. It was almost pathetic. I mean the way he couldn't tear himself away from the desserts *or* the books. He would shyly ask one of the girls for another piece of cake or strudel and glance about the room as though to reassure himself that no one was watching. Don't worry, I wasn't upset. More touched, really."

"Sweets are his one concession to the world of the senses," I said. "Aside from opera. He doesn't drink alcohol. He doesn't even eat sweets that contain alcohol."

"Yes," Frau Sachs said, "I suppose I can understand that. He *has* his intoxicants. Still, it might do him good to indulge a little, you know. He's quite serious."

"Indulge in women or wine?"

"Either, I suppose."

The combination of wine and women and Adolf almost made me laugh out loud.

Before I left I kissed Frau Sachs on my own, that is, on my own initiative, you would say. This was the first time I'd done that during that entire afternoon. I could smell the wine and taste its penetrating sharpness on her lips and tongue. I placed my hand on the small of her back and she leaned backward and closed her eyes. It made her seem as young and yielding as a girl.

Walking through the streets of the Josefstadt, and then on the tram, I don't recall feeling six inches taller or cocky or even faintly proud. I felt simply more ordinary in a way. It was as though a burden had been lifted from me. I used to feel that people could somehow tell I was inexperienced—the converse, I suppose, of my classmates' claiming they could tell whether a young woman had known a man by the way she walked. In my case, I thought, they just somehow *knew* my condition. It was something that could not be hidden, not from my classmates, not from strangers, and certainly not from the prostitutes who seemed to follow me with their smirking eyes ("Are you going out, lad?" "Oh, you look like you need it terribly, sonny. Just two kronen is all." "Not good enough for you? How would *you* know, now tell me?") I felt as though my virginity were tattooed across my nineteen-year-old forehead. I even wondered whether I could fool them by crossing my legs right over left, or left over right, or not at all, or letting myself slouch a bit and yawning with ostentatious boredom, as though I'd spent a long night with my insatiable mistress. Now, in a single afternoon, Frau Sachs had released me.

When I left the apartment in the Josefstadt, it was too late to have my usual dinner at the Conservatory canteen, so I took the tram back to the Mariahilf district. I was used to returning reasonably early each evening to avoid Adolf's questions. When I got back to the room he was sitting erect at the small desk as usual, reading.

"You don't have to tiptoe in," he said, without turning around.

"I wasn't. I'm just tired, you know."

"Here."

He turned suddenly and handed me a sketch. It was Herr Sachs! I recognized it instantly—an abstract profile, but the high forehead with receding hair, the clifflike nose, slight frown, and prominent chin were unmistakable. Below, *Ex Libris* in Gothic lettering and a space for the inscribed name.

"What do you think? You look stunned. Then it must be good. I am thinking of presenting it to Herr Sachs. He can have it printed and use it as a bookplate in the front of his books. Do you think he would mind if I kept these a few more weeks? The philosophical sections in Fichte are difficult, very difficult, more so than Schopenhauer. But the political thinking is clear and quite excellent. He is a true father of German nationalism, with very good ideas, forcefully expressed. He speaks of a *Volkskrieg*, or people's war, to unite Germany, and denounces the joke of parliamentary democracy, calling instead for a direct dialogue between the German people and a leader."

I followed him with my eyes and massaged my chin, my habitual way of trying to appear intent and thoughtful.

"We Germans, he says, are an exception, unique among European peoples." He was now up and pacing. "Our language is rooted not in Latin but in a distinctly Teutonic tongue. It has been infiltrated by foreign influences, but freed from those influences, it could give rise to the expression of pure—and purified—German thought. He says we think and act differently from other Europeans. What an inspiration! It is no wonder Bismarck admired him. He believes in an utter subordination of the individual to society, but a society based on a pure German language and German culture. He affirms utterly the value of the *Volk*, an open, honest, truth-loving *Volk* capable of enthusiasm and sacrifice.

"We are at a turning point in history, Eugen, a turning point that has yet to reveal itself, true, but one that will lead to a complete transformation of cultural, political, and economic life. This is a book we should own one day for our library." He closed the volume on his desk and placed his hand on it, like a benediction. "I have carefully marked several pages I would like you to read later," he said. "Just a few. Consider it part of your education. It will make you forget your fatigue."

I sat on my bed, staring at Herr Sachs in heroic profile. I felt nauseated. The smell of sour poultry permeated the room.

"Yes—yes, of course," I managed to say. "I'm sure Herr Sachs would let you keep the books as long as you'd like." I handed the sketch back. "It's a good likeness. I knew it right away."

"Excellent, though I still have more to do with it. I will never be good at real portraiture, but if one can grasp the essential features, one can produce a true graphic likeness. Stage design is very similar, in a way."

I rose, almost listing like a drunk, and went to the piano. The nausea had come over me like a wave. I made a perfunctory attempt to work on a composition for one of my classes, but after a while I gave up and went to sleep. Adolf had lit the candle and was still at the desk, reading and sketching. When I woke in the morning, he was asleep, his arms rigid at his side as usual, fists clenched, his head back and mouth open. I could hear him breathing. The books and a pile of sketches were stacked on the floor alongside the bed. There was a sour, metallic taste in my mouth, but the nausea was gone. I washed and dressed, and went to class.

I spent the late afternoons and early evenings the rest of that week and the next at the Sachs's. Emilie was gone. I cancelled my other lessons.

We would spend the late afternoon in bed, either in Emilie's bedroom or Frau Sachs's own, larger bed. Victor had his own bedroom, which was a relief to my prickly conscience. It seemed not to have been used in some time. To this day, I associate having money with husband and wife having separate bedrooms.

We had a routine. I would, with ironic deference, unbutton Frau Sachs's dress and remove her camisole and shift. She would fold them, then remove my collar, and I would undress while she lay naked on the bed watching me. Once, I put the collar back on and crawled into bed wearing nothing else, and she was wonderfully amused by my concession to respectability. I am a man now in later middle age, malnourished and exhausted after five years of war, inhabiting a thin body with no real musculature and which seems to experience only an occasional, random twinge of desire. I look back on this, and my excitement and endurance, even my sense of humor then, amaze me.

We would talk in bed. I found out the story of the Japanese prints in the library. They had been a wedding present from her husband, a kind of joke, really. Apparently, in Japan young women about to marry were shown these lithographs and were horrified to see the monstrous, heavily-veined penises. Then came the wed-ding night and the realization that their new husbands were far more reasonably endowed; the brides were greatly relieved and would relax, and a night of blissful happiness ensued. Frau Sachs said Emilie would probably not require this trick, as she had a boyfriend who was a law student at the University, was (Frau Sachs suspected) no longer a virgin and in any case preferred reality to fantasy, one reason she detested opera. Of course she had seen the prints, which she considered "silly" and referred to as "Father's cartoons."

"Are you still a Protestant?" I said one afternoon as we lay in bed after making love.

She looked at me with surprise. "I have never set foot in a Protestant church. Neither did my parents. They paid a fee to convert and completed the papers."

"Well, are you a Jew, then?"

"On the tax rolls, yes. We pay the 'Jew' tax. Why do you look so skeptical?"

"I don't know, I just am. It seems strange, like something from another world."

"Every Jew in Vienna, depending on his income and district, pays a special residential tax. In addition to the usual taxes paid to the city. This is what allows us to live here. I wouldn't expect you to know that."

"What about Victor—your husband? Is he Jewish? I mean, does he consider himself Jewish?"

"Jewish, yes, but German. Victor is German. You have seen the library."

I thought of the rows of leather-bound sets of Goethe, Fichte, Schopenhauer, Holderlin, Schiller, Kant, Novalis, Nietzsche. The whole Pantheon.

"Austrian German?" I said.

"If you'd like."

"Or German Austrian?"

She looked at me impatiently.

"Or 'Nouveau' German? No, no, *you* are 'Nouveau' German."

She smiled. "All right, then, 'Nouveau' German."

"Does Victor believe in God?"

She sighed. "He does not believe in a God who punishes and rewards, no."

"And Emilie?"

She laughed. "Must you ask? Emilie long ago abolished relics and superstitions. Soon she will do so for the rest of society."

"And what do you believe in?"

"All these questions!" She raised her chin and narrowed her eyes. "I believe"—she ran her fingers through my hair—"in talent." She leaned over and kissed me on each cheek and then on the mouth. Her breasts brushed against my chest, a sensation that obliterated all thought and all questions. I pulled her down to me.

My inexperience continued to be a source of amusement and an opportunity for bemused instruction.

"When you put the prophylactic on, pull back the foreskin as well." Frau Sachs would demonstrate with the same motherly competence with which she adjusted my collar. "If not, the head of the penis will have two coverings, the prophylactic and the foreskin, and sensation will be greatly diminished, Eugen. The head, and in particular its underside, called the glans, here"—she drew an oval with her finger—"is where most sensation originates. It is sensitive to light touch and to pressure. The glans of the uncircumcised penis is especially sensitive. During unprotected intercourse, the foreskin moves back and forth over it, increasing stimulation. The risk, of course, is that ejaculation will occur too quickly. You know this from using your hand."

"I do not use my hand."

She laughed. "All boys use their hand."

"I am not a boy."

"Young *man*. All young men use their hand."

I wanted to tell her that there was one young man—who slept with his fists at his sides for the sake of the future of the German race—who did not.

"How do you know all this, anyway, Frau Professor Doktor?"

She lay back and sighed. "Emilie."

The daughter was instructing the mother!

"Emilie?"

"When she is a physician, she plans to institute frank sexual education for all Austrian schoolchildren aged twelve and older. She also plans to build orphanages for girls."

"Good luck," I said.

"No, that is how it should be. Things are moving too fast now, and the risks are too great. There is no point in hiding things."

"Ahhh," I said. "*That* is why Stefan Epstein says Jewish men make better husbands, and why he smiles in that way."

Frau Sachs raised herself up on her elbow and looked at me.

"*Why* is that?"

"Stefan is one of my classmates. His father is one of my professors and a splendid violinist, who could have a profitable career in performance tomorrow if he chose to. Now, if the head of the circumcised penis is, as you say, slightly dulled to sensation, then erection will last longer, the man will be compelled to strain more vigorously for greater stimulation, and the wife will be more satisfied. I had thought he meant that they, Jewish husbands, were better providers, you know, more adept at business and so on."

"This is what you talk about at the Conservatory?"

"Well, with Professor Dr. Epstein, no. But with his son—do Jews and the southern races in general have longer and more robust penises, which they use to greater effect? And do Aryan women prefer them?"

"What?"

Frau Sachs sat up now abruptly, making her breasts bob, and poked me in the forehead with her finger.

"Dr. von Liebenfels—"

"*Him.*"

When Adolf was gone, I had been dipping out of curiosity into *The Science of the Sodomite Apelings and the Divine Electron.*

"He says that Germanic women prefer men of the darker races for precisely this reason, that this is the 'tragedy' of the Aryan penis, which is smaller but technically better proportioned, and that it has resulted in a decline in the purity of the German race. And, of course, that it has demeaned and belittled—"

"—so to speak—"

"—all German men. I agree it sounds rather far-fetched."

"Your roommate confounds me," she said. "One moment it is Schopenhauer and Wagner, the next the worst of the gutter press of Vienna. The answer to your question is, I have *no* idea, and the only Aryan penis I have any interest in at the moment is yours and it appears, with some encouragement, to be doing very well, frankly."

She gave me her affectionate, reproachful tug on the ear lobe.

"I *do* have some news that will interest you and your depraved classmates, but you mustn't quote me." She ran her finger along my thigh and gave me a teasing smile. "I visited Klimt's studio."

At the time, the controversy over Klimt's murals for the University was still raging, and Adolf and I had seen his Beethoven frieze at the Secessionist exhibit. But what interested my depraved classmates (and me) most was Klimt as erotic visionary: the Watersnakes paintings, the sketches, the slender naked women floating through glittering, phantasmagoric landscapes. Klimt's studio on the Josefstadtstrasse, only a few blocks from the Sachs's apartment, was supposed to be straight out of the Marquis de Sade. And Klimt was rumored to have had children by almost all his models. It was hard to imagine when the man had time to paint.

"I went there with Ida Kirsch," Frau Sachs said.

"The 'doyenne'?"

"'Doyenne' only because her husband collects."

"*Well?*"

I grabbed her shoulders and she laughed. We'd become much more relaxed with each other. It is interesting what going to bed with someone does for a friendship, isn't it? It has been many years, and I have forgotten this.

"I shouldn't tell you. You'll likely run straight out of the room, forgetting to put your trousers on, and tell all your student friends at the Conservatory. Calm down." You could tell she was enjoying this. "The house itself is hidden by a tall brick wall, maybe ten feet, on all sides, you can't see it from the street. Inside the wall, though, is the most wonderful garden—riotous, overgrown, like a real English garden. With a small fountain and patio. But what you notice immediately is how quiet it is. Silent! You can't hear the city at all. And when you walk into the house—the studio, that is, the whole house, which isn't large, has been made into a studio—it is just as quiet. You might hear a cat meowing or the birds in the garden, that is all. Windows from floor to ceiling face the garden, which is east, of course.

"When we came in, Klimt was sitting on a scaffold working on a huge canvas, it must have been twenty feet high and twice that across. He was wearing a smock that seemed to have come straight from the Flöge salon—big, blousey, all the way down to his feet, with some colorful design at the neck and across the shoulders. There were two young ladies—now you must listen very carefully because Stefan Epstein is going to ask you for all the details and you must know them or you will disappoint everyone—there were two young ladies, entirely without clothing, handing up to him a tray with sandwiches, a bottle of wine, and a wedge of cheese. I couldn't tell what the canvas was, he was just starting it and sketching in a very loose, off-hand way."

I must have been grinning like an idiot in antici-pation because she grabbed my ear and gave it a quick, hard tug.

"Now! There were four or five other girls—they were working girls, not middle-class girls, you could tell—in a state of complete undress, or perhaps wearing flimsy, diaphanous robes, or a chemise and nothing more. Most couldn't have been older than twenty, barely older than Emilie. Certainly none older than twenty-five or thirty. And thin, as slender and attenuated as the figures in his paintings. There were armchairs, a couch, two or three beds. The girls were strolling aimlessly or had draped themselves over the furniture and were either dozing or stimulating themselves— you know *perfectly* well what I mean—or lying on the beds, caressing each other. The only sounds were a few soft, satisfied moans and the birds chirping. Otherwise, silence.

"Klimt has absolutely forbidden them to talk. It is a condition of their employment. Ida says that when he sees something interesting, he clambers down from the scaffolding, rearranges the limbs a little, issues a few instructions, and sketches. Occasionally, if he is in the mood, he doffs his sandals and throws off the smock—he never wears anything under it—and has one of the girls right there. Satisfied? And the sketches—the place is littered with them. They are all over the floor, like leaves in autumn. Truthfully. And many are quite interesting, quite good. The girls just walk over them. One of the cats was playing with a drawing, stalking it and batting it about, shredding it. Again, no one talks. Klimt simply issues a few orders, sketches, paints. You see, it is more than even you hoped for."

"Did he—did he talk to you?"

"He spoke with Ida. About a commission and other works he thought she would be interested in. The canvasses were leaning against a wall, the floor around them cluttered with sketches of the girls. Most seemed to be large preliminary sketches for future paintings. He is going to design for Ida and her husband a big cabinet, floor to ceiling, like an altar, to house the works she and Hugo have bought, since apparently they don't feel comfortable displaying them on their walls. I suppose they'll take them out and admire them and then put them back, like religious scrolls.

"And yes, Ida introduced me. He gave me a brief nod and looked at me, or *through* me, with those steel-blue eyes. He seems like a remorseless man. He doesn't smile. He is all business, no small talk, no pleasantries. The only time he displays anything like emotion is when he scoops up one of the cats and scratches its head. Ida says he doesn't go out in the evenings and refuses all invitations. He waves off the girls at the end of the day and goes home. He lives with his mother and two sisters, who are unmarried. They cook and keep house for him and apparently dote on him."

"He should paint you, Adele! In one of your Flöge dresses, you are *just* the sort he likes."

"A rich Jewess, you mean."

"No, no, no. I mean your features. The large, um, alluring, yes, alluring eyes—"

"Oh—alluring, now!"

"And a little bored, a little aloof."

"Alluringly aloof, no doubt."

"Yes, and slim, slender, elongated-looking, especially in one of your gowns. You would be perfect."

She tousled my hair.

"You are flattering. But I am afraid he doesn't need the commission and he has his choice of subjects. Besides, Ida says he sleeps with the women he paints, this is almost a requirement. And that won't do. He is humorless and short, and stout, built like a bull. Or a butcher. Talented, yes. But men should have a few endearing qualities."

"I am afraid inexperience is my most endearing quality."

"That's one—"

She pulled me towards her and took my head in her hands.

"You are staying for dinner, no?"

"Yes, of course. But I mustn't stay too late. Adolf will wonder where I am."

Frau Sachs fell back, her arms splayed outwards in an attitude of feigned exasperation.

"Your *roommate*," she said.

"I would rather not have to answer questions."

"By what right does he ask? What sort of hold should he have over you?"

I sighed and lay alongside her and stared at the ceiling, which was painted tin, pressed into elaborate patterns. My penis had shrunk to the size of a button.

"After Adolf left for Vienna the first time, alone," I said, "I used occasionally to visit his mother, who was still quite weak. This was before she got worse again, just before Christmas. She told me she thought the reason Adolf stays up all night reading and sketching is he doesn't like the dark. He sleeps better after the sun starts to come up. More to the point, really, she said that after his father died when he was thirteen, he starting having nightmares. He would wake shrieking and screaming. She couldn't console him. After that, he just stayed up. When I first came to Vienna in late January, we looked for a place for me but I ended up moving in. It was easier, even with the behemoth Boesendorfer. But I also think he doesn't like to be alone at night, even with me asleep.

"And then there is the odd way he feels about women," I said. "Why else would someone like me come back late, or not at all? I don't really drink. My classmates like to talk but most of us don't, well, *carouse* very much. Even Klimt, as you say, goes home to his mother in the evening."

What else could I say? That Adolf had inspired me to change my life? That he had helped me find the will and desire to act on my deepest ambitions? That I felt bound to him in a secret pact propelling us into the future, in which I would become a composer and he an artist, and that we would build our *Conservatoire* and from there change the course of the German-speaking world? That it all seemed like some mad dream? That I felt sorry for him?

Frau Sachs nodded.

"Well, then," she said evenly, "we should get dressed and ask Fritzl to bring us something. All right? Perhaps a little wine, too, or a liqueur."

One of the things I liked about Frau Sachs was that she always listened. She always tried to understand other people's attitudes, even when she disagreed or found them inconvenient. I suppose this was because she was older, although I am fifteen years older now than she was then and it is not clear to me that I am any more tolerant or better at understanding people. She was a good and perceptive listener. *I* was a good listener! Though I'm not sure I really had a choice—after all, how else could one be a friend to Adolf? Of course, eventually he had whole crowds, and then a nation, and then a world listening to him. Who is to say how much choice *they* had, in the end?

One night I did stay. The cook and Fritzl prepared a fine dinner. We had smoked meat and dumplings, crepes in plum sauce, and drank champagne. I played Brahms and Debussy and Alkan for her. We soaked in a bath. What luxury! To have a private bath smelling of rosewater and citrus, instead of the bathtub at our building on the Stumpergasse with its rust-colored streaks in a hall lavatory filled with the piercing odor of ammonia and feces. You had to breathe through your mouth while you were in there.

We went to bed, perfumed, our skin still warm and pink from the hot water. We gossiped about the Conservatory, about the ladies on the board of the *Gesellschaft*, and I confided to her my plans to become a conductor, which I had not mentioned to my classmates or teachers, or even to Adolf. She talked about her classmates when she was in school, about Emilie, and about trips she had taken to Paris and London—she had been to the Paris Opera and Covent Garden. I wanted to know every detail, every impression. At the time, except for a short trip with my father to a client in Braunau on the Inn, just over the border, I had never been out of Austria. I am hardly better traveled now, almost forty years later.

Frau Sachs said nothing unflattering about her husband. In fact, I had the impression she rather admired him. She wanted him to spend more time in Vienna and less at the factories, if only for Emilie's sake. His mistress she had no real opinions about one way or the other. But the sexual illnesses and their consequences had made things difficult, very hard to repair. I do not think she could forgive him.

We made love again under the perfectly weightless duvet, a treat in itself as I normally slept under a pair of stiff, heavy woolen blankets that contained the corpses of hundreds of *Bettwanzen* and smelled like a stable. Sometime during the night, we made love a second time.

Sleeping alongside the smooth, warm body of Frau Sachs, with its faint scent of citrus and apples, and the clean smell of her hair, was a sensation beyond my power to describe then or now. *Le plaisir, c'est le droit.*

In the morning, I went straight to my classes at the Conservatory. I returned to Frau Sachs's apartment in the afternoon, and then to the Stumpergasse in the early evening.

Adolf was at the desk when I came in. He said nothing. I put my briefcase on the bed, took out my notebooks, the compositions I was working on, several scores I had brought back. I placed them on the piano and lifted the lid over the keyboard. I lay down on the bed for a moment and stared at the cracked and stained plaster of the ceiling. I could feel my heart beating.

Usually I could count on a brief perfunctory response when I came in. He would be frowning at whatever he was reading or sketching and grunt without looking up. Reading in particular was deadly serious business and not to be interrupted. In an hour or two he would push back the chair. I would stop playing. Then would come The Summary, a condensed version of whatever he had been reading or a building he had been studying and drawing.

He would pace in front of the desk. Sometimes he would quote long passages entirely from memory and (as far as I could tell) with remarkable accuracy. It was as though he were going through an exercise meant to impress what he had read—or at least those parts of it he found most persuasive or which agreed with what he was inclined to believe—to stamp these on his brain in a way that could not be erased. He seemed to be placing one more stone or tile in an enormous mosaic, a mosaic that would eventually represent a picture of *something*, something huge, a cathedral or panorama whose shape and outline were for now impossible to trace. I would simply listen or ask a few brief questions. If The Summary involved music or mythology, if he'd been dipping into one of Wagner's sixteen interminable volumes, then my questions might be a little more pointed. I could respond with a little disquisition of my own, or even, in the mildest and most diplomatic tones, and with all due respect, disagree, a little. These were my favorite moments. I'd imagine that Adolf, in a fit of irrepressible enthusiasm or outrage, had come from the studio or library of our *Conservatoire* and into the cork-lined study where I composed and practiced, and was treating me to his latest brainstorm.

Tonight, nothing. Silence. The scratching of the pencil, a page turning, a clearing of the throat. At one point, as though asking a question, I said "The rent is due this week." No answer. The back remained stiff, a page turned, there was no shift in his posture. Eventually, I went to sleep.

The next day, I visited Frau Sachs in the afternoon. She asked about Adolf. I shrugged off the question, and she did not insist. Emilie would be returning in two days and I did not want to spend our time talking about this. Perhaps I felt complaining would be unmanly. (Wasn't manhood, mine anyway, the point?) It was a situation I should deal with on my own. I should not need advice or coaching from a woman more than twice my age.

That evening, the same. The stiff back at the desk, the precise turning of pages, the irritating scratch of the pencil as he took his habitual notes, the hiss of the kerosene heater.

"They are working on the Burgtheater," I said. "The facade is covered with scaffolding and they've put up barriers."

I could hear the distant clatter of the tram on the Mariahilfer Strasse.

"You can talk, you know."

He asked, without turning around: "Is it the mother or the daughter? It is the mother, is it not so? I can practically *smell* it on you." He made a few notes and turned the page.

I put the lid down over the keyboard without a sound and looked at the back of his head. In the faint light, the wood of the Boesendorfer shone. I wouldn't let a week go by without cleaning and polishing it, even the hinges and pedals. I felt my throat tighten.

"How—" I coughed. Suddenly I felt weak. I must speak, I must speak, I must speak. "How—is this—your business?"

"When you enter this room, when you return to this room, *our* room, reeking of filth, it is my business."

I spoke with effort. "Perhaps—like most people—I prefer what is real to what is imagined."

He still had his back to me.

"Perhaps," I said, "I prefer not to stand on a bridge for years."

He closed the book and pushed the chair back from the desk. "What is that?"

I said nothing.

He rose from the chair and with his head down and hands behind his back began to pace. His hair was longer now, unruly.

"When you choose to wallow—"

"I bathed afterward. You needn't worry about my infecting you. I do not plan on having sexual relations with you."

"I suppose I should be thankful for *that*." He paused, closing his eyes. He pressed his palms against either side of his head like a vice, then ran his fingers back through his dark, shining hair. He spoke as though straining for patience. "Why—are humans—*so* blind? Why can they not see that their actions affect not only themselves but others, even generations of others, coming before and after? Each individual action is implicated in a wider culture and contributes—every thought, every action—to the raising or lowering of that culture, and to its ultimate triumph or desolation. There is evidence, there is scientific evidence, that even a single instance of intercourse, even without fertilization, can have genetic consequences—"

I could not help myself. I was on my feet, by the piano, shouting.

"Who are you quoting? Von Liebenfels? And what is his real name, anyway? The man is half-mad!"

"Mad? Why? Because he doesn't belong to the mighty Conservatory or sit on the faculty of the University and cloak himself in the gown of academic respectability? Do you think every talented or successful musician or composer attended the Conservatory? What makes you think that a degree from the Conservatory is a guarantee of originality or talent or success?"

"Of course I don't think that. That is not the point."

He continued to pace.

"One must examine all ideas," he said with infuriating steadiness. "This is what *I* do. Whether they come from a scholar's small apartment in the Leopoldstadt, a magazine from a tobacco kiosk, a newspaper—"

"What did your friend say was needed?" I was drumming my fingers on the piano. "'Intervention', yes! 'Intervention in the erotic lives of men and women.' He sounds like a horse-breeder!"

Adolf paused. He still had not looked at me. He extended his arm towards our pathetic airshaft window, and then reaching back he made a sweeping gesture that seemed to take in the entire world. "Look at this," he shouted. "This city is a human sewer! Is this what you want? You were made for higher things! I have done nothing but encourage you in this direction! Listen to me—"

There was a tentative knock on the door. I could hear Frau Zdenek asking "Hello?" in her tiny, worried voice.

Adolf fell back into the chair. His eyes on the floor, he began to rock back and forth, rubbing his hands along his thighs rapidly. I had seen him do this before, when Dr. Bloch was examining his mother not long before she died. I felt frightened, and I sat back down on the piano bench. "Why," I asked quietly, "must you always have the last word?"

There was another soft knock on the front door, and Frau Zdenek's gentle voice. "Hello? Herr Hitler?"

"Why," he repeated, as if the word itself was puzzling. "Why?"

He brought both fists down on the desk three times. "Why! Why! Why!" Then he jumped up and barged past me, nearly tripping over one of the legs of the bench in the narrow space between the piano and the bed. He threw open the door and brushed by Frau Zdenek, who stepped back quickly. I could hear him running up the tiled stairs to the ground floor.

I approached Frau Zdenek, and unable to speak I held my finger to my lips and nodded. She nodded at me and put her own finger to her lips and I closed the door. I knew enough not to run after him.

When I woke the next morning, he was lying asleep on his bed, fully dressed. His arms were rigid at his side, hands balled into fists, and he was breathing hoarsely through his mouth.

The next day was the last before Emilie Sachs would return from Warnsdorf. I went straight from classes to the grand apartment in the Josefstadt. Frau Sachs nodded politely and without speaking we went to her bedroom, where I undressed her in the way I had become accustomed to, and then myself, allowing her to remove my new collar, smaller and less conspicuous than the "choker" I arrived in Vienna wearing. We made love until the light was gone. We shared a bath and dressed and had a small dinner, and then crepes and fruit with champagne, and then small glasses of pear brandy, which had been a favorite, she said, of her father's. The amber bottle actually held a twig with a tiny pear growing from it.

She said that Herr Sachs was thinking of building another mill in Reichenberg near

Warnsdorf and giving it to one of his brothers to run. He had asked her and Emilie to spend part of that summer in Bohemia. She was not sure about this. The area reminded her of the awful time at the spa years before. Also, the factory was in a part of Bohemia that was largely ethnically German and there had been trouble between the Germans and the Czech workers. If things got worse, the Jews would get it from both sides, from the Germans because they weren't German enough and employed Czechs in their businesses, and from the Czechs, who saw them as siding with the Germans because they were German-speaking, went to German schools, and thought of themselves as German. I was young but not unreasonable. I did not ask when I would be able to see her alone again.

For a few days, Adolf and I moved carefully around each other in our small room. In fact, I thought he might move out, but there was no sign of that. He continued to sleep into the early afternoon, and read and sketch and pace all night with the same nervous energy. He dusted everything as usual with his boric acid powder and spent a whole afternoon and night using carpenter's putty to seal new cracks in the floor and baseboards. We did not speak. I did not expect an apology. I had known him almost four years and had never heard him admit to being wrong, or apologize, once in all that time, not even to his mother.

Then after a few days, at night, while he was at the desk and I at the piano, he said suddenly, without turning, "You've given Frau Zdenek the rent?"

"Yes, of course."

"Good."

"Performances of Gluck's *Iphigenie en Aulide* start in two days at the Court Opera," I said. "Shall we go?"

He paused, then continued sketching.

"Of course. We saw one of Gluck's just after you arrived. Which was it?"

"*Armide*."

"Yes, I do not recall liking it much."

"It was a good production. The opera itself is nothing to write home about. It was a surprisingly poor choice. This should be better."

"Perhaps. The *Völksopera* is preparing a production of *Tristan*."

"You have seen *Tristan*, by your own count, twenty-nine times since you came here," I said.

"Of course. You will accompany me, I trust, to the thirtieth. I am just starting to know it."

"Will I have to revive you once again, if you faint during the opening chord?"

"No."

"Then I will come," I said, and continued playing.

It was a somewhat stiff, strained little exchange. I felt enormous relief.

Later, Adolf would claim to have carried a copy of the score to *Tristan*—as well as the complete works of Schopenhauer—in his pack throughout the entire Great War.

That July, the weather in Vienna was splendid. At my suggestion, we went on a little excursion, a hike in the woods west of the city. Beethoven had lived in these hills during the warm months and composed many of the works of his heroic period here, having mastered his despondency over his approaching deafness and a resulting wish to die. We took the train out to Semmering and from there hoped to walk to one of the nearest summits, the

Rax, I think. No traditional hiking costume—the Bavarian get-up of lederhosen, hiking boots, knee socks, embroidered shirt, hat and feather—and no tagging along with a group of *Wandervogel*, bursting with smiles and Teutonic health and singing about the "Holy Reich of all the Germans." Just the two of us, poor students, in our worn trousers and shirts and old shoes.

It was the first time we had been out of the city. The landscape—after five months in the Mariahilf, with its grime and sooty tenements, dim courtyards, prostitutes, and our own small room with its dank walls, crumbling plaster, and the constant stink of paraffin—had the intensity of a dream. The train wound towards Semmering, listing along the edges of a ravine, and struggling through black tunnels that opened onto staggeringly clear views of the hills and nestled villages. I was bracing for one of Adolf's monologues—how many miles of track, the difficulties of blasting through stone, which *kind* of stone, etcetera, because this was the sort of thing he tended to know by rote. But no! He was like an enraptured child, staring out at the forests of birch and pine, outcroppings of rock, and the distant fields below us, streaked with the color of the first wildflowers of the season.

By the time we left Semmering on foot, though, and reached the summit of the Rax, the sky had clouded over. This is a part of Austria famous for its dramatic and unpredictable weather, the floods that will suddenly sweep through a valley and wash away half a town. We hiked down the side of the Rax as fast as we could but the storm caught us. The rain fell in sheets and soon was streaming down the hiking paths with such force that it could take your feet right out from under you. After fifteen minutes we spotted a hut—the hills there are dotted with these "hiker's huts"—and crawled on our hands and knees some fifty meters up the side of the mountain.

The huts were meant to be used as resting places for climbers, and also to spend the night during longer hikes or if one was caught on the mountain at nightfall. They had no windows, a few bales of hay, and roofs covered with tarpaper. We were drenched. Just taking a step would squeeze rainwater out of our shoes. We ducked inside and I pulled the door shut and latched it.

Adolf had begun to shake terribly. His teeth were knocking, he was clutching himself and stamping, shifting his weight from one foot to the other, almost hopping, as though he couldn't stop. I asked what was wrong; he seemed unable to answer or even look at me, but simply shook his head and kept stamping. I managed to strip off his shirt and trousers, and removed his shoes and socks, and then I stopped. This was someone who in the seven months we had been living together had never undressed in front of me, at least while I was awake. He kept his informal shirts buttoned to the neck and at the wrists. I couldn't recall ever seeing him in a short-sleeved shirt. In Linz, he had never joined in the naked swimming in the river, or in the ponds near Urfahr beyond the river, which was so common among boys. He would become furious if his younger sister Paula walked in while he was in the bath.

I pried loose his clasped arms and peeled off his undershirt. He held his arms up as I did so but continued to tremble and stamp his feet. He didn't resist. I removed his underpants. He was wet, glistening, all shank, tendon, stringy muscle, bone. Every rib was clearly etched under his skin, and his abdomen was flat, almost sunken. The long hair was plastered to his head and neck. He looked like a dancing skeleton.

I took fistfuls of hay and dried him off as he stood there hopping and shaking. There was a pile of burlap squares, five or six feet wide, in the hut. They were dry. I laid one out, and coaxed Adolf into lying down on it, and then wrapped it around him, with his arms at his sides inside the cloth. I rolled his shivering body from side to side so I could toss the sheet over him, wind it around him, and pull it tight. He was trembling so profoundly that even in this burlap cylinder from his feet to his neck he was knocking against the rough wooden floorboards. I made a bed of hay, moved him onto it, then covered him with more hay.

I stripped naked myself, then wrung out our clothes and hung them over a beam that supported the roof. I dried myself off with hay, made a bed of it, covered it with burlap, lay down and pulled another square of burlap over me. By this time, Adolf had stopped shivering, his eyes were closed, and his breathing was loud and hoarse. I wondered whether I had wound the cloth too tight, or whether I should try to get further down the mountain to the nearest village and to a doctor. I decided no, and fell asleep to the hypnotic drumming of the rain.

In what seemed like minutes, I opened my eyes and sat up. I had dreamed that we were in the cemetery in Leonding in the pouring rain—Frau Hitler, Dr. Bloch, my parents, and I—and we were burying Adolf and his sister Paula. My mother turned to me and said, "Now there are six." But there was Adolf, standing in the doorway of the hut. He must have rolled out of the burlap; it was thrown over his bony shoulders like a cape. He was looking out over the marvelous landscape and foothills of the Rax. The sun was rising and the air had the electric clarity of air in the mountains following a hard rain. It was like breathing ether. I realized that in the years I had known Adolf and then lived with him, this was the only time I had seen him awake in the morning.

My first term at the Conservatory ended in late July. I received honors in two of my classes, composition and harmony, and several of my songs were performed at the student and faculty recital held at the end of each semester.

My parents came to the performance. This was a small triumph for me. My father had been worried that I might not be admitted to the Conservatory and that if I was I might not be able to handle the courses, because of my lack of truly formal training in Linz. Reluctant to leave Vienna and Adolf, I would end up working as a journeyman upholsterer in one of the large Viennese sweatshops, or trying to scrape by as a violist or pianist in the cabarets or cafés that featured musical entertainment.

It was a vindication for Adolf, too. My father had worried that his reasons for recruiting me were purely selfish and his high opinion of my musical abilities suspect. "Try not to join our Tribune in his fantasies," he had told me. My mother was worried for the same reasons, and because she worried about everything I did. In the metropolis of Vienna, I think, she expected me to end up an unemployed, syphilitic wreck at nineteen.

Adolf joined my parents and me backstage after the recital. My mother, doing a poor job as always of hiding her concern, whispered to me that he seemed thinner than when he left. My father asked me to invite Adolf to stay with us in Linz for a few weeks during the summer; one of his new clients was a Linz clothier who would "fix him up," and my father would foot the bill. I had not told them that Adolf was not a student at the Academy of Fine Arts.

I planned to spend August and September in Linz. The night before I left, we went to see Gluck's *Iphigenie* at the Court Opera. We both liked it, stood through all three acts, and I paid the *Hausbe-sorger* his twenty heller to let us into the building after the "curfew." I slept, Adolf read. I remember, as I fell asleep, listening to him pace and recite under his breath—from what, I can't recall—passages he was committing to memory.

The following afternoon we stood on the platform of the West-bahnhof. I put my suitcase down (this time it did not smell of cheese and smoked meats). I did not know what to say—we had said little and avoided looking at each other in the few blocks from the Stumpergasse to the station. Adolf stood erect, hands clasped behind his back, chin up. He seemed to be searching the gray sky for an appropriate passage to quote. Suddenly he grasped both my hands, gave them a hard shake, and whispered, "Godspeed!" He turned and walked away briskly, almost breaking into a trot, and disappeared into the crowd milling on the platform.

At home, I let my mother spoil me. I ate like a pig. My clothing was mended and I acquired several new white shirts and a new suit for recitals and opera-going from the same clothier my father had promised would "fix up" Adolf when he visited. I was asked to play in several chamber recitals at my old music school, where as a local student at the national Conservatory I had become some-thing of a celebrity. I even had a go at the massive *Die Welt als Wille und Vorstellung*, Schopenhauer's great tome. Wagner was our god, Schopenhauer was Wagner's god (he was said to have reread the entire thing every year), and I couldn't make head or tail of it. Here and there a passage on music and death or the wisdom of resignation made some vague, passionate sense. Schopenhauer said that to understand him one first had to understand Kant, so I obediently obtained, from one of Adolf's old lending libraries, a volume of the great Kant of Königsberg. It was impenetrable. I would rather have read about the Sodomite apelings and their attempts to copulate with the electric god-men of the North. Or about the World Ice Theory, which had also attracted my whimsical roommate's interest.

I spent several hours each day in my father's shop, taking down old sofas and chairs and the other larger pieces he had been asked to rebuild and reupholster. But he did not press me to spend a full day with him and even discouraged it. He seemed to sense that I had worked hard during the semester and needed a rest. He had seen the Conservatory with its towering colonnade of red marble and gilt murals of Orpheus and Eurydice, he had met my professors, he had heard my songs played at the year-end recital, and in his quiet, undemonstrative way he seemed quite proud. And a little surprised. When I was taking down an old splintered sofa bristling with nails a bit too roughly, he cautioned, "Slow. You must not risk injuring your hands."

I received a nice letter from Emilie Sachs, thanking me for my help. She was applying to the University in a year but in the meantime asked if we could resume our lessons when I returned in October.

Frau Sachs and I had not met privately since Emilie's return from her visit to her father in June. Still, I stayed for dinner sometimes after lessons—arousing Adolf's suspicions—and Frau Sachs and I treated each other with an ironic and knowing courtesy which I found immensely satisfying. Did Emilie notice? Did she suspect? Perhaps; perhaps not. At that time, in that place, many things were glimpsed, suspected, winked at, and went unspoken. As I have become older, this is an attitude I have learned to appreciate, especially after years under Adolf's National Socialism and the "Nazification" of Austria. It is an attitude of discretion and tolerance which I still associate with money, with culture, with big cities. It is not an attitude one comes by easily in Eferding, the provincial town west of Linz where I have been forced to spend most of my diminished adult life.

I received a letter from Professor Georg Gauthier, one of my performance teachers—the Vienna Symphony was in need of a second violist for rehearsals and some performances. It was a commitment, but it came with a healthy stipend and would, he was sure, leave me time enough for my Conservatory studies. The contact with professional musicians and conductors alone could prove useful. And the additional money would allow me to help Adolf. We could move to a larger place, possibly outside the Sixth District altogether, with a little sunlight and fewer *Wanzen*. Not quite the *Conservatoire*, but a step up.

The same day I received a letter from Adolf—"Dear friend! My dear Reczek!" He asked me to send him *The Guide to the Danube Town of Linz* by Krakowitzer—"much more detailed with more accurate scale than the one published by Worhl"—and demanded information on the new Bank of Upper Austria and Salzburg in the center of town—"Is there a photographic postcard? Send one, please!"—as well as the new Post Office building, and railed against "the bumblers and fools on the Committee for the Delay of the Rebuilding the Opera House, that Old Shack and Eyesore." He was still rebuilding Linz, in his head! "The nights have been very warm and the *Bettwanzen* are restless," he wrote. "I am fighting murderous battles with them! They prefer my blood, Reczek. Perhaps they are little Teutons and themselves seek the Holy Reich of All The Germans"—an uncharacteristic touch of humor which I found encouraging. He ended, as always, "My best to your esteemed parents! Please extend my thanks to your always concerned mother for her package of cheese and cakes. They were gone quickly."

He did mention that he was "writing a good deal. A play that will perhaps transpose the heroic ideals of old into a modern setting." I winced. Heroic fantasy and myth, I thought, were a gold mine for Richard Wagner; without Wagner's vision and titanic talent, they were a straight route to failure and obscurity. I had continued to encourage my friend to send pieces of cultural and architectural criticism to the *Neue Freie Presse* and other—legitimate—newspapers, but as far as I knew, he sent nothing. What was it? Was it his pervasive scorn for the accepted institutions of Austrian life? A fear his stuff would be rejected by the "academic crowd," the "righteous gatekeepers," as he called them? I did not know. I was reluctant to press my case.

One day I received a letter with a postcard enclosed displaying a photograph of the town square of Freiberg in Moravia. It was from Frau Sachs.

Dear Herr Reczek,

I have taken the opportunity to escape the Viennese heat and I am visiting relatives in Freiberg. Emilie is with me. I want to thank you for the patience and diligence you showed in teaching my daughter during these past several months. I will have you know she finished the year receiving distinction in all subjects. She would be terribly embarrassed and angry with me if she knew I had mentioned this to you, as she considers such honors "meaningless."

I know you are not foolish enough to regard these things with scorn and wise enough to regard my daughter's strong-headedness with amusement. In any case, I am quite proud of her. Along similar lines, I was delighted to see that three of your Lieder *were included in the July recital and consider them good examples of your work. There is more to come, I'm sure. As you know, plans to nationalize the Conservatory have gone ahead. This should not interrupt your training in any way and can only add to the Conservatory's prestige, even if it makes some of us sad.*

If your good father is in Vienna on business (as you said he sometimes is) this fall, you should bring him to the apartments to see the redecoration. He would be pleased to know, I'm sure, that you are neglecting none of your talents.

With all hopes for an enjoyable summer,

Fr. Adele Sachs

Frau Sachs's restraint was an interesting contrast with Adolf's more dramatic and exclamatory style. I stood in the doorway of my family's home staring at the photograph of the tidy Moravian town and at Frau Sachs's flowing and impeccable hand, perfectly even, across the sheet of stationery. For an instant, I felt the light-headedness that came over me when I brought my hands to her white, sloping neck as she lowered her head and I started to unbutton her dress.

I went upstairs and lay down on my bed. Adolf's watercolors of the *Conservatoire* and the Villa Eugen were still pinned to the wall. I pulled the Villa from the wall and studied it. Adolf had drawn it in ink and then painted in watercolors. It was not much of a villa. The outside was tan, suggesting stucco, but it was three stories and the top floor bristled with garrets and turrets. A Gothic villa. It was set in the hills outside Linz with no other buildings in sight. It would house a chamber for recitals and a library with specially oversized shelves to hold scores. Well, Adolf had said when he presented it to me, are you going to desert the *Conservatoire* for your villa, or perhaps spend time in each? We decided that I would spend August at the villa and visit on occasional weekends the rest of the year. But if I were deep in composition and needed to avoid the distraction of the city and the busy cultural life of the *Conservatoire*, I could repair to the villa at any time. A housekeeper would live there year round.

I pinned the watercolor of the Villa Eugen to its spot on the wall and returned to Frau Sachs's letter. I read it a few more times, following the slanting, perfectly formed cursive (the product, she had told me, of years of training at the *Mädchenlyceum*). I ran my fingertips over the sepia ink. Next to the bed, the volumes of Schopenhauer and Kant sat on my night table like bricks. That afternoon I went back to the lending library and found a few of Mr. John Galsworthy's books in translation and started reading them that day—parents, children, money, sex, love, disappointment, ambition. These I understood.

I came back to Vienna in early October. Although I'd sent Adolf a card, he was not waiting on the Westbahnhof platform, which was unusual. I walked briskly to the Stumpergasse, my suitcase weighed down by yet another food package from my mother. The door to room 17 was ajar. I put down my suitcase and gave it a nudge and it swung open—the room was bare. There was only one bed. Adolf's books and clothing were gone. The wardrobe was empty. The gleaming Boesendorfer was gone.

"Herr Hitler left two weeks ago," Frau Zdenek said. "I thought you knew! He paid his rent through the end of the month and I had gotten your rent money in the post. He thanked me but he did not want to talk. He could barely look at me and he seemed in a hurry. He wouldn't say where he was going—in fact, I assumed you both had found a new room, perhaps one closer to the Art School. I had to have the men from Fegelein's take the piano. I am so sorry, Herr Reczek. Tell me, where am I to find two such tenants like you and Herr Hitler—two artists, completely devoted to your work and your studies, no drinking or smoking or bringing girls, or whoever, back to the room at all hours? In all Vienna, two such young men do not exist. I will find only filth, the same filth."

I recall the first thing that occurred to me when I saw the empty room: I was glad I had taken the sketches from the bench and brought them home; he was gone, I would never see him again, and this is all I would have of him. At home, I had several of his watercolors on the walls of my bedroom—the Villa Eugen, our *Conservatoire*, a redesign of the *Landestheater*, Linz's opera house. Under the bed, in a wooden box, I kept his cards, letters, and dozens of sketches and watercolors he'd given me. I had a close copy of the sketch he had done of his mother on her deathbed, which I had asked for. I never told him about the long conversation I'd had with Frau Hitler only months before she died.

I went to the Sixth District Police Station—any move had to be registered immediately with the police in the district of the new address. It was the first thing one did when moving, even to a sublet apartment or a rooming house. I thought he might have found a cheaper room somewhere in the Mariahilf, but the police had no record of it. I checked with the police in all the less affluent districts he might have been able to afford, even District Eleven, the Leopoldstadt. He had failed to register with any of them.

This did not surprise me. In Austria at that time, all young men at the age of nineteen were required to register with the Army to perform two years of service. I was lucky. Since I was a student at the Conservatory, I was allowed to register for the Reserve Army, to put in my service over the summers when I was not in school, and to serve for one year rather than two. (Of course, in the case of war, like all men of twenty-five years and under, I would be called up immediately.) But Adolf did not register at all, which was considered a punishable crime. I warned him, but he refused. Absolutely. He would never serve the corrupt empire his father had devoted his life to—had, quite literally, been a "servant" of, in his white trousers, blue-and-gold tunic, and pathetic civil servant's saber. This corrupt, decomposing, maggot-ridden corpse of an empire! This Babel of races! (I recall the little speech he gave, pacing and sawing the air with his hand.) I told him he would be found out. By that time, he said, he would be long gone. Then they would deport him, I said. The Austrian bureaucracy was very efficient at certain things, and this was one. He doubted it.

I continued to look. I visited the two or three large lending libraries I knew he subscribed to, but it turned out he had recently withdrawn his membership and of course there was no forwarding address. I went to the Vienna Museum Association, which he belonged to, but the story was the same there. I even went to see that man von Liebenfels. I heard him shuffle to the door in his carpet slippers. He was still wearing his smoking jacket and licking crumbs from the corners of his mouth. No, he had not seen or heard from Adolf recently. Was anything wrong? That would be a shame, as Adolf had expressed such strong interest in his revival of the Order of the Knights of the New

Templar at the Castle Werfenstein. In the meantime, would I like to come in for some strong coffee and a little *Streuselkuchen*? I excused myself and made my way through the throngs of peddlers and prostitutes to the trolley.

Several weeks later, at Christmas, when I was with my parents in Linz, I went to see Adolf's older half-sister Angela, who had taken in Adolf's younger sister Paula after Frau Hitler died. No, she hadn't seen or heard from him and didn't want to. She had heard that Adolf had visited his mother's sister, the hunchbacked Aunt Johanna, and tried to "extort" a loan from her, and that he had "come crawling" to the guardian Mayrhofer and tried to persuade him to release the rest of his patrimony before his twenty-fourth birthday, which Mayrhofer had refused to do. He was a parasite, she said, who thought only of himself and if you—"and people like you, but *especially* you"—had not persisted in indulging his fantasy that he was, or would become, a great artist, that he was special and had a unique destiny, or something of the sort, perhaps he would have found a job with a future like any responsible human being and even contributed to raising his orphaned sister. Instead, with my encouragement, he remained a lazy, selfish, swollen-headed dreamer, a parasite, a know-it-all, the worst kind of—

I apologized for bothering her and left. As I recall, Adolf would later employ Angela, after her husband's death, to run his house-hold at the elegant Prinzregentstrasse apartments he bought in Munich and then at the palatial Berghof, the spectacular "Alpine Chancellery" he built on the Obersalzberg in Berchtesgaden. Angela's daughter, also Angela, or Geli, would kill herself with Adolf's revolver in her room at the Prinzregentstrasse quarters.

At the time, I could think of only one reason why Adolf would have vanished. Shame. He was running out of money. Aunt

Johanna had refused him, the guardian Mayrhofer had refused him. He would continue nibbling the rinds of cheese wheels and stale biscuits and looking more and more like the impoverished, eccentric, self-taught artist and "scholar." A social and academic reject. Soon even standing room at the Court Opera would be beyond his means and he wouldn't have the clothes for it anyway. What he owned was already disintegrating on his back. And without the library memberships he wouldn't have access to the kinds of books he preferred and felt he needed. His halitosis would become positively toxic.

He would not get a job. That would mean submission, it would be the first, irreversible step towards a life he detested. In fact, his defiant refusal to work was as important to his sense of himself as standing through *Tristan* or *Lohengrin* forty times, or his artwork, or reading until the sun came up. In the meanwhile, his roommate would continue his glorious ascent at the Conservatory (the irony of this makes me choke), enjoying the patronage (and favors) of Frau Sachs and the other sponsors and friends of one of Europe's great training grounds for musicians and composers. When I sent him Krakowitzer's *Guide to the Danube Town of Linz*, I had included a note telling him of the possibility of my becoming a part-time violist with the symphony and my plans to move us to a better room and to help him financially. Had this offended him? He was proud and uncompromising, perversely so.

Was he secretly embarrassed by the incident on the Rax, when I had undressed and dried him, and rolled his gaunt, trembling, naked body into the burlap sheet? Perhaps he had some feelings about this, but if he did he said nothing. Otherwise, I had never touched him. Not a clap on the back or a hand on the shoulder.

I knew how sensitive he was about this.

Perhaps, with his near-phobia of germs and syphilis, he worried that he would catch something from me. After all, I had fallen, I had succumbed, I had sullied the "Flame of Life." I had been exposed. Maybe the syphilitic agent could be transmitted through using the same wash basin or tub, or via the blood-sucking *Bettwanzen*, or through the air as he slept. Who knew?

It did not take me long to find a new place to live. I took a room with the family of my third-year classmate Michael Oberhupel, the violinist in our quartet. And a room not in an apartment but in a real house, a home, with a garden and patio and surrounding wall, in the Weiden or Fourth District, closer to the Conservatory.

Several nights each week I dined with the family. Michael had a cork-lined practice room I was allowed to use, and I could sit on the patio on Sunday mornings in the summer, scanning the essays and reviews in the *Neue Freie Presse* or pretending to read Schopenhauer. After six months in that grimy room in the Mariahilf with Adolf, I could breathe. Frau Oberhupel bought me a dinner jacket to wear when the family had one of its "evenings," at which our quartet sometimes played. It was here, in this house, that I would meet my wife, Sabine, who was giving music lessons to the younger children. On our first real date, I took her to see *Rheingold* at the Court Opera. We did not stand.

I knew Adolf could contact me at the Conservatory, if he wanted to. Under the circumstances I doubted he would. After six months at *Haus Oberhupel*, I again checked with the police in those districts where I thought he might be living. He remained unregistered. Of course, if he were homeless or living in one of the crowded men's shelters, he would not be required to register, and I assumed that something like this had happened. My friend had disappeared into the vast, teeming squalor of the city. It would be thirty years before I would see him again and learn the truth.

them on, promptly, to the next man on the list. Since we have several copies of each, on most days any man who signs up will have his time with them. The Americans consider this important; it is a way of participating at a distance in the democratic "reconstruction." More to the point, the trials in Nuremberg are beginning to dominate the news.

I have made my own contribution: a "concert series," held every Wednesday afternoon. Colonel Lewis has procured a phonograph, and my wife has brought part of my record collection from home. I give a brief talk beforehand, play the piece, and talk a bit more. Wagner is "off-limits"; he seems to be regarded as the court composer of the Third Reich. Bayreuth was clearly identified with Adolf and the Nazi regime, and apparently Wagner's music was played over loudspeakers in the concentration camps as inmates were marched to work. I have offered to play excerpts from *Tristan*, an opera devoid of German chauvinism, but Colonel Lewis has said no. He has also asked me not to play pieces composed or conducted by musicians associated with the regime—Strauss, von Karajan, and Furtwangler in particular. Bruckner, my landsman from Linz, is permitted.

This is not exactly the role Adolf had envisioned for me when we were roommates in Vienna and he had me leading the "Reich Mobile Orchestra"—a full-sized professional orchestra on wheels—giving lectures and conducting symphonies and chamber pieces of my choosing. I am the *Capellmeister* of Glasenbach, giving my little talks to a drowsy handful of the more or less "incriminated." And they *are* drowsy. Routinely, several of them doze off during my introduction or during the music. They ask few questions. One of them—Koppenberg, the former, and now massively obese, president of the National Socialist Cycling Association—snores openly. They are not convincing representatives of "the most musical race in Europe." Sergeant Hardie, the mathematics teacher who is my acquaintance among the guards, listens and asks perceptive questions about harmony and orchestration. Privately, in the library, we listened to Mozart's 39th Symphony, which I used to illustrate points I have made previously in our talks.

This morning, Colonel Lewis gives us a talk on "The Murder and Enslavement of Civilians." He starts with Dachau, the camp for political prisoners built only a month after Hitler became Chancellor in 1933; then he discusses the mass shootings by the SS squads in the East, the use of mobile gas vans, the herding into ghettos, and the construction of the first camps at Chelmno, Belzec, Treblinka, and elsewhere, which used gassing and cremation. He describes the massive deportations later in the war to Auschwitz, Majdanek, and smaller camps, and the increasing use of slave labor from the conquered territories as more German men were conscripted into the army. He also discusses the "euthanasia" program within Germany, the gassing of the handicapped and mentally ill.

Much of this we have heard before (although the "euthanasia" program inside Germany is new to me). This time, though, he includes photographs we have not seen, projected onto a sheet at the front of the room: excavated mass graves in Polish forests, the unloading ramp at Auschwitz, inmates used as subjects in "medical" experiments, "operating" rooms, the "showers," the ovens, a freight car that arrived with all its human cargo dead. There is also a photograph of Russian prisoners of war in a field: countless frozen stick figures and tattered clothing covering a snowy landscape all the way to the horizon. There is a warehouse the size of a football field filled with women's hair (7.7 metric tons worth, the Germans had weighed it). Another photograph shows a workshop of some kind in one of the camps; on a table is a row of naked decapitated bodies, on the floor alongside a large metal tub holding dozens of shaven human heads, like a bowl brimming with apples. What is especially distressing is that the eyes of many are open, the lips drawn back and the teeth showing, the faces set in a fixed, smiling grimace. Schlosser, my bathmate and Kaltenbrunner's adjutant, stares at the floor.

Colonel Lewis turns on the lights and asks "Reactions? Questions?"

Lange the chef seems dazed. He looks like he has been hit with an anvil.

Jobst the lawyer, who thinks he speaks for all of us, is as usual the first to raise his hand. "This is all very unfortunate," he says. "But who knew? Who *could* know? As you say, this was not advertised."

"Still," the Colonel says, "people were disappearing. That much was clear."

"Yes, but to be resettled, perhaps. You obviously have never lived in a dictatorship. Information is tightly controlled."

"True. But this happened on your doorstep. In your name. As a result of policies with which you were familiar. That is something to think about."

Back on the ward, during our cigarette break, we mill about the high windows on one side of the room and look out over the grounds to the perimeter fence fifty yards off. The sun is high, there is a growth of new grass, and wildflowers, little dots of color on the rocky soil. It is a bright day, a beautiful day. On the far side of the room Dincklage the clerk paces with intense concentration, head lowered, hands clasped behind his back, and calls out "Bad Hofgastein approaching!"

Jobst the lawyer twists his cigarette out fiercely in the ashtray on the windowsill. "The photographs are doctored," he says. "That is obvious. It is simply too grotesque. What do you know of the Americans' intentions?"

"Intentions?" Burckhardt the Farben engineer says. "That is why thousands—hundreds of thousands—fled west from Breslau and Königsberg and elsewhere, desperate to surrender to the Americans rather than the Russians?"

"The lesser of two evils," Jobst says, lighting another cigarette. "The Russians are animals. Lower than animals. You know that."

"I know I saw a field covered with dead frozen Russian prisoners," Burckhardt says. "Like matchsticks. There were so many you couldn't even see the earth, or make out the bodies. It looked like an abstract painting."

"That was what you were told you saw," Jobst says. "*Greuelmärchen.*"

Greuelmärchen—literally "strange" or "gruesome fables." This was a favorite expression of Goebbels'. He used it first in a famous speech in Vienna, right after the *Anschluss*; he was referring to reports that hundreds or thousands of Viennese Jews were committing suicide. It found its way into radio propaganda, in response to claims by foreign governments regarding the treatment of Jews and other minorities, and also political opponents, inside Germany.

Burckhardt is smiling and staring out the window. He glances over his shoulder at Jobst, then turns slowly. "So who is today's fount of truth, the 'Reich Plenipotentiary for Total War'?" he says. "Excuse me, Herr Goebbels is not here to speak for himself. His notion of 'total war' was to kill himself, but only after first making certain his loyal wife had killed their six blond children and then herself. More *Greuelmärchen*? Truth?"

"According to your *Berliner Zeitung*, which is written entirely by the Americans and British."

"Yes, of course. 'History from the winners'."

"That is exactly right."

Burckhardt has taken a step towards Jobst. Lange places a restraining hand on his shoulder.

Sergeant Hardie watches us from across the room. He is perfectly still. Dincklage the clerk has stopped his pacing.

"When I was in Frankfurt"—Burckhardt, who is older than most of us, was conscripted towards the end of the war and taken prisoner—"we ate the same rations as the American soldiers, we had access to the same doctors and medicines, we were given a place to shit, we slept in identical barracks. We were not herded inside a fence like animals in a field and left to starve or freeze to death. Or be eaten. *That* is truth. That is history."

"Because it—"

"Because it 'suited their purposes,' their 'program.' You've said that, yes."

"In any case," Jobst sighs, looking out the windows into the distance, "we are not responsible."

Burckhardt laughs, grim, mocking. "Of course," he says, "we are not responsible for what never happened. You are not responsible. I am not responsible. Hitler is not responsible. Schlosser and Reczek and Koppenberg are not responsible. Who is responsible?"

He stubs out his cigarette, shrugs off Lange's hand, which is still resting on his shoulder, and leaves the room. Sergeant Hardie watches him closely but doesn't move.

We listen to the ward doors squeal on their hinges and flap closed. There is a long silence. Finally, Dincklage the clerk, as if to no one in particular, says "Do you think Hitler knew?"

We turn, a little surprised. It is rare for Dincklage to interrupt his "tour," and—other than announcing his next "destination"—he generally says little.

Schacht, a low-level aide of von Schirach's in Vienna, throws his head back and opens his arms. "If *only*—"

We laugh, ruefully.

After the *Anschluss*, there was a saying, *Wenn der Führer das Wüsste*—"If only the Führer knew." People would shake their heads and say this after hearing about some wrong, a case of corruption or a grave injustice, about which there was no recourse. The expression was common in Germany as well.

"What does it matter whether Hitler knew?" Schacht says.

"It is not the whole thing," I say. "But it is not unimportant. It is something."

Several of the others nod.

The following day, I tell Sergeant Hardie about the presentation and ask whether he thinks Hitler knew.

"Well," he says, "what do you think?"

Ah! Just like the Americans: turn the question around. But that is what they are taught to do. I understand that.

"I think," I say, "I think that in this sort of society, or government, it is unlikely that much would happen without his knowledge or direction. But there are others who think, assuredly, that he did not know and could not have known. That he never would have permitted it. That the SS was a state within a state and Himmler was a powerful man."

"And do you believe that?" Again.

"At times I don't know what to believe."

"Well," Sergeant Hardie says, "if you believe that, then there is a structure spanning the East River in New York City in which I would like to sell you shares."

I look at him.

At that moment, the doors to the ward swing open and Colonel Lewis and two other officers walk in.

Sergeant Hardie claps me on the shoulder. "I'll explain later," he says.

I have thought about this. Am I the sort who would buy a share of the Brooklyn Bridge in New York? Am I really that credulous? Another hero worshipper? Another face in the crowd along the side of the road, cheering and gaping like an idiot? A dupe? Do I believe something simply because someone else believes it with great strength and conviction? When Adolf would quote Schopenhauer and Wagner and Fichte—sometimes at length, often from memory, always forcefully—in our room on the Stumpergasse, pacing and sawing the air with his hand, how much of it did he really understand? In architecture and art, I could see his tastes were a bit narrow, repetitive, overblown really, even though his grasp of detail was impressive for someone with no training. In music, I knew he knew Wagner and not much else. That was certain. But he knew every passage, every note, every word, every orchestral effect, every aspect of lighting and stage design. It was astounding. Did he really not see the overreaching and tragedy and resignation, until he was forced to live through it himself? Even then: Our curriculum here includes his "Last Will and Testament," dictated hours before he put a bullet in his head. It is filled with clichés about German destiny, predicts the future "radiant renaissance of National Socialism," describes the German cause as the "most glorious and valiant manifestation of a nation's will to existence," and ends by blaming the war on the Jews. Jobst the lawyer, of course, doubts its accuracy. More "history from the winners."

Part Three

Linz, Bayreuth, 1938

I HAD EXPECTED HIM TO BE in uniform. Instead he wore a rumpled blue serge suit and tie, and a stiff white collar fastened with an imitation-gold pin. His face had filled out, he was a little stout around the middle, and he wore a toothbrush mustache the width of his nose. He still parted his hair on the right, and it still fell over his forehead. The eyes were the same: clear, luminous, penetrating. He stood in the doorway of the side entrance to the speaker's platform, flanked by two brownshirts with truncheons on their hips. His head was bowed, his hands folded in front of him, and he stared at the floor. There was no podium, just a simple table and chair, and a pitcher of water and a glass.

The hall had become quiet. The man sitting next to me said, "You see that tall fellow in the corner?" Standing below the speaker's platform on the far side was a man in a large, loose overcoat and hat. One hand was thrust into the pocket of the coat and he watched the crowd closely. "That is Ulrich Graf, his bodyguard. He follows him everywhere, he is at every meeting. He speaks to no one but Hitler. His hand is always in the bulging pocket of the coat, wrapped around a revolver."

In September 1921, after I'd been living in the small provincial city of Eferding four years, I was walking home from my office in the Municipal Hall and spotted a notice on a kiosk in the town square:

ADOLF HITLER

Speaker for the National Socialist German Worker's Party

Kindlkeller, Munich

25 September, 8:30 pm

Germany Awake!

I stared at the notice for several minutes. There was no photograph, and under *Germany Awake!* only the image of the single-headed German eagle over a shield. Munich was two hours by train from Linz, and the rough-and-tumble beerhall politics of the city drew a good crowd from among the ethnic Germans of western Austria. Hitler was not a rare German surname, but it wasn't common either. So this is where my friend had ended up— competing with the other shouters in beer cellars for the attention of a few hundred drunken veterans of the Great War!

I had heard about this crowd. They were merciless hecklers, often unemployed, and consumed astounding quantities of cheap beer. Fights would break out, speakers would be tossed from the platform, the police were often called in. There seemed to be hundreds of small right-wing nationalist parties; on any night, speakers from four or five would be scheduled, and they would bring their own cheering sections, complete with clubs, brass knuckles, and the occasional army-issue revolver. Truly a tough, pathetic racket.

How many years had passed? Fourteen? He would be thirty-three.

I decided to go. I took the train and arrived at the Kindlkeller early. It was the typical Munich beerhall: meeting rooms upstairs, downstairs a vast low-ceilinged hall with long wooden tables and benches. At one end was a speaker's platform, raised just a few feet. Rows of folding chairs had been set up in front of the platform, around the beer tables, and in the back of the hall. At eight o'clock the place began to fill quickly. There must have been four or five hundred people; some had to stand. I listened to the conversation around me. It was a strangely mixed crowd: small shopkeepers and their wives, artisans, minor civil servants. Some had never heard Adolf speak, but most seemed to be hearing him for the fourth or fifth time. The beer tables were filled with veterans, big-bellied thick-necked men with cropped hair, working on enormous stone tankards of beer; they laughed and cuffed each other. Busty waitresses in traditional Bavarian peasant dress moved through the crowd, holding up three or four tankards in each fist. What seemed odd was that the first two rows of chairs, by the platform, were filled with well-dressed, almost prim middle-aged women. This did not seem to be their first meeting.

At exactly eight thirty, two rows of brownshirts—very young men, most in their twenties or even younger—filed in and lined the walls on either side of the hall. They stood with their feet apart, hands behind their backs, and wore the same stern, chiseled look. The hair on the sides of their heads was close-shaven. The man sitting next to me said, "These are the men of the Recreational and Sports Division." He seemed perfectly serious. "Look," he said, pointing. And there he was, by the side entrance, in the shabby blue suit, flanked by two of his men, his eyes fastened on the floor. It *was* him. The three of them walked to the center of the platform. The two brownshirts took a step backward, and Adolf stepped forward to approach the speaker's table, but then stopped. In the audience, a man in overalls had climbed poured himself a glass of water from the pitcher, sipped, looked up. "Would you like to begin?" he said.

A torrent of applause.

"I am a nobody from Vienna. When I was eighteen I left my hometown in Austria and traveled to that ancient capital of German culture, hoping to become a painter. An artist. Perhaps a stage designer for opera. But the Academy of Fine Arts in Vienna, in their wisdom, would not have me. The experts"—he looked down and pointed to the ceiling with one finger—"had spoken. So I eked out a living painting watercolors and postcards. But I studied and I listened and I watched. I learned something."

He paused. His voice—which had been thin and rather high when we lived together—was soft, but rich and deep, and projected across the hall. He brushed his hair back from his forehead and began to pace, but slowly.

"I learned, for one, of the utter squalor in which the average worker and his wife and children live. I learned what it was like to wake in the night covered with bedbugs. I learned the moral squalor of the young daughter forced into prostitution. And I learned, in this school of suffering, to be hard. Did I have a choice? I don't think so." He paused to pick up his water glass; he rotated it in his hand, in one direction, then the other, like a man inspecting the facets of a gem. Then he sipped and placed it on the table. "And I listened. The German of my youth was the dialect of lower Bavaria and I could not learn, or like, the soft, almost effeminate Viennese drawl. I listened to the swirl of languages around me—the yiddling of the Jews in caftans and beaver hats, to the whole Babel of tongues, Czech, Croatian, Hungarian, Italian, Romanian—and I asked myself: Is this German?"

Several in the audience shouted "No!"

"Exactly. So as soon as I could afford to, I came to this most German of cities, this marriage of primordial German power and fine artistic mood. And when war was declared in 1914, I fell to my knees and thanked God for the opportunity to prove, and to shed, the German blood that flowed in my veins. Thus began the greatest and most important experience of my life—but you know this. You know it too well. In the final month of the war, I was gassed, I was blinded. They sent me to a military hospital outside Berlin to recover. It was there, my lungs and eyes still burning from the gas, that I learned of the Armistice. I threw myself on my bunk and for the first time since I stood over her grave and watched the gravediggers shovel dirt on my mother's casket, I wept. I wept for our two million war dead; I wept for the desecration of everything German. And blind as I was, the betrayal was clear. I knew what I must do."

A woman spoke from the front rows. "But would you have war, Herr Hitler?"

Adolf thought for a moment, then he walked from the behind the table to the edge of the platform. In a gesture that seemed almost chivalrous, he bent from the waist. "Madam," he said, "war is terrible. Slavery"—he paused again—"is worse."

The hall erupted in applause. The men at the tables stood, banging their tankards.

"Economic slavery," he went on. "Political slavery. Racial slavery. Interest slavery. And who will rescue us from this slavery? The politicians of the democratic Republic who sold us into slavery in the first place?"

"No!" The crowd was on its feet.

"The Bolsheviks in Berlin?"

"No! Never!"

"The Kaiser?"

"No!"

"The profiteers who import oranges from Italy while you stand in line for bread?"

"No!"

"The Jewish finance capitalists who behind the scenes are doing their best to see that your money is worth less every minute?"

"No!"

He turned, walked back behind the speaker's table, and refilled his water glass. "Sit, my friends. There is much for us to discuss."

He spoke for over two hours. After five minutes, he had the audience's rapt attention; after ten minutes, they were drinking it in; after two hours, they were drunk. He returned to the same themes: the November criminals, the cowardice of the Weimar politicians, the continuing humiliation of Versailles, the menace of the Bolsheviks, the treachery of the Jews, the malice of the Slavs, and, finally, the capacity of Germans for heroism and sacrifice and the role of Germans as creators of culture. There was no mention of Sodomite apelings or the plight of the Aryan penis. At one point, describing the German soldier being "stabbed in the back," he alluded to "a knife the length of a spear" and then smiled as if to himself, and I smiled: I knew he was thinking of Hagen's spearing Siegfried in the back in *Götterdämmerung*. He moved from sly mockery to thunderous condemnation in the blink of an eye. But the tone always was one of utter sincerity, utter certainty—as it had been with me. Often, he would pose a question and then answer it in a series of escalating, suspenseful insights, laced with innuendo. He was like a skilled violinist who never allows himself to come quite to the end of his bow, leaving an anticipation of the next note, the next tone. Only in the final twenty minutes did his gestures become more emphatic—splaying his fingers around his throat and lifting his eyes—and he shifted to the frenzied, guttural style that so fascinated and appalled listeners. The Communists, the Socialists, the Jews, all the stabbers-in-the-back, he promised, would be *beseitigt*—got out of the way, removed, literally "done away with." At the time, it did not seem a sinister or inappropriate word to use.

I had debated whether I should approach him after the speech. Would he embrace me? Ask me to leave the hall with him? Try to persuade me to join the party? I decided I would stay hidden in the crowd. I did not want him to know what I did for a living, how I had . . . turned out. It wouldn't have mattered. The instant he finished the speech, the two brownshirts who had flanked him stepped forward, and he turned and left the hall. The two columns of brownshirts poured onto the stage and followed him out the door. The crowd was applauding wildly, shouting, rattling their beer mugs, but he had vanished like some magician.

On the train back to Eferding, I thought about him. Was he still sketching and painting and going to the opera? Then coming home and staying up all night to redesign the entire production? Did he go from the beerhall to his room to read and draw and and pace and hunt bedbugs? Was politics simply how he made his living? The uniforms of the thuggish young men and the fighting—none of that surprised me. This is how it was at the time. Every party had its own little army, composed of veterans of the first war, for whom violence had become a way of life, and largely uneducated young men out of work. You came to the speech and then out into the street to fight the Reds! Even private companies without any political purpose had their own "units," or *Freikorps*, to protect the plant, to intimidate, to deal with the unions and with recalcitrant workers.

I felt a tightness in my chest, remembering the disciplined, unhesitating way the uniformed boys grappled the man in the overalls, the piston-like rhythm with which the one who held his neck kept punching him, the sound of the skull hitting the wall— you could hear the heavy *thunk!* even over the shouts and cheers of the audience. When I left, I followed the thin trail of blood from the wall, across the back of the hall and out the door, down the stairs, and into the street.

When I got back to Eferding, I went up to our attic. I pushed aside the boxes and trunks until I found the trunk which I knew held Adolf's cards and drawings. I had kept them in my parents' home while I finished Conservatory, while my wife and I were in Marburg, during the dark days when we tried to find work back in Vienna, and I retrieved them once we were settled in our own home in Eferding. I had never shown them to my wife. I removed the tissue wrapping and sorted through them: the large, triptych-like cards from his first trip to Vienna, the letters and cards from Vienna in the months before his mother's death, and the dozens of sketches and watercolors—the Villa Eugen, the *Conservatoire*, buildings and sights in Linz and Vienna, a whole set of stage designs for *Walküre*, a watercolor of Semper's Burgtheater—a building Adolf already considered an example of neo-Classical perfection—with a startling gold domed roof, and at the bottom of the pile, the bloody, smoking scenes of Wieland's revenge and triumph. I rewrapped them carefully and put the suit-case back in its place, hidden by the trunks, cartons, the bric-a-brac and random objects that filled our attic. One of these was the hard leather case that contained my old viola.

Nine years before, in 1912, I had graduated with distinction from the Conservatory, and I was offered a job—a real plum—as second conductor of the Opera at Marburg on the Drau. This small city was "the perfect place to cut your teeth," as one of my professors told me, perhaps an hour by train south of Graz. It was more than three-quarters Austrian German, and its cultural and public lives were entirely in German hands. With the prospect of a salary, Sabine and I married.

The director of this small but competent company was old and declining rapidly, and within a year I was first conductor of most productions. I took Mahler as my model—I even acquired pince-nez to make myself appear a little older and more Mahler-like. I was exacting and uncompromising, but not cruel. I insisted that the players have a thorough understanding of story and character and the emotional context of every line of dialogue. I did away with the cadenzas and embellishments that were so popular with singers at the time, and stressed rigorous attention to the score. I combed my hair straight back, grew it longer, and let it become, well, a little artistically disheveled, especially while I was conducting. I tried to fit more Wagner into the repertory, but this was difficult as even *Dutchman* and *Meistersinger* required a larger orchestra and chorus, more first-rate singers, and a larger space than we had available to us. I often imagined that Adolf was in the audience—this time, sitting. (Later, I would learn, that this was the period when he was living in the Mannerheim, the men's hostel in Vienna.) At the end of my second year,

I was offered a job as second conductor of the Opera of the City Theater of Klagenfurt, a step up, and I took it.

But war broke out in 1914, and within a few months I was part of a division of the Austrian army fighting the Russians in the Carpathians, with winter coming on. You know that my lungs had never been good, and my endurance was frankly poor. I contracted double pneumonia, was sent to a military hospital in Hungary where I spent more than eight months, and from there was sent back to Marburg to wait out the war. Even after I "recovered," I could not walk more than thirty meters without becoming short of breath. The doctors recommended a sedentary job. Not that it mattered—by the end of the war, the Klagenfurt Opera had been disbanded and Marburg was no longer part of Austria.

At a loss, my wife and I moved back to Vienna for a while. Half the city seemed to be starving. There was no fresh meat or vegetables. The butcher shops were empty and should anything worth eating appear on the shelves it was gone in minutes. I took any job I could find—I played piano in the cabarets and cafés that were still open, I played viola in the orchestra pit of a cinema featuring American silent comedies. At night, I played Strauss waltzes and tunes from operettas (oh, God) on an old upright in the parlor of a "hotel" or brothel. Now and then I'd slip in a little Brahms or Schubert, but the dancing whores would put their fists on their hips and glare at me. Prostitution was still thriving in Vienna; after all, in these times, what else did one have to sell? From another point of view, what else was there left to enjoy? The more enterprising girls on the streets, taking a cue from their colleagues in Berlin, had begun wearing items of clothing—green boots with gold laces, scarlet boots with black laces, and so on—to denote the particular perversions they specialized in. I suppose the Conservatory students had even more information to exchange in the canteen when they weren't battling over Brahms and Wagner, and now Schoenberg. I can't imagine what must have been going on at the Spittelberggasse.

I went to see my old professors at the Conservatory. While they were sympathetic, none had any suggestions for employment other than finding what private students one could. Professor Epstein gave me a few names but could promise nothing; Stefan, who on graduating from the Conservatory had taken a job with the Vienna Symphony, had been killed at Ypres, and the old man seemed empty and distant. I even considered visiting Frau Sachs, whom I had not seen in the six years since my graduation, to find out whether she and her friends were still hiring musicians for their "evenings," but decided against this. The truth is I was ashamed. When I took the job in Marburg, I imagined, I daydreamed—I wince to think of this now—that I would work my way back to Vienna: Marburg, Klagenfurt, Graz, Salzburg, then Vienna, even as a guest conductor. I would have a seat held for Frau Sachs in one of the front rows; after I took my opening bow, before turning to the orchestra, I would pause, look directly at her and smile, then bow one more time, to her. At times the fantasy was positively grandiose: I was conducting the premiere of my own work, a symphony titled "Homage."

Why is it that everyone whose career was destroyed by the "Great" War feels like an out-and-out failure? We might as well blame ourselves for being caught in an avalanche. Still, the result is the same. Even if you are a joke of history, you are still a joke.

After a few months in Vienna, I heard through a friend of my mother's that the small city of Eferding near Linz was looking for

an administrator with a background in music. I applied for the
job and got it. There was a fair amount of boring and repetitious
desk work—seeing that people paid the various town taxes,
dealing with sewer contractors, and so forth—but it also involved
organizing the cultural life of the city, and in an Austrian city that
meant music. I would be in charge of renovating the city's small
opera house, persuading traveling companies to make Eferding
one of their stops, organizing a subscription recital series, and
devising a music curriculum for the grade schools and the *Realschule*. It was less physically demanding than performing and
conducting, and these jobs didn't exist anyway. I would be a civil
servant! Of course, there was no longer an empire to serve, and I
would have to do without the tunic, saber, and boots. But a drab
suit would do fine and the gray pallor and look of permanent
disappointment came with the job. Plus, I might pick up a few
viola and piano students in the evenings to supplement my
income. My wife would certainly have an easier time of finding
music students in a provincial city than in Vienna, and a metropolis awash in prostitutes wearing green boots with gold laces was
no place to raise children. Also, decent food, farm produce and
fresh beef, was a bit easier to come by in the provinces. My wife
was a better than average cook and she somehow equated having
a stout husband with success in life.

It never even occurred to me to look for other conducting positions. The jobs simply were not there, and even if they had been,
my physical exhaustion wouldn't have allowed it. Mahler died at
fifty-two. On the losing end of a war, what more could one hope
for?

*

The year I saw Adolf speak at the Kindlkeller, our money became increasingly worthless and the notices more frequent and larger (still no photographs); the speeches were now held in the larger halls in Munich, even the Circus Krone. Adolf was no longer a speaker for the NSDAP but its leader. Then, in November 1923, I turned on the radio and heard that Adolf had tried to take over Bavaria. I went out to get the newspapers and tried to piece together what had happened: The Prime Minister of Bavaria, von Kahr, had been holding a meeting in one of the largest beerhalls, the Burgerbraukeller. Adolf and his men, armed, burst in and commandeered the meeting. He forced von Kahr and his ministers into a side room. There, pacing frantically and waving his revolver, he declared himself the leader of a "new Reich" and demanded that von Kahr order the police and army units stationed around the city to join them in a march on Berlin, where they would toss out the government and take over the country—a tactic obviously modeled on Mussolini's march on Rome the year before. The whole thing ended with Adolf and a small band of his people facing off with the police in a square outside the City Hall. A few dozen Nazis were killed, Adolf fled in an automobile, and Göring, one of his top men and a national war hero, was shot, of all places, in the groin. According to one journalist, Adolf was decked out in spats and tails and looked more like a lion tamer or the head waiter of an expensive restaurant than the leader of a political movement.

What a farce! I sat in our kitchen and stared at a photograph taken at night of a crowd being dispersed by the Munich police. Adolf, I was sure, would be caught and tried for treason, and executed or imprisoned for life.

Well, the trial came and for the first time Adolf had a national platform. The stab-in-the-back, the November criminals, the vindication of history, the defeatism of the government, the humiliation and betrayal of the German race—the newspapers carried all of it. And Germany listened. Overnight Adolf became a celebrity, instead of a local Bavarian crackpot who wasn't even Bavarian, as the newspapers portrayed him. At one point, the judges allowed him to orate for four hours without interruption. Even I hadn't listened to him that long without saying *something*. "If your father were alive," I remember my mother telling me, "he wouldn't even know what to say."

Adolf was sentenced to five years' imprisonment in a castle in Landsberg, where he was surrounded by huge parcels of food and sweets sent by well-wishers. He received visitors, dictated *Mein Kampf* (typed by Rudolf Hess on paper and a typewriter donated by Winifred Wagner, the wife of Wagner's son, Siegfried), and after a nine-month "incarceration," he drove off in a new Mercedes provided by one of his wealthier sponsors.

Local branches of Adolf's party began to spring up in Austria, even in Eferding. I would see them on my lunch hour in their makeshift brown uniforms and armbands, handing out flyers on street corners. I never joined. Politics interested me no more than it had when I was practicing on the Boesendorfer in our room on the Stumpergasse, especially the kind that featured torchlight parades and raucous meetings in beerhalls.

Things cooled down for a bit, and one heard less about Adolf, who had been banned from speaking in public after his release from Landsberg. But in October 1929, the New York Stock Exchange collapsed and with it the German economy. For some reason, the more frustrated and humiliated people felt, the more appealing they found Adolf. I suppose to some extent it was that way with me, when I was spending all day in my father's shop covered with sweat and horsehair, and practicing my viola and trumpet and going to our little opera house at night barely able to keep my eyes open.

In August 1931, I took my wife to the cinema to see an American comedy. Before the movie started, we were shown a newsreel which included a report on the annual party rally in Nuremberg. I felt a chill down my spine before I knew what I was watching—the overture to *Rienzi*! He had chosen to open this massive event not with a speech but with this inspiring overture, built around the tender, stirring melody of "Rienzi's Prayer." Years before, I had sounded out the piece on the piano and played it as Adolf croaked out the lines in our living room, and my parents listened, moved by the melody as well as my friend's sincere yet awful rendition. He had also used excerpts from *Meistersinger* as well as the funeral music from *Götterdämmerung* (admittedly not the most hopeful omen, but providing the right note of reverence and solemnity). And the enormous columns of light used during parts of the rally—they were the pillars of light that flanked Wieland as he entered the court of Nothar in the sketches my roommate had done for our aborted opera, *Wieland the Smith*! According to the announcer, Adolf had orchestrated and designed the whole thing, from the opening torchlight parade winding through the 500-year-old streets of the city to the uniforms worn by the Youth League, from the legions of stormtroopers and party officials to the flags and party standards. This wasn't a political event—it was the world's largest and most spectacular opera, and one I had seen a preview of at Stumpergasse 31, door 17, when I was nineteen years old.

Himmler's contribution was *Death and Immortality in the World-view of Indo-Germanic Thinkers*. Riefenstahl, the filmmaker, gave him a first edition of the collected works of Fichte (Fichte, again!), published in 1848, bound in cream-colored vellum, the pages edged with gold leaf and the spines bearing a hand-painted quadrant in red pastel with the titles and volume numbers in gold.

Adolf himself had begun to commission special "Führer" editions, including the complete works of Shakespeare bound in hand-tooled calfskin and embossed with the ever-present emblem of the National Socialist eagle clutching the wreath, flanked by the initials "AH." One of the largest contributors, according to the article, was J.F. Lehman of the famous Lehman Publishing House, who had inscribed over fifty separate volumes, including one that could have come from the pen of that Viennese lunatic von Liebenfels titled *Terminating Reproductive Capacity for Racial-Hygienic and Social Reasons*. Winifred Wagner had sent a priceless contribution: the bound original score of *Lohengrin*.

I put down the newspaper. I remembered Adolf's reading Carlyle's biography of Frederick (and his treating me to a "summary" that must have been longer than the book) in the tiny bedroom crammed with books off his mother's kitchen in Linz. I could still see the books from the lending libraries in Vienna stacked neatly in our room on the Stumpergasse, and his handling the two volumes Herr Sachs had lent him with a special cloth, turning the pages with a single fingertip to avoid leaving prints. You'd think they contained some magical and pristine substance. He treated them the way I treated the big Boesendorfer grand.

I found a sheet of blank stationery (I cringed at the thought of using the town's official letterhead) and composed a brief letter congratulating him on becoming Chancellor, and said I was glad to see that the terrific weight of responsibility had not interfered with his devotion to his reading and that his book-loving instincts had survived politics intact. I said nothing about myself. I addressed the envelope—this still amazes me—to Reichchancellor Adolf Hitler, The Chancellery, Berlin, Germany.

Of course, I heard nothing. Then, seven months later, I received this, on heavy, official stationery, from the party headquarters at The Brown House, Munich:

My Dear Reczek,
Only today was your letter of 2 February placed before me.
  From the hundreds of thousands of letters I have
received since January it is not surprising. All the greater
was my joy, after so many years, to hear from you and
receive your address. I would very much like—when the
time of my hardest struggles is over—to revive personally
the memories of those most wonderful years of my life.
Perhaps it would be possible for you to visit me. Wishing
yourself and your mother the best, I remain in the memory
of our old friendship,
  Yours,
  Adolf Hitler

There were no spelling errors and I assumed the letter had been dictated. He had used the familiar and affectionate *Du* form of address. In the upper-left corner of the page was his design of the stern-faced eagle—with the long torso and lower limbs it resembled a man in an eagle suit, its talons around the wreath and the letters "AH." On a separate slip of paper, Adolf had enclosed the name of one of his senior adjutants, whom he said I could contact to arrange a meeting in Berlin or in Munich, where he was still spending much of his time.

I did not contact the adjutant. I could not imagine talking with Adolf again and telling him how things had gone with me since we'd last spoken. I saw myself ushered into an office the size of a concert hall for a five-minute meeting, a brisk handshake, and then finding myself, a middle-aged Austrian desk clerk with thinning hair, out again on the streets of Berlin. I enclosed the letter in tissue, slipped it into a larger envelope, and put it in the trunk in the attic.

Five years later, in February 1938, we would hear rumors almost every day that the Germans were about to march into Austria. Almost everyone I knew expected this and wanted it. Perhaps it would be more accurate to say they longed for it. They had longed for it for years, but union between Austria and Germany had been forbidden by the Versailles Treaty. We were still in the grip of the Depression, almost half of Austrians were out of work, and Germany supposedly now had full employment. (Of course, this depended on conscription into the workforce and massive rearmament, but that is another matter.) Adolf had defied, one after the other, every clause of Versailles; he had redeemed Germany, he would redeem us. And how could he not? He was Austrian! I later read that he had been impelled finally to act by listening to Bruckner's Seventh Symphony—Bruckner, as you know, was born in Linz, raised on a farm outside the city, and is buried there. I had taken Adolf to hear the Seventh at the *Musikverein* in Vienna and he later insisted that I play a piano transcription of it, the entire symphony, on the Boesendorfer in our little room on the Stumpergasse.

Then in mid-March we heard that the Wehrmacht had crossed into Austria. Adolf himself crossed the border at Braunau am Inn, his birthplace, and was said to be driving towards Linz, but as Austrians poured in from the countryside and lined the roads the convoy had become more of a slow procession.

I got into my small motorcar and drove towards Linz. It is hard to say exactly why I did this. I did not care much whether Austria was a part of Germany or not. I had no interest in joining the party, and I did not want to be part of some cheering mob. I wanted to see him. I wanted to talk with him again in the town in which we'd met and grown up, before he died, or I died. As if that could prove that my past had been real, my talent had been real, my life a real life.

The roads were crowded and people were walking alongside the main highway. I had to leave the car on the outskirts of Linz and walk. It was getting dark and people were streaming into the city from all directions, down every street. We could hear an undulating roar in the distance, and as we got closer to the city square we could begin to make it out: *Ein Volk! Ein Reich! Ein Führer!* They were stamping their feet three times with each chant, on *Volk! Reich! Führer!*, and the ground—the streets themselves—was shaking beneath us. Overnight, the city seemed to have draped itself in the red, white, and black banners of the Reich. The sidewalks were strewn with flowers. Behind the thunderous chant, you could hear the continuous peal of church bells; every Catholic church in Linz must have been ringing its bells.

I wound my way along the edge of the immense crowd towards the Hotel Weinzinger, which faced the Danube and where I knew Adolf would stay—he had always admired the building and, frankly, it was the only decent hotel in Linz. The crowd had engulfed the place. A line of official-looking automobiles—mostly open-topped Mercedes—had snaked its way across the bridge and river, up to the entrance of the hotel, and come to a stop. The street and sidewalk in front of the hotel were covered with white carnations; where these flowers had been found in the middle of a cold March, I don't know. It looked as though it had snowed.

I approached one of the men in uniform outside the foyer and showed him Adolf's letter and note from The Brown House mentioning the senior adjutant. The fellow frowned at the letter, looked at me, asked me to wait, and disappeared inside. A few minutes later, the adjutant, Albert Bormann, whom I would later learn was the younger brother of Reichsleiter Martin Bormann, appeared and handed me back the letter, which he had stamped and signed himself. He apologized, telling me that the Führer was very tired and was not receiving visitors at the moment, but had decided to spend the entire next day in Linz. Would I come back at two o'clock in the afternoon, bring the papers, and ask directly for him, Herr Bormann? I thanked him and went off to find myself a room for the night in one of the many guest houses that overlooked the river in that part of the city.

Despite all the tumult and people, I had no trouble finding a room. I could not sleep. The crowd did not leave, it grew; the chanting was ceaseless and the walls of the guest house shuddered. I remember reading later a remark by a foreign journalist, "To say that Hitler entering Austria was received with absolute delirium would be an understatement." The church bells went on ringing all night.

*

Promptly at two o'clock the next day I presented myself at the entrance of the Hotel Weinzinger. Bormann met me, brought me into the foyer, and asked me to sit.

"So you," he said, "are *Hitlers Jugendfreund!*" ("The Friend of the Führer's Youth"—I had already been given a title!) "I have a question for you, Herr Reczek," he said, placing his hand on my arm in a gentle but beseeching way. "Has the Führer always started the day during the afternoon? He seems to wake between noon and perhaps two o'clock, takes a glass of milk or a cup of tea and a slice or two of *zwieback*, collects himself, then speaks first with his senior adjutants, who have been waiting for hours in the corridor outside his door. You cannot imagine what kind of obstacles this presents! Since most decisions must emanate from the Führer himself, the machinery of government simply does not function in the morning. Anyone who understands the importance of morning hours for work in a government ministry will appreciate this.

"For example, a government states its position on the important political events of the previous day after they are published the following morning. Publicity releases, replies, demands, and so forth, have to be prepared in the morning for an afternoon press conference or before the afternoon newspaper deadlines. The daily Armed Forces Communiqué often isn't ready for the two o'clock news broadcast or even the afternoon newspapers. Lunch takes place at four o'clock and dinner at midnight! On any given night, some of us might be asked to join the Führer for tea and cake, and, of course, to listen to the Führer. But this might go on until three or four in the morning. After that, he retires to his study and we sleep for a few hours and go back to work! Don't misunderstand me. I take every opportunity to expose myself to the incomprehensible genius of the man. My admiration is unbounded. But the routine is not efficient, and it can be exhausting! You are smiling, Herr Reczek. You are familiar with this?"

"Yes," I said.

"And?"

"I'm afraid you must take Herr Hitler as you find him."

"May I ask one more private question?"

"Of course." I felt like some kind of oracle.

"Does the Führer have a sense of humor?"

I almost laughed. "Well, yes," I offered diplomatically. "But it is not always evident. He prefers to keep it hidden behind a rather stern facade."

"Our conversation has been confidential, of course?"

"Oh, I assume—"

"*Eugen!*"

I turned. Adolf, with a look of alarmed disbelief, was walking towards me cautiously, the way one might approach a very compelling ghost in the night. He was wearing a tight, single-breasted military jacket, a wide belt with cross-strap over the shoulder, white shirt and tie, dress boots, wide riding breeches, and a peaked officer's cap. There was an Iron Cross over the left breast pocket, I remember. He had been talking with a group of men—all of them uniformed as he was—and spotted me from across the Weinzinger's large foyer. The men had fallen silent and were watching him.

He stopped a few feet away and stared at me with a mixture of gravity and disbelief. "Come," he said. "The suite of rooms they have given me is on the second floor."

He took me by the elbow and led me up the staircase to the landing. We did not speak or look at each other as we walked to his rooms.

No less restless than when I had known him, he paced with his hands behind his back, frowning at the carpet.

"You have not failed, Eugen," he said. "You have been betrayed. There is a vast difference."

I had told him about my last years at the Conservatory, the job in Marburg on the Drau as second conductor and my attempts to expand its repertoire, discipline the orchestra, and attract first-rate singers; and about the job at Klagenfurt, which never materialized after I was sent to fight in the East and ruined my lungs. I told him about my work in Eferding, my attempts to reform the teaching of music in the schools, the recital program, and my most recent project: a small but professional symphony orchestra, which only in the past few months had begun to give regular concerts. He was astonished that I had been able to do this in such a small town and wanted to know every detail—how many musicians, how were they recruited, how well trained, did certain sections outnumber others and if so what was the resulting imbalance in orchestral sound, which instrumentalists were in the shortest supply, what was the current repertoire, could it be expanded to include opera in some rudimentary form? And how large was the hall, were the acoustics adequate, could I describe the design, when was it built and of what materials, were there further plans to renovate and what were my budgetary constraints?

Between us, as I sat on the sofa and he paced, was a cart holding various fruit juices and the sort of sweet nut cakes his mother had made for us as boys. He had told me about his gastrointestinal difficulties, his treatment by Dr. Morell, and his conversion to a vegetarian diet.

"Perhaps," I said, "I have been betrayed by history."

"The betrayal is much more specific. And it will be avenged. It is being avenged and it will go on being avenged." He sighed. "You see the men I was speaking with downstairs? I owe something important to each one of them. They are not unintelligent. And yet they would not sit through *Die Walküre* unless they were being served beer continuously. If opera, if music drama, were performed in beerhalls they would become passionate devotees. A little food and drink and entertainment! You tell me you have failed—yes, you are not conducting or performing—but you are doing everything you can to expose others to the keenest, most concentrated expression of the will known to any human being. More than that, a tool to evoke, shape, and intensify the will. This is especially true for young people, and it has profound implications for the future. For *our* future. Every city or town the size of Eferding should have a symphony and opera, even on a reduced or simplified scale. In a few days, Austria will be absorbed into the Reich. Every aspect of its daily life will be coordinated with those of the Reich."

He slumped into a chair and closed his eyes.

"You must come to Bayreuth, Reczek. It is in August, I can arrange it. The scale, acoustics, performance, interpretation, design is exactly as Wagner intended. I am certain of it."

He reached for another slice of sweet nut cake. "You—you said you have children, didn't you?"

"Yes, three sons. All three are musical—my wife has been instructing them since they were able to crawl. The youngest is fourteen, he may have the makings of a true virtuoso, he already has that kind of facility. The other two—both woodwind players—are just as talented, just as musical, but—well, perhaps conducting, composition, teaching. It is hard to know in what direction things will go. Or where—where life will take you. Their discipline and devotion, though, amazes me."

Adolf got up from the chair, went to a desk, pulled open a drawer and withdrew a binder.

It was a check register. He leaned over it, scratched away forcefully with a fountain pen, placed a daggerlike letter opener on it, and tore across the page. I noticed at the handle-end of the dagger the Eagle clutching the wreath. He leaned over the desk and handed me the check.

"It should cover the secondary musical education and Conservatory training of your sons."

I blinked at the pale green rectangle and saw the hurried, heavily slanting cursive I was familiar with from his letters and postcards more than thirty years before. I held the check in both hands and studied it.

"I'm not sure I know what I can say."

"Say nothing. I'm going to die, Reczek. Morrell says no, but I can tell he is simply putting me off. He is brilliant, he has worked miracles for others but I do not think he will work one now. Half the time I do not know what he is injecting me with. The ingredients seem to vary from week to week, and I am afraid he is at the end of what he knows. Sometimes, at night, my hands will shake for hours." He was up and pacing again. "I am moving too fast for the generals, I am moving too fast for the German people, I am moving too fast for Göring and the others, most of them. But I have no time."

"Why," I said suddenly, "why did you leave? Frau Zdenek said you left only two weeks before I returned. The rent had been paid through the end of the month."

He paused and looked at me. Then he turned to the windows and looked out over the river and the hills beyond, towards the Freinberg, where we had walked that night after seeing *Rienzi*—he striding, his eyes fixed, me trying to keep up and keep my balance on the wet, spongy earth.

"I had been rejected, Eugen. A second time. I had submitted my portfolio again, even added new material, watercolors, sketches we had made for *Wieland the Smith*. They rejected me. Flat. Outright. They would not even let me sit for the examination. Under the circumstances, I couldn't face you. Had things been different I would have stayed. Perhaps I would even have accepted the financial help you were offering, moving to a new place, away from that dank little dungeon on the Stumpergasse."

I rose out of my chair and stood behind him. "I looked for you," I said. "I looked in the Mariahilf, and went to the police station. I looked in the Neubau, the Leopoldstadt, the Landstrasse. I even went to your lending libraries to see if they had a forwarding address. You had disappeared."

He glanced at me over his shoulder and back out over the river. I thought he nodded, slightly. After a long moment, he said, "My God, Rezcek. It is still there. That wretched bridge. It's still there."

I looked down. The wide, low, steel-frame footbridge from Urfahr—the bridge on which we had waited each afternoon at five o'clock for Stefanie—was only a few hundred meters off. Motorcars were using it now and in the bright afternoon light an unmoving line of them stretched across it, stranded by the immense, ecstatic crowds that were still streaming into the city and had stopped all traffic.

"Yes," I said, almost laughing to myself. "It's still there."

Not for long, I thought.

Less than forty-eight hours later, I sat in the kitchen of my home
in Eferding listening on the radio to Adolf address a quarter of a
million roaring people crammed into the Heldenplatz, the
"Heroes' Plaza," where we had stood on my first night in Vienna,
at dawn, watching the forms of the gods assume their shapes on
the roof of the Parliament building, from which he was now
speaking. We had stood there in the early dawn, under a canopy
of chestnuts; except for the lazy *clop-clop* of an occasional milk
wagon, the streets were empty and silent. "It is beautiful," he had
said, staring at the Parliament, "but there are too many steps, and
it makes the building seem smaller and distant." This was one of
the few times I'd heard him say there was too *much* of something
rather than too little. "I would cut them by half, and move the
statue of Pallas Athene back, closer to the colonnade. And shorten
the drive." Perhaps the Parliament was in for a few alterations.

A few days after this, a local party official paid me an unexpected visit to announce that I was now an *Obergruppenführer*
of the new local branch of the "Strength Through Joy" organization. (On meeting the other members of the chapter, I decided it
should have been called "Joy Through Strength.") I was rather
surprised to find myself a *Führer* of a party of which I wasn't
even a member. As it turned out, I wasn't really required to do
anything more than what I was already doing—supervising the
music program in the public schools, organizing recitals, and
running our little symphony.

Amid all the happiness and celebrating, though, disturbing
things were starting to happen. Colleagues of former Chancellor
Schuschnigg's and others active in social and political groups had
begun to disappear, and in the towns and cities in the eastern part
of the country, especially in Vienna, very bad things were

happening to the Jews, often openly, in the streets. There were many suicides. No one spoke about this. I heard it over the BBC, which had begun to broadcast one news program each evening in German. (Listening to foreign programs was somewhat risky, and after a time radios were routinely confiscated.) Of course, in Eferding there were almost no Jews, and very few in Linz. I thought of Frau Sachs and her husband, and Emilie Sachs. I had no way of knowing whether they were still living in Vienna. Perhaps, I thought, they had got out. The library in Eferding had a directory of telephone listings that was several years old; they were listed at the same address on the Josefstadt Strasse, but the telephone number was no longer active. I know because I called it. Visiting the city was out of the question; it was filled with German troops, bands of young Austrian Nazis roamed the streets, and approaches to the city by motorcar were carefully controlled.

I made inquiries and through a friend of my mother's I learned that Adolf had ordered the Gestapo to guard Dr. Bloch's home. (He was still practicing and still known as "the people's doctor.") Dr. Bloch was allowed to sell his house and emigrate to America, where he settled in New York—his daughter and her husband, also a physician, had left Austria for New York less than a year before. Not long after this, Dr. Bloch published an article in an American magazine called *Collier's Weekly* titled "My Patient, Adolf Hitler." It was an account of his experience with Adolf as a young man in Linz and of the terrible circumstances of Frau Hitler's death. It is not in our "library" here, but Colonel Lewis gave me a copy to read, thinking I might find it interesting, since I'd known Bloch and the Hitler family. I thought it quite accurate. I remembered our conversation that afternoon in his consulting rooms, his fatigue, his concern over Adolf's response to the approaching death of his mother. But I was unaware of how deep an impression this seemed to have made. "In all my career," he wrote—and this was a man who was no stranger to death-bed scenes—"I have never seen anyone so prostrate with grief as Adolf Hitler." He even recalled how much trouble we had persuading Adolf to leave the gravesite after the funeral in Leonding.

There was nothing for several months and then in June I received an envelope from The Brown House in Munich. It contained a formal invitation to the Wagner Festival in Bayreuth in late July as a "Guest of the Führer." There were paid reservations at a small hotel in the town of Bayreuth for one week and tickets to five operas: *Tristan*, followed by the entire Ring cycle. The party insignia had been printed on the tickets. I thought this presumptuous as the festival was still run by the Wagner family—in fact, by the daughter-in-law Winifred, English by birth and the widow of Wagner's son Siegfried, who had died only a few years before. Her name had been linked romantically with Adolf's for some time. I'd read that she ran things with a strong hand but consulted Adolf on the choice of conductors, singers, and set designers. Perhaps the insignia simply indicated that mine were "Führer-tickets."

When I got to Bayreuth, this quaint medieval town was bedecked with hundreds of the black, white, and red flags of the Reich; they hung from every shop, home, cottage, and municipal building. I can't say I was surprised since, within weeks of the *Anschluss* in March, most towns in Austria looked very much like this, and all organizations, whether they promoted cycling, singing, gardening, or bowling, had become officially National Socialist. Often, if they involved some form of recreation, they were affiliated with "Strength Through Joy." The Bayreuth book-shops displayed and sold *Mein Kampf* right alongside *Mein Leben*, Wagner's 600-page autobiography, and souvenir shops sold trinkets and flags and even kitchen utensils featuring the images of both men. The festival program itself featured a sketch of The Master, in floppy beret, with the heavy eyebrows and fierce, beakish nose, on the front cover, and one of Adolf, with his toothbrush mustache and stern, far-seeing eyes on the back cover. The streets were full of men in brown or black uniforms who appeared to be always climbing in or out of open-topped Mercedes. They moved with a sense of energy and purpose that seemed out of place in that sleepy Franconian village.

When I checked into the hotel, I was told that I would be picked up in front of the building at three o'clock the next day; it was assumed, I suppose, that I knew who was picking me up and where I was going. When I got to my room, there was a note requesting that I wait outside the hotel at three o'clock; there was also a booklet containing Adolf's most recent speeches to the Reichstag.

I leaned out of the window: The crowds were milling in the cobblestoned streets, and in the distance I could see the wide, tree-lined avenue leading up the famous "Green Hill" to the squat, brick Festival Theater, and off to one side the gardens surrounding Wahnfried, the Wagner family home. I wondered whether when I saw Adolf—I assumed it would be inside the Festival Theater—I should ask him where the line for standing-room tickets was. I remembered the adjutant in Linz asking me whether the Führer had a sense of humor.

The following day I was driven in an open Mercedes up the

Green Hill (the avenue had been renamed the *Adolf Hitler Strasse*) not to the theater but to the family home. The building was stone, all imposing right angles, the sort of severe neoclassicism that appealed to Adolf. Before the car came to a stop at the entrance, Adolf had stepped outside and was reaching for the door of the Mercedes.

"I want to show you something, Rezcek," he said.

There was no foyer. One walked straight into an enormous, vaultlike room whose ceiling was the very roof of the structure. The floors were marble. There were several massive fireplaces. The shelving built into the walls housed hundreds of operatic scores. In the center of the room: the huge grand on which Wagner composed, the keys slightly yellowed with age, the wood lustrous, a colorful throw over the bench, his pair of rimless reading glasses still sitting on the ledge above the keyboard, and alongside a coat-tree from which hung several of the embroidered silk robes Wagner typically wore at home when he worked. In the rear was a stairwell, the stairs Cosima Wagner descended the morning of her thirty-third birthday—Christmas morning—to find a small orchestra serenading her with her birthday present, the just-completed Siegfried Idyll.

Against the wall near the piano was an ivory Buddha seated on a wooden bench, eyes closed, his fingertips touching in his lap. And I remembered that "Wahnfried" meant "Peace (or Freedom) From Illusion." The home was built after Wagner had come under the spell of Schopenhauer, and then composed *Tristan* and the Ring cycle. How strange that Wagner—a revolutionary, a man who tried to impose his will on everything and everyone, for whom no opera house was good enough, big enough, or right enough until he had designed and built his own, who insisted that people not race from their jobs to the theater to see his music dramas but abandon the work of the world entirely and travel like religious pilgrims to an isolated countryside to see and hear his operas as *he* intended them to be seen and heard—would be captivated by a philosophy of such profound renunciation of striving and ambition. Perhaps he really was tired of it all. You would never know it.

"You are Wolf's friend! Herr Reczek!" Frau Winifred Wagner swept into the room in a silk evening gown. She was a strong, broad-shouldered, big-boned woman, but rather handsome. "It must have been a great advantage for Wolf to see my father-in-law's work, at such a young age, in the company of a musician and Conservatory student. Are you a Nazi?"

Adolf held up his hand.

"This is beside the point," he said. "If everyone had Herr Reczek's understanding of your father-in-law's work we wouldn't have needed a party."

"Well, of course that's so. Being a party member guarantees nothing, does it? I've told Wolf that the uncultivated apes he brings with him from Berlin have no—"

"Rough work requires rough men, Winnie."

Adolf seemed to be in a remarkably tolerant mood.

"Perhaps," she said. "But in my book Herr Göring is worth the rest of the lot twice over."

"Yes, you have said that. Herr Reczek, let me show you something."

"Visit us at our box," Frau Wagner smiled.

Adolf took me through a set of glass doors and into the garden behind the house. He glanced at me, and—I thought—almost smiled in a rather weary but understanding way.

"You seem very comfortable here," I said.

318

"I am, Reczek. In the old days, when I was racing between Munich and Berlin, I would stop here at night to tuck the children in and tell them gruesome fairy stories, acting them out complete with sound effects. Then I would allow myself to be amply fed, get a few hours' sleep, and be on my way. The children thought I was some sort of Robin Hood. Perhaps they were right. When Chamberlain was still alive and here, I would talk with him, a little, that is, on the days when he was clear-headed enough. And Frau Wagner is a splendid woman. She was with us from the beginning and believes thoroughly. Her husband was a great disappointment to her. Cosmopolitan, spineless, a homosexual. It has no doubt been hard for her."

"There are rumors, of course—"

He waved his hand.

"There have *always* been rumors. Yes, she has suggested marriage. But that is impossible. I would only marry if I knew that at the end of the ceremony I could put a bullet through my head."

Well, that stopped conversation. After a moment I said: "I am sorry I won't be able to hear Toscanini conduct." At the time, Toscanini was perhaps the world's best known conductor and one of the great attractions of Bayreuth. I had read that he conducted Wagner with the clarity, precision, and understanding of a Mahler. The German critics attributed this to his being a "Northern Italian," or simply "Northern"—in short, Nordic, a misplaced Aryan! The year before he had refused to return to Bayreuth to protest the treatment of Jews and others within the Reich, and he made no secret of this. After his friend Bruno Walter had been prevented from conducting in Leipzig and beaten up, he wrote to Frau Wagner, "These sorrowful events have wounded my feelings as a human being and an artist. It is therefore my duty to inform you that for my tranquility, for yours, for everyone's, it is better not to think of my ever returning to Bayreuth, or to Germany." I have this from one of our books in our little library here at Glasenbach. I recall thinking about Toscanini a good deal as I was organizing our "symphony" in Eferding. I bought every recording of his I could find, I hoped someday to hear him conduct in Vienna or Munich, I knew he had traveled to England and America. I imagined his world to be one of continual, exhilarating possibility. At the time, the German and Austrian press were tightly controlled and all we knew was that he would not be conducting at Bayreuth that year.

"Frau Wagner was distraught," Adolf said rather uncomfortably. "For her sake, I tried to persuade the Maestro to return. I was not successful. Here. Here it is."

At the back of the garden was a clearing and in its center an oval of English ivy. The ivy shivered in the mild breeze; embedded in it was a long slab of polished granite.

Then I noticed the engraved dates of birth and death. No name.

"His grave," I said, under my breath.

He nodded. "And Cosima's."

Adolf bowed his head and closed his eyes, and I bowed mine. Then I felt him grasp my hand tightly, and we knelt, on both knees, our heads still bowed. My heart was racing, and I tried, like an uncertain dancer following his partner's lead, to kneel exactly as he did, solemnly, without allowing myself to be pulled down. We were on one knee, then both, our heads lowered in unison. Adolf's hand was surprisingly soft and damp, but his grip was strong. We stayed this way for what seemed a long time, but probably was no more than a minute. I was afraid to open my eyes and glance at Adolf, and so I determined not to rise until I could feel him either release his grip or begin to rise himself. At some point, his hand fell away from mine and we both got to our feet slowly. I could practically see Wagner's spirit, rising like a vapor from the earth, forming his image, the deeply set eyes narrowed and determined under the shaggy brows, uncompromising, undefeated. And we stood, our hands folded in front of us, our heads bent under the hawkish, implacable gaze of The Master.

I was not prepared for this. In opera houses at that time, the lights were left on throughout the performance, so people could see and be seen. At most they were dimmed. Here, a fanfare of horns from the theater balcony called you in, you found your seat, you could hear all the doors close at once, and the house was plunged into darkness. And then *sound*, gradually, which seemed to come from everywhere at once, and the first light on the stage. The orchestra was invisible—the musicians played in a sunken semicircular area well below the level of the proscenium and covered with a black canopy that somehow didn't prevent the music from projecting with uncanny clarity throughout the theater. At times, it was hard to tell from where it was emanating.

The seats were raked so steeply you were unaware of the person sitting in front of you and oblivious to the persons on either side. There were no columns; every view was complete and unobstructed. You might as well have been asleep and dreaming.

Although the town was draped in the flags and other paraphernalia of the Reich, there was none of this inside the Festival Theater. As you entered after the sounding of the fanfare, you were handed a notice instructing you "at the personal request of the Führer" to refrain from singing the "Horst Wessel Lied" (the unofficial party anthem about a heroic and selfless stormtrooper who, I later discovered, was an ex-convict and pimp) or "Deutschland Über Alles," and not to applaud until the end of the final act. There were no bows, curtain calls, or encores. The conductor and singers would not reappear. There were the dying strains and fading light of the last scene, a pause, and the doors opened simultaneously.

There was also a full hour's intermission between acts. This allowed—encouraged—one to stroll about the Green Hill and nearby woods, which were filled with deer who didn't seem at all startled to find themselves grazing beside dazed and overwhelmed opera-goers trying to clear their heads before the start of the next act. (Adolf had banned the hunting of animals, as well as medical experimentation using animals, within the Reich. He told me he would have banned the eating of animals, too, if he could. "I seem to be presiding over a nation of corpse-eaters, Reczek," he said. Gruesome. A gruesome expression. I've never forgotten it.) During intermissions, Adolf was usually surrounded by Frau Wagner and other members of the Wagner family, as well as his own entourage. Still, he did seek me out more than a few times between acts, and we paced the Hill discussing performance, interpretation, design, and staging the way we had as boys in the night-time streets of Linz and Vienna.

What was there to criticize? The orchestra was no orchestra—it was made up of the best players from companies throughout Germany and Austria. The conductors seemed to have spent their lives studying the scores. The singers were all exceptional, or better. The chorus—especially important in Wagner's works and modeled on the chorus of Greek tragedy—was beyond praise, a single, complex, crystalline voice. Every member was already a leading singer in his or her own company, or should have been. Adolf had a few quibbles with lighting and design—for him, not many. He said that as a policy he refrained from interfering with the choice of conductors, singers, and set designers. He had decreed only that no scene could be seriously abbreviated. Everything that Wagner wrote had to be played. At the end of these talks—usually the guests were staring; who was the thin stranger with whom the Führer was lost in deep and excited conversation?—we would hear the horns and Adolf would say, "Well, that has been enough time for my colleagues to fill their tanks." We would shake hands and return to our seats.

For the final opera of the Ring, I was invited to sit in the Wagner family box, called The Annex. It had been built for King Ludwig—"Mad" Ludwig—of Bavaria. He wanted it angled and hidden so he had a clear view of the stage without being seen by anyone else in the theater. Ludwig's Annex was less a theater box than a small house inside the Festival Theater, poised over the stage on one side, with a window to the outside that could be blacked out with drapes. There were several rows of raked theater seats, but also sofas and refreshments. The adults sat in the first two rows and the children behind them. I sat on one side of Adolf and Frau Wagner on the other.

This time, instead of pacing "The Hill," we stayed in the Annex during intermissions and Adolf explained the lighting. He seemed to have memorized the positioning of every rig and crane, every spotlight and bank of lights, and the entire sequence in which these dimmed and brightened in varying combinations to heighten the emotional and dramatic action of the four hours of *Götterdämmerung*.

He hadn't changed: He watched with the same pale, glistening eyes I had seen in the rapt sixteen-year-old as we leaned against our "posts" in the standing area of the *Landestheater* in Linz. As

Valhalla burned and the gods perished—the end of the world in a Wagnerian torrent produced by 120 players furiously busy under that black canopy—Adolf brought Frau Wagner's hand to his lips and with eyes closed kissed it gently; he then lowered it and placed it again in her lap. It was a curious gesture, one of both exaggerated courtesy and complete submission.

The following day Adolf left Bayreuth. The train of open Mercedes limousines descended the Green Hill from the Festival Theater, the avenue lined with thousands of cheering, saluting people. I wasn't near the front of the crowd, but I could see that Adolf was standing in the first car, saluting one side, then the other. Suddenly, his car came to a stop and the others unceremoniously braked behind it. Adolf opened his door, left the car, and walked briskly towards the crowd. Two rather surprised SS men jumped from the car behind his and followed. The crowd, rather than engulf Adolf, fell back in an awestruck wave, clearing a path for him to walk towards me: He had spotted me from his automobile, among thousands of people. He stopped, took me by the shoulders and said: "*Zur Kunde taugt kein Toter. So leite mich denn, mein lebendes Schwert!*"—"The dead can tell no tales. Then lead me, my living sword!" These are Siegfried's words when he kills the giant, Fafner. I wasn't sure whether he was warning me, exhorting me, or exhorting himself. Perhaps all three. To this day, I'm not quite sure what he meant.

We embraced; he pressed his chest to mine, and, leaning his head over my left shoulder, clapped me on the back with both hands, then the same with his head over the other shoulder—as though he were bussing me. Then he stepped back, looked at me with those pale, penetrating eyes, nodded, and he turned and walked back to his staff car, as the crowd filled in the space behind him, to the edge of the avenue. They left an expanse of several meters around me, as though I now lived inside a nimbus that hadn't existed moments before. A few stepped forward to grasp my hand, others nodded. An hour later, as I walked down The Hill to the town, my heart continued to beat hard and my hands trembled.

The next day, I returned to my desk in the basement of the Town Hall, a large, dusty, poorly lit room which I shared with two municipal clerks. One of my clerks, Herr Fischer, was gone. His desk had been cleared. Herr Fischer was perhaps ten years older than I and had been working in the Registrar's Office longer than anyone could recall. He was an odd duck. He had lived for years in a rooming house in the center of the city, only a block or two from the office, and he was always at his desk when Herr Solmitz, the other clerk, and I arrived. He was the only one in the office who would regularly attend the chamber recital series I'd arranged as well as the performances of our "symphony." The morning following a performance, I could count on an appreciative little appraisal from Herr Fischer, who had studied violin as a child. We would discuss the piece, and I would confide my troubles with the musicians and my battles with Eferding's aldermen over our budget. He used to write stories in the evenings, he told me, and had filled a shelf of notebooks with these over the years; he would cover his table lamp with a towel to keep his hectoring landlady from realizing he was burning the electricity late at night. I would call him "Herr Shakespeare," and he would call me "Maestro." Having spent part of my youth in cosmopolitan Vienna, I thought of him as My Jewish Acquaintance in Eferding.

"Gone?" I said to Herr Solmitz. "What do you mean 'gone'? Fired? Quit?"

Herr Solmitz was hunched over a document.

He threw up his hands impatiently and shook his head. "Frau Kopenik says we should have a replacement within a week."

I pulled open the drawers of Herr Fischer's desk, one after the other: empty. Not only had the desk been cleaned out, the desktop had been polished and the blotter replaced. As I stood over it in the half-light of our basement office, it almost shone; I could see the dark, blurred outline of my looming figure in its glossy surface.

I recalled the word Adolf had used when I heard him speak at the Kindlkeller seventeen years before. *Beseitigt.* To remove. To get out of the way. To do away with.

Beseitigt.

A few weeks later, in the evening, I stopped by the office—I forget the reason—after a performance of the chamber music series I ran. When Herr Fischer's desk had been emptied, his personal belongings had been efficiently boxed, the box wrapped in heavy brown paper, tied neatly with string, and deposited on top of a metal cabinet in the main office upstairs. It would probably stay there for years until someone noticed it; as far as we knew, Herr Fischer had never married and had no surviving relatives in Eferding or elsewhere. I looked at the box. Standing on a chair, I carefully slid it from the top of the cabinet, untied the string, unwrapped it, and lifted the top: a folded muffler and pair of gloves, an old dictionary with cracked binding, a thesaurus, a copy of Pushkin in translation, his own pencil sharpener, a woven bookmark with tassels, and a beautiful Pelikan fountain pen—green bakelite with a gold clip and bands (odd, I had never seen him use it in the office).

There was also a small bound notebook of the sort Adolf used to carry with him when we were boys, with a brown leather cover and heavy, unlined paper. Only the first several pages had writing. They were short entries: a description of people having lunch on the benches outside the Town Hall, scenes in restaurants, sketches of the other tenants in his rooming house, a description of a streetsweeper. There were ideas for stories, an interesting description of Herr Solmitz (referred to as *Der Maulwurf*, "The Mole," for the way he hunched over his work and burrowed into it), and a clever parody of Frau Hornemann, our busty, officious office manager. And a brief entry I appreciated: "To a performance of Eferding's new symphony last night. Mozart's 'Prague.' Not bad under the circumstances." I was surprised Herr Fischer would leave something like this at the office; perhaps he had not meant to.

In the box were also three small shriveled apples. Herr Fischer once told me that our great German poet, Schiller, could not work without the scent of rotting apples. The apples, no doubt, had been found inside Herr Fischer's desk, and dutifully included with the other items. I held one up, examined its wrinkled skin, and breathed in the pungent, half-rotting smell. I sat with that box, and the notebook, for a long time that night. Then I replaced the contents, wrapped it again, tied the string, and pushed it back in its place on top the cabinet.

Just last week, in our small makeshift library here, I read something that interested me. At that festival, in mid-August 1938, Adolf first discussed with his chiefs of staff—everyone who was anyone was in Bayreuth—his plans to demand the "return" of the Sudetenland, that part of northern Czechoslovakia which was almost half ethnic German and also home to the country's coal-mining industry. If England and France would not agree to this, he told them, he would simply move troops in and expel the Czech majority. In fact, he gave them then the tentative order to invade on 1 October, if England and France had not already agreed to the annexation.

General Franz Halder, the leader of the High Command, was certain that France and England would declare war if Adolf went ahead with this, and that Adolf, whom he considered a dangerous amateur, would lead Germany into a war it would ultimately lose. Halder wasn't alone in this fear. Despite Adolf's enormous popularity, most Germans and Austrians were afraid he would provoke another European conflict.

And so, that August, while Adolf and I were strolling the mani-cured hills outside the *Festspielhaus*, Halder met with his generals: If the order to invade was given, they would arrest Adolf and kill him that night—he would be shot "while trying to escape." He was too dangerous to be left alive. A "coup" would be declared and the High Command would re-establish a functioning Reichstag and perhaps the monarchy as well. At this point, all the generals, most of them old Prussian aristocrats, were in agreement. On the last day of September, Halder actually wrote out the warrant for Adolf's arrest. Later that day, Chamberlain conceded the Sudeten-land in order to bring "peace in our time," as the famous phrase went. The troops moved in and the Sudeten Czechs, those who hadn't already left, were either arrested or expelled. The Greater German Reich had become even greater, once more without having to go to war. Adolf's popularity soared. Halder felt that any further attempt at a coup would now be too risky and likely to fail.

*

"Tell me again, Herr Reczek, what you discussed with Hitler in Linz."

The American officers always look beautiful to me. Their uniforms are pressed and fit nicely, their caps folded and tucked under the epaulette on the right shoulder. They have beautiful teeth, large, evenly spaced, and incandescently white. They are polite and nod often. They have never been abusive towards me. They encourage me to talk, they ask questions, they listen, they try to persuade. Except when I am speaking with the American psychiatrist, whom I dislike, I am always cheerfully cooperative, and I think they appreciate this.

"We spoke about my children's musical education," I say, "and my supervising the music curriculum in the schools in my town. We spoke about my mother, who was older and a bit infirm at this point, and also a little about *his* mother—that was always a hard subject for him. She died at Christmas, you know, and he said that each Christmas—he called it the 'Yuletide Festival,' never 'Christmas'—he became very depressed and needed to be alone. We drank fresh fruit juice and ate sweet nut cakes. He wondered why when he bought the same nut cakes in a sophisticated city like Berlin, it was never quite the same. He talked about his plans."

"Plans?" My American interviewers often have a bemused expression when they speak with me.

"Well, you know, how it was possible to expand Linz without ruining its character as a Danube town. He wanted to build two new bridges, very large, over the river, and a Museum of German Art, an enormous project as he conceived it, which was to house paintings from museums throughout Europe. He also wanted to expand the Music Conservatory dedicated to Anton Bruckner—

Bruckner was a native of Linz—and turn it into a true national Conservatory, like the one in Vienna.

"But the conversation didn't concern only Linz. He thought that every large town or city in the Reich should have a symphony and opera in residence, on some scale, of the kind I had founded in Eferding. And that a mobile orchestra and opera company, of real quality, should be established and tour continuously. This was very important to him. He felt that adults could learn a great deal about German psychology—'spiritual' psychology, he called it, to distinguish it from Jewish psychology—from German music, and that exposure to certain composers could color the emotional lives of young people in a positive, helpful way, and even motivate them."

"What is 'Jewish' psychology?" The colonel sits up and strokes his chin.

"I suppose the psychology of Sigmund Freud. He sometimes referred to this as 'materialist' psychology, but I cannot really tell you what he meant by that."

"And 'German' or 'spiritual' psychology?"

"That would be, I think, a psychology which stressed certain notions of heroism and self-sacrifice. But, again, I can't say more than that. It was not something we ever discussed at length, either in Linz or Vienna or more recently. I've never had much interest in such things."

Colonel Lewis sighs. "Tell me again, Herr Reczek, how it is you became an *Obergruppenführer* of the 'Strength Through Joy' organization without ever being a member of the party, at least officially."

"Oh, I was never a member of the party, officially or not. I always assumed it was a request of Adolf's which he passed on through one of his adjutants."

"And what did you do as *Obergruppenführer*?"

"Nothing, really, that I wasn't already doing. The symphony and recital series had already become National Socialist organizations, but so had everything else. They wanted me to start a choral organization, but I knew very little about voice and choral conducting, and frankly I think what they really meant was a kind of 'glee' club that could sing inspiring songs at party meetings, the sort of songs that healthy young men and women sang while hiking. I had no interest in such things."

"Are you aware," he says, very deliberately, "that after you spoke with him in Linz in March 1938, Hitler's entire itinerary was changed? The speech in Vienna was moved back by a day, and the route to Vienna taken by the motorcade changed completely. The concern was assassination."

"I wasn't aware," I say, earnestly, "but I can easily see it. Emotionally the crowds were frenzied. It was frightening, really. People stopped what they were doing and walked or drove to wherever they heard he would be next. And I was surprised at how much direct contact he had with them, from the open car, and getting out of the car to greet them and even talk. With all the commotion and the large and unpredictable crowds, it would have been very easy to kill him. I read that as *Reichchancellor* he spent much of his time in Munich and still took his lunch— for him, breakfast—at the Osteria Bavaria, an unpretentious cafeteria and restaurant there, as he had done for years. If you wanted to meet him, you simply went to this place every day at noon or one and waited for him to come in. He would always exchange a few words. And if you were a pretty girl, he would invite you to join them."

"Were you aware of any assassination—plots?"

"No, of course not. I had no political contacts one way or another. Of course, since I ran the Registrar's Office, I was involved in town politics, but this mostly involved how money was spent."

"If you did know of a planned assassination, would you have told him?"

"Of course. He was my friend."

Colonel Lewis looks at me. I see Adolf standing over his mother's grave in Leonding in the rain, his head uncovered, swaying, my mother and I trying to persuade him to go back to the waiting carriage, until my mother takes him by the shoulders gently and turns him.

Colonel Lewis asks, "Herr Reczek, have you read *Mein Kampf*?"

"Yes? Well, no. Yes. I mean, I tried. Perhaps I got through fifty or sixty pages. I found it tough going. The writing actually reminded me a good deal of Wagner's—sprawling, dense, overblown, very repetitious. As my friend Sergeant Hardie would say, it's a 'real snoozer.' I read somewhere that his original title was *My Three-and-One-Half-Year Struggle With Lies, Stupidity, and Cowardice* and that an editor changed this, simply, to *My Struggle*. I actually didn't know anyone who *was* able to finish it. When we met in Linz, at the hotel, I was afraid he'd ask me about it and I would have to lie and say something favorable that would sound terribly false—he was keen about this, he could sense this sort of thing right away. When we were living together, he was always pressing some book or other on me, and I would make a show of reading it, but he knew. In Linz in 1938, and later at the Wagner Festival, he never asked me about the book, even though I under-

deutschland ("Greater Germany") as it was now being called. Perhaps this was fantasy. He had shown such excitement and detailed interest in what I was doing in Eferding, especially in my organizing the symphony. I could have evaluated the musical life of selected cities, analyzed the music curriculum in the schools, and even thrown in a little analysis of costs, which I had learned a bit about in my administrative capacity in Eferding. When I got home, I made a list of small- and medium-sized cities in Austria which I knew had no public symphony, and began to list every cost of our symphony in Eferding, from musician's salaries—pathetic! most held other jobs—to heating the concert hall, to paying for the sheet music for each section of the orchestra. I even had a plan for every *Völkschule* and secondary school student in the Reich to learn to play an instrument. *Every* student, in a *Real-schule* or *Oberschule* or *Gymnasium*, or even a vocational school. And the percentage would be determined by each instrument's role in a professional orchestra—there wouldn't be twenty million violinists and three contrabassoon players. Perhaps there would be a few more violists than we really needed, but then it had always been a difficult and under-appreciated instrument.

And maybe something like this would have come to pass if the war hadn't intervened and everything been put on hold. Why? Why did he have to do this? Did we really need more space to live in the Ukraine? In Belorussia? Did we need more manganese from the Caucasus? A super-autobahn connecting a Germanized Kiev and *Salzburg*? What would have been the point? We already had almost all of Europe and Scandinavia. England? It's an island, and in any case their finest composer is a German. We could have introduced the glories of German music—and Bach, Bach in particular, especially the keyboard music, infinitely

diverse, intricate, delightful, reverent—to the French "tinklers"!
And the gigantic, engulfing Nordic sound of Sibelius deserved a
wider audience. There was plenty to do.

And then there were his other—preoccupations. Other things.
Beseitigt.

What happened with the rebuilding of Linz? As I've mentioned,
Stefanie's bridge was replaced and the side entering the city flanked
by statues of Krimhilde and Siegfried. (The Allies, of course,
removed this Wagnerian accent when they arrived.) Oh, yes. The
Hermann Göring Steel Works, a lasting cultural monument, *was*
built. The Anton Bruckner Conservatory of Music? Adolf decided
that the best place for this was St. Florian, the vast Benedictine
monastery on the outskirts of the city, where Bruckner had played
the organ and was buried. He threw the monks out and brought
in all of Bruckner's manuscripts, which were in the library of the
Vienna Conservatory, where Bruckner spent his last years teaching.
He restored the organ, arranged for the publication of Bruckner's
collected works, and set up the Bruckner Study Center at the
Conservatory. All out of his own pocket. He even produced
sketches for a new bell tower for the building which would play a
motif from Bruckner's Fourth Symphony, the *Romantic*—a work I
had introduced him to when we lived in Vienna—every hour. The
project went no further. And the centerpiece of the future cultural
capital of Europe, the Museum of German Art? Thousands of
canvases, from museums and private collections throughout
Europe, were stored, waiting, in salt mines—where the Allies
found them, those that hadn't been incinerated in the ceaseless
bombing during the last two years of the war.

There is one thing I haven't been quite honest about, simply
because I haven't mentioned it. When we met in his rooms at the

Weinzinger, Adolf offered to find me a post as a conductor in one of the smaller cities in the Reich—as "restitution," he said. I imagine this would have involved removing someone from his job and installing me, a real nobody. I said no. When I took my first job at Marburg I was straight from the Conservatory. I could read and interpret scores with great facility. I had ideas. I had energy. I had a fine ear, and I had my health. I knew how to deal with musicians. Thirty years had passed; it was not even a matter of being, how do you say, filled with rust and needing a little oil. I would have embarrassed myself and created resentment, too. I thanked him. He seemed to understand.

I read recently in one of the local newspapers that towards the end of the war the Americans bombed Bayreuth—out of spite, perhaps, since it was a town of bed-and-breakfast lodgings and souvenir shops with no military value whatsoever. I had heard this before and assumed that the Festival Theater and Wahnfried had been destroyed. But it turns out this is not the case. Only the back of the *Festspielhaus* was blown off; this part of the building contained the multiple receding proscenia which gave the stage an impression of remarkable depth. The rear half of Wahnfried was wrecked as well. Wagner's desk was destroyed. His music library, the salon, and his 1876 Steinway were undamaged. About the ivory Buddha, I don't know. I suppose he took the whole thing calmly. The Siegfried Wagner House, built alongside Wahnfried by Wagner's son, had become the headquarters of the local Army Counter-Intelligence Corps.

Of course, the Festival was cancelled. The Festival Theater was now an informal shelter for German refugees from the Sudetenland. At the end of the war, the Czechs had expelled them—they put many of the Sudeten German families on trains which let them out somewhere on the edge of the Baltic Sea, where they were told to find shelter and food, if they could. The rest fled west and south, into Germany. Three hundred thousand Sudenten Germans. I suppose they were lucky: had the Russians gotten to them first, their fate might have been considerably less pleasant.

According to the *Berliner Zeitung*, those homeless living in the Festival Theater without adequate clothing appropriated the costumes, and apparently refugees for miles around could be seen wandering in the garb of characters from one Wagnerian opera or another. Dances for American GIs were held in the garden behind Wahnfried, and it was reported that "muscular black soldiers danced with blond German girls." American soldiers were seen jitterbugging on Wagner's grave.

There is a photograph in the *Salzburger Tagblatt*. It was taken two days before Adolf shot himself. I wanted to tell Colonel Lewis about it—as an illustration, really—but was afraid I might seem too enthusiastic, even unbalanced. In it, Adolf is in uniform and crouching, his hands propped on his knees; he is gazing at an architect's model of a city which takes up most of the room and is set waist-high. He had the model taken down into the bunker, cleared out a room, and had lights arranged to create the effect of the city seen in morning, afternoon, in the early evening, and by moonlight. The lights were on a timer and ran continuously.

I recognized it instantly. Linz! Redesigned on Adolf's instructions by the architect Hermann Geisler of Munich. Much of it as Adolf had described it to me on our afternoon and early evening walks when we were sixteen. The city center has been enlarged, and the

Landstrasse, the avenue running from the center to the river, is now the size of a Parisian boulevard. It ends in a bridge which sweeps upward, like a highway to the sky, then down into Urfahr on the other side. The Post Office and Bank of Austria are still there. The *Landestheater* is in the same place but redesigned, on the scale of an opera house in a major city. The Museum of German Art is located along the river, with a Parthenon-like facade presumably hundreds of meters long. Across from it, on the far side of the river, where only farmland had been, is a complex of buildings, a university, and beyond that a stadium meant to seat 300,000 people. I have studied the photograph closely, with a magnifying glass.

According to the article, Adolf spent many hours alone with this model in his last days, as the Chancellery overhead shuddered under Russian bombardment. The walls of the bunker were concrete and twenty feet thick.

I do not think I have conveyed to you how beautiful a city Linz is. When I was a boy, it had little industry; it was an agricultural and trading town, surrounded by hilly countryside and farms. The city center was tidy, spotless; the buildings had colorful Renaissance facades and Baroque ornamentation; the cobblestones looked as though they'd been scrubbed that morning; from most of the larger streets you could catch sight of the wide, glinting Danube, usually with a barge or two gliding by, bringing goods or taking them away. At night, the sky was perfectly clear, and the sweet, unmistakable smell of the earth would sweep in from the farms on the other side of the river.

I dreamt about him again last night. We were walking through the halls of the Conservatory in Vienna. I had persuaded him to forget the Academy of Fine Arts and to apply instead to the Conservatory, and he had been admitted. I was enormously pleased with myself for suggesting this; we were roommates, and now we were fellow Conservatory students. I was showing him about. We turned into one of the two concert halls in the building. I understood that this was our first written examination. Tables had been set up, at each a different set of exam questions. This surprised me; we rarely received written examinations at the Conservatory and never in this hall. I moved from table to table and realized, with confusion and mounting anxiety, that all the questions concerned history and politics. I had been caught unprepared. I looked to Adolf, who showed me his examination booklet: he had already filled it, in his neat, slanting handwriting, with long, detailed answers. I knew he wanted me to copy them. I realized then that I was no longer holding my examination booklet. I patted the pockets of my suit jacket; it wasn't there. I must have left it on one of the exam tables. Desperate, I ran from table to table, scanning each and ducking my head to check the floor beneath.

I woke. I was lying on my stomach on my cot, one arm over the side; I was feeling frantically under the thin mattress as though for something I'd hidden there. I rolled onto my back and stared at the ceiling of the ward. It was early morning. My heart was pounding, and I took slow, deliberate breaths.

He is with me still.

This afternoon, the American psychiatrist. He has not shaken my hand once. He pauses by his chair, indicates that we should sit, and we sit. If he did shake my hand, I suspect his own would feel flabby and soft, suspicious. I am biased, I admit.

"You are aware," he says, "that Colonel Lewis has downgraded your classification from 'incriminated' to 'less incriminated'?"

"Yes."

"And how do you feel about that?"

"Good. How am I supposed to feel? I have been here fourteen months. I am tired of eating turnips. I am told this means I may be released in a few months, at most."

"Uh-hmm. Perhaps."

Oh, God.

There are the usual questions, or variations on them, about my early friendship with Adolf, our time as roommates, about Frau Hitler, about supposed masturbatory activities, and so on. I believe this man would employ a periscope to spy through the vaginal canal on a fetus to see whether he was fiddling with himself. And how do you feel about your impending birth, Herr Fetus? Is this what Adolf meant by a "materialist" psychology? Still, I suppose it's his job to produce certain information, satisfy his superiors, and justify his existence.

"Did you know that the Führer was a sexual masochist?" he says today.

Why does he always refer to Adolf as "the Führer" when the other interviewers simply say "Hitler" or "Adolf Hitler"? Is he trying to evoke some guttural, fascist response?

"A what?"

"A sexual masochist."

"I don't know exactly what you mean."

"In his sexual life, he persuaded, or even ordered, women to abuse him—specifically, to urinate and defecate on him while abusing him verbally, even kicking him—as he masturbated to orgasm. This seems to have been his preferred method of arousal.

He may have been entirely impotent with women, in the normal sense. We have this from reliable sources, several in fact."

He widens his eyes, tilts his head back and nods, as though he has just conveyed to me some ultimate and explanatory truth.

"I suppose anything is possible," I say. "Frankly, it seems to me a little far-fetched."

"You knew Angela Raubal, the Führer's niece?"

"I didn't really know her. She was a very young child when I visited her mother in Linz. I was looking for news of Adolf after he had disappeared from our room in Vienna."

"When Miss Raubal was eighteen, she lived with her uncle in his Prince Regent Square apartments in Munich. Her bedroom was next to his, in fact."

"She killed herself, didn't she?"

"She shot herself in the chest with her uncle's revolver, or she *was* shot, perhaps to keep her from talking. It's not clear. She appears to have been involved in—or coerced into—a relationship with her uncle of the type I've just described. He also seems to have persuaded her, or forced her, to pose naked—that is, to adopt obscene postures enabling him to sketch her genitalia. Hundreds of sketches, in fact. Her face does not appear in these sketches, which is a revealing omission, as such people have difficulty forming relationships with the whole person. Somehow, these sketches came into the possession of one of his Prince Regent Square neighbors, who blackmailed him for a considerable sum. The sketches were found in a safe in the rubble of the Brown House at the end of the war. Miss Raubal may have felt so ashamed, so impossibly ashamed, of this relationship that she took her own life rather than continue to submit to it."

I try to fight back my natural feelings of revulsion and choose my words cautiously.

"Adolf could be very jealous and possessive, almost proprietary, in his relations with others," I say. "If he became deeply attached to Angela, sexual relationship or no, he might have, you know, in a rather strict, paternal way, controlled her, or tried to—who she could see, what she could do, where she could go, and so on. She might have felt stifled, imprisoned—especially if she had fallen in love with someone her uncle disapproved of. That would be just as likely an explanation of her killing herself, if that is what she did. Even when he was younger he could be that way, possessive I mean. He was this way with me."

"Yes?" His eyebrows shoot up. I sigh.

"When we were in Linz, he wanted to know whether I saw other boys, and expected me to be—how to put this?—available to him, exclusively, in the afternoon and evening to take walks around the city and to go to the opera. In Vienna, things were different since I was at the Conservatory and met many more people—in class, at recitals, and so on. He understood this. Still, he was a little suspicious, wanted to know who I knew and how well, where I was going when I went out at unusual hours. A bit nosy. He certainly never asked me to do any of the things you say he demanded of his niece."

I look at the psychiatrist. I can never tell whether he believes me or not.

"Well, what were his attitudes towards women, then? You know, the kind of perverse inclinations I've described have their roots very early in life, in childhood. It seems to me unlikely that you could have seen him every day for almost four years and

then lived with him for six months—all during the sexually vola-
tile period of adolescence—and seen no evidence of this." He
gives me a look like a lizard.

"Well," I reply, "I think it was rather normal, really, as I recall.
There was the boyhood crush on Stefanie, from a distance, which
I told you about. Other than that, I can't recall his having any
direct relations with girls or women, other than his exceptional
devotion to his mother. In fact, he was rather conservative—
rigidly so—about these matters, you know, about sex before
marriage and so forth. Many of my Conservatory classmates had
gone to prostitutes, or said they did, anyway. I recall Adolf's
mentioning some youth group that required men and women to
pledge to remain sexually abstinent until the age of twenty-five,
but I don't think he actually had anything to do with these
people. He was fairly isolated then. He studied, sketched, painted,
we went to the opera. That was all."

"Is it, really?"

"Yes. It is."

There was another photograph in the *Salzburger Tagblatt* this
morning, of the bare room Adolf used as his bedroom during his
last days in the bunker. It is almost as small as his bedroom off the
kitchen of his mother's apartment in Linz. The room has obviously been plundered. There is a narrow wooden bedframe, quite
simple, with exposed bedsprings and no mattress. The small closet
is empty, the hangers in disarray—the clothing has been taken.
There is a low, square table alongside the bed frame. In the fore-
ground, at the foot of the bed, is a black strongbox. (Under these
circumstances, why a strongbox? What could he possibly have

been keeping in it?) The front of the strongbox has been cut open with a welder's torch.

There are only two aspects of the room with any personal meaning. The first is a framed photograph—the only one I recall—of Adolf's mother, on the wall above the bed. She is still a young woman. Her hair is worn up and knotted tightly, her face is roundish and healthy, her eyes are large, pale, transparent—unmistakable. Her expression is unsmiling, but open and imploring in a curious, reserved way.

And then there are books. Several large volumes lying stacked flat on top of the strongbox. You cannot see the spines but the volumes are the size of the encyclopedias Adolf used to enjoy having about. On the low table, there are three or four scattered volumes. One of them, on the corner nearest the bed, is thick and handsomely bound, and the spine, with bright lettering, faces the camera. Even with my magnifier I cannot make out the title or author.

Apparently, an American officer made off with more than eighty volumes from this room. He has donated them to the library of Brown University in Rhode Island in America.

A letter from my wife yesterday:

> *Dearest Eugen,*
>
> *It seems a long time since my last allowed visit, even though this was less than one month ago. I can understand why we are not permitted to meet alone or speak in private. Still, I resent this. You are not a criminal nor do you have anything to hide.*
>
> *The* Volkschules *and the* Realschule *have begun classes again, and I am starting once more to receive referrals of*

private pupils. There are not enough teachers—too many of the younger ones have been lost in the war—but still classes are being held. Herr Saukel, the music teacher, was killed in Breslau during the last months of the war, and so he is not here to conduct classes or give lessons. Perhaps, then, more referrals will come my way. I do not mean to seem heartless. I liked Herr Saukel.

But here is another idea, one which I have mentioned before and wish you to take seriously. I have just learned that Frau Klepper is giving up her seamstress' shop. This is an excellent location and size for a drapery shop. You know I have a talent for this and students' mothers, seeing the drapery in our own home, have often asked if they could commission me to do work for them. You could advise me. I am only asking you to think about it. I could continue giving lessons in the evenings.

I received another letter from Gustl. He says he is managing to scrape by on the few students he already has, although I don't see how this could be. But! The Conservatory in Graz has announced it will reopen in July, and he will be able to resume his training then, although this is later than he hoped. It is an irony that the man who financed his education is the one who disrupted it. But he is alive. Thank you, God, for scoliosis of the spine!

I do not understand, frankly, why you are still in Glasenbach. It has been fourteen months. I know you say the Americans have been fair to you. But I do not see what more you have to offer them or why you must be "de-Nazified." You were never a Nazi and they know that. They only want to keep you because they think you

345

know things about Hitler they can use, or perhaps
because of your involvement with the ludicrous
"Strength and Joy" group. As for "de-Nazification," I
think it is a difficult matter, if not hopeless. Millions
were guilty. Millions were innocent. Millions were
somewhere in-between. How can they ever sort this out?
  Have you been able to see the American dentist?
  Your loving Sabine.

Yes, the drapery shop. My wife is a very good seamstress and
a hard worker, and personable. All her students like her, and their
parents in particular like her. I bet she could "make a go of it," as
you say. I could help her. I helped Frau Sachs; she had a good eye,
and she liked my taste. It is interesting that skills learned long
ago, and which we expected never to use again, may come in
handy. This is important as so much of life seems difficult to
predict, even improbable.

When I enter my "writing room" this afternoon, there is a copy
of the *Linzer Volksblatt* on the table, which is odd. The newspaper seems to have been placed there; it looks fresh, unread. I
have come to this room, which Colonel Lewis allows me to use,
hundreds of times, and so far nothing, not a scrap, has been left
here. It is simply an empty room, with a wooden table and
chairs, concrete floor, whitewashed brick walls, nothing else. I
know the officers use it for meetings at times, but they have
never left anything before, and only a few of them speak or read
German.

The local German-language newspapers have begun to publish
again. At first in editions no more than four or eight pages in

length, but now they are longer. There is no censorship, as far as I can tell, but I am sure the American and British occupiers read them carefully. There have been a number of articles lately about the concentration camps that were liberated late in 1944 and last year. The trials in Nuremberg continue.

The article in this edition is about the Mauthausen concentration and slave labor camp, and the many smaller slave labor camps that grew from it. I had not heard of it before, but it was built only twelve kilometers from Linz. Twelve kilometers! Adolf and I took hikes into the countryside longer than this, with our army canteens and our packs filled with big chunks of ham and pastries from his mother, or mine. It was built alongside a quarry where my father and I had gone swimming on summer days, on our way home from visits to our sometimes naked client in the castle. Once, Adolf and I picnicked on the edge of the quarry overlooking the water. I described to him—now and then, it was my turn to deliver a monologue—how Beethoven in the *Pastorale* had used certain passages and particular instruments, motifs really, as well as shifting keys cleverly, to convey the approaching storm and its redemptive aftermath in the last movement. I had been studying the score and was flush with insights and detail. Adolf ate and listened without asking questions. I was excited and proud of my little analysis, the day was hot, and I wanted badly to strip naked and take a swim. It was late in the summer and the water, so cold even in June it made your head throb, would be tolerable and refreshing. We could dry ourselves with our blankets. But I lost my nerve: even then I knew how Adolf felt about being seen unclothed, and I had no desire to risk his silent scorn by asking. I dropped the idea.

But I digress. I sit down and open the newspaper and continue to read. Originally, the writer says, the purpose of building the

Mauthausen camp at the quarry was to produce the enormous quantity of granite required to build the new and larger versions of many towns in Germany and Austria, including Linz. The other purpose was "extermination through labor" (*Vernichtung durch Arbeit*). The slave laborers would be worked until they died of exhaustion, starvation, or disease. If they had become too weak to work they would be killed with injections of phenol. According to the article, the slaves came from all over Europe— not just Russians and Poles, but French, Belgians, Dutch, as well as Germans and Austrians who were considered politically "incorrigible." Many were university professors, lawyers, doctors, scientists, artists—an obvious attempt to do away with the intelligentsia of the conquered nations. The flow of these slave laborers became so great that a twin camp was built in Grusen, ten kilometers away. Slave laborers were rented out to local businesses, especially farms, as more Austrian men were conscripted into the army to fight in the East.

Apparently, despite the horrible conditions under which they worked, the slave laborers weren't dying fast enough to accommodate the arrival of new slaves from throughout the Reich. So after twelve-hour days in the quarries, the laborers were subjected to grueling and pointless exercises—playing leap-frog in the hot sun or freezing cold, for example. Beatings became more frequent. Prisoners were forced to carry fifty-kilogram blocks of rough granite up the "steps of death" in the main quarry at Mauthausen. If they survived this, they might be made to form a line at the edge of a cliff ("The Parachutist's Wall") and given the choice, at gunpoint, of being shot or of pushing the laborer ahead of them off the cliff. A "mobile gas van" shuttled day and night between the camps at Mauthausen and Grusen. Eventually, a gas chamber and crematorium were built at Mauthausen.

In May 1945, Mauthausen was taken by soldiers of the 41st Reconnaissance Squadron of the US 11th Armored Division, 3rd US Army.

There is a photograph accompanying the article. In it, American soldiers, only their eyes visible above surgical masks or towels or shirts tied over their faces, are delicately lifting the bodies of slave laborers and laying them out. The bodies are naked, barely more than skeletons draped with skin, and the shaven heads hang flaccidly as the soldiers carry them. According to the writer, on arriving the Americans found bodies stacked throughout the camp. The single crematorium had been in constant use and unable to keep up, and the guards had fled. Hearing moans, the soldiers decided to disentangle and separate the bodies. A few laborers were still alive and were taken to a local military hospital.

That hospital, I realize, is the Sisters of Mercy on the outskirts of Linz. It was closed years ago and apparently has been converted to a military hospital by the Americans. It is where Frau Hitler was operated on by Dr. Urban, a surgery attended at her request by Dr. Bloch—Dr. Eduard Bloch, who had visited Frau Hitler every day during the critical periods of her illness, encouraged Adolf in his painting and displayed one of Adolf's watercolors in his consulting rooms, and summoned me privately to express his concern that Adolf might commit suicide following his mother's death. Dr. Bloch was allowed to emigrate in 1940; the money from the sale of that grand house on the Landstrasse with his office on the first floor was appropriated by the Gestapo. In the United States, he was barred by law from practicing medicine. He ended up living in a single room in the Bronx, a part of New York City, impoverished and alone, and after only a few years he died there. This does not surprise me. *Er Lebte füer seine Patienten*, my mother used to say—he lived for his patients.

There is another article in the *Volksblatt* today. Apparently, Mauthausen and the camp at Grusen are thought to be part of a network of nearly one hundred slave labor camps, throughout northern Austria, producing not only granite but munitions and airplanes. This seems odd to me. In Eferding, during the war, we never saw soldiers. Men disappeared into the army, first the younger, then the older ones; I knew that because of my age and health I would not be conscripted. My co-worker Herr Fischer disappeared. We went to work; listened to the radio, which was controlled by the state, until radios were confiscated; and we listened to the drone of bombers overhead—towards the end of the war for days at a time—but never seemed to attract their attention. (Linz and Salzburg were bombed.) We worried about our sons; our eldest was studying in Vienna and applying to the Conservatory, and our second son was at Conservatory in Graz, which was bombed, but not extensively. We worried constantly about food shortages. The Russians never reached us from the east; the British and Americans did, from the west, quietly, and by then we were expecting them. It was a gray, hungry time, full of worry, but not a dramatic one, really. That there were nearly a hundred slave labor camps in the nearby forests, invisible, producing granite, bomb sights, mortars, infantry guns, fuselage, tires, airplane engines, batteries for U-boats—it seems fantastic, almost difficult to believe.

During the two weeks that Emilie was gone and I spent part of the afternoon and evening each day with Frau Sachs, I felt I could tell her anything. I would lie on my side, propped on one elbow, and she would lie a little higher in the bed, almost sitting up, a pillow behind her head, her hands folded on her belly, the duvet covering her from the waist down, listening, nodding, smiling a little. Her dark brown hair was fanned out against the pillow and fell over her shoulders. Her full, round breasts with their large, pale nipples lay inches from my face. I remember thinking, This is what it is to be a man: to be relaxed and talking with a handsome woman who is naked. She was the first person with whom I shared my plans to become a conductor. I hadn't yet studied conducting—I was a first-year student, and even the ambition was a bit premature—but I was nervous about it.

"Why nervous?" she said. "I saw you play the Beethoven with Michael Oberhupel and your quartet, and again here that night in the library with the other students. I thought you were quite good, and confident also. An expression of mild concentration on your face, not struggling with the music, as though it were nothing special, simply something you did every day."

"Yes, but that's different," I said. "If things don't go well, you can split the blame four ways. With conducting, it's only you. There's no one else to blame. How do they know whether the musicians didn't have the discipline, or motivation, or—God forbid—the talent and understanding to go where you wanted to take them? To follow, you know, the ideas and vision you've set for them? There are too many of them. All the audience can do is blame you, the conductor."

"You hope too much," she said.

I looked at her.

"You hope too much," she repeated matter-of-factly. "I have seen this in you a few times now. You hope that Herr Professor Doktor Epstein will be pleased, and your friend Stefan Epstein will be pleased—and a little jealous—and hope Michael Oberhupel and Herr Professor Doktor Stulpnagel will be pleased. And the rest of the faculty. But you are afraid they won't. So the fear is connected to the hope, always. If you stop hoping, you will stop being afraid. Is there much to do when you conduct?"

"Much? Everything! First, you must know the score almost by memory. You have to be able to close your eyes and hear the entire piece in your head from beginning to end—this is why I really think Beethoven's losing his hearing, while a very sad thing, was not really a great disadvantage, either for composing or conduct-ing. You glance at the score now and then just to remind yourself and then your eyes are up again, watching each section like a falcon, hearing everything individually and together, so if something is missing or off you hear it instantly and correct it instantly. *If* you are any good. And the motions! People seem to think—I'm serious—that this is mostly for show, you're just setting the tempo and cheering the musicians on. Every gesture— large or small, tight, flowing, smooth, choppy, delicate, violent— is directed and precise, shaping every phrase and passage, determining whether a musical line is merely quiet or lyrical, loud or commanding. You leave no aspect of the music untouched. They are right, really—if it's a mess, it *is* your fault. I think the ideal conductor should have three heads and six pairs of arms. And a tail, to keep the beat. I haven't even touched on the diffi-culties of conducting opera."

"Well," Frau Sachs made a face and lifted her hands from her belly, "I don't even see how you have time to hope, then. There is far too much to pay attention to. You should conduct without hoping. It's only a distraction. And if you cease to hope, you will cease to be afraid. Isn't that, after all, what you tell Emilie, or what she tells me you tell her?"

I looked at Frau Sachs. She leaned forward, reached back and gathered her hair into a thick brown rope and draped it over one shoulder. Her breasts lifted and then fell as she lay back.

"When she plays something for you? Mechanics and sound, mechanics and sound, that is all she should be aware of. She should even forget you are there." She sighed. "You know, sometimes I think your teachers do you no favor by being so formidable and German."

I nodded to myself. I must have been aroused or excited because Frau Sachs looked down and then at me, and made the clicking sound with her tongue. I placed my hand behind her neck and kissed her, as I had become accustomed to do.

By the time I graduated the Conservatory at age twenty-two— no, just twenty-three—I had taken several courses and tutorials in conducting, and I had conducted at least one piece, some my own, in each of the recitals held at the end of every semester. When I went to Marburg in the summer of 1912, I knew what I wanted to do and how I would do it.

In June 1945, a month before I was brought to Glasenbach, I read that the American Red Cross in Vienna, with the help of the Russians, had begun to distribute lists of those deported to Chelmo, Treblinka, and the other camps in the East. The Germans had kept meticulous records. I took the train to Vienna on some excuse; I did not want to tell my wife why I was going.

Vienna had been bombed, by daylight, during the last months of the war, almost as an afterthought. Nearly one-third of the city had been destroyed. It had been divided into Russian, American, British, and French sectors. The American, British, and French zones communicated freely; the boundary with the Russians was marked by a wall of brown sandbags decorated with barbed wire, a wall that ran through the city like a jagged scar. On the American side, there seemed to be a guard every twenty meters, but they carried truncheons instead of guns, and with the olive uniforms wore tight white belts and white helmets.

The sight of the Westbahnhof took my breath away. The steel-and-glass roof of the station was entirely gone, and the stone pillars which had supported it were badly damaged. The ceiling of the stationhouse had collapsed. The place was open to the air, nothing but tracks and a platform—the platform on which I had arrived thirty-seven years before as a nineteen-year-old with one suitcase of clothing and another filled with my mother's meats, jams, and pastries, and Adolf had taken me by the shoulders and declared that my future awaited me.

I walked into the dusty light of the streets; it was—except for the throaty roar of jeeps and military trucks—strangely quiet. As I walked towards the Ring, right away I noticed something else: the huge chestnuts had lost many of their limbs; some had been reduced to charred, splintered trunks. By the time I reached the Heldenplatz—which had been covered with chestnuts forming a canopy so dense that during the summer and early fall it seemed like a little forest—they had been blasted almost to the roots. The plaza was a field of blackened stumps. The chestnuts that had lined the Ring were the same. More than anything, more than the rubble and the craters and the smell of drifting ash, this gave the city an atmosphere of desolation.

There were women with young children on the streets, but the only men of adult age I saw were American and British soldiers. The bombing seemed to be nearly random, buildings blown right down to the foundation, the rubble spilling across the street and over the trolley tracks, alongside buildings that seemed to have been untouched. I did not see any trams running. The squeal-and-rattle that I had fallen asleep to each night in 1908, when I lived with Adolf on the Stumpergasse, was gone.

I found the Red Cross housed, of all places, in the offices of the Court Opera, which had been partly destroyed. Folding tables had been set up and behind them sat women in civilian clothes with the red-and-white armbands, combing through typed lists in large binders. The place was surprisingly empty, and the whispered voices echoed off the high ornamented ceilings. You'd think an opera was being performed and they were keeping their voices deliberately low.

I approached one of the women and I told her I'd come to seek the whereabouts of Viktor Sachs, Adele Sachs, and Emilie Sachs of Josefstadt Strasse 1009.

"Are you family?" she said.

"Friend. Friend of the family."

She nodded and I produced my papers from inside my coat. She glanced down at my Czech surname and back at me, and scanned the rest. They still bore the National Socialist letterhead, the eagle Adolf had designed clutching the wreath encircling a swastika. She handed them back to me and began to leaf through one of her binders, then a second, and a third. She moved off to consult with a woman at a different table, leafed through a set of this woman's binders, then came back and continued searching her own books. She was obliging and thorough. Frau Adele Sachs and Doctor Emilie Sachs, a pediatrician, and the two daughters of Doctor Emilie Sachs, had been sent to the Theresienstadt camp outside Prague and from there to Auschwitz. None had survived. Emilie's husband, a gentile lawyer who refused to divorce her, had been sent to a forced labor camp in southern Germany; his fate was unknown. I thanked her and left.

I decided I would walk along the Ring to the Eighth District, or Josefstadt, which was in the American sector. I picked my way through the mounds of rubble; a pall of dust—mortar, brick, pulverized stone—seemed to hang in the air. It had a wet, ashen smell and through it one could see the dull disk of the sun. The Ring in the Eighth had been hit, but the Josefstadt Strasse looked undamaged. I found Frau Sachs's building, 1009. The entrance was boarded and chained, and the windows shuttered, but otherwise it was as I had known it: the wide grey facade, the double-headed eagle over the entry, the rows of tall windows spanning each floor, a row of plump, naked, curly-headed boys across the top, one hand on a flirtatiously thrust-out hip, the other raised and holding up the projected roof of the building. After I'd been coming for Emilie's lessons each week, at times twice a week, the doorman, Karl Josef, had come to know me and address me by name; during the two weeks that Emilie was in Bohemia and I came every afternoon from the Conservatory, he'd simply smile and nod and hold the door, and I would ascend the spiral marble staircase, draping one hand over the wrought-iron art nouveau balustrade with its arabesque of swans and lilies, to the second floor, and I would tap the brass head of Pallas Athene against that massive door, and she would open it and nod and smile slightly without saying hello.

"Do you think I will ever live in a place like this?" I asked one afternoon. We were in Frau Sachs's own bedroom this time, not Emilie's. I was naked and standing in front of a mahogany bureau with a marble top, which she said she'd purchased in Italy the year before; it was covered with small, stoppered bottles holding liquids of different colors, which I was inspecting. Frau Sachs was propped up in the bed, watching me.

"No," she said. "Of course not."

Ah! I thought. Here it is at last, the contempt of class! I will sponsor you, I will invite you into my home, into my bed, I will kiss you and wrap my legs around you and clasp my hands to your back. But you can never have what I have. Do not think about it.

"Yes? Why is that?"

"Come here," she said. "Sit." She patted the bed.

I paused, deliberately, and moved to the bed and sat, and crossed my legs. I folded my arms over my lap.

"Don't look like that," she said. "Tell me. Are you willing to come to work each morning at five o'clock to make sure the calcium and phosphate are added to the washed sugar just so, and the impurities skimmed off just so, and then the sugar crystallized under the vacuum just so, and then dried and stored at exactly the right temperature? Just so? And check every shipment of cane to make sure your suppliers aren't cheating you? And worry that some angry worker will set fire to the factory, or the Germans who believe the Czechs have the jobs that by rights belong to them will come and they will set the fire? And the insurer will refuse to pay?"

"Yes, but—"

"Wait! I have forgotten to send you to school—for how many years?—for your degree in chemistry and engineering, and you can forget about Brahms and Schoenberg and Wagner." Again, the finger under my chin and she turned my head to her. "Listen to me. If you are unwilling to do these things, then you will never run, or own, a sugar refinery like my husband, and you will never live"—she made a face and darted her eyes around the large bedroom—"like 'this.'" She lifted my chin an inch with that commanding finger. "Don't look at my breasts, look at me. This is important. You will be a professional musician. You will never be rich, but you may be comfortable, and people who live 'like this' will come to hear you play, or conduct, or both, and they will invite you to supper in their homes and treat you with respect and genuine interest, and they will write checks to your symphony or institution. This is worth something." She folded her arms over her chest and fell back against the pillows. "And when you come to Vienna to conduct, I will expect the best seats, and Emilie will come, and you will have supper and perhaps a reception in this home."

"Will you come to my hotel room after the performance?"

"I do not know what you have in mind and I will be a some-what older lady then. But I will want to congratulate you and hear all about your family and children. And if your wife is as beautiful and talented and jealous as Alma Mahler, I don't think you will get any ideas."

I must have looked crestfallen—I never got the better of Frau Sachs in an exchange—because she frowned again and extended her leg and rubbed my shoulder gently with that small, soft foot.

"There is an expression in English," she said. "We say *So ist das Leben* or *So läuft es nun mal,* you know, 'Such is life! That's how it goes!', which is so mundane, so common. *C'est la vie* is a little better but it is facile, like an excuse. The English say: 'This is the way of the world,' which sounds philosophical, more profound. Say it."

"*Der vey uf da vorldt.*" I have always had a problem with the soft 't' in English. 'W' is hopeless.

She laughed. "That's good!" she said. "Good enough. Come here."

A roar, the crunch of gravel under tires, and two white helmets in a jeep were in front of me, the vehicle's motor idling loudly. I produced my papers, which they inspected, folded, and handed back to me. They reminded me of the curfew and to be off the streets one hour before nightfall, and that trains out of the city would not run between midnight and nine o'clock the following morning. The jeep was off again, spitting gravel and dirt from the rear tires.

I looked up at Josefstadt Strasse 1009. The woman at the American Red Cross had told me that they had no information about Herr Sachs; his two brothers, the surgeon and engineer, were not listed either, but their children and grandchildren were. With the exception of the niece who had emigrated to England with the violinist Frankl, almost everyone who had heard us play the Brahms in the library that night—the night Adolf came with me and startled us all by kissing Frau Sachs's hand—had perished.

"Well," Colonel Lewis says, "are you going to interview me today? This is a rare event."

"I asked to see you," I say, "for a specific reason."

"I gathered."

"The papers I gave to the NSDAP archive—"

"You mean Rudolf Hess?"

"Yes, I told you that Hess had visited me in Eferding after I returned from Bayreuth in September 1938. Given the people who surrounded him, I found him surprisingly intelligent and soft-spoken—"

"You mentioned that."

I manage a smile. "He asked me to record my memories of Hitler for the archives in Munich. I had no problem with this. Why should I? They gave me an office in the local party head-quarters, and a typewriter, and time off from work. I gave him perhaps fifty pages of material, mostly about Hitler's enthusiasm for opera, history, art, the inspiration he seemed to draw from the biographies of great Germans. I left out, of course, the difficulties involved in being his friend and in living with him. Hess was satisfied. He also asked me for letters, watercolors, and so on."

"You've told me. But, you know, shortly before he killed himself Hitler dispatched Bormann to Munich to destroy the personal files kept in the Brown House—which was heavily damaged in any case only weeks later in the bombing. Hitler himself destroyed the files kept in his apartment in the Chancellery."

"There is more."

"More of what?"

"Postcards, letters, notes, watercolors, sketches." I cannot bring myself to look directly at Colonel Lewis. "Hundreds," I say. "More than one hundred."

"Where?"

"In my attic. In the wall. I gave Hess only a fraction of what I had."

Colonel Lewis holds up both hands. "Herr Reczek. Let me take a step back. This is material you would have saved from the years—when?—1904—"

"1905 to 1908."

"Yes. For a long time it was valueless. You didn't even know Hitler was still alive until the early 1920s. Why keep it around?"

I shrug. "Memorabilia. Memories."

"Did you think of selling them? I'm being perfectly serious. There is a man in London now, a Swiss, who is peddling—for five hundred thousand pounds—eight hundred pages of what he says are Bormann's transcripts of Hitler's private monologues, the so-called 'Table-Talk.' Have you heard this? I always see you reading the newspapers."

"I have no interest in selling them."

"Money is scarce," he says.

I wave my hand. "I will manage."

Colonel Lewis pauses and rubs the heel of his hand against his forehead. "Why—in the wall?"

"I walled them up the day I returned from Bayreuth in 1938. Suddenly people knew me. They would come nosing around. Hess arrived a week later. People's homes—even those of party members and officials—were searched almost routinely in those days, on the slightest pretext. That same month, my mother's apartment in Linz was searched, most likely without Hitler's knowledge or approval. The officials were polite. Still, it was unpleasant."

"Herr Reczek." Colonel Lewis looks at me with a kind of friendly exasperation, an expression I have come to know. "Why are you telling me this now?"

"You have dealt decently with me," I say. "I will instruct my wife to allow you in the house. There is a small window in the attic. To the right of the frame, you can see where the wall has been plastered and repainted. It is obvious. The paint there is lighter. When you have the materials, show me, and I will tell you the meaning, you know, the setting, the—"

"Context."

"Yes, the 'context.' Is that all right?"

Colonel Lewis usually calls for a guard to accompany me back the ward. Today, for the first time, he thanks me and sends me back on my own. He says that my withholding information of this sort will not affect my status. I remain "less incriminated." I will most likely be released in one or two months.

Walking along the corridor, I look out at the barren ground behind the building and at the barbed-wire fence in the distance. The day is overcast and gray, and there are flecks of snow swirling, like bits of paper. My wife has been to the Registrar's Office several times and they tell her they have no idea whether I will be able to return to my old job. Perhaps the drapery shop would be a good idea for us both. I could even take on small upholstery jobs—chairseats, cushions, and so forth. One never loses these skills.

In 1922, when I returned from Munich after seeing my old friend speak in the Kindlkeller, I went up to our attic and spent hours going through the sketches and cards and watercolors I'd saved, wrapped in tissue, in a trunk. My old viola was up there. I hadn't touched it in years. The case was expensive, hard black leather, tight enough to keep moisture out, and specially upholstered with cotton and silk. The instrument itself was inside, wrapped in felt. Perhaps I could have continued playing, or given lessons, or played in an amateur symphony or in chamber groups. Perhaps.

But you see, if you allow someone else to live inside you, and you make a hero of him, you give away a part of yourself that is hard to get back. And I believe, strongly, that everyone should try to be the hero of his own life, even if life makes that difficult or impossible at times. You may fail, but you must try. I think that this is one reason the memory of Frau Sachs has stayed with me so vividly, because she encouraged me in just such a direction. Those wild, adoring faces in the newsreels the Americans never tire of showing us—how different am I from these people? I cannot say, really. But I know—and have known from the moment I sat down to write this—that I am not the hero of my own story. I know, with a clarity and force I have never before felt, that if you give this role to someone else, then you take a risk. The results may be unfortunate, or terrible.

I am not special; I have no special destiny. I will never live in the Villa Eugen. I will never live in the *Conservatoire*. I will never write an opera with a soprano part for Stefanie. I will never conduct for Frau Sachs; I will never nod and smile mysteriously at her from the conductor's podium, like a man with a precious secret. I will not revolutionize the role of music education in the Reich or transform the place of music in the public life of its cities and towns. I will return home. I will help my wife, and help my three grown sons, and I will try, like every other person who has been fortunate enough to survive Adolf Hitler, to stumble out from under the ruins of this broken world. This will be enough.

Author's Note

In November 1905, August Kubizek, then fifteen, met Adolf Hitler, who was a few months younger, at the opera in Linz. The boys became nearly inseparable, and the friendship involved both their families; it culminated in their sharing a small room together in the commercial Mariahilf district of Vienna for six months in 1908, when Kubizek was a first-year student at the Vienna Conservatory and Hitler was "studying" art. Kubizek's memoir *The Young Hitler I Knew* (1953) chronicles that friendship and, despite its flaws, offers a fascinating and credible glimpse of the personality and mental attitudes of the adolescent Hitler. Perhaps because an earlier version of the memoir had been written at the request of the party for the NSDAP archives, it was often ignored by historians. In 1999, however, Brigitte Hamann used the memoir in her excellent social history *Hitler's Vienna*, and it was used as well by Ian Kershaw in the first volume of his superb biography of Hitler.

I have used many of the incidents of the boyhood friendship described by Kubizek, and many more have been entirely fabricated. One subject in particular, Hitler's anti-semitism, deserves mention. In his introduction to the current edition of Kubizek's memoir, Kershaw writes:

(Kubizek's) story of Hitler denouncing to the police a kaftan-clad Jew was probably an embellishment on a well-known episode in

Mein Kampf . . . the description of a visit to a synagogue sounds equally dubious. The claim that Hitler joined the Anti-Semitic League in 1908, and registered Kubizek for membership at the same time, is plainly wrong. No such organisation existed in Austria at the time. Kubizek's passages on Hitler's anti-semitism, in fact, deserve generally to be treated with scepticism.

Hitler, in *Mein Kampf*, chose to portray his anti-Semitic views as having originated during his stay in Vienna; Kubizek, who wrote his original memoir for the NSDAP archives, may have been trying to align his own story with Hitler's. Hitler is now thought to have become a fanatic anti-Semite only at the end of the First World War, when there was a general rise in anti-Semitic feeling in Germany as Germans attempted to find a scapegoat on which to blame their humiliation; Jews were one of many possible candidates. In this novel, Hitler is depicted as attracted to the racist and pan-Germanic ideology of *Ostara* and similar publications, but not yet an overt anti-Semite.

One should remember that the narrator of *The Tristan Chord* is writing at the very end of the war, in 1945–6, when the scale of the German atrocities in the East were only gradually becoming known, and often met by Germans with skepticism and even outright disbelief. One should add to this the unique complication of Adolf Hitler having been the inseparable and idealized friend of the narrator's adolescence, followed by their reunion as adults. And add again the usual myopia of a pointedly apolitical man. It is not surprising, then, that Eugen Rezcek's ability to acknowledge and reflect on the full horror that his boyhood friend accomplished is in its early stages. Still, Reczek seems to me to have come a long way by the end of his story.

The portrait of the adolescent Hitler in *The Tristan Chord* is not flattering. He is selfish, self-centered, rigid, grandiose, and contemptuous. He refuses to work. He refuses to return to school, where he would have to compete against students his own age. At the same time, he is capable of experiencing loneliness, intense disappointment, and grief. He is capable of friendship; and as long as that friendship provides him with a source of significant, if not unlimited, admiration, he is capable of loyalty and encouragement. He is also capable of patiently placing a sliver of ice on the tongue of his dying mother, who is unable to drink as a result of the medical treatment she is receiving. Some readers might be offended by this picture. To them, I would paraphrase the documentarian Marcel Ophuls, that viewing Hitler and men like him simply as monsters is a form of moral and intellectual complacency. Certainly, it would be more comfortable and reassuring to view even the adolescent Hitler as merely a younger version of the adult monster, as a member of a different species. But it would not be true. He does not belong to another species. He belongs to our species.

I first read Kubizek's memoir when I was in college. I felt drawn to certain aspects of his situation: that of a person who, despite considerable talent, found his life and career derailed by vast forces of history; and who found his adult life shadowed by the strange, overbearing friend of his youth, who would become for a time the most powerful man in the world, and a notorious mass murderer. But the narrator of this novel is not Kubizek: his personality and voice are his own, and the conflicts which nearly rupture his friendship with the young Hitler are not those of the friendship between Kubizek and Hitler. However, the personality of the adolescent Hitler portrayed here is, I think, quite consistent with the one described by Kubizek—a personality which in its final, adult form has become only too familiar.

Acknowledgments

With special thanks to Peter Scotto, Luanna Devenis and Peter Wright for their support of this book.

Thanks to Emily Sweet, without whose diligence, thoughtfulness, and professionalism this book would have never seen print.

Thanks to Katy Guest, DeAndra Lupu, Rachael Kerr, Anna Simpson, Alex Eccles and everyone at Unbound, who are unafraid.

Thanks to Mike Bundy, Tina Bailes and the reading group of Louisville, Tennessee, Ken Ballen, Julia Prewitt Brown, Mary Christin & John Becker, Bob Christin, Luanna Devenis, Amy Gershenfeld Donnella, Erica Ferencik, Dominic Green, Martin Hanley, Ken Kalfus, Larry Miller, Peter Marks, Julia Matthews, Kevin Monahan, Paul O'Malley, Sergio Munoz, Daniela Plesa, Robin Ratcliff, Steve Rioff, Sofia Starnes, Mori & Percy Tzelnic, Howard Wach, Peter Wright, and Andrea Yelle.

Unbound is the world's first crowdfunding publisher, established in 2011.

We believe that wonderful things can happen when you clear a path for people who share a passion. That's why we've built a platform that brings together readers and authors to crowdfund books they believe in – and give fresh ideas that don't fit the traditional mould the chance they deserve.

This book is in your hands because readers made it possible. Everyone who pledged their support is listed below. Join them by visiting unbound.com and supporting a book today.

M.G. Allen
Tina Bailes
Kenneth Ballen
Graham Blenkin
Julia Brown
Aifric Campbell
Harriet Cunningham
Fyfe Design
Amy Donnella
Erica Ferencik
Mark Gamble
Dominic Green

Katy Guest
Thomas Hemnes
Tom Hrycaj
Mark Iocolano
Ken Kalfus
Dan Kieran
Mit Lahiri
Paul Levy
Meng Howe Lim
Peter Marks
John Mitchinson
Kevin Monahan

Tom & Karen Nort
Paul O'Malley
Leah Parker-Moldover
Daniela Plesa
Justin Pollard
Deborah Primiano
Steven Rioff
George Sobek
Sofia Starnes
Michael A Sweet
Mori Tzelnic
John Warren